Holy Flame Trilogy, Book 2:
Operation: A.N.G.E.L.

C.J. Peterson

Texas Sisters Press, LLC

ISBN: 978-1-952041-23-5

Published by Texas Sisters Press, LLC. Lufkin, TX U.S.A.

Texas Sisters Press, LLC.
2020

Second Edition

This book is dedicated to my loving husband and dear family who love and support me. You all mean more to me than you will ever know! Thank you! I love you!

It is also, dedicated to those brave men and women of the military, along with the firefighters/paramedics and the police officers who work night and day to keep us safe. Thank you!

A portion of the proceeds of this series will go to Airborne Angel Cadets of Texas – a non-profit group of hardworking volunteers who send care packages to our soldiers overseas. You can find them at: http://www.airborneangelcadets.com

To learn more about C.J. Peterson, you can find her online at: http://cjpetersonwrites.com/

'While the stories are fiction, the journey is real.'

The characters and incidents portrayed and the names herein are fictitious, and any similarity to the name, character, or history of any person is entirely coincidental and unintentional.

<u>Summary</u>

This is the second book in a trilogy that follows firefighter/paramedic Casey Carter and a special ops unit known as A.N.G.E.L.. As their worlds collide, Casey has to figure out how to live two lives at once, balancing her firefighter family with her military family.

Unbeknownst to her, things had gotten 'hot' around Casey. The A.N.G.E.L.s have stepped in to cover where Jack and Mac could no longer be, by providing safety and security for her on a twenty-four-hour basis. But did she find something more than security within their ranks?

See how the A.N.G.E.L.s, with help from a unique band of characters, were able to heal not only Casey's body, but also rescue her mind and soul. See how events completely turn Casey's life upside-down once again. Did it end up being for good…or will these events finally do her in? Will the Angels be able to protect Casey from those hunting her?

I Peter 5:8:

Be sober, be vigilant; because your adversary the devil, as a roaring lion, walketh about, seeking whom he may devour.

Table of Contents

<u>**Preface**</u>

Scenes from: THE CALL TO DUTY

(Book 1 of the Holy Flame Trilogy)

While she was in the hospital, Casey had a nightmare. It began with the smell of rancid, burnt flesh, much the same as when the man at the fire scene stumbled by her. Then, it compounded with the pungent sulfuric stench of brimstone on fire. She slowly opened her eyes to find that she was in a cold, rough catacomb structure that weighed heavily in desperation and despair. The chambers were about five feet long and two feet tall. They lined the walls of the cavern, stacked about five or six high depending on the height of the cavern at that point, and she was in the second one up from the ground.

Casey rolled over, and what she saw petrified her. Moving or breathing was the furthest things from her mind as she saw things her mind could not conceive. Fire coated the walls, but it did not consume them. There were hideous creatures walking around that were dark red, almost black in color. They had skin made of scales like a reptile. They had large wings like a bat, talons for nails, and yellowish-green eyes that darted around everywhere, searching for any sign of movement from their prey. They had fangs dripping with saliva as they scoured the scene before them, as if it were a Thanksgiving feast.

There were people walking around with only parts of their clothing still on them, some with chunks of their flesh hung off their bodies. The people walking around were in shock as they wondered around aimlessly and despondent.

She continued to scan the area the scene was almost indescribable. She was not sure she would ever be able to explain it to anyone. About thirty feet away from her was a vast, literal lake of fire. As the fire danced atop of the water, it reminded her of when someone sets a puddle of gasoline on fire. The emanation of brimstone was powerfully potent. It was suffocating to her. It overpowered any other scent, making it even difficult to breathe.

Then, just when she thought she had seen it all, she noticed there were people in the lake…and they were alive! All she could do was lay there watching people reach out, grabbing others, pulling them back, deeper into the abyss. The hands had absolutely no flesh on them, yet the people were alive!

She studied the scene for a brief moment, almost mesmerized, when suddenly one of those hideous, reptile-like creatures appeared right in front of her. His tight, leather skin crinkled as he folded his arms, resting them on the side of the catacomb. He leaned down near her face. "Well, hello there," he sneered, drumming his claws on the rock.

She could not form a single thought in her head. Words were not an option. Her heart raced as she stared at him in terror. For the first time in her life she was literally scared stiff.

"Welcome, Mzzzzzz Carter," he hissed through his fangs.

She had to consciously remind herself to breathe as the saliva dripped off his sharp teeth, landing in tiny puddles less than an inch from her face.

He reached his claws out and gouged her arm, digging his claws into her skin. She closed her eyes and a scream finally escaped her mouth.

*   *   *

Casey sat there for several moments, debating it in her head. This was the biggest secret of her life. However, in order for him to understand the struggle, he needed to know.

"Whatever you decide," Mac finally said. "If you want me to, I will file it in my head and never mention it again, unless you come to me and ask to talk about it."

"Mac, it's huge."

"Talk to me. I swear to you. I make a vow to you that I will not say anything."

"If you do, so help me, I will kick your –"

He shook his head. "I won't."

She took a deep breath, before she blurted out, "Somewhere out there is a child of mine."

*   *   *

"Hey, Morgan!" Dale called out to a drop-dead gorgeous guy who got out of his car. Casey had never seen him before.

Casey watched him, stunned. "Who is that?"

"That is our rookie, Hunter Morgan," Dale said. "He just started this last week, you know since Tucker retired. His retirement party, by the way, is next Friday. You coming?"

She nodded, not talking her eyes off Hunter. "Actually, I probably can since 'C' shift is on."

Hunter Morgan looked to be about thirty-six or thirty-seven years old. He was six-foot-three, and had short, light brown hair that was slightly feathered on the sides and in the back, and the top was parted on the side. He also had amazing bluish-gray eyes. His tanned body, told how enjoyed his time off at the pool. Casey was sure Zoey and Bobbi Jo were already drooling over him. Unfortunately for them, it was against regulations to have relations with someone on your own shift.

"Hunter, man, come get some lunch!" Dale waved him over.

"He's a rookie?" Casey asked, making sure she heard them right.

"He's a transfer from outta Chicago," Matt explained.

*   *   *

"Man," Casey shook her head, as she nervously chuckled, "what's with you and the big questions?"

"Just curious as to what I'm dealing with here," Hunter said.

Her heart skipped a beat. "What do you mean by that?"

"Well, I don't want you jumping every time I touch you."

"Why would you be touching me at all?"

"Such paranoia!" He laughed. When he settled, he said, "Look, let's be realistic, there's an obvious attraction between us."

"Such arrogance!" Casey stood up, offended.

"No. Just honest."

Casey crossed her arms.   "I don't trust you."

"But…are you attracted to me?" He looked up at her with a smile of satisfaction.

*   *   *

Hunter stayed where he was, not wanting to scare Casey again. He liked her a lot. She captivated him. He forced himself to keep in mind his mission, but he was struggling inside. He saw her heart, and wanted more than anything to help free her from that which was holding her heart prisoner. He wanted to be her hero.

*   *   *

"I've held on for you. Please don't ask me to stay. I want to live in peace with our Father. You can bet, though," he wiped the tears off her face with his thumbs, "that I'll be getting a room ready for you up there. I will always look out for you."

She fought to get her sobbing under control for his sake. "You always have."

"Then know that I've done my best. I've fought for you, my country, and have even won a few battles for Christ as well while I was at it. I love you, Casey."

"I love you too, Jack," she said, resting her head on his chest. She listened to his staggered breaths as his heart rate slowed.

He reached his arms around her and held her as tight as he could. He kissed her head. "I love you," he quietly cried.

"I love you too. Thank you for everything you have done for me. Please, go be at peace with our Daddy. You're free."

She heard the rhythm of his heart monitor lag as his breathing faltered. She felt desperate as she cried, "I love you, my Jumpin' Jack!"

"I love you too…Space Case," he whispered, and he was gone.

*   *   *

Chief took a moment before he continued, "While I know this is something we had to go through not more than eight months ago, I have the confidence that we will come through it stronger than ever."

Panic churned so strongly inside Casey, that she thought she was going to throw up. "Chief?" She stood up. Jesse held her arms so she couldn't go anywhere. "Chief, where's Mac?" Casey nervously asked. She did not see Mac or his partner Carl Warner in the room. "Where's Warner?"

"Carter," Chief shook his head. Barely able to get the words out, he said, "I'm sorry."

She gulped. "He's in the hospital, right?"

He shook his head.

"No," she whispered. Her eyes locked on Chief, she said, "This can't be! No, he wouldn't do this to me!"

*   *   *

The Colonel gestured toward them. "This is what's left of the squad."

Casey pulled a chair from the table and sat down across from Mark and the Colonel.

"You've already met Captain Mark English." The Colonel nodded toward Mark. "This is Major Derek Cruise." He nodded toward the man in the chair to his right.

Derek Cruise looked to be about thirty-nine-years-old. He was about five-foot-eleven and had blue eyes. His short, dark brown hair was mixed with gray. As he sat there, Casey noticed that he was fit, but not nearly as muscular at Mark.

He nodded toward the man on the left. "And this is Major Keith Mariano."

Keith Mariano was about thirty-seven years old. He had dark brown hair, brown eyes, a natural slight tan, and was about six-foot-two.

"Guys, as you all know, this is Casey Carter, Jack's sister," Colonel continued. The men nodded as they sat in their seats, on edge.

"What's going on, Colonel? You're dead, but you're not. Mark over there is in the same position. Are you two dead?" She asked Derek and Keith. They nodded, so she turned to the Colonel and demanded, "Explain!"

"In doing what we do, we need to not exist."

"That was cryptic. Mind clearing it up a bit?" she snapped. "I'm not in the mood for games."

He sighed, as he shook his head with a smile on his face. "You're amusing. I give you that."

"Colonel," she warned.

He looked up at her and said, "We aren't here. This never happened."

"Fine! Just explain!"

"We do work for the government, specifically special ops in the Air Force."

"Tell me something I don't know." She crossed her arms in a huff.

"We're not allowed to exist in order to do what we do. We go in and out of the law all the time. We go into places that no one should ever see. We are exposed to things that if the average person saw it, it would give them nightmares. If we told you exactly what we did, it could literally put your life in danger."

*   *   *

"While your discretion is appreciated, it's misguided here," Derek pointed out. "We're on your side. We've been protecting you for years. We just wanted you to be aware of it, so you wouldn't be paranoid if you caught sight of us."

"If you guys have been protecting me, what happened in Columbia?" Casey asked the Colonel.

"That was Marcos's assignment," he said somberly.

"Okay. And who is that?" she asked.

"Marcos was Jack's partner. He was weak from being sick, but he still wanted to pull his weight," Keith explained. "Columbia was his last assignment. He died while he was down there."
Wide-eyed, she gulped, as he continued, "When you were attacked, he was dying in his hotel room. When you called Jack, we knew something happened to him. His job was to protect you, and if something happened to you, then something had to have happened to him."

"We scrambled after we got your call," Derek continued. "We had to get Jack cleared for his leave-of-absence, and get our behinds down there to find out what happened. While Jack went to you, the rest of us looked for Marcos and found him dead in his room."

"So," she put her hand up for him to stop, "if I'm following you right, you're telling me that everywhere I ever went in the world one of you guys was following me?"

"Yes," the Colonel said. "We would trade out so one person was watching you at all times, while the rest of us were on assignments."

"So, in doing that, you probably saved me from getting hurt, with the exception of Columbia."

"Yes," Mark said.

"When did this start?" she asked.

"From the day Jack first became an A.N.G.E.L.," Mark explained.

*   *   *

Once again, around nine-thirty Casey got a knock on her door. "Really?" She sighed as she got up off the couch. When she pulled the curtain back, she saw Mark standing there. She slightly opened the window, and told him to go to the back.

When she opened the sliding glass door, she said, "This is getting to be a really bad habit."

"Just checking in with you," he said, sitting on the couch.

She sat in the chair near the end of the couch where he was sitting. "I'm fine. You guys don't have to hold my hand."

"The Colonel said he had a rather disturbing conversation with you at Jack's grave the other day," Mark said.

"You can't be serious! Do you guys tell each other everything?"

"When it's something as important as your relationship with God, then yes."

"Are you a Christian?"

"Yes. I found Jesus through the Colonel about ten years ago in the field. We were in Cuba at the time. We were being held prisoner in a rebel camp when I just about lost it. They tortured both of us, but got nothing. We were there for about two weeks when the Colonel sat in the shed, singing. I was furious. How could he be singing in the middle of that? He said he had a peace within him. I wanted that peace. I wanted to feel free, even though I was being held captive. Well, long story short, I accepted Jesus as my Savior in that little shed in the middle of the forest in Cuba, and haven't steered from Him since. God is a God of love, Casey."

"I don't know. While I appreciate your concern, I'm angry with Him."

"How can you be?"

She looked at him, furious. "He took everything from me!"

"He gave everything for you!" Mark shot back. "Jesus gave His life for you. He sacrificed just so you could be with Him in Heaven. Isn't that what you told Jack?"

"I did," she admitted. "But that was before He took Jack and Mac away."

"Casey," he rested his hand on her knee, "you're being tested. God has something really big in store for you, or He wouldn't be taking you through this test. You are strong. You have a tremendous heart. God loves you and knows what you are made of."

"Then He might want to check the owner's manual on me. In case you missed it, I was in the hospital, remember?"

Mark sighed, shaking his head. "I've watched you for years. I have seen you grow up and turn into this amazingly beautiful woman. You purposely go into fires to help other people. Do you understand how much courage that takes?"

"Yes."

"Think about it this way: the fires you go into are nothing compared to the fires of Hell. Jesus went down there for three days, only to come back out with –"

"I know the story," she cut him off.

"Do you understand why though?"

"Yes. I fought to trust Him for a long time. That's the part that infuriates me. I trusted Him, only to have Him rip away any security I had in this world."

"Maybe He wants you to rely solely on Him. Maybe He wants you to feel your security is in Him, and not in people. Maybe, just maybe, He wants you to fully trust Him."

"I do." She sighed. "Well, I did."

"Casey, God loves you. He really does. He wants you to trust Him again."

"How can I? I don't feel comfortable trusting anyone right now. If I get close to them, are they going to die?"

Stunned, he asked, "Where did that come from?"

"My parents? Jack? Mac? I loved all of them, and they died."

"You don't seriously think you did that, do you?"

"Sometimes I wonder," she admitted.

"Casey, maybe Mac was with you to show you something. God may yet give you another man to share your life with."

"Why? So, He can take that person away too?"

"You're reading this all wrong. Mac's time was done. Jack's time was done."

"Well, I'm kind of tired of people being done when they get close to me."

* * *

After lunch, they took the trail that headed out to the mountain ridge where Casey accepted the Lord as her Savior. Casey fought the flashbacks of Mac, as she scrambled down the ledge with the others.

"How are you doing?" Jesse quietly asked her as they sat down on the rock.

"Doing okay," she said, staring out at the canyon before her.

"I can see it."

"See what?"

"The memories going through your head."

"Are you two going to whisper the whole time?" Brennon scowled. "It's like you guys have a secret. Want to share?"

"Just talking." Jesse shrugged. He sat back and crossed his arms.

"Well, you two have been 'just talking' a lot lately," he pointed out.

Jesse huffed. "Jealous?"

"They're close. Get a grip, Hanson." Kim rolled her eyes.

"What's your problem?" he snapped at her.

"I'm just tired of you complaining about it. No one else seems to have a problem with it."

"They do too," he said. "They just don't say anything."

"Why would anyone have a problem with us being close?" Casey asked.

"Probably because we just buried your fiancé about a month ago, and you're already joined at the hip with him."

"Hanson!" Jesse snapped, almost in a yell.

Casey looked at him, appalled.

"How dare you!" Jesse growled.

"It's true. I dare you to say different," Brennon challenged. "Where one is, the other one is not far behind."

"Jeff and Jay are like that, but you don't accuse them of anything inappropriate," Casey pointed out.

"Hold up!" Jeff put his hands up to stop the conversation. "Jay and I are not gay!"

"We know that." Casey rolled her eyes, as Kim and Sally giggled. "The point is, Jesse and I are not in any way, shape, or form, romantically involved either."

"Jack made me her brother on his deathbed," Jesse explained. "We're close because of that."

"And Kara's affair had nothing to do with how close you two are, huh?" Brennon challenged.

Jesse looked like he wanted to punch Brennon. He probably would have if they were not separated by six other people and on the ridge of a mountain.

"She said it was because you were either spending time at the station or with her," Brennon said.

Jesse glared at him. "How would you know?"

Brennon stood in front of Jesse with his arms crossed. "Who do you think she had the affair with?"

Jeff and Jay immediately jumped on Jesse, who went to lunge at Brennon. There was a momentary struggle to control Jesse, before Will got up and pulled Brennon up the path to a safer spot. Kim followed them up, and together they both forced Brennon back to camp.

It wasn't until they were out of sight, that Jeff asked Casey, "Is it clear?"

She stood up and looked over the ledge. Brennon was nowhere in sight, so she nodded.

"Good." Jeff looked back down at Jesse. "We're going to let you go, and you're going to go back over there and sit on the rock so we can talk. Got it?"

Jesse didn't move. You could see the anger in his eyes. Every muscle in his body was tense.

"Jess?" Jay asked after another minute of silence.

Tommy and Sally stayed beside Casey. They hadn't breathed since Brennon's confession.

"I will never forgive him for that!" Jesse seethed.

"Let's talk about this, okay?" Jeff tried to calm him down. "We're going to get up, and you're going to go over and sit by Casey. Can you do that for us?"

Jess looked at Tommy, Sally, and Casey, before he turned back to Jeff and Jay and nodded. Jeff and Jay got off him, and Jesse slowly sat up.

"Jess?" Casey asked. "Can I come down?"

He nodded, so she went over to him and gave him a hug. When she hugged him, she felt the anger inside of him. Jesse and Kara were dating for almost two years before it happened.

"Come on over to the rock, okay?" Casey coaxed.

He shook his head.

"Please? We're too close to the ledge here. I'm pretty sure if Jeff and Jay didn't jump on you, that you and Brennon would have gone over the side."

Jesse stared at Casey for several tense moments before he said, "I loved her."

"I know," she nodded in understanding, "just as much as I loved Mac. That's another bond we share."

He sighed before he turned to the others, and asked, "Why would one of my brothers do this to me?"

"She did it too," Sally point out. She was furious with Kara. They had been best friends for over five years.

"But he had an option of saying no, and he obviously doesn't regret it." Jesse got off the ground. A combination of hurt, shock, confusion, and fury churned inside him. "Why would he do that to me?"

"Jealousy is an ugly beast," Tommy said, as he and Sally came down off the rock. "He has liked Casey since she came to the station. He was beside himself when she and Mac started courting. Then, watching the two of you bonding more and more over the last several months, becoming closer than you already were, you could see the jealousy raging inside him. I wouldn't be surprised if he got together with Kara and they planned it."

"But, we have a brother/sister relationship. Why couldn't Kara see that? I would do anything for my family."

"We know that. Brennon can be pretty persuasive though," Jeff said. "I know he planted that seed in my head too."

"About us?" Casey asked, stunned.

"Yep. There were several of us keeping an eye on you two. He was trying to get something on either one of you, to get one of you guys either fired or transferred," Jay added.

"Why would he do that?" Casey asked.

"Probably because he wanted you for himself." He shrugged. "He put it by us as the rule was being broken. Out of fairness, it was our duty to make sure the rule still held."

Casey whistled in astonishment. "Wow."

"We need to get back and figure this thing out." Jeff reminded them, "We have to go to bed sometime here in the next couple of hours, and I would rather not do it with all that rage stirring around."

"Do you think you two can have a civil conversation?" Jay asked Jesse.

"I doubt it." He shook his head. "Maybe I'll just go home."

"You can't!" Jay and Casey objected at the same time.

"You've got my house!" Jay referred to the tent.

"And you came in with me," Casey pointed out.

"Besides the fact that we'd miss your smiling face," Sally added. "Come on, stay?"

He looked at them for a moment, before he finally relented, "All right."

"We have to talk to Brennon. Think you can stay here with Casey while we do? I think we need some referees before you two get together again," Jeff said.

"Yeah," he agreed.

After they left down the path, Jesse went over and sat down on the rock. He closed his eyes as he crossed his arms. Then he stretched his legs out in front of him and took a deep breath.

"Want some company?" Casey asked.

"Yeah, come here." He patted the seat next to him. When she sat down next him, he said, "I love you like a sister."

"I know."

"While I do love you, it's not the same love I had for Kara."

"I know. I feel the same way."

"There's nothing I wouldn't do for you."

"Same here."

*   *   *

The zipper on her tent slowly opened, waking her up. It had to be about three or four in the morning.

She slowly reached into her pocket and pulled her knife out as a foot came into her tent. Her heart raced, but she did not dare move. As long as the person did not know she was aware of them, she had the upper hand.

"Case?" She heard Mark's voice as he poked his head in.

"My word! This is daring!" she whispered in shock.

"Come outside," he said, before ducking back out of the tent.

Casey scrambled out of her sleeping bag. She cautiously climbed out of her tent, looking in every direction. She didn't zip it back up, because she wanted to be able to slip back in without unzipping it.

He grabbed her wrist and pulled her to the tree line, his eyes continuously darting in every direction. He took her there, so he could see what was going on at camp without anyone seeing them.

"What's going on?" she whispered.

He didn't say anything. He just grabbed her face and kissed her. She reached up and rested her hands on his wrists as she joined him in the kiss. The passion, electricity, and excitement behind the kiss made her not want to stop.

Several minutes later, Mark took a step back. He looked at her with a lot of intensity, as he rested his hands on her face. "I'm sorry. I just couldn't hold it in any longer."

"Where did…? That was…wow," Casey stammered, as she rested against the tree to catch her breath.

He took a step forward, bending so he was eye level to her, as he said in a low voice, "I have had feelings for you for years, but you were untouchable. You were my assignment. You are not supposed to get emotionally close to your assignments. But as we got closer over the last couple of weeks, and then you hugged me today…." He sighed. "Feeling you so close to me…I'm sorry. We don't have to mention this again, if you don't –"

She cut him off by kissing him again. He ran his hands tightly down her sides to her waist, as he strongly returned the kiss. "Is this…possible?" Casey asked in between kisses.

"If we're careful…yes….There will be times…when you won't see me…maybe for weeks at a time….You think…you can handle that?" he asked in between kisses as well.

"Yes," she said…and the kiss exploded!

She wrapped her arms tightly around his neck, as he pulled her closer to him. Their bodies tingled. Their thoughts were lost in each other's kisses.

"Wow!" Casey said as she breathed heavily. She leaned against the tree to catch her breath.

He looked up at her and admitted, "I've waited for so long. Jack and I even talked about it."

"What did he say?"

"He said if circumstances were different, he would whole-heartedly approve. The problem was that you weren't to know we existed."

"And now that I do?"

He looked at her and very seriously asked, "Can you lead two different lives?"

Chapter 1

Hellfire

The sand was thick in the air, while the sweltering, stagnant atmosphere hung around them. Mark, Derek, and Keith were tucked into a rock cave on the side of a mountain. The sun began its descent from the sky as it neared five in the afternoon, but it didn't ease the heat. Once the sun went down, the ground would give away its heat into the air, dropping temperatures nearly thirty-five to forty degrees.

The red and tan stone of the surrounding terrain of Kirkuk, Iraq, allowed the trio to blend in with their camouflage of brown, tan, and khaki. The way the heat danced off the ground would frequently create a mirage that messed with what one saw, creating a haze that was difficult to see through once on ground level. Mark knew this could make their job that much harder.

Derek wiped the sweat off his forehead. "Man, it's hot."

A layer of dirt coated each man. When the sweat dripped off their forehead, it left long streaks on their face.

Mark sighed, as he pulled out his binoculars. "Yeah, the Colonel is enjoying camping on a cool seventy-five-degree mountainside, while we're sitting in the stifling, ninety-seven-degree, blistering heat."

Keith raised an eyebrow at Mark. "Are you jealous of the Colonel camping, or the person he's watching?"

Mark shot him a dirty look before turning back to the binoculars.

Derek looked from Mark to Keith in confusion. "Wait. What did I miss?"

Keith huffed. "You couldn't tell?"

"Tell what?"

"Shut up!" Mark snapped, as he was sandwiched between Derek and Keith.

"Man, don't you see how he looks at her?" Keith said, satisfied of the accuracy of his assessment. "They also talk...a lot."

"What do you mean?" Derek asked.

"They meet every night he is on and she is off and talk for hours?"

Mark narrowed his eyes. "How do you know?"

Keith rolled his eyes. "Did I ever tell you what I do for a living?"

"Did I ever tell you that you need to get a life?" Mark shot back.

"Is he right?" Derek asked, stunned. He did not see that one coming.

Mark shrugged it off. "She's interesting. That's all."

"Interesting?" Keith chuckled. "Is that the best you got?"

"I'm warning you."

"Come on," Derek pressed.

"Look," Mark said, innocently, "she's a sweet kid."

"Kid?" Keith's jaw dropped. "Open your eyes, brother! She's no kid. She's a woman."

Derek nudged Mark. "And a pretty one at that."

"You two can shut up now," Mark grumbled.

"Just saying. You might wanna open your eyes," Keith pointed out, adjusting to get a better position to look through his sight tool. He had to make a plan on where to place the charges once he got his opportunity.

"She just lost her fiancé," Mark pointed out. "What makes you think she's even looking?"

"By the way she looks at you."

"She does not."

"Focus." Derek slapped Mark's arm when he saw movement in the camp below through his binoculars. "Movement."

Mark put the binoculars to his eyes and groaned. "They're moving Harrison to interrogation again." Mark got a knot in his stomach, knowing they were going to torture Harrison within an inch of his life. They would have to sit there listening to his screams, not being able to do anything until the sun went down. "They don't deserve this," Mark said, disgusted.

"They know what they signed up for – same as us," Keith pointed out. "While we hope we make it out alive, we know the possibility of not coming out is realistic. It's a sacrifice I am willing to make."

"But to go like that?" Mark cringed as they heard shrieks of pain in the distance. He dropped his head onto his hands, feeling sick to his stomach. He didn't want to listen to it anymore. He really didn't want to have to wait until sundown to pull them.

"We need to wait," Derek said, reading Mark's body language. "You know there is a better chance of success if we do it in the dark."

"What time is evac?"

"0200."

Keith swore before he said, "You mean we have to wait until a quarter 'til two in the morning to get them out?"

"It's the best he could do. The fact that we have any evac is a miracle. They're only going to wait until 0215 before they take off, so it has to go off without a hitch. There's not a lot of room for error here," Derek said.

Suddenly a bomb went off in the city about a half mile away. The debris shot into the air, spraying portions of a cement building all over, while a vehicle spun over on top of itself. Mark shook his head again. "I'm getting too old for this."

"Was that them or us?" Keith asked.

Mark put the binoculars to his eyes, adjusting for the distance. What he saw made him angry. "Ours. It was an IED versus a Humvee," Mark said, referring to an Improvised Explosive Devise.

"How many?" Derek asked.

"We lost at least three." Mark swallowed hard, knowing three more of his fellow brethren had fallen. He wanted more than anything to be able to pull the three currently in danger before they lost anymore.

Derek grabbed his arm when Mark went to get out from under their rock alcove. "No. Not yet."

"We have to do something!"

Keith tugged him back into the alcove. "We can't. The evac is set for 0200. Just wait."

Mark settled back down in his position, visibly agitated. "I don't understand. Why is it that all we can do is watch?"

"This is what we were sent here to do," Keith said. He sighed before he continued, "Look, I don't want it to end here. Harrison, Miller, and Matthews don't want it to end here. If that God of yours is looking out for us, it won't. We have to wait in order for all of us to make it out though."

"What's holding you back?" Mark asked, referring to past conversations between Keith and him about God.

"In looking at all of this," he gestured toward the blown-up countryside, "You need to ask? Why would a God of love ever let this happen? Why would He let war even exist? War is evil. It takes men, women, and children alike with no mercy. Why would this God of yours, who is supposed to love everyone, let Harrison go through that?" He pointed at the building in the compound where Harrison was being tortured. The trio heard him screaming from where they were perched on the mountainside.

"Unfortunately," Mark said, "that's where free will comes in."

"That's your answer?" Keith asked, stunned. "Are you kidding me? That's the best you've got?"

"That's the only answer I can give you," Mark said. "Free will affects the choices we make…that they make. It's their choice to torture for information. It's their choice to treat other humans with such distain and disrespect that it propels others to fight for their freedom. It's our choice to step in and fight for their freedom…for the continued freedom of our families and friends. It's our choice to stand up for what is right, when others run the other way or duck behind orders. We're not supposed to be here. According to the orders these men were given, they will not be acknowledged. They knew the risks, but did what they felt was right. They were rewarded for it by being left behind. However, God had a different plan in mind. That's why we're here. That's why I'm here."

Keith let out a string of swear words under his breath.

"Easy," Derek said, trying to calm down both men.

"What about the other A.N.G.E.L.s you've met over the years? Didn't you learn anything from them?" Mark questioned Keith. "You know this is bigger than any of us. Sacrifices need to be made."

"F-18s," Derek said.

Hearing the jets in the distance, Derek instantly recognized their unmistakable roar. He was the ears of the team, because his range was better than the rest of the team. Over the years, the sounds of war had taken its toll on their bodies, hearts…and souls.

"What are they doing here?" Mark looked over to Derek for an explanation, as Derek was mission leader on this one.

"No idea. No one is supposed to know we're even here. I wasn't expecting company until zero-two-hundred."

The men ducked further into the shadows of the rock alcove as the jets neared their position. A surface-to-air missile shot into the air from inside the camp below them. The lead jet answered the surface-to-air missile with a stinger that hit its target on the first shot, but not before the missile smashed into the mountainside. The mountain shook near the trio. They ducked to cover their heads as the rubble rained down on them.

Keith swore. "We need to pull them now! They're going to kill them!"

"They're eight hours early, but are you ready?" Derek asked Keith. Keith's job was to get C-4 ready to use as a distraction so the others could escape.

Keith grabbed the bag containing the explosives, offering a nod before the men scrambled out of their protective hideout and ran toward their mission. Running and sliding down the hillside, while ducking gunfire and debris as the F-18 distracted their targets, the elite band of men went to work, diving into the hornet nest of what only minutes before was a calm camp.

Mark knew exactly where they were holding the men. While he and Derek went after the men, Keith set the C-4 charges. Then Keith retreated to a safe distance behind a tall boulder for his own cover a hundred yards outside the camp where he would cover the escape.

In losing the element of surprise, Mark decided the first rally point, set for a half-mile away near the base of the mountain, was out of the question. The second rally point would be their goal – set out a mile away from the camp. Watching the camp through the day, Mark knew the men would be injured, so going on foot was not going to be an option. They would need a secondary way of escape. He tapped Derek's arm as they crouched next to a building on the edge of camp, and pointed toward a couple of vehicles near the building where the prisoners were being held.

Derek nodded in response. That would be their way out.

The men were well armed for their mission. Keith carried the C-4, along with a MK-23 and a M-4 with a 203-grenade launcher. He was on his own until the trio met up at the Blackhawk. In the meantime, Derek and Mark each carried a MP-5 with a MK-23 for backup. They each also carried a Socom knife to use if push came to shove and they were out of ammunition.

Derek and Mark moved through the tiny camp as clean as they could amidst the firefight that raged around them. The strategically placed missiles of the F-18s hit their targets all around them, clearing the way, but the dirt and debris made the air thick, and harder to breathe.

When the men turned the corner near the building where the prisoners were being held, two men with AK-47s awaited them. With instinct and adrenaline propelling them forward, Mark and Derek fired their MP5s, leaving the guards mangled bodies in the dust. Hearing the yelling and men from the camp running in their direction, they bolted for the building. Mark kicked the wooden door in while Derek stayed outside to keep watch.

The three prisoners squinted up at the bright light of the setting sun that suddenly penetrated their cement cage. "Time to go, boys!" Mark grabbed the arm of the man nearest to him.

Harrison didn't resist when Mark pulled him out of the windowless concrete building that was their holding cell. Matthews and Miller quickly followed, now knowing the explosions that rattled around them meant their freedom. When they ran toward the vehicles of escape, a building they ran past exploded from a grenade thrown by one of the insurgents from the camp. The men hit the ground with a thud while debris blew out the windows.

"GO! GO! GO!" Derek shoved Miller and Matthews forward.

They stumbled to get their feet under them as adrenaline coursed through their bodies. Mark threw Harrison over his shoulders, knowing Harrison didn't have much else in him.

In the meantime, Keith had set charges in several key areas. Hearing the building blow up, he looked through his binoculars to see the men scrambling to their feet. He set off a charge that exploded the ammunition storage for the camp first, before setting off another that blew up one of the buildings on the other side of camp. The explosions allowed the men to get to one of the insurgent's vehicles within the camp. As Derek covered the bodies of the three prisoners in the back of truck with his own body to shield them from further injury of the soaring debris, Mark hotwired the vehicle, throwing it into drive with his foot down on the gas as fast as the truck would go.

Keith looked up in time to see a man with a RPG-7 drive out of the camp in a Jeep, along with two other guys with AK-47s. They came to a halt twenty feet from Keith. The men within the camp slammed the wooden doors shut behind them, leaving the three to defend the stronghold from the outside. The man with the RPG aimed at the F-18s. Keith pulled the pin and threw a grenade at the Jeep. It bounced off the back seat and blew, propelling the men's bodies into the air, flipping the Jeep on top of one of them. As the two thrown from the vehicle landed, they twitched for only a moment before they stopped moving.

The more charges Keith set off, and targets the stingers from the jets blew up, the thicker the air around him became. From his position, Keith heard the wonderful sound of the extrication crew. He knew the helicopters were on the way, so it wouldn't be long. He set off two more of the charges inside the camp, watching as Mark and Derek crashed the truck through the closed wooden gates of the compound, before spinning the tires in the direction of the second rally point. He took that moment to run as fast as he could, knowing he would have to sprint over three-quarters of a mile to the safety of the helicopters.

He stopped about halfway there, and set off the remaining four charges, sending the camp into a fireball. He thanked Mark and Derek's God when he saw the two Blackhawks and four Apache helicopters silhouetted against the setting sun. For good measure, he spun around and sent a couple rockets into the camp, making sure there would be no trouble for the extraction crews.

In the distance, he saw the two Blackhawks waiting with engines rotating. He saw Derek enter one with Miller, dragging Harrison in with them, while Mark and Matthews jumped into the second one. Seeing that, he knew he was targeting to jump into Mark's Blackhawk.

The Apaches rained down a round of Hydra 70 rockets and a Hellfire to give Keith the chance he needed to get to the Blackhawks. He looked toward the blazing inferno behind him to see a truck spin out from the encampment. He couldn't believe anyone had survived the firestorm from the air support and the fireball he created.

Keith ran as fast as he could. He heard the bullets whizzing by his head from the incoming truck, and dove for the ground with only a precious hundred yards to safety. Mark jumped out, spraying the area providing cover fire, as the Apaches sent another barrage of Hydras toward the truck, creating a wall of fire as the truck exploded. Keith scrambled to his feet.

"MOVE!" Mark roared as he emptied his MP-5.

As Keith dove for the helicopter, two of the Apaches sent in another round of the Hydra 70's and a Hellfire for good measure, finishing off what was left of the camp. Mark reached out, yanking Keith into the safety of the Blackhawk.

Keith looked up to see the relief of four crewmen of the Blackhawk at seeing him alive. He quickly clipped himself in, and the Blackhawks took off in the opposite direction they had come. The four Apaches flanked the Blackhawks with the F-18s overhead. When they were cleared and headed toward safety, with a tip of the wings, the F-18s broke off. The helicopters finished the journey on their own.

Lost in their own thoughts, neither Keith nor Mark said a word the entire flight. That was too close for Keith. He might have resisted this God of theirs for the last time. Seeing his life flash before his eyes when he dove for the ground may have pushed him over the edge. He and Jack were the last two holdouts of the A.N.G.E.L.s. They did what they could to support the unit, but seeing everything they had over the years made their hearts hard. When Jack came to Christ, he pleaded with Keith to listen. By that point, Keith was done with the world. His heart was jaded. He looked toward Mark who was lost in his own thoughts. Even in the midst of the chaos that ensued, he could still see the peace Mark had on his face. Mark reached in his pocket, pulled a photo out, and gently rubbed his thumb over it.

Seeing the camp in the distance, knowing they would be landing soon, Keith made a decision. He didn't want to die without God. He had been through Hell on Earth. From what he understood over the years, he would have that forever if he didn't make a decision to follow this Jesus. It was his understanding that Jesus was the one and only way to eternal safety.

Matthews rested his hand on Keith's arm. "Thanks, man."

"Anytime, brother. You would do the same."

"Anytime, anyplace," Matthews agreed. "Gotta ask," he said, as the helicopters lowered to the ground, "what unit are you guys?"

"We're A.N.G.E.L.s," Mark said as he hopped out of the helicopter. "We were never here."

"You guys are real?" He stared at him jaw-dropped and eyes wide. "I thought you were a myth! I've heard stories, but had no idea you were real."

"We were never here," Mark reiterated with a stern tone.

He nodded in understanding and appreciation. "Yes, sir."

Mark and Keith slipped out of the helicopter, meeting Derek in between the two Blackhawks as medics assisted the other three. "Need to meet with Keller. They came too early and almost got all of us killed." Derek was angry, yet relieved at the same time. He was glad they were able to get the men out, and that everyone escaped, but no one was supposed to come in until zero-two-hundred. "Go get showers. I'll meet you at the mess hall. We leave in the morning."

"Yes, sir." Mark and Keith said, and then headed one way, while Derek headed another.

Mark and Keith were quiet during their showers. It carried over to when they sat at the table, eating. Finally, Keith looked up at Mark and asked, "Who's the picture of?"

Mark raised an eyebrow. "What picture?"

"The one in your pocket. Who is it?"

"What are you talking about?"

"You were looking at a photo in the helo. Who was it?"

Mark froze for a minute, before he set down his fork. After a couple of moments, he reached in his pocket and reluctantly pulled out the photo. He glanced at it one more time before he passed it to Keith.

Keith's eyes popped. "When and where did you get this?"

Mark gave him a knowing look.

"This is recent."

"About a month after Jack passed."

"Why?"

Mark wasn't sure he could explain it. He thought of how to answer his question before he said, "She is why I'm here."

He handed the photo back to Mark, who tucked it safely into his pocket. "I don't understand," Keith said, shaking his head.

"Casey was at the station one day, and you know the crap they play on each other."

"Yeah." He chuckled. He had witnessed several of the practical jokes himself.

"She pulled one over on a couple of the guys, and the smile that lit her face...." He sighed dreamily. "I just wanted to remember what I'm giving my life for. What I'm sacrificing for."

"What's that supposed to mean?"

"John 15:13 says, "Greater hath no love than this: to lay down one's life for one's friends." Casey is more than a friend. She's family. When it comes to doing what we do, there is a bigger picture. It's more than just my own life at stake."

"I get that. That's why we're here…to protect freedom."

"I don't want to die, but I'm willing. However, I'm here for a greater purpose than those men we rescued today."

"Meaning?"

"The most I can do is give my life for my country," Mark said. "But, Jesus gave His life for the world – past, present, and future. I'm here to do His will."

Keith shook his head. "I don't get it. How can some guy who died thousands of years ago help me today? That doesn't make sense."

"John 3:16 and 17 says, "For God so loved the world that He gave his one and only Son, that whoever believes in Him shall not perish but have eternal life. For God did not send His Son into the world to condemn the world, but to save the world through Him." God sent Jesus so we, meaning you and me, can enjoy Heaven when we die. As you said earlier, we've seen the evil this world has to offer. Do you want that for all eternity?"

"Uh, no thank you. Hell on Earth for this lifetime is more than enough for me."

"Well, hate to tell you, but you're on track to face that for all eternity too."

Furrowed brow, Keith asked, "What if I don't want to?"

"Not an option. Let me explain it this way…there are two teams in play. You have to pick one or the other."

"What if I don't want to play the game?"

"It's not an option, brother." Mark shook his head. "You're already on one team. You actually have to choose to leave it to go to the other one. You're playing whether you want to or not."

Keith scoffed as he crossed his arms. "How is that a choice?"

"We're all born into the team headed to Hell for all eternity. God, gracious as He is, gave us another option through the blood Jesus shed on the cross. You don't have to stay on that team anymore. You can opt out and go to the other team – the team the Colonel, Derek, Jack, and I are on."

"And if I don't?"

"You'll end up in a firestorm like you set today…forever."

Keith shook his head, upset. After a long minute, he looked up at Mark. Knowing what he had to do, he asked, "How do I do that?"

A pleased smile crossed Mark's face as he said, "Matthew 7:7 says, "Ask and it will be given to you; seek and you will find; knock and the door will be opened to you." All you have to do is pray and ask Jesus to be your Savior. You need to ask Him to forgive you of your sins, and to show you His purpose for your life."

"I have a purpose."

"Right now, your purpose is to put your life on the line for others. When are you going to do something for yourself?"

He shook his head in confusion. "I do stuff for myself all the time."

"What about your eternal security?"

Keith sighed, knowing what he meant.

"Now, don't do it just for fire insurance."

"Ha!" Keith chuckled. "That's a joke! I'm the pyromaniac of the unit. Fire doesn't bother me. On the contrary, it fascinates me. However," he held his hand up to stop Mark from interrupting, "I understand what you're saying."

"And?"

"I don't want to die at all. And, I really don't want to die without this Jesus of yours either."

*   *   *

Mark's camouflage-painted face was less than a few inches from Casey's, when he asked, "Can you lead two different lives?"

Casey gasped as she sat up straight in her sleeping bag. It took her a moment to remember she was camping with the fire company in the woods. She dropped her head into her hands, bracing her elbows on her knees. The argument between Brennon Hanson and her best friend, Jesse McFadden, ran through her mind…then she remembered the dream she had of Mark English.

Mark was one of the A.N.G.E.L.s from her brother's squad. The A.N.G.E.L.s had been looking out for Casey since she was thirteen. She remembered the long talks she and Mark had on the nights she was off work over the last two weeks. While Jesse helped Casey work through the deaths of Jack and Mac, Mark took on a different roll. He reminded Casey as to why she trusted God in the first place. He reminded her why Jesus was so important to her, and why she treasured the guidance of the Holy Spirit.

"Wow." She let out a slow breath of air, remembering what Mark looked like in the woods earlier that day. He was in camouflage from head to toe. His brown eyes blended with the face paint colors of green, brown, and black, while his blond hair stood out on his six-foot frame.

Then it hit her. The dream. The kiss. The passion. Her face flushed in embarrassment as she reprimanded herself again. Mac meant the world to her. How could she be dreaming of another man? This was too soon. She wondered if the dream had any element of truth to it. Did Jack and Mark ever talk about the two of them?

"Stop it!" she whispered, angry with herself.

She couldn't shake the dream, so she left her tent in hopes that the coolness of the night would clear her mind. She was surprised to see Jesse sitting on a log next to what was left of the fire. She sat down beside him. "What are you doing up?" she asked, as she picked up a stick and played with the embers that still burned among the coals.

"I can't sleep."

"Were you and Brennon able to work things out?"

"We worked things out enough to put up with each other until we can return to the station and talk to Chief. If you can't trust the person watching your back not to stab you in the back, it makes it extremely difficult to go into a burning building with them."

"This is true."

"If we can't work together, Chief may change our shifts." He watched her for her reaction. When he saw the shock on her face, he quickly added, "I don't want to though." Turning his attention back to the coals, he picked up a stick to play with a piece of charcoal that escaped the cluster and sighed. "The people on 'A' shift are like family to me."

"If we have a vote, Brennon is the one who gets transferred," Casey said, as the anger that was an almost constant as of late, surged through her once again. "I don't want to lose you on my shift either. I would quit first."

"What? You can't!"

"You have to stay on my shift. If you're not there, it'll be a nightmare."

"That's sweet."

"I'm serious. I'll quit if Chief transfers you. You're right. You have to trust the men who have your back on a fire scene. I don't trust Brennon. If Chief leaves him, and transfers you to another shift instead, I promise you I will quit."

"Don't do that. You're too valuable."

"So are you. Give yourself credit."

He shook his head.

"Jess, you have to stay on our shift. I'm going to talk to Chief about it too. This is something I feel strongly about."

"All right." He sighed. "I know better than to argue with you when you're this emotional."

"Good." She stood. "Then go back to bed. I know I am."

"Case?"

"Yeah?"

"Thanks."

"No problem. I know you would do the same for me."

Casey fought most of the night to sleep. She tossed and turned. The feelings left over from Brennon and Jesse's fight intermingled with Casey's feelings regarding her dream of Mark. The emotional mixture brought up her struggles to work through Mac's death. How long would it take her to move on? Could she move on?

She finally decided the only thing she could do about her feelings was pray. That made her angry again. She was angry with God about taking Jack and Mac in the first place. She didn't want the anger in her body anymore though. It wore her out. She would often wake up exhausted. All of the emotional turmoil gave her a headache.

She took a couple aspirin before she went to bed. She prayed to God in her head as she cleared her mind, heart, and soul. She knew the first step in moving forward, was to repair her relationship with her Father, the Lord God. She longed for Him and missed His presence in her life.

*   *   *

The next morning, things were still tense between Brennon and several of the firefighters. They could not believe Brennon had an affair with Jesse's girlfriend, Kara – you don't mess with a fellow firefighter's mate. Trust was critical within the firefighter community. Working side-by-side for long hours each week formed a strong bond. Sometimes that bond was stronger than an average family, which was why Brennon's betrayal cut so deep. The equivalent of Brennon's crime would be one brother sleeping with another brother's wife in a real family.

The 'B' shift guys came in at about ten that morning. Before they arrived, as a group, 'A' shift decided to keep silent about what happened between Brennon and Jesse. If someone asked about the tension, they agreed to say they had a fight, and it was between them. No one was to give details.

Hunter sat down next to Casey, where she ate her lunch next to the fire pit. "Hey." He put his arm around her and asked, "So, how about a hike after lunch?"

"Um, what?" she asked, taken aback.

"Well, I think we need to talk."

She reached around and took his arm off her shoulders. "Well, I don't think we do."

"Now, why are you going to be like that? There is an obvious attraction between us. Why are you denying it?"

She shook her head in irritation. "Hunter, are you really going to start this again?"

"Why are you fighting it?"

"Because I don't want it."

"Sure you do." He grinned. "How could you not?"

"Could you be any more arrogant?" she snapped.

He looked at her for a minute before he leaned back in his seat, folded his arms, and tried a different tactic. He learned in working with her that she was different from most women. This made his assignment more difficult than he had anticipated. He knew people were counting on him to get certain information. He had a perfect track record, and he wasn't about to let one woman destroy that record. He had to figure out a way to get her to trust him. "So, what's going on with Hanson and McFadden?"

"They had a fight." She shrugged. "That's between them."

"About what?"

"You need to ask them." She took the last bite of her burger.

He let out a frustrated breath of air. "Oh, Casey, Casey, Casey."

She looked at him out of the corner of her eye as she chewed her burger.

"You know you want me."

She shook her head.

Matt snuck up behind her. "Boo!"

Casey gasped as she jumped, and what was left of her burger lodged in her throat, blocking her air. Her hand immediately went to her throat. She swallowed in an attempt to get the bite down while she strained to breathe.

Hunter sat up in his seat in alarm, but tried to contain himself in case he was wrong. "Casey?"

"What?" Matt came around and knelt in front of her. "Are you okay?"

She shook her head 'no' while she tapped her throat to signal to him that she wasn't getting any air. Her face got redder by the second.

"Casey." Hunter put his hands on the arms of his chair ready to spring when her face turned red.

"Is it blocked? Are you chokin'?" Matt asked her.

Casey nodded, so Hunter jumped up out of his seat. He pulled Casey out of her chair and wrapped his arms around her in the Heimlich maneuver to release the food.

It shifted with the first abdominal thrust, but it didn't release. Casey fought the black cloud that tried to consume her. A crowd started to form as her face shifted to a reddish purple. Since they were mostly paramedics, they stood back and let Hunter and Matt handle it.

"Did it work?" Hunter asked Matt.

Matt shook his head 'no' while he watched Casey's face. As Hunter did another abdominal thrust, the bite of hamburger and bun flew out of her mouth and hit the ground about five feet from them.

Casey sunk into Hunter's arms. She felt weak, and her head pulsated with each pound of her heart. She was mortified, yet relieved at the same time.

Hunter lowered them to the ground while Matt coaxed, "Come on, you're starting to get some more color there. Take deep breaths…not too fast now."

Casey took a few minutes to get her breathing under control.

"Getting better." Matt nodded in approval as people dispersed.

Jesse knelt down next to Hunter, who still had Casey in his arms. "What happened?"

"I scared her, not realizing she had food in her mouth. I'm sorry, Casey." Matt felt horrible. She could tell by the look on his face.

"You didn't…know," she said in between breaths.

"So, why is it that I keep finding you in my arms lately?" Hunter looked down at Casey. He winked at her with a grin on his face.

Casey's head pounded, but Hunter had aggravated her one too many times. She glared at him while she moved her arm forward, then jabbed her elbow back into his mid-section as hard as she could.

*   *   *

The Colonel watched the scene from a distance. He just about spit his water out of his mouth as he laughed when he saw Casey elbow Hunter. He decided to check into him deeper when the others got back, because he reminded the Colonel of someone from his past. He knew it couldn't be him though, because that man was old enough to be Hunter's father, but could it be the sins of the father were passed down to the son?

*   *   *

Hunter wasn't expecting Casey to elbow him, and he immediately doubled over in pain. "Oww! What was that for?" He scowled, holding his ribs.

Casey slid over near Jesse. He put his arm around her, as he glanced from Hunter to Casey in shock. After a moment, he asked, "What did you do to her?"

Matt watched what was going on in front of him, stunned. He didn't expect that from Casey. When he worked with her, she was laid-back and easygoing.

"I didn't do anything!" Hunter groaned, rubbing his ribs.

"Casey?" Jesse asked her.

"He won't leave me alone," she defended herself.

"I just saved your life, and this is the thanks I get! You are so not worth this!" Hunter held his side as he got up, leaving them sitting there.

"What did we miss? Why is everyone so tense around here?" Matt asked Jesse. "You and Hanson look like you're ready t' punch each other out, and Carter just got Morgan in the ribs."

Jesse sighed, shaking his head. "It's a long story."

Chapter 2

Lost

Casey lay down for about an hour after everything settled. When she woke up, she still had a headache, so she took a couple more aspirin before leaving the tent.

As her eyes adjusted to the sunlight, she saw Matt at the table eating lunch. She grabbed a handful of chips and put them on a plate before she sat down beside him. "Hey."

He smiled. "Hey, darlin'."

"Have things improved at all out here?"

"A little. It helps that Hanson left about an hour ago. How are you feeling?"

"I took a couple of aspirin, but it's tolerable. My head has been hurting since last night."

"I'll bet. I've heard rumors about what all happened around here yesterday, not to mention the things that happened in your personal life lately."

"You have no idea." She sighed. Then she realized what he said. "Um, what do you mean by rumors?"

"Some of the kids were talking about the yelling between Hanson an' McFadden. They weren't sure what it was about though. They just didn't like the yelling."

"It wasn't fun," Casey admitted.

"Hey, sis," Jesse sat on the other side of Casey, "how's your headache?"

"I took a couple aspirin," she said. "Give it a bit to work, and I should be fine."

"Why don't you go sit in the lake like you did yesterday? It was cool, and you were relaxed, right?"

"Yeah, that sounds good."

"Well, I'm going to go play some hoops. Why don't you grab something decent to eat and then cool yourself down? Chips alone are not healthy."

She rested her head on her hand. "All right."

"You don't feel well, do you?" Jesse asked in concern.

"I'm fine. I'll go cool down by the lake."

She went to her tent and pulled out her navy-blue hooded sweatshirt, tan shorts, her on-piece black bathing suit, her towel, hairbrush, and a pair of socks for her hiking boots for when she got out of the lake. She put on her shorts and bathing suit, while she carried the rest of her belongings.

When she got to the lake, she set down everything, making a spot for herself on the shore. It was bright and hot at the campground that day. Casey noticed the incoming clouds and prayed rain wouldn't ruin the retreat. She enjoyed the outdoors – the fresh scent, the flowers, the animals running around in their element. She also took delight in the way people acted out in the open air. They seemed relaxed, more laid back…free to be themselves.

She slipped off her shorts and left them on her towel on the shore. Then she headed over to the shallow part of the lake away from the kids. The water was still on the chilly side, so she had to admit it was a good idea.

Casey sighed as she soaked her legs in the waist-deep lake water. She leaned back with her arms braced behind her in the cool, refreshing water while watching the flurry of activity around her. It was nice to see the families having fun together. She appreciated watching the parents with the children the most. She missed that growing up and longed for it. She knew she would never have it though. It wasn't meant for her.

The more she reflected on the parent/child relationships around her, the more she thought about Angelina. Casey knew Angelina had what she would never have. She knew she had a set of loving parents who would take care of her for a long time. While Casey's parents did love her, they were busy and unfortunately were only around until she was eight. While she realized it wasn't by choice, it still deeply hurt her.

She was so into her thoughts that she didn't hear Hunter come up behind her until he sunk in the water beside her and stretched his legs out in front of him.

She groaned, rolling her eyes. "Ohhh, what do you want now?"

"You look nice in a bathing suit." He nodded in approval, as he looked her over while sitting beside her in only his swim trunks.

Casey shook her head, disgusted.

"So, tell me…." Hunter started.

She looked over at him, irritated, and impatiently snapped, "What?"

"Why did you punch me earlier?"

"Because you won't leave me alone. Obviously, I didn't do it hard enough because you came back."

"Ouch! Such hostility." He cringed. "Okay, what if we start over?"

"Why?"

"Well, if I'm going to be a member of 'A' shift, I think we should be able to have a conversation and one of us not get hurt."

"You're going to what?"

"I got a call from Chief a while ago. It seems Hanson needs to change shifts. Not that I think anyone here will object, seeing the glares flying around earlier."

"Why are you the one who's changing though?"

"I guess because I have the least amount of seniority, with the exception of the new guy starting here in a couple of days. He gave me the option of staying on 'B' or coming to 'A' shift. The new guy got the other one. I chose to go to 'A' shift."

"I see."

"So, do you think we can get along?"

"Maybe. Whose partner are you going to be?"

"Richter's, I assume." He shrugged. "That is, unless you want me to switch with Van den Bergh?"

"Nope." She shook her head. "Pete and I get along just fine."

"Pete, huh?"

Casey sighed in irritation. Her headache came thundering back with a vengeance. "What is with you?"

"What do you mean?"

"You have a one-track mind. All you seem to be focused on are romantic relationships – mainly mine. There's more to life than that."

"Such as?"

"Such as family, friends, the work we do every day when we are on shift. You know, saving lives and people's precious memories," she said with a touch of sarcasm.

"So, there's no room in there for romance? Do you not want a family of your own? Don't you want a husband and children?"

"I doubt that will ever happen. I'm thirty-five years old. Children are close to being biologically impossible. And before you say it – no, I'm not going to have sex with a guy just to get pregnant." She was rapidly losing patience with him. He went from annoying to aggravating in one conversation.

He chuckled. "So, you don't want children?"

"Why are you so fixated on me? Why don't you go after Martes like this?"

"Because she's taken. Besides, you're a challenge."

"A challenge? What's that supposed to mean?"

"You are loyal and giving. You're a great cook. You know what you're doing on the ambulance and in a fire scene. Mac was always talking about you. He loved everything about you – including the photos you take. He loved your heart the most, though. I admit that I was jealous. But…" he added as she went to object, "you are also a tough person to get close to. When you do let someone in, they seem to get stronger around you. Look at McFadden for example."

"What about Jesse?"

"Since you two have gotten close, he has become deep, more thoughtful. Mac was always that way, but he began to lighten up and enjoy life more when you two got together. You bring out things in people they didn't know they had."

"Do I want to know what I bring out in you?"

"You bring out the thinker in me."

Casey raised an eyebrow.

"No really." He laughed when he saw her face. "What you said the night in the engine bays hit home. You're right. I don't keep relationships with women because I don't know why they want me. You on the other hand, I know you don't want me for my looks, so it pushes me to be more."

She shrugged as she looked back out at the lake. "Looks are temporary."

"You're beautiful too." He peeked at her before he shifted back out to the water.

She glanced at him out of the corner of her eye. "Are you asking for it again?"

He laughed as he shook his head. "That's what your brother said."

"I'll take that as a compliment."

"Ready for our hike yet?" Jesse came into the water with Will and sat down beside her, squeezing his way between Casey and Hunter.

She looked at him in confusion before he winked at her. He was running interference for her with Hunter.

"Yep. Oh, Jesse, did you know Hunter is going to be joining our shift?" Casey asked.

"Really?" He narrowed his eyes at Hunter. "How'd ya swing that one?"

"It seems Hanson wants to change to 'B' shift for some reason." Hunter shrugged him off. "Chief called and wanted to know if I minded changing shifts."

While Jesse nodded in understanding, he didn't trust Hunter as far as he could throw him.

Will lightly nudged him from behind to get him to focus. "Um, hike?"

"Yeah. Ready?" he asked Casey.

"Can I go?" Hunter asked.

Jesse shrugged as they got up out of the lake. "Sure, why not?"

Casey slipped her shorts, socks, and hiking boots on over her bathing suit. Then she tied her sweatshirt around her waist for later, before tossing her towel and brush into the tent, and they left.

Jesse, Casey, Hunter, Will, Jeff, Jay, Kim, Scott, and Pete went on the hike. Everyone else stayed in camp. Captain Hartley yelled something about dinner being at six as they walked toward the woods.

While there were marked trails, they intersected, twisted, and turned with others, and the group took whatever way they wanted, mixing them up. After about an hour, the group headed off the paths toward some hills they saw in the distance that would give them a great view of the surrounding valley. Casey was a little concerned as they headed off the trails, but the others in the group assured her they would be fine since they camped there frequently. She and Jack used to do survival training while they were camping, so the thought crossed her mind to mark the trail, but she trusted the others, so she left it alone. About an hour and a half into the hike, Casey became disorientated as to what direction they were heading, let alone what direction they came from. She did not have the least bit of confidence that she could get them back, so she was glad the others with her said they could get back to camp.

They hiked in the woods off the trails over four hours, until they reached a ridge where they could sit down and rest. It wasn't their intended location, but it was picturesque. The ponderosa pine trees sent off their natural fragrance that reminded Casey of vanilla. It mixed with the Douglas fir scent that was reminiscent of Christmas. The animals scurried in and out of the thick underbrush, as well as in the valley below them. As they sat along the ridge, the surrounding flora and fauna added to the sense of contentment to the small company of crewmembers.

"Magnificent!" Casey sighed as she rested back on the rock. Kim was on one side of her with Jesse on the other.

"Yeah. I'm glad we did this. I definitely needed to see this," Hunter agreed. "It's stunning."

They chitchatted for over an hour, until Scott glanced at his watch. "Hartley's going to be looking for us for dinner. We've been gone for five and a half hours."

Jeff stood up and brushed his shorts off as he said, "We should get back anyway. We only have a couple more hours of sunlight and we need to be back to the trails by then."

They headed back up the hill from the ridge. When they got to the level ground, an argument ensued as to which direction they needed to go in order to return to the camp.

"I know it's this way!" Will pointed toward a medium-sized oak tree in the east that stood out within the lush green of the pine and fir trees due to the fall coloring of the leaves. "I remember that tree over there."

"You mean the one that looks identical to the one over there?" Kim pointed to an oak tree toward the west that was similar in color and height. The two areas looked eerily similar.

"Oh no." Hunter hung his head and sighed. "We're lost."

Remembering that Hunter received a call from Chief at Camp, Casey asked him, "What about your cell phone?"

"It barely worked at camp. I couldn't move at all when I was talking to Chief. I lost the call a couple times and even had to call him back." He took it out of his pocket and showed it to her. "See? Nothing."

"Great." She sighed as her headache came back full force. The aspirin had worn off about an hour ago, but she'd been able to brush it off because she thought they would be heading back to camp soon. She rubbed her temples as she sat on the rock. "You guys promised me we wouldn't get lost."

"I'm sorry, Casey." Scott shook his head, upset. "We turned so many different directions that I'm not sure which way to go."

Will nervously ran his hand through his hair. "And if we go wandering around in the woods, we could get lost even worse."

Jay sat down on the rock next to Casey. "If we stay out here, they may never find us. Not to mention the fact that we have no food."

Kim held up her half-full water bottle. "And there is only a little water."

No one moved or talked for several minutes, before Casey growled in frustration. "We need to do something." She crossed her arms. "At the very least, we need to find a water source. We can do without food for a couple days, but water is a must."

Jeff nodded. "I agree."

"Then that's our first priority." Scott stood. "Let's go."

"Which way?" Kim asked the obvious question. "I don't remember where the streams were."

"We need to go," Casey pushed, feelings of anxiety churned inside her. "Let's go this way." She headed east, which was the direction Will originally suggested.

The group walked with Will and Scott in the lead. Jesse, Casey, and Hunter were in the back, leaving everyone else in between.

They walked for at least an hour before they stopped to rest and evaluate. During their walk, Casey snapped twigs here and there to mark the trail so they could backtrack if needed. She made them all about the same level so it would be obvious to her which ones were hers.

"All right guys, we're rescue paramedics." Jay shook his head in frustration. "We need to rescue ourselves here. What's the plan?"

"To find water," Casey reiterated.

"And if we can't?" Scott asked.

"That's not an option." She rubbed the back of her neck to calm her headache. "That's the first priority. We can only do without water for a maximum of three days."

"But we don't even know where we are," Kim objected. "And to top it off, we're now lost again."

"Casey's been marking our trail from the ridge," Hunter pointed out. "Worst case scenario, we hike back to the ridge exposing ourselves for a recue chopper."

Pete looked up at the setting sun. "We don't have any flashlights. If we're going to do it, we'd better do it now. We have less than an hour of sunlight left."

Jeff turned toward the group. "I would say it's a pretty safe bet that we're spending the night in the woods. We'd better head back now. I agree with Pete. We should go back. We need the light to find our way back to the ridge."

With that, Casey led the way back. They got back to the ridge in time to see the sun sink past the mountains on its way out of sight. While the sunset was breathtaking, it was also discouraging. With the passing of the daylight, their chances of getting spotted before morning dwindled with each passing minute. They were definitely stuck for at least one night.

After the sun set, Casey got a chill, so she slipped her sweatshirt on. The others followed suit as the temperature dropped.

With everyone scattered throughout the ridge, deep in thought, Casey ran the track the group took through her mind to see if there was a way she could figure out how to get them out of the situation. Unfortunately, they hiked all over. It wasn't a matter of going in one direction…there were too many to count. They were so deep in the woods that she was not even sure what direction the campsite was located from where they were in order to head in the right direction. If she knew the direction of the camp, she could figure out where to go. She knew the others were as upset as she was, but they did their best to hide their feelings.

After another half an hour, Casey had to go to the bathroom. Kim said she needed to go too, so she went with her. Hunter, Will, and Jesse accompanied them to look out for any wild animals. Meanwhile, Jeff, Jay, Scott, and Pete stayed at the ridge to yell if they got lost, giving them a direction to head in the darkness. The only light they had to work with was the moon, and it was a cloudy night.

They stopped about twenty feet into the woods. Kim nervously looked around as she asked Casey, "Um, how do we do this?"

"Well, hmmm…" She felt the trees around her. The guys were about ten feet away from them in order to give them space. "Here." Casey handed Kim a good-sized oak leaf.

She looked at her, appalled. "We're supposed to use this to wipe with?" If they weren't in the situation they were in, Casey probably would have burst out in laughter. Even in the darkness, she could see the whites of Kim's eyes.

"We're a little short of toilet paper, Kimmy. You have a better idea?"

"No." She inspected the leaf, distraught. "This isn't poison ivy or anything, is it?"

"No. Poison ivy is soft. Sorry to say without the light, I picked a rough one to be on the safe side."

"Good idea. Um," she nervously glanced around as she admitted, "I've never gone anywhere without a toilet."

"I know, but that's not an option right now."

"You guys okay?" Jesse called.

"Yeah. We're working on it," Casey said. "Give us a few."

"Geez! Women." He chuckled, shaking his head. The other guys made several jokes about women and bathrooms before Casey told them to shut up. She and Kim were having a difficult enough time without the commentating.

Finally, Casey decided she couldn't wait on Kim anymore. She took her sweatshirt off and Kim held it to block for her. Of course, it took her a couple of minutes before she was able to go the bathroom knowing the guys were so close.

When she finished, Kim handed her the leaf to wipe. Casey was sure it was the most uncomfortable thing she'd ever wiped with, but she didn't have a choice. When she stood, she handed Kim another leaf and said, "Your turn."

Kim gulped. "I don't know if I can."

"I don't know when we're going to get back out here for another bathroom break. You have to take it when you can."

She sighed. "All right."

Casey left her sweatshirt off to give Kim some privacy while she went to the bathroom.

Casey sighed after five minutes. "Any day now."

She shook her head with tears in her eyes. "I can't."

"Try doing the multiplication tables aloud, or running a long poem through your head."

"Good idea." She nodded. Then she quietly said, "One times two is two. Two times two is four. Four times two is eight. Eight times two is sixteen. Sixteen times two is thirty-two. Thirty-two times two is sixty-four. Sixty-four times two is one hundred twenty-eight…." She kept this up until she got to somewhere in the thousands. Casey was astonished she did the math without paper.

When Kim got to the ten-thousands, she finally went. Casey would have cheered if she wasn't afraid Kim would stop out of embarrassment, so she quietly rejoiced as she stood there.

When she was finished, she stood. "All right, done."

"Feel better?" Casey raised an eyebrow at her. Kim went for a solid two minutes.

She blushed as they walked over to the guys. "Yeah."

Jesse jokingly glanced at his watch. "Twenty minutes later."

Casey rolled her eyes while she slipped her sweatshirt back on. "Let's just get back to the others."

"We have to go too. We were waiting until you two finished," Will said.

"Yeah, give us a couple minutes," Hunter mentioned as he, Jesse, and Will spread out in the woods about ten feet away from Kim and Casey.

"They're guys. This isn't fair." Kim crossed her arms in a huff. "They just whip it out and go. We have to squat."

"And the scariest part of that?" Casey smiled. "Is that we can't see what we're squatting on. It could be an animal."

"Why are you so comfortable out here?" she asked, watching her after a minute.

"Because my brother and I went camping a lot."

"And?"

"And he was military." She shrugged. "He would run survival training on the trips so I would know what to do in case of an emergency."

"Smart guy."

Jesse came over after another minute. "Done."

"That was fast," Kim said in amazement.

Will came back as well. "It doesn't take long for guys."

Hunter walked out from the bushes. "Yeah, I told you to give us a minute. Let's head back. I don't like being in the woods at night. I would rather be on the ridge with rocks to our back."

"Me too. Let's go." Kim rubbed her arms when she got a chill. "It's starting to get cold."

Pete looked up, as they walked to the ridge a couple of minutes later. "We were beginning to wonder."

Jesse glanced at the girls. "Some people had bashful bladders."

Casey sat down on the ridge. "At least we went."

"True."

They settled against the rock wall, huddled together. When they sat down, the guys wanted Kim and Casey toward the middle to protect them.

After a few minutes, the group found themselves lost in their own thoughts as they gazed out at the mountains that surrounded them. The full moon filtered down through the clouds, trying its best to give them some light. Rain was a possibility, but Casey prayed that it was not a probability.

* * *

The Colonel sat perched on a rock in order to see Casey without anyone seeing him. He was decked out in full camouflage, including a hat and face paint in order to blend in better. Watching the group, he shook his head. He couldn't believe they got lost. The Colonel, being an experienced survivalist, made sure he knew what direction he was heading the entire time, and how to get back. He knew if he could get Casey alone, he would be able to get her going in the right direction.

What concerned him was that Casey wasn't looking the best. Under normal circumstances, he was sure she could have gotten them out without his help, but he knew she'd had a headache since yesterday, and today she looked flushed. He was sure she had a fever with the headache, and that it was clouding her sense of direction.

* * *

Derek, Keith, and Mark sat in the recreation tent playing an intense game of Texas Hold 'em poker after their mission briefing with a couple guys from the flight crew. The fluorescent lights hummed, casting light into as many shadows as it could. Clusters of men and women playing a variety of games laughed and told stories of friends and family they left back at home, doing their best to forget that they were in the middle of a war. Someone had connected their iPod to the speakers, which blasted the angry, hard rock music that did its best to drown out the mixture of feelings each soldier had swirling inside of them.

The rusting fan in the corner worked to pull in the cold air, but it also added to the dust that coated everything and everyone. Mark sighed. There was no escaping it. He could brush his teeth as much as possible, but he could still feel it, and would be more than happy to bid it good-bye in the morning.

While not much scared him, being that he had been all over the world and faced many things head-on, the camel spiders were one of the few things that gave him the creeps. Moving at speeds of ten miles per hour, and hopping like crickets two feet into the air, these things sized up to eight inches in diameter. To Mark, the spider almost looked inside out. It looked like a dried spider with its skeleton on the outside. While he knew they were not poisonous, their bite stung like a hornet, and had been known to cause nasty infections. Mark had enough brushes with the spider and killed his share of the vile creatures to last a lifetime. He shuddered as he remembered the crunch he felt under his boot when he stepped on one earlier.

"What are you going to do?" Anderson, the guy to Mark's right, asked.

Mark knew he had an ace and jack of the same suit in his hand. The flop gave him an option of a pair of aces, while the turn gave him a possibility of a royal flush with the queen and ten in it. He weighed if he should bank on the king being on the river.

Mark tossed a twenty-dollar bill into the pot. "All right."

Derek took a deep breath. "Okay." Mark had the perfect poker face. While he could hide his feelings from his face, he couldn't keep them out of his eyes. Over the years, reading his eyes was the only way Derek could break through his tough exterior. In looking at them, he knew Mark had something good. "I fold."

"Mariano?" Anderson asked. Anderson was the dealer, and outside of Mark and Keith, he was the only other holdout on the hand.

"Hmmm," Keith rubbed his chin. He glanced up at Mark before looking at Anderson. Even the two soldiers playing their harmonicas to the tune on the iPod couldn't distract them from the intense game.

Mark sighed in frustration. "C'mon, Mariano, are you in or out?" He wanted to get back to Colorado, but he had to wait a couple more hours. With the sounds of bombs and gunfire in the distance, it kept him continuously on edge – a feeling he had lived with most of his life. The only time he seemed to be able to relax was around Casey. He sighed again. Casey. She had grown to be a beautiful, strong woman.

Keith tossed in his cards. "I'm out."

Anderson smiled at Mark. "Looks like it's just you and me." He had him right where he wanted him.

Mark let out an impatient breath of air. "Yep." He wanted the game to be over. As a matter of fact, he wanted the night to be over.

As soon as Anderson flipped the last card, Mark's heart skipped a beat. It was the king he needed. He tossed in two more twenties, knowing he had the hand.

Anderson's stomach sank. "Really?" In looking at the cards, he realized what Mark had and he groaned. "Fold." He tossed in his cards. "It's yours."

"Thank you, gentlemen." Mark collected the pot. "And, as a side note, I know when to walk away." He smiled, tossing the cards in the middle of the table.

"You have to give us a chance to win it back!" Hamilton objected.

"I've given you guys five hours to get it back. I need some air," Mark said. He collected his winnings and left the tent.

The temperature had dropped a good forty degrees, making it around fifty-three degrees outside. He glanced at his watch. They still had two hours before they flew out. He shoved his hands into his pockets. The shift in temperature between night and day wreaked havoc on his internal thermometer.

Looking up at the half-moon, he wondered what Casey was doing. It would be ten o'clock at night where she was. She was probably sitting around the fire, talking with the men and women of her fire company, roasting marshmallows for s'mores. He knew how much she loved s'mores. He shook his head and sighed. He couldn't get her off his mind no matter how hard he tried. The time they spent talking over the last couple of weeks was priceless. He had been alone for so long. Was it an infatuation, a wanting for company…or was it something else?

"Where are you?" He sighed as he looked up at the starlit skies.

*   *   *

Kim shuddered. "I'm cold." It was only ten o'clock, and it already was chilly.

"We could cuddle for heat," Will suggested.

Casey leaned forward to see what Kim thought. Kim looked over at her and shrugged as she said, "It's only going to get colder."

Casey scanned the ridge for open areas enough for groups to cuddle. "How would we do this?"

"And, how do we keep an eye out for the rescue party?" Jeff asked.

"Yeah. Hopefully when we don't come back, they'll send out a search party," Scott said. "If we're asleep and huddled together, they might not see…." He felt rain drop onto his head and legs. "Oh! Are you serious?" Scott growled in irritation.

"We need to huddle together." Pete broke the silence the raindrops and Scott's outburst had caused. "If it rains hard enough, they're not going to send anything out until the morning. In the meantime, we could end up with hypothermia."

After fifteen minutes of debate, as the cold rain pelted them, they broke into two groups of four. They left Scott and Hunter on the outsides of the huddles since they were the biggest guys.

It took quite some time of quietly talking before some of the group drifted off to sleep. A couple of the guys struggled to stay awake, mainly for safety reasons. They didn't know what dangers they were facing out in the woods. Casey was sure she heard howling, but wasn't sure if they were coyotes or wolves. She also heard a couple of owls, along with normal sounds one would hear in the woods at night, such as rustling of leaves and snapping of twigs. This left the group on edge, so they finally decided on sleeping in shifts for the night.

Chapter 3

Survival

When Casey woke up the next morning, she stretched as best she could. She was sore, cramped, and freezing, but she took comfort in noting that the others were not doing any better. The collective group decided to take the positive approach for as long as they could. They were alive and determined to find food, water, or better yet, the camp that day.

"Let's go," Scott said, as he was the first one off the ridge for the upper ground. "Do we want to take a vote on the direction?"

"Let's think about this logically." Casey scanned the area for a sign of something familiar, while the rain continued in a steady flow. She shuddered as several icy raindrops snuck past her hooded sweatshirt and ran down her spine. She took a deep breath. "Okay, when we left the camp what direction did we take?"

"That doesn't make a difference." Jesse shook his head. "We turned nearly every direction thanks to us mixing up the trails."

Casey went to the ledge and looked out at the valley below, hoping to get a feel for what direction were north and south. With the sun hidden in the clouds, it made it more difficult to determine direction. Kim got on her knees next to Casey to look for any bodies of water.

While it was not a heavy rain, the continuous steady drizzle was wearing. Casey enjoyed the sound and smells of rain, but not being able to get warm left her with a permanent chill. Her fingers and toes were even wrinkled.

"Um, what's...cool!" Kim excitedly peered over the ridge. She tapped Casey's leg. "Look!"

As the guys made their way back down the ridge, Casey saw what excited Kim. A tiny waterfall poured from the rock about a hundred yards down the mountain. A sense of relief washed over Casey to see the precious water so close.

"Where's the stream feeding that waterfall?" Casey crouched down to get a better angle to see below the towering trees.

"Right there." Jeff pointed to a stream that flowed toward the rocks, forming the waterfall as it went over the ledge. "Let's hike down to it."

"Is it still okay to drink?" Kim asked. "Shouldn't we boil it first?"

Will looked at her over his shoulder. "Do you have matches?"

"No."

"Then where do you plan on getting fire to boil the water?" he sarcastically questioned.

Kim shot him a nasty look as Hunter tried to calm down everyone. "Guys, we need each other. Let's not fight out here."

"If we can't boil the water, will we get sick?" Kim asked Casey.

"We could." She nodded. "But on the flipside, we can only live without water for about three days."

"I have an idea." Jesse rubbed his chin as he thought through how to word it. "What if a couple of us stay here to work on a fire, not only for a signal, but for the water as well, while others go for the water?"

"That sounds smart," Jay agreed.

Kim nodded in agreement as well.

"So, the obvious question would be how to divide up?" Casey asked.

Scott glanced around the group. "Does anyone know how to make fire without matches?"

Casey shook her head. "The wood and underbrush are wet. It will be really hard."

"But, can it be done?" Scott asked her.

"It can." She nodded as she crossed her arms in thought. "But, as I said, it will be really tough."

"Case." He rested his hands on her shoulders. "Can you do it?"

"I don't know." She shook her head. "I can do my best."

"That's all we ask." He smiled. "So, who's staying?"

Casey raised her hand. "I guess I am."

Hunter's hand immediately shot into the air. "I'll stay with her."

"Me too." Jesse raised his hand, glancing suspiciously at Hunter. Hunter's hand went up too fast for Jesse's comfort.

"I will too." Jeff raised his hand, feeling that a referee might be needed between Jesse and Hunter.

Scott nodded in approval. "Great. Then we'll go get the water and maybe see if we can find some food while we're at it."

"Give us your water bottles so we can refill them," Kim said, as she took Casey's water bottle. Jesse and Jeff handed theirs to Pete, while Hunter handed his to Will. With that, they were off.

"Okay, Timberland Tina, how do we do this?" Jeff winked at Casey, trying to lighten the mood.

Casey chuckled at her new nickname. "Well," she cleared her throat, "We need wood – the dryer the better. We also need some kind of kindling. I don't know." She glanced around at the ground that was soaked from the overnight rain and sighed. "Maybe some dry underbrush if you can find it."

Jesse nodded. "Sounds good."

They scrambled up the ridge and fanned out in the woods. They collected rocks, tree branches, and some underbrush that was not drenched by the rain before they met back near the ridge.

"Are we going to want it on the ridge with us?" Casey asked Hunter and Jesse, as they gracefully finagled their way down the ridge with the rocks and branches in their arms.

"Are you saying no?" Jeff asked her.

"It's going to be hard enough to get this thing sparked," she pointed out. "I think it would be easier on the dirt ground than on rock."

Jeff dropped the rocks he had in his arms onto the ground. "These are getting heavy anyway."

Jesse went up to the high ground with Hunter. "All right. Let's get this thing started."

"Um." Casey scanned the ground for the best place to set up a campsite. She shook her head out of frustration. Everything was wet. While she was honored that everyone seemed to have confidence in her abilities to get the fire going, in looking at the wet forestland around her, her self-confidence quickly diminished.

After a moment, she picked a spot in a clearing that was partially dry due to the trees that surrounded the open ground. The guys stacked the rocks they brought from the woods in a circle to form a fire pit. She pawed through the assortment of collected items in order to find the driest sticks she could, along with a handful of underbrush. She set some of the underbrush on the ground in the middle of the rock circle before she laid six sticks in a horizontal position about an inch apart over the top. Accordingly, she placed another handful of underbrush on top of that before she arranged another set of six sticks an inch apart in the opposite direction. Afterwards, she picked up the four sticks she planned to use to start the fire. She then said a prayer in her head for a miraculous intervention because she knew it would take that to get the fire going.

The wood was damp, but she prayed it would be dry enough to catch. She took the first straight stick and dented it in the middle with her pocketknife. Then she took the second stick and cut a notch on each end before she pulled the lace from of her boot and made it into a small bow. Afterwards, she took the third straight stick, which was approximately fourteen inches long, and made a point on each end to use with the bow in between the top and bottom sticks. Lastly, she took a fourth piece of wood and carved out a small divot in the middle. After she was done, Hunter held the bottom stick, while she took the fourteen-inch stick and picked up the bow. She slid the stick about halfway down the bootlace bow and twisted it around the stick once before she put one end in the stick Hunter held, topping it with fourth stick to hold it in place. After she did all of that, she used a sawing motion with the bow to twist the fourteen-inch stick, creating the friction at the bottom stick Hunter held. While Casey set up the other sticks, Hunter placed some dry underbrush where the base of the fourteen-inch stick would be placed. If Casey got it going fast enough, while Hunter continued to blow on the smoke once it generated, and the wood was not too wet, the underbrush should ignite...at least that was her plan.

Hunter watched while she worked, knowing as soon as she took the lace out of her boot and notched the ends of the stick to make a bow, that she was using the bow drill method to build the fire. He learned how to do it in S.E.R.E. (Survival, Evasion, Resistance, and Escape) training in the Navy, and understood it was her best bet. He admired her skills and resourcefulness. Truth be told, he admired her. If things were different…if this wasn't an assignment…he could see himself falling for her. He loved her smile and seeing her laugh. He adored her, even when her green eyes were blazing in anger toward him. He enjoyed her presence and loved what she seemed to pull out of him. He sighed in frustration as he shook his head. This assignment was going to kill him on the inside. Normally he didn't mind messing with the hearts of women to get what he wanted…but not her, not Casey. She was different.

*　*　*

As the Colonel ate a protein bar, he watched from a distance. He had to admit he was proud of Casey for doing exactly what he would have done, but he grew more concerned with her physical condition. She looked ashen and her cheeks were flushed. He saw her periodically rubbing her temples or the back of her neck, and it irritated him that the others didn't see it and made her sit there working on a fire for hours. The men could have easily done what she was doing, especially since Hunter seemed to know what she was doing when she started.

Hunter. The Colonel decided to keep a close eye on him. He saw what Jesse saw, and that made him uncomfortable. When the Colonel made his initial checks, most of the men in the department seemed squeaky clean, but it seemed there was something he might have missed. Hunter looked as if he knew exactly what Casey was doing when she set up the fire. He seemed just as comfortable as she was in the forestland. He half wondered if Hunter could get them out. Was he keeping them there so he could get close to Casey?

*　*　*

A couple hours after they left, the others returned. "Hey, guys," Scott said as he walked into the mini campsite with the others. "Get anything?"

"A little smoke." Hunter tossed the acorn he was fiddling with into the woods, as it was Jesse's turn to hold the bottom stick.

"That's progress." Scott was disappointed, but decided to do his best to keep a positive attitude within the group. "Keep it up. You'll get it soon," he encouraged Casey.

She tucked the piece of her hair that escaped her ponytail behind her ear, before she rubbed the back of her neck for what seemed like the umpteenth time that day. "I need a break. My head has been hurting since yesterday, and now my arms feel as if they are about to fall off."

Kim handed Casey her water bottle. "Here."

"Did you guys drink this?" Casey questioned. Specks of dirt floated around in the bottle…at least she hoped it was dirt.

"We don't have a choice." Pete shook his head. "If I recall, it's three days max without water, right?"

"Right." Casey nodded, glancing nervously at the water bottle.

"And without a signal fire, they won't know where we are, so we need to drink." Will sat down next to Casey. "It's not that bad. It's kind of like drinking spring water."

"But animals use this as a…." Casey shuddered. She held the untouched water bottle up to the light to get a better look at it.

"Got a better idea?" Jay looked at her, a little irritated by her ungrateful attitude for the water.

"No, I guess not." Her training told her that even filtering it through someone's t-shirt would have been better than drinking it straight from the stream, but she didn't want to discourage them, since they seemed so proud of the water.

"You guys didn't happen to find any food while you were out there, did ya?" Jesse asked.

Will shook his head. "Sorry, they haven't built any restaurants out here yet."

Casey sighed in discouragement as she looked down at the branches and underbrush. "We need a fire."

Pete didn't like the hopelessness that had infused its way through the group over the last couple of hours. In an attempt to lighten the mood, he said, "Ya know, this is kind of like one of those reality shows."

"Only we don't have a host to give us fire if we vote someone out," Casey reminded him.

"And there's no million-dollar prize at the end," Jeff added.

Jesse cracked his back and stretched from holding the stick for Casey for so long. "A million dollars sounds great. I know I could use it."

"What would you do with a million dollars?" Hunter asked him.

"Take a trip to Australia."

"Why Australia?" Casey asked.

"I've always wanted to go there," Jesse explained. "You know, swim in the Great Barrier Reef, enjoy the exotic wildlife, see the Sydney Opera House, Mount Uluru, and watch the wild kangaroos hopping around."

"What about you?" Pete asked Hunter, hoping the conversation would distract everyone from the situation.

"Take a safari trip to Africa." He smiled as he thought about it. "I would love to see the different animals for myself in their natural habitat, preferably before I die. I'm saving up for it."

Jay nodded in approval. "Sounds cool."

"What about you?" Hunter asked Jay.

"What would I do with a million dollars?" He looked up in thought. "Well, I would buy a house for myself – modest, nothing big. I would also pay off my mom's house. Since my dad died a couple years ago, she had to go back to work just to keep it. I keep making extra payments for her even though she doesn't know it." He sheepishly grinned when he noticed the way Kim looked at him. "It's the least I could do."

"What else? There is still a lot left after that." Kim pointed out. She'd admired Jay since the academy. She was thrilled when she found out they were not only going to be on the same company, but also on the same shift.

"Hmmm," Jay said, mulling it over in his mind. "I would probably set part aside for the day I find the woman of my dreams. You know, for a beautiful wedding and honeymoon, and a starting nest egg. What about you?" he asked Kim.

"I would pay off my schooling, my car, and my credit cards. I would also buy a house for myself. Then, with what's left, I would probably put it into a money market account, and use some of the money it generates to go on a vacation every year…that is, until I retire."

Scott nodded in approval. "For someone so young, that's wise."

"What about you?" Kim asked Scott.

"One million dollars, huh?" He looked down, running options through his mind for a moment before he answered, "I would probably buy a house on the beach and a boat. I would go out to the house every year for my vacation time until I retire, and then retire out there when it's time. Of course, I would also buy myself a Harley." He nudged Jesse. They both shared that passion.

"Me too," Jesse agreed. "That would have to be first on my list after I got back from Australia. These are great ideas."

"Yep. What about you, Pete?" Scott asked.

"I don't know." Pete shook his head. "That's a lot of money. I would want to do something good with it, that much I know. I would probably give some to my parents so they could do something they have always wanted to do. I would then put the rest in an account and give some money to a different charity every year until I retire. Then I would use the rest for retirement. This country's social security system stinks." He rolled his eyes. "By the time I retire, there's not going to be anything left."

"That's true." Scott nodded. "I know it's a concern of mine and I'm older than you."

"What about you?" Hunter asked Jeff.

He smiled at the thought of having a million dollars. "A million dollars? That would be wonderful."

"But, what would you do with it?" Hunter pressed.

"I would like to see the Seven Wonders of the World. With all the ugly we see on a daily basis," Jeff said, "I would love to see the beauty this world has to offer for my own eyes."

"Wow! That was deep," Casey said, taken aback.

"Especially coming from you," Will shot at him.

"What about you, funny man?" Jeff glared at him. "What would you do with a million dollars?"

As Will thought for a moment, while Casey went to work on the fire again, with Jesse holding the bottom stick for her. Fire was a priority.

"I don't know." Will shrugged. "I agree with what everyone has said so far. There is so much you could do with it. The possibilities are endless."

"Such as?" Kim challenged.

"Such as: pay off my house, pay off my parent's house, help my sister since she's a single mom, and still have some left for me to retire," he listed.

Kim nodded. "That's admirable."

"Yeah, helping my parents finish paying off their house is a good idea too." Jesse ran several more ideas through his mind.

"I know taking care of my mom would be high on my list," Hunter mentioned. "My mom raised me by herself since I was a teenager."

"What happened to your dad?" Kim asked.

"They got a divorce. My dad was in the Navy at the time, so when the divorce came, he threw himself into work. I didn't see him much after that." He sighed. "Not that I care. He wasn't around often before that anyway."

"Tough break, man." Scott patted his shoulder. "Sorry."

"Things are tough all over," Hunter said. Then he glanced over at Casey and asked, "Aren't they, Casey?"

She froze. She looked up at him, startled, forgetting about the twigs for a moment. "Um, what?"

"Each of us has at least one parent…except you."

Casey narrowed her eyes at him, while she sat there unmoved, tense and angry with him.

"You're an orphan, right?" he asked.

"Back off, Morgan," Jesse warned, on edge.

"You don't have any parents?" Kim looked at Casey, taken aback by the idea that Hunter knew something so important about Casey that she did not.

"No. I don't," Casey said flatly, not taking her eyes off Hunter. When she told him, it was in confidence, not for him to publicize it.

Kim rested her hand on Casey's shoulder. "I'm sorry. What happened?"

Casey was furious with Hunter for even bringing it up. "It's a long story."

"Um, who's left?" Jay nervously glanced around the group. "I think we need to change the subject back to something good."

Hunter looked over at Casey. "Well, that would be our lovely Timberland Tina over there. That is, if she ever gets the fire going."

"I think we need to move on to a less tense subject," Pete said as he watched Hunter and Casey. Being her partner, he knew Casey well enough by this point that her body language told him she was about to punch Hunter.

Jeff tried to lighten the mood. "Case, what would you do with a million dollars?"

Casey worked on the fire once again. She went slowly at first before gradually getting faster. She took a deep, cleansing breath before she shook her head. "I don't know." She would keep a closer eye on Hunter from that point forward. She did not want to be caught off guard again.

"Let your mind wander. What would you do with it if you had it?" Kim sounded genuinely excited. "Daydreaming about it is fun."

Casey shook her head. "I don't know." Then she turned to Will and smiled. "Maybe build a restaurant out here." As everyone burst out in laughter, Casey hoped that would send the subject off her. She did not like to be in the middle of conversations.

"Seriously," Hunter pressed. "What would you do with a million dollars?"

Casey sighed out of frustration as she stopped working on the fire. She sat back on her feet for a moment, glaring at Hunter. She calmly, but sternly said, "I haven't had a mom or dad since I was eight. I don't have my brother or Mac anymore. The things that were important in my life are now no longer even on this planet. While charities and helping parents are wonderful concepts, they do not pertain to me. I don't have a charity I am passionate about, nor do I have family. Now, if you really want to push the issue with me, we are going to end up where we were earlier," she warned him.

"Why won't you talk to us, Case?" Hunter pushed. "Every time we touch something sensitive in our conversations, you pull back. Why are you afraid to open up? Why are you afraid to trust us?"

She glared at him, daring him to keep pushing. "I do trust you."

"Then tell us why you don't trust men," he challenged.

"That's enough, Morgan!" Jesse snapped. "Just back off!"

"What's your issue with me talking to her?" Hunter asked. "Can't she defend herself?"

Casey stood up as she threw the sticks into the rock circle in frustration. Hunter jumped up and grabbed her arm when she went to leave. "Talk to us!"

"Let me go," she warned, fire flashed across her eyes.

"Why won't you trust us?" he asked.

"I do!" she growled. She glanced around at the others in the group, who intently watched the scene in front of them. They knew there was something Hunter and Jesse both knew that Casey was not telling.

Hunter tightened his grip on her arm. "Then tell us!"

She tried to jerk her arm back, but he was too strong. "Let me go!"

"Tell us!"

"I don't have to tell you anything!"

"What are you hiding?"

"That's none of your business."

Hunter sighed as he released her arm. Casey walked down to the ridge, furious with him. She saw a nook tucked in a corner of the ridge and ducked into it. As she slid down the ice-cold stone wall to the seat on the rocks. Wrapping herself in her arms, she did her best to shove the tears back that threatened to overflow. She was done with this trip. She had reached her maximum with Hunter a long time ago as well. She also knew she was tired of being cold, tired of her head pounding, and tired of her stomach growling. She needed some space to think things through and cool down. She was having a hard time believing that in the middle of nowhere, she still felt smothered.

*   *   *

"Yes, sir," Derek said into the satellite phone. The Colonel was on the other end, still tucked deep within the Colorado Woodlands. Derek plugged one of his ears to hear, as an F18 took off on the landing strip behind him. He groaned on the inside, knowing how the conversations had been going with Mark regarding Casey. "Yes, sir, I will fill them in." He nodded in response. "Understood."

"Major, we're taking off," the Staff Sergeant called to him from the loading hatch.

Derek nodded in acknowledgement. "They're taking off, Colonel. I'll contact you when we land." He listened for another moment before he said, "Thank you, sir, we'll be in the air about fourteen and half hours. I will contact you when we land."

He climbed into the plane, sitting in a row of three in between Mark and Keith. They were on the top deck of the C5 Galaxy. It was noisy, packed, and even though the heat was searing within the plane from baking on the tarmac, to them it was the desired choice over the daily, blistering heat of Iraq. It also beat having to be in a C130, which would have taken three times as long to get home. Derek looked cautiously over at Mark, who slouched in his seat already half-asleep. Derek had no idea how he did it with how loud the flight was, but it worked for him.

Derek hated the way the C5s took off. On the top deck, the seats faced backwards, so when they took off, the inertia that normally threw his body back into the seat, would throw him forward instead. Seatbelts were a necessity, because it was the only thing that kept one in their seat. He knew once they reached altitude, the plane would quickly cool down, so he didn't mind the temporary heat within the plane either.

"You talk to the Colonel? Everything okay with Casey?" Mark asked, sitting up to put his seatbelt on as the engines ramped up for take-off.

Derek was grateful that the engines suddenly groaned louder, making it difficult to be heard. The plane shuddered and started the take-off, so he could put off the conversation with Mark and Keith he'd dreaded, but knew he would have to have eventually. The faster the plane went, the louder it got, whining as its massive body climbed into the air. It didn't take long for the albatross of a plane to reach altitude and level off.

After a few minutes, Mark was so tired that he didn't care about the turbulence. He took his seatbelt off, and slouched in his seat with his arms crossed over his chest. He wanted to get back to see Casey. He even didn't care to talk anymore.

Derek waited for what he thought was the best time to bring up the conversation with the Colonel. An hour or so into the flight, he said, "Guys, we need to talk."

When Mark didn't move, Derek reached over and jostled him awake.

"You have a death wish?" Mark growled.

"No, we need to talk."

Mark looked over at him without moving his head. He was tired from being up all night, and done with this trip. He was already asleep and in dreamland when Derek shook him out of a deep sleep.

"What's up? What's going on?" Keith asked. The tone of Derek's voice, along with his body language, told him something was wrong.

Mark leaned forward to look at Keith. The stress in his voice brought Mark out of his temporary comatose state. In seeing his furrowed brow, he questioned Derek, "Did something happen?"

"Yes…" Derek said. In looking at Mark's body, which was suddenly on edge as he sat up in his seat, Derek quickly added, "And no."

Mark narrowed his eyes. "You'd better start talking!"

He took a deep breath, bracing for impact before he said, "Casey's lost in the woods." When Mark and Keith fired off a barrage of questions, Derek continued, "That's not the only thing." They shut their mouths, waiting for the rest of the news. "Good news is Jesse is with her." Well, that was at least a relief to Mark. "Bad news is, Hunter's with her too…and she's sick."

"She's what? Who is with her?!" Mark was furious. "Was he not watching her? How could this happen?"

"Calm down." Derek tried to soothe Mark's agitated state. "He's watching her. He's waiting to get her alone in order to give her directions back to camp."

"If she's sick, will she be able to do it?" Keith asked.

"How sick are we talking here?" Mark asked.

"From what the Colonel could tell, she looks as if she's got a fever and a headache. Depending on how high her fever is," Derek said, "she may not be able to get them out."

Mark apprehensively asked, "What's his plan?"

"To get her alone and give her directions."

"And if she's too sick?"

"He'll think of something."

"How can you be so callous about this?" Mark scowled in irritation.

"Because the Colonel won't let anything happen to her."

"He already has!"

"You need to calm down," Derek said. "We still have over twelve hours of flying."

"You'd better start talking, or this is going to be one of the longest flights you've ever had in your life," Mark growled. "I want answers, and I want them now!"

*   *   *

The silence was evident from the location of the fire pit. She knew it was her fault – another emotional hurricane brought to you by Casey Carter. She knew she needed to get a grip on her emotions. By this point, it was even frustrating to her. She could not imagine what the others thought.

Much to her relief, after about five long minutes, Scott picked up the sticks to work on the fire with Jay's help, while the others talked lightly amongst themselves. This gave Casey some time to think. She knew Jack and Mac were in a better place, but she also knew where her parents went, and that she would never see them again. After losing them at such a young age, the only way she remembered what they looked like were by the photos around the house. The only other memories she had of them were their laughter and light-heartedness.

While she knew God did things for a reason, she could not comprehend as to why He would take loving, caring parents away from a young child. No child should have to be without a true mother and a father. They need both in order to function properly in society. While Casey did not have her parents, she did have a brother who raised her. As far as she was concerned, he did a great job. He even had some of the military wives keep tabs on her when he was in the field. This allowed her to have varied perspectives from her "surrogate parents" through her teen years. Nothing would replace her real mother and father though, and she prayed that someday God would reveal to her the answer as to why He took them when she was so young.

After about thirty minutes, Hunter came down and sat beside Casey. "We need to talk."

She narrowed her eyes and crossed her arms. "No, we don't. You've talked enough."

"Talk to me, Case."

"I don't trust you."

"Why not?"

"Because what you said was personal."

"We were all sharing something personal." Then he added, "Well, everyone but you."

She got up from her rocky perch. "Leave me alone."

He grabbed her arm as he pulled her up the ridge to solid ground. "You and I are going to take a walk."

"No, I'm not!" she snapped.

* * *

The Colonel appreciated Casey's temper. She didn't put up with being pushed around, and at this point that included Hunter, much to his relief. He was proud of her, but he was also on edge. While she was angry, she was sick. If push came to shove, he would jump in and help her. He would not let anything happen to her. He was her responsibility.

* * *

"No one is going to intervene," Hunter informed her. "They want me to talk to you. We need to work this out."

"There wouldn't be anything to work out had you kept your mouth shut!" Casey pointed out.

"Trust us, Case."

"What I carry with me is my own burden."

"Look, I'm not doing this to hit on you or anything. I'm doing this because whatever this is obviously has you wound up."

"This is none of your business."

"Oh, yes, it is. Remember, 'what happens to one happens to all,'" he reminded her of the station motto. "We are a family. If you are hurting, the rest of us are hurting too."

Jeff walked over to them, draping his arm over her shoulder. "He's right. We love you, Case, but you close off your feelings all the time. Is there something going on, or that went on, that has you so on edge? Anytime anyone mentions family or their past, you get tense and clam up. What are you hiding?"

Jesse looked up from where they worked on the fire, as he sat between Kim and Scott. "Guys, don't push her," he warned.

Hunter looked at him for a minute before a look of realization came across his face. "You know, don't you?"

"Just leave her alone," Jesse reiterated.

"What is it?" Kim asked Casey.

Hunter studied Casey. "She's hiding it deep."

Casey sighed as she crossed her arms. "Leave me alone. I don't want to talk about it. I shouldn't have to tell you if I don't want to either. This isn't some court of law where I'm forced to tell."

"Hey, I'm an open book," Hunter boasted. "Anything you want to know, just ask."

"I don't want to. I want you to leave me alone." She turned and headed toward the trees in hopes of finding more food, and a chance to calm the pulsating pounding that had completely taken over her head. She wiped where the rain mixed with sweat on her flushed face.

"Whoa!" Scott ran up to her about ten feet into the woods and grabbed her arm.

She jerked her arm back. "Quit pushing."

"Calm down."

"No! He won't leave me alone, and you guys won't back off either. This is personal. My life is personal, not an open book," she shouted at him. "There's too much for you to even remotely understand."

"We deal with pain every day, Case, you know that," he calmly pointed out.

"Nothing like this. You still have your family to rely on. You can call your parents, your brother, or your sister. I don't have anyone to call."

"You can call us."

Casey glared at him. She got within several inches of his face and hardheartedly asked, "What do I do on Christmas day? When I'm sitting there alone by myself in front of my Christmas tree – if I decide to have a tree this year – which one of you guys do I call then? Do I call Jay or Hunter who are celebrating with their moms? Or do I call Tommy or Marty who are celebrating it with their wives or children? Or do I call you guys who are having your traditional family gathering – opening presents and sharing family stories of Christmas's past? Where do I go, Scott? Who do I call?"

He stared at her as her reality sunk in. He wasn't sure what to say. "I'm sorry, Casey," he said compassionately. "You're right. Your life is harder than any of ours. Your secrets are your secrets. At the end of the day, we do have family to go to. You don't. I wouldn't want trade places with you…not even for a million dollars. You had a rough start, and it's been an even tougher year. I'm sorry for you. You don't know who to trust, and I don't blame you. Please know that we do love you and sincerely care about you."

She sighed. "I know you do."

"Then come help us survive this place. Out of all of us, I'm pretty sure you are the only one who knows what you're doing out here."

She nervously chuckled. "Yeah."

"Then give us a hand. We need fire, food, and to get out of here."

"I know."

"Then know at the end of the day there is no million-dollar prize. There is no voting off anyone. It's just us." He hugged her before he let her go. "Let's go survive."

She nodded, so they turned around and headed back to camp.

"I'm getting hungry." Jay took a sip of his water. "Where would we find food?"

Casey shook her head. "Jay, I don't think that's wise." She wiped her face again from the sweat that dripped. She couldn't figure out with how wet and cold it was why she was sweating.

"What?" Jay asked.

"Drinking that."

"We don't have a choice. We need to drink about a gallon a day. So here, you need to drink too." He tossed her the water bottle.

Casey took a sip. She knew the unfiltered water from a stream wasn't good for her, but it felt icy and cool going down her parched throat.

Jay smiled in satisfaction at seeing the relief on her face. "Now, what about food?"

"And fire?" Kim shuddered. "We're wet and cold, and this stinking rain is not stopping any time soon."

"What if we make a shelter of some kind to get out of the rain?" Jeff scanned the area for supplies. "We could break some trees to make a roof."

"This is too wet." Pete tossed the wood into the pile of rocks out of frustration. "We are never going to get this lit."

"Okay, then it's settled," Hunter said. "We work on shelter and food."

"Sounds good." Scott nodded. "You, Jesse, Will, Jay, and Kim want to work on the shelter, while Jeff, Pete, Casey, and I go look for food?" Scott suggested, giving Casey a break from Hunter. He thought that by dividing the two of them, it might bring about some peace in their camp if they could both calm themselves.

"Sounds good." Hunter agreed, but cringed on the inside. He wanted to stay by Casey as much as possible, hoping to break through her inner defenses.

"I'll keep working on the fire." Kim knelt down and picked up the sticks. "This is important."

Casey knelt down to show her how to do it before her group left. "No, you have to do it like this."

Scott lifted branches to see into the surrounding bush as they walked into the woods. "All right, where do we start? We don't have a lake, so we can't fish."

"We don't have fruit or coconut trees," Pete smirked, "so those are out."

"Insects are a good source of protein," Casey offered.

"Aww, no way." Jeff shuddered, disgusted. "I cook my food. I don't want it crawling off my plate…or worse yet, crawling across my mouth while I'm trying to swallow it."

Scott laughed at Jeff, and then asked, "What kind of insects?"

"Well," Casey started, "crickets –"

"No," Jeff cut her off, adamantly shaking his head. "Come on, Carter, work with me. Find us some fruit or something."

"I don't know if there is any," she said, looking through the underbrush around the area.

Scott turned down the path. "Let's walk."

Casey marked the trail by breaking twigs again as they went down the trail. After forty-five minutes of wandering around, Casey saw a couple autumn berry bushes about six-feet into a thick area of the woods.

Casey pointed toward them. "Will that work, Jeff?"

He grinned. "Are those…? Yeah!"

They ran over and picked the berries off the bushes. Casey flipped her sweatshirt up to carry them. Jeff filled his sweatshirt as well, before they hiked down to the stream to wash them.

Scott took off his sweatshirt. Then he took off his t-shirt and collected all the berries into it before he put his sweatshirt on again. They used his t-shirt to wash the berries, as well as stop them from floating down the stream.

While they washed the berries, Pete saw movement out of the corner of his eye. He looked down and saw, "A fish!"

Scott's head swiveled in Pete's direction. "What?"

"There are fish in this stream," Pete excitedly exclaimed.

Jeff's heart skipped a beat. "No way! Really?" The idea of meat and protein made him excited.

The fish were there, but they were few in number. "How do we catch them?" Casey asked, running her fingers through the berries to clean them. "We don't have a fishing line."

"Hmmm…" Scott glanced around the area, wracking his brain to come up with an idea. "Looks like we are going to have to be creative. We could use a branch for a fishing pole."

"Um, hate to play Polly Pessimist here," Casey said, "but we don't have any rope for a line. I would say to use insects for bait, tree branches as poles, but as far as the fishing line, we have to work on something else, because a shoe lace won't cut it. The fish will see that a mile away, think it's a snake or something, and will avoid it."

Scott thought for a moment before he said, "We could make a fish trap, but that's a lot of work. Let's work on the fish another day."

"Hopefully we won't be here another day," Pete said. "Nothing personal, but I want to get out of here."

"The problem is, if we move around, we could end up in a grid they've already searched. We kind of need to either stay here or figure out exactly where the camp is. We can't go at it half-baked," Casey reminded them, hoping they would understand the intentions behind her words. She didn't want to discourage anyone. She only wanted them to think through their actions before they made the situation worse.

Jeff threw his hands in the air in frustration. "We need to get out of here!"

"I agree, but be smart about it," Casey cautioned. "If we move around, we could stumble into an area they've already checked. We know how the search parties work. We've been on enough of them. They search grid to grid, and you know it."

"That's true," Scott agreed. "We shouldn't go anywhere. What we should do is work on a signal fire."

Jeff huffed. "Which we can't do without dry wood. Casey's already tried. All we got was smoke. Don't you understand that we are in trouble here, people?"

"Then we keep trying." Pete shrugged. "If the fire is the key, then we get our behinds back there and get it done."

"Are they clean yet?" Scott asked Casey.

"Yeah." She ran her fingers through one last time to be sure, as he continued to hold the t-shirt.

He scooped up the t-shirt full of the berries out of the water, letting them drain a bit before the group started back toward camp. When they arrived, the others were working on what looked like a lean-to. It went to the ground on one side and had a slightly tilted flat roof for drainage. They used other trees to brace the tree branches they used for a roof. Those who built the shelter weaved the tree branches to make it sturdy before they tied the end branches with bootlaces to ensure it wouldn't fall over in the middle of the night.

"Um, what if we get some more branches for the sides?" Scott logistically inspected it. "That way those on the end won't get soaked."

"Good idea," Hunter said as he got up off the ground to fix the ends.

"Very creative." Pete nodded in approval. "I'm impressed."

"You like that?" Jesse grinned. "It was my idea."

"Good job." Casey looked it over before she sat cross-legged on the ground next to Kim. "How are you doing on the fire?"

She rolled her eyes at Casey.

"That good, huh?" Casey chuckled.

Kim brushed away the hair that fell across her eyes. "Please tell me you guys had better luck with food."

Scott held the berries for them to see. "How about autumn berries?"

She grinned in excitement. "That'll work!"

"The other option from Timberland Tina over there was insects." Jeff shuddered.

"Insects? Really?" She looked at Casey for an explanation.

"They're a good source of protein," Casey said in her defense. "If it wasn't for the berries, we would be eating grubs."

Pete wiggled his eyebrows. "Or raw fish…scales and all."

Kim shuddered. "I'll take the berries any day."

"What's wrong, Kimmy?" Casey smiled in amusement.

"I just…I'm not accustomed to this type of...." She shook her head.

"Listen to you." Casey burst out in laughter. Kim looked up at Casey with a nervous smile. Casey mimicked her in a snobby voice as she stood, "I'm not accustomed to such primal living." Kim joined the group in laughter as Casey went on, "No toilet, no silverware or plates, and no restaurants. Ugh. How can you people live in such barbaric accommodations?"

Kim laughed at Casey's antics. "Stop!"

"I want a shower, caviar, and some tea…if you please." Casey fluffed her hair, which at this point was wet and stringy at best.

*   *   *

The Colonel laughed from where he sat, watching the scene in the camp. He was glad the group's spirits were high considering the situation.

*   *   *

Kim laughed. "You're incorrigible."

Hunter grunted. "Hmm, me like living in jungle." Then he pounded his chest, "Ahhh-ah-ahhh-ah-ah-ah-ah-ahhhhhh."

"Geez!" Jesse wiped the tears from his eyes.

Hunter stood in front of Casey and asked, "Me Jungle King…you my wife?"

*   *   *

The Colonel rolled his eyes as he took a sip of his water. Did Hunter seriously think he was a jungle king? He prayed Casey wasn't falling for his pathetic attempt for her attention.

*   *   *

"No, me Casey. I am no one's wife." Casey shook her head and crossed her arms. Some of the guys held their stomachs from the laughter.

"You pretty lady. I take you. You live in jungle with me."

"Absolutely not. I am unaccustomed to such primitive accommodations. I must have silverware, plates, pots and pans, a bathroom, shower, toilet paper –"

"Hmm," he huffed, looking down in thought. Then he looked back to Casey and pouted as he said, "I not have that here."

"Then I am sorry. You need to find another wife." Casey crossed her arms. "I am more civilized than this…this…pathetic attempt at civilization. I need proper accommodations," she said with a tone of playful distain. She had trouble keeping a straight face, and wasn't sure how much longer she could keep it in.

"Hmm," he huffed. "I find another wife?"

"Yep."

"Hmm," he huffed again. "I get a-com-o-da-tion changed, you be my wife?"

Casey snubbed her nose at him. "Nope. Sorry. I like my men more civilized. You need to find a new wife."

*   *   *

The Colonel nodded in approval. "Good girl. Don't even give him an inch."

* * *

"Hmm," he huffed again. Then he looked down at Kim. "New wife." He scooped her up and flipped her over his shoulder.

Kim screamed, as she pounded on his back while laughing. "Let me down!"

"You not be my wife either?" He pouted.

"No."

He sighed, setting her on the ground. "I go find gorilla then."

Scott patted his back. "How about finding our camp, big guy."

"I find."

Casey suspiciously watched Hunter. "Do you have an idea?"

"No." He shook his head. As the group settled down, Hunter discouragingly added, "Except to get that fire going."

"Back to reality, huh?" Jesse watched Kim pick up the sticks to work on the fire again while Jay helped her.

"Speaking of reality." Casey started toward the woods. "Nature's calling."

"Need an escort, or are you okay by yourself?" Scott asked.

"No need. Thanks to the always-thinking Kimmy, we created an outhouse of sorts for you guys." Jesse pointed to a small hut about fifteen feet away from camp. "We dug a hole too, so don't worry about little critters. You can just squat and go."

"Do I want to know how you dug a hole?" Casey asked.

Hunter shrugged. "We used our hands. If it'll make you guys feel more comfortable, we'll do it."

Casey smiled appreciatively. "Thank you."

"Now, just so you know, there are no grocery stores around here, so you have to find your own toilet paper," Jay pointed out.

As Casey walked by a tree, she grabbed a leaf (that was a lot softer than the one from the previous night), before she headed over to the tiny hut. It was three sided, but the open side faced away from camp. Casey was grateful for the privacy and felt more comfortable.

When she came out from going to the restroom, she saw something out of the corner of her eye. She searched the woods for a long moment, before she saw the Colonel in the distance. He pointed toward her, before he pointed toward himself, and then he made a talking motion with his hands. She nodded in response. She would have to figure out a way to get away from the others without them suspecting anything in order to talk to the Colonel. It was her prayer that the Colonel knew how to get them out of there.

When she walked back into the camp, Will asked, "You like?"

"I like," she said. "Thanks."

"Good. Then drink." Scott shoved Casey's water bottle toward her. "We have to get more, but I know you have only drunk half your bottle. Since we're eating our dinner here, sit down and enjoy." He gestured to a spot next to him. Everyone sat in a circle eating the berries while drinking the water, taking a break from working on the fire.

"You marked the trail to the berries, right?" Jesse asked Casey.

"Yep," she said, grabbing a couple berries.

"We need to figure out where we are, so we can figure out how to get out of here," Hunter said, thinking aloud after several minutes of silence.

"We need to be sure before we move anywhere though," Scott said. "Our loving Timberland Tina reminded us about the grid search. You can be sure they're looking, but if we stumble into a grid they've already searched, then we're back where we started."

"Good point." Hunter nodded. Then he pressed the issue, "We know it's not east. And we know we can't go north," he smirked, because north was over the edge of the ridge, "which only leaves south and west."

"Do we want to look or stay here?" Kim asked. "They brought up a good point about getting ourselves lost again in one of the already-searched grids. That's not smart."

Casey had a wave of nausea mixed with a hot flash. She slowly got up and lay down under the hut with her head on her arm.

*   *   *

Colonel sat up, slightly on edge. When Casey stood, he saw her face, which looked sickly pale, while her cheeks were a bright red. She was getting worse. If she didn't get better soon, he would have to move to plan 'B.' He would have to figure out a way to get the group out soon before anyone else got sick.

*   *   *

"Head still hurts?" Scott asked, concerned.

"Yeah." She nodded with her eyes closed. Her head almost felt as if it was spinning off her body.

He crouched beside her and touched her forehead. "You've got a fever too."

"Really?" Jesse asked. "Here, use my legs for a pillow." He sat on the ground next to her with his legs stretched out in front of him, tapping his legs for her to lay her head on them. "That better?" he asked.

"Yeah." She nodded, relieved not to have to lay her head on the ground. "Thanks."

"Go to sleep." Scott said, worry written all over his face. "Maybe when you wake up you will feel better."

"In the meantime, let's head down to the ridge and see if we can figure out a way out of here." Hunter stood. "Maybe we can see something over the ridge that will direct us home." He felt a twinge of jealousy when Casey rested her head on Jesse's lap, and kicked himself for not suggesting it before Jesse. Their close relationship was going to be a problem. He would have to not only figure out a way to be the hero to get them out of the woods, but also find a way to break the friendship between Casey and Jesse in order for him to make any headway in his mission.

While the group headed down to the ridge, Jesse reclined back with his hands behind his head to take a nap. Scott continued to work on the fire by himself, using his foot to brace the bottom stick.

*   *   *

After a couple hours of drilling him for any and all information Derek might know about what had been going on with Casey since they took off for their mission, Mark was finally satisfied that he had it all. He sat back in his seat with a million things flying through his mind at once, as the chill of the plane pierced through to his bones. The heater in the plane did its best to keep the temperature under control, but the vastness of the plane prevented it from doing much good.

Derek looked at him, relieved not to be under interrogation anymore. Mark didn't have to use violence in interrogations – his presence was intimidating when he was angry enough. He felt bad for the Colonel, knowing how angry Mark was at that moment. He prayed Casey would be fine when the plane landed. The Colonel had exactly ten hours to get Casey to safety, or Mark was going to have his head.

"You done?" Keith leaned forward.

"We got all the information, didn't we?" Mark snapped.

"Yes, you have all of the information I have," Derek said.

"So," Keith laced his fingers together, with an evil smile on his face. Now it was his turn to interrogate Mark, "Why are you so upset?"

Mark narrowed his at him. "She's the only family we have. Why aren't you that upset?"

"Is that all?"

"What are you insinuating?"

"You tell me," Keith said. "You are visibly angry."

"Of course. He let her get lost and sick."

Keith stared at him, letting Mark stew in his emotions for a moment. He watched as his face shifted from anger, to a moment of confusion, before landing back on anger.

Mark leaned back in his chair, deep in thought. Could there be more to his feelings? No, Casey was family. He watched her grow up, for goodness sake. He was only three years older than she was, but he had been around her since she was seventeen and he was twenty. He was prior enlisted before going to Officer Training School (OTS) after getting his degree in political science at the age of twenty-eight. Since he worked with the A.N.G.E.L.s in intelligence as an enlisted man, when he graduated OTS, the

Colonel snatched him up, and he became a permanent part of the team.

"Is that the only reason you're angry?" Keith asked Mark, interrupting his thoughts. "This looks deeper than that. While we are upset that she's lost, she's not really lost. The Colonel is watching her. He won't let anything happen to her."

"He already has," Mark said in aggravation.

"He can't control if she gets sick."

"No, but he can get her out of there instead of letting her stay in the wilderness, hoping she can get them out of there with a fever and a migraine. She's not an A.N.G.E.L. for crying out loud!"

"No, but she is trained. Jack taught her survival skills. Trust her. Trust the Colonel."

Mark sighed. "I don't have a choice."

*   *   *

Casey's growly stomach woke her. She couldn't remember when she felt so empty and drained, cold yet hot, and sick to her stomach, while her head pounded out of control.

Feeling her stir, Jesse asked, "How are you feeling?" He was in a seated position with Casey lying on his lap, while he leaned against a tree snacking on some berries.

"I'm hungry, but…." She put her hand on her stomach as a wave of nausea came over her. She quickly covered her mouth, praying the vomit wouldn't come up. That was the last thing she needed. She was already mortified from her conversations with Hunter. If she threw up, she knew she would never live it down.

"How about some water?" Scott handed her a water bottle. "While the rain is giving us moisture, we still need to drink water."

"Is it raining harder?" She scanned the area, as she sat up and stretched. She closed her eyes for a moment and took a couple deep breaths to clear her head. She felt as if she was going to pass out.

Jay sighed in frustration. "Rain, rain, and more rain."

"I don't think I have ever felt so weak." Jeff rested his arms on his crossed knees. "I mean, yeah, we ate yesterday, but with the lack of food and being low on water…I guess I'm used to eating a lot more than I have been. We haven't eaten anything of substance since yesterday morning."

"They'll find us," Kim said confidently. "Give them time."

Casey quietly drank her water, while she looked around the makeshift camp. They had food. They had water. They even had shelter and a bathroom of sorts. Casey was impressed that for nine city-people, the camp was coming along smoothly.

"Can I check your temperature?" Scott asked, as she finished her water bottle.

Casey nodded in response.

When he touched her forehead, he shook his head, upset. "Getting higher. How is your head?"

"Still hurts," she admitted. "Feels like one of those horrendous migraines."

"My head has been hurting this morning." Kim rubbed the back of her neck. "I think it's from a lack of food though."

Scott went over to her and touched her forehead. "Hun-uh," he shook his head. "You have a fever too. It's a low-grade one though."

"Oh, this is just wonderful." Jay rolled his eyes. "We get lost in the deep forestlands of Colorado, only to start passing a virus."

"Relax, there are only two," Scott said calmly. "Let's not panic."

"More water." Jeff got off the ground. "If we keep our system's flushed, maybe it will lessen the effects of this virus."

"Good thinking." Pete helped gather the few empty water bottles. "What do you think? One more good fill for the night?"

"Everyone suck down what's left of your bottle, and we will go fill them," Hunter said, as he stood up to join Pete and Jeff.

Casey lay back down on Jesse's lap, while the trio took off for the stream to fill the bottles. Everyone, except Jesse, Casey, and Scott, went down to the ridge for a change of scenery. After a few minutes of watching her struggle to get to sleep, Jesse said, "I hate to do this, but I have to go to the bathroom."

She sat up so he could slip out from under her. "Go ahead."

While he was gone, Scott sat down beside Casey and quietly said, "Okay, I'll admit this only to you, but we have serious problems."

"Worse than the mess we're already in?"

"Honestly, there is a virus of some kind crawling around us. My head hurts too, and I never get a headache. That's in addition to the fact that we've been wet for over twenty-four hours, and it's raining even harder than before. We don't have any dry clothes or fire, so that isn't helping either."

"I know."

"You're the sickest, yet you are the one we probably need the most."

"What do you mean?"

"We're all rescue paramedics, but you're the one with the survival skills."

She sighed. "A lot of good it did for the purpose of fire."

"Hey, we got smoke. It's more than we would have had." As he thought aloud, he said, "If they're looking for us, they have to do it on foot. The choppers aren't coming out until this rain slows down."

"I agree."

"That means we have to do this on our own," Jesse said, as he came out of the woods and sat down with them.

Scott jumped at hearing Jesse's voice. "How much did you hear?"

"Enough to know that you're a good actor." He looked him in the eyes, seeing the same fear and concern that he felt. "You're sick too, huh?"

"Are you?"

"Yeah. I've had a headache for a couple of hours now. That's why I didn't mind Casey sleeping on me. That way I wouldn't have to do anything."

"I need to lie back down again. I feel like I'm going to throw up." Casey lay down on her arm, curling up on the ground.

Jesse adjusted to a better position, before he had her lie on his lap again. "Here ya go," he offered.

"We're going to have to huddle to stay warm again tonight," Scott pointed out.

Jesse rolled his eyes. "Yeah, like that's going to help with containing this virus."

Casey rolled over, looking up at him. "It's either the virus or pneumonia."

"Good point." He said, as he lay back on the ground with his hands behind his head. He sighed. "If there is a God, then I pray He has mercy on us, and gets us out of here…and soon."

Chapter 4

A Spark of Hope

As soon as they landed, Derek called the Colonel on the satellite phone. While the trio listened to the Colonel's report, it didn't make them feel any better. He said Casey was getting sicker, and if she couldn't get away to talk in the next day, he was going to step in and get them out of there on his own. For him to say that, it meant the situation was nearing a dangerous level.

"We need to get out there," Mark insisted.

"No. Stay put," the Colonel said over the phone. "I have the situation under control."

"Let us come out there as a hunting party and get them out that way," Mark pleaded.

"No, Captain," the Colonel said sternly. "I'll make it an order if you push the issue."

"You can't seriously expect us to just sit here."

"I don't. I expect you to acquire a hospital ID and uniform. When she gets out of here, she is going to have to get to the hospital as soon as possible, and we are going to have to sneak in to keep an eye on her."

The words hung in the air for a moment, before Keith looked over at Mark and asked, afraid of the answer, "Just how sick is she, Colonel?"

"She's hardly moved over the last several hours. Her fever looks as if it's climbing, but she's quit rubbing her head from the headache. I don't know if that's good or bad. By the looks of her, I can't imagine her fever's any lower than one-hundred-and-three or four."

"Why are you letting her stay there then?" Mark's face got red in anger. "Pull her now!"

"Captain!" the Colonel's voice came across the phone in a sharp tone.

Mark took a deep breath to calm himself. "I don't understand why you are risking exposing her longer than she needs to be. If she's that sick, then get her out of there."

"I don't want to risk my exposure."

"You'll risk her life though?"

"I've got it under control, Captain," the Colonel warned.

Mark walked off to cool down. He intertwined his fingers on the top of his head as he took deep breaths. What was wrong with him? Why couldn't he keep his emotions under control anymore?

"I'll take care of it," Derek said into the phone.

"Understood," Keith responded to the instructions the Colonel gave Derek and Keith.

"I will contact you in four hours. If you don't hear from me by then, assume the situation is critical and come in for her," the Colonel instructed.

"Yes, sir," Derek acknowledged, and then hung up the phone.

Mark scoffed, as he looked over at Derek and Keith, who were watching him. "Really? If it's that bad –"

"Don't start!" Derek snapped, cutting him off.

"Don't start?" Mark growled. "He's gambling with her life!"

"She's not bleeding. Nothing is broken. She only has a fever and a headache."

"And at least a five-hour hike to get to help. Do you honestly think she's going to make it out on foot?" Mark challenged.

Derek sighed, shaking his head. While he knew Mark had a valid point, he also knew the Colonel's orders. "Look, you can go in and see her as soon as they bring her into the hospital. Get me a badge so I can change it out for you."

Mark knew Derek was doing him a favor by letting him be the one to go in, but it didn't make him feel any better. "All right," he conceded. Then he looked up and added, "But if she's not out by the morning, we're going in after her."

"I agree," Keith said. "I'm not sure what he's thinking. She's an adult. She can only go so long before she won't be able to bounce back."

*   *   *

Casey slept most of the next day, off and on. When she did wake up, she noticed more people lying around than the day before. Pete rested against a tree with Kim on his lap. Her face was flushed as well, but she slept comfortably. Near the fire pit, Scott and Jesse looked ragged, while it looked like Hunter, Will, Jay, and Jeff might have been carrying most of the load, by taking turns running for autumn berries and refilling the bottles of water.

Casey started coughing around five or six that night. It woke her up for a bit, but she tried to conceal that she was awake. Every time she remotely picked up her head, Scott would shove more water down her throat. She didn't think it helped, but it seemed to make Scott feel better. The water didn't seem sanitary to her, but she understood the idea 'you do what you can with what you are given.'

*   *   *

Mark pulled into the hospital visitor lot in the navy-blue Dodge Ram 1500 the unit shared.   He walked into the main entrance toward the elevators as if he knew where he was going. He got off on the next floor, and walked through to the staircase door, back down to the bottom floor to make sure he was not being followed.

He then headed toward the ER, reading the signs that directed him toward the staff locker room. He had been in enough hospitals over the years to know what to look for. While most hospital set-ups were different, a few basic elements were similar enough to find what he was after.

After wandering around for about thirty minutes, he finally found what he needed. He looked both ways before he ducked into the men's locker room. No one was in the immediate area, but he heard someone in the shower, so he knew he had to hurry. He picked the lock of a locker about four in from the end. That locker was empty except for toiletries, so he picked the lock of the locker next to it. Jackpot! The male nurse who owned that locker had left his badge on his scrub top in the locker. Mark knew some of the staff members did that out of habit. It took him only a second to swipe the card and relock both lockers. He slipped out of the locker room without anyone noticing…with the ID tucked away safely in his pocket.

He met Derek and Keith at their hotel room and tossed the ID on the table. "There. Do your magic," he said to Derek.

Derek was the mastermind behind creating false IDs to get the unit into places they wouldn't otherwise be able to access. He had no doubt in his mind that Mark would be able acquire an ID – he did it all of the time. He had to give Mark credit. He had no idea how he got over half of the IDs he obtained over the years, but he was grateful. With a real ID in his possession, it made his job that much easier. "Do you have a set of scrubs?" he asked Mark.

Mark held up the bag from the local surplus store, before tossing it on the table next to the badge. Keith had the news on, which had a story about the missing firefighters, so Mark sat on the bed opposite Keith, interested in the story.

"Still missing, the local heroes of Engine Company Fifteen are at the top of our storyline for today," the news anchor began her broadcast. "Disappearing near Longs Peak two days ago, the search continues for a group of –"

"Tomorrow morning, right?" Mark looked at Derek.

"If they're not found by tomorrow morning, I have permission from the Colonel to go in as hunters and get them."

"Is she going to last until morning?" Keith asked.

Derek looked at him for a moment before he said, "She has to."

* * *

When Casey woke up again, it was about three in the morning. She had to go to the bathroom. As she looked around, she had four guys either sleeping on top of or immediately next to her, huddled together for warmth. The fact that she was able to slip out without waking any of them shocked her, because it was still raining heavily, and the temperature could not have been more than fifty-five at best. That's when the thought of how weak they were dawned on her. A feeling of despair washed over her.

She sighed, knowing she shouldn't go by herself, but she didn't want to disturb the entire group since they were sleeping so well. She looked around, debating on what to do, before she gently shook Hunter since he was on the end.

"Hunter?" Casey tried again for the third time with no success. While she didn't mind going by herself during the day, it made her nervous to go at night. She wanted someone to know where she was going due to the unknown creatures of the night or in case something happened to her with how weak she felt.

Finally, after trying a couple more times to wake Hunter, she sighed, resigned to going by herself.

She started toward the bathroom hut…only to run into the Colonel. He covered her mouth as he pulled her towards him. "Shhhh!" he said by her ear when she gasped. "Come over here before you wake anyone."

He pulled her by the hand deeper into the woods, away from the others. "What are you doing?" she hissed when they stopped.

"Watching you." He shook his head as he crossed his arms. "I can't believe you guys got lost."

"Do you know how to get us out of here?"

"Yes. Just be quiet. If they wake up and you're gone, they're going to panic. Speaking of which, why are you by yourself?"

"Because I have to go to the bathroom."

"Why didn't you try to wake someone?"

"I did for a few minutes, but I really have to go, and this rain isn't helping." Casey nervously looked around as she shifted her feet.

"Go ahead and go. Here." He handed her his coat to wrap around her so she wouldn't have to take off her sweatshirt. "Go behind that tree. I'll stay here to keep an eye out."

She practically ran behind the tree. As she felt around for a leaf, she gasped and jumped when a spider crawled across her hand.

The Colonel ran over to her. "What's wrong?"

"It was…nothing." She shook her head in embarrassment.

He gave her a look.

She rolled her eyes with a sigh. "Fine. A spider crawled across my hand."

"It's okay," he chuckled, but tried to keep himself composed for her sake. "Go ahead and go. I'll be over here," he said, and then went back over where he could keep an eye on the rest of the group.

It took her a couple minutes before she was finally able to go. She had to go so bad that it hurt. When she walked back over, she handed him his coat.

"I'd let you keep it if it wouldn't get you caught."

"I know."

"I'm sorry I couldn't get to you sooner, but you were never alone. Things around camp aren't looking too good, so I took the chance when I saw you were alone. In the morning, head west. You should find a trail about three hours west. Take that trail until you find one of those lovely 'you are here' maps," he said, doing his best to make sure she would remember. With as hot as she felt, he prayed she would be okay until morning, and that she would remember his instructions.

Just then, a bolt of lightning struck a tree on the mountain next to them. It sent an almost instantaneous clap of thunder that rumbled the ground under Casey's feet, waking up everyone with a start. Casey gasped and covered her ears at the deafening cannonade of thunder that resounded through the valley, as the Colonel pulled her to the ground, covering her out of instinct.

"You okay?" he asked when the sound calmed.

She nodded as he helped her off the ground. "Your camp is awake," he said. "You need to go." He shoved her in the direction of the others, as he heard people waking up from inside the camp.

Due to the excitement, her heart raced, which made her head pound harder. With the fever, her pounding head, lack of food, and racing heart, she was so dizzy that she rested her hand on a tree in order to catch her breath. She would have probably thrown up if she had more in her stomach. She took several steps forward before turning back around to say something to the Colonel, but he was gone.

"Casey!" Jeff sat up in alarm, feeling around the ground around him. "Where's Casey?"

"I'm right here." She ducked back under the lean-to.

"Where were you?" Scott yelled. His heart raced when the thunderous boom woke him out of a deep sleep with a start.

"I had to go to the bathroom."

"You don't go anywhere by yourself here." While Scott was upset with her, part of it was also the adrenaline from the thunder and the ground shaking below him. "It's dangerous!"

"I tried to wake people up, but they wouldn't wake up," she said, as she sat down on the ground next to him. She wrapped her arms around her legs, hugging them close to her as she dropped her head onto her knees. Her head was almost spinning out of control. "And I really had to go."

"I mean it," Scott said, sternly. "You don't go anywhere by yourself until we're out of here. Got it?"

"Yes, Daddy."

Scott looked at her as his heart rate slowly returned to normal. "Case, I'm serious. We're in the middle of the woods, it's raining and slippery, and it's the middle of the night. If one of us did that, wouldn't you be upset?"

"I had to go. I tried to wake Hunter several times."

"Sorry." Hunter sighed, understanding the wasted opportunity. He kicked himself for missing the chance to be alone with her in the woods.

"I can't believe you people slept as hard as you did with it raining so much either."

"Uh, Scott," Pete said as he looked out at the mountain across the valley from them.

"What?" he snapped, still angry with Casey.

Pete didn't say anything. He pointed to where the lightning struck a tree on the other mountain. Casey groaned at seeing the unmistakable flicker of fire.

"Oh! No way!" He shook his head. "Unbelievable! If we had any luck at all, it would be bad."

Casey looked up as the lightning crackled, leaving trails of light across the sky while the thunder rolled all around them, shaking the mountains.

Will huffed. "This just keeps getting better and better."

Casey took a deep breath, attempting to keep her emotions under control. "We need to get out of here."

"We still have two more hours before daylight. And as bad as this storm is, I doubt we're going to have a lot of sunlight," Jay pointed out.

Kim perked up. "Rain!"

Jay shook his head. "Kimmy, go back to sleep."

"You moron. It's raining."

Jay rolled his eyes. "It has been for two days now."

"But it's actually raining hard." She scrambled out from in between Will and Pete. She ran down to the ridge with her bottle and took the lid off, setting it on the rock. "Fresh water. Come on. Fill up."

"She's right. It's clean." Hunter got up and followed her down to the ridge, opening his bottle for the rain to fill. The others spread out along the ridge, following suit. They used leaves to direct the water into the bottles.

Casey sat on the ridge for a couple minutes with lightning, thunder, wind, and rain pelting them from all directions, before she slid back against the rock.

Jesse looked over his shoulder at her. "What's wrong?"

Her head pounded fiercely as her stomach churned under her hand. "My head and stomach."

He put out his hand. "Give me your water bottle."

As she got up to give it to him, she ended up scrambling to the edge of the ridge, where she threw up over the side. Hunter wrapped his arm around her waist so she wouldn't go over the side when she threw up again. "Ohhhh," she moaned, putting her head down, covering her face with her hands.

"I hope the rain puts that fire out," Pete said, keeping an eye on the orange glow across the valley. No sooner did he say that, then the rain went from heavy to a torrential downpour.

"Could this get any worse?" Casey yelled up at the sky toward God. She was angry…sick…tired…drenched…and hungry.

"We have to fill these. We need the clean water." While Jesse felt bad for Casey, she had to fill the bottle with clean water while she could.

Casey nodded, crawling over to the rock near him. While she lay her head down on her arm, she held the water bottle with her other hand. He held the leaves for her and his bottles.

"They're not sending a rescue crew in this," Scott said, looking around as the water dripped off everyone.

"West," Casey mumbled, remembering what the Colonel told her.

"What?" Jeff looked over at her.

"We need to go west," she said again.

Will wiped the water out of his eyes. "No, we need to go east."

"West." She glared at him. "We tried east. It-didn't-work."

He scowled at her as he held his bottle.

"She's right." Pete nodded. "We need to try a different direction."

"Gee, then why don't we try north? Oh, wait! Because that will land us over there." Will pointed over the ridge.

"Don't be an idiot." Jay shook his head in irritation.

"Well, what if we flip a coin? We'll let the coin decide the direction we need to take?" Scott asked.

"West." Casey insisted. She knew the Colonel would not steer them in the wrong direction. She prayed she remembered it right, knowing her fever must have been slowly climbing over the last twenty-four hours.

Jesse reached over and touched her forehead. "You're hotter."

"No, I'm not." She brushed his hand out of the way. He looked at her for a moment before she leaned over the side of the ridge and threw up again.

Scott crawled over to her when she finished, and felt her forehead. "He's right. You are hotter…a lot hotter."

She shook her head. "I can't be."

"Come on back here and rest." Scott pulled her away from the ledge as she wiped off her mouth.

"We need to go west," she mumbled, as she lay on Scott's shoulder, facing out toward the valley.

"Don't worry about it. Just go to sleep." He had his arm around her, holding her under a rock ledge, hoping to keep her somewhat dry. "Hopefully things will dry out in a couple of hours."

"Fire's out," Pete said as the rain finally snuffed the fire across the valley.

"Good." Will exhaled. "Hopefully that's a sign that things are finally turning around for us."

"It's a spark of hope," Jesse agreed.

*   *   *

The pine canopy made it difficult to see the direction Mark was headed. He cautiously made his way through the forestlands searching for Casey. He had a feeling of urgency convulse through his body as he thought about her being lost in the woods.

The storm generated roaring thunder and a spectacular lightning display around him, making the ground shudder below his feet. That's when he saw the orange glow in the distance. If that fire was near her, she could be in serious danger.

He saw a small camp about fifty feet ahead, with the fire about an acre wide and less than a hundred yards away. "Casey!" Mark shouted. He knew he shouldn't be yelling, but he didn't want anything else to happen to her. "Casey!"

That's when he saw it. The forms of her fellow firefighters were burnt to a crisp near the hut. His heart sank as he dropped to his knees. The pain that ripped through his body shattered his heart into a million pieces. On one of the bodies he saw her necklace. It was the cross necklace she always wore whether she was on duty or not. She never took it off.

He reached over and wrapped his fingers around the cross. He would never forgive the Colonel for leaving her in the woods when they could have pulled them so long ago.

He looked up at the sky, and cried, "NOOO!"

"Mark!" Keith shook him. "Wake up, English!"

Mark sat upright in his bed, his heart racing while rapidly breathing. "Casey."

"Got that." Derek sat down on Mark's bed, relieved they were finally able to wake him. He had yelled in his sleep for over five minutes before they were able to wake him out of the nightmare.

He caught his breath as he dropped his head onto his knees. "A wicked thunderstorm ripped through the woods and surrounded her."

"Like the one outside?" Keith pointed out.

Mark looked toward the window to see the lightening penetrate the sky again, closely followed by a crack of thunder. His looked at the sight in wide-eyed shock. "We need to get to her!"

"We are. We're leaving at eight o'clock unless we hear from the Colonel."

"What if we leave now?" Mark asked. "That dream makes me nervous to leave her out there."

Derek looked at Keith, who shrugged. "Sure. We can go now. It's going to take us a bit to get there. I'll contact the Colonel on the way."

Mark nodded in appreciation. "Thanks. I only hope it's not too late."

*   *   *

"Okay, time to wake up, sleepyhead." Scott gently shook Casey a couple of hours later.

"My head," she groaned, grabbing her head.

"We need to get us out of here, and it doesn't look as if we're getting any help right now," Scott said as the rain continued in a strong, steady flow.

"West." Casey sighed, lying on her arm. "We need to go west."

"Don't worry about it," Hunter scooped her up in his arms to carry her. Casey was so dizzy, she closed her eyes, not caring which direction they were going at that moment or who carried her.

Scott felt her forehead. He shook his head as he said, "It has got to be up there."

"Like what? 102? 103?" Kim looked up from where she wrung out her sweatshirt.

"Feels higher than that."

"Great." She sighed, shaking her head. As the water cascaded out of her sweatshirt onto the ground from where she wrung it, she said, "I don't even know why I'm doing this. It's going to get soaked again."

Pete wrung his out as well. "To get rid of some of the excess moisture."

Casey moaned. Her head went side-to-side. She felt horribly dizzy.

"Let's go, folks," Scott said, and the group took off heading south.

*   *   *

"You folks are out early this morning." Casey heard the Colonel's voice a couple minutes later, as he came out of the woods. She looked over to see him dressed like a hunter. His face was painted, and he had a camouflage hat, coat, and pants on along with his military boots. He also had on a bright orange vest that hunters were required to wear, and carried a crossbow with a pack of arrows on his side.

"We're a little lost," Scott admitted.

"Where are you guys camped?"

"Over near Longs Peak."

"Well, you're going the wrong way for Longs Peak," he said. "Is she okay?" He nodded toward Casey. Hunter pulled her closer to him, not knowing who the Colonel was.

"She's sick. We need to get her back to camp," Scott explained. "Would you be able to help us back?"

"Sure. No problem. I hunt up here all the time. I know this place like the back of my hand. This way," he said, almost parting the group as he went the opposite direction they were heading and turned toward the west.

"I told you west," Casey mumbled.

"Shhh, just go to sleep." Jesse rested his hand on the side of her face for a moment. He shook his head and asked, "How far away are we? She is really sick."

"About three hours to the trails and then another hour or so. What's wrong with her?" The Colonel touched her forehead. She was too hot for his comfort. "Just a second," he said before he disappeared into the woods.

"Where's he going?" Scott looked after him.

Will shrugged. "Don't know."

The Colonel came back less than a minute later with a handful of balsam fir needles in his hand and asked them for her water bottle. The Colonel took a plastic bag out of his pocket and crushed the needles inside the bag with a rock. When the needles were the consistency of a paste, he poured the leftover water into the bag with the needles and worked it until it was well mixed. Then he poured it back into her bottle.

"What's that?" Scott crouched down next to him.

"These are balsam fir pine needles. They're a natural analgesic used to reduce fevers. She's not going to make it back with that fever," he pointed out. "It's too high." Then he stood up and vigorously shook the bottle before he put his hand behind Casey's head and tilted it forward so she could drink. "Here, you need to drink this," he coaxed. She shuddered at the taste. "Keep going. You need to empty the bottle," he encouraged.

She retched a couple of times, doing her best to keep down the bitter, ginger-flavored mixture. Knowing who he was, she knew he wouldn't give it to her to hurt her, so she forced down the horrid mixture.

When she finished, he handed the empty bottle to Jesse. "Come on," the Colonel said, "we need to get her back, preferably before she gets worse."

"Thanks, man," Scott said, relieved to finally get help.

*   *   *

"We need to go now," Mark said as he paced the hotel room, wearing out the carpet.

"The Colonel called, and he's guiding them back to camp. We have to sit and wait," Derek insisted, as he sat at the table. On their way to the mountain, the Colonel had called and told them he was getting them out, and to stay put at the hotel.

"He said she looked sick, and that Hunter of all people was carrying her. She would have to be really sick not to pitch a fit that he's carrying her," Keith pointed out. "I have to agree with English on this one."

Derek sighed. He hated it when the Colonel put him in this type of position. He knew the Colonel knew what he was doing, but he had to convince Mark and Keith. "His orders were for us to stay here. He said he would contact us when he was clear."

Mark stopped pacing and glared at Derek. "If she doesn't come out of this okay, I will never forgive him."

"Neither will I," Derek said, deep in thought. "Neither will I."

* * *

The group walked for almost three hours before KC Cross from 'C' shift saw them in the distance. He picked up his radio and said, "Chief! I found them!"

"Where are they?"

"East of the trails by a half-hour. Carter's being carried by Morgan, and Richter's being held up by Van den Bergh and Kendall."

"Copy. Get them here as soon as possible. I'm calling in life flight."

"Copy that. ETA will be about an hour and a half."

"Get them here sooner if possible," Chief said with heavy concern on in his voice.

"Will do."

* * *

Mark walked onto Casey's floor in a pair of scrubs. A couple of nurses looked at him for a moment, before they saw the badge and then went back to work, thinking he was supposed to be there.

He confidently went behind the nurse's station, sliding Casey's chart out of its holder. He shook his head at what he saw. With her temperature still hovering around one-hundred-and-four, the antibiotics they administered several hours ago should have kicked in long before now.

He slid it back into its holder before he went into her room. When he walked in, all he heard was the rapid beeping of the monitor, along with the oxygen being fed into the nasal tube. He checked the antibiotic to see how much of the Levofloxacin was left of that dose. Then he looked down at her and brushed his finger across her bright red cheek.

He knew the antibiotic she was on was potent, and knew they used it as a last resort. Using an antibiotic that strong meant she was critical. He shook his head at her condition. He hadn't spoken to the Colonel since he got back. He knew deep down in his heart that he would never forgive the Colonel if she didn't make it out of the hospital.

He picked up a washcloth from the stack of towels in her room, and went into the bathroom off her room. He drenched the washcloth in cold water before he wrung it out. Then he walked to her bed and brushed the sweat off her face.

"You need to snap out of this," Mark said in a sigh. "We have a lot to talk about."

Casey squinted up at Mark.

"Casey?"

She nodded.

"How are you feeling?"

She shook her head before she closed her eyes again. As her head dropped to the side, Mark's heart sunk. He knew he would have to sneak back in again in a couple of hours to find out how she was.

"Who are you?" a nurse asked when she walked in the room.

Mark quickly glanced at her name-tag. He recognized her as Casey's nurse. "Dr. Ellis had me stop in and check on her. He'll be here in a bit to look at her, but I was on my way into work so he asked me to stop by."

She glanced down and saw his name-tag. "Well, he'll be happy to know that her temperature has dropped a degree since she came in yesterday."

Mark cringed at that news. That meant it was hovering around one-hundred-and-five by the time she got in there. "Good." He nodded. "When's her next dose of antibiotics?"

She glanced at her watch. "Around noon. They are set for every four hours. Dr. Ellis will have my tail end if she's even a minute late." She rolled her eyes. "He already made that clear."

"She's one of his favorites." Mark smirked.

"Tell me about it. He looks after her as if she was his own."

"Well, keep a close eye on her. I'm sure he'll have me stop by later. I live only a couple of blocks from here."

"Must be nice. I live forty-five minutes away. I guess it's convenient for you to stop by."

"Dr. Ellis is a great guy to work for…provided you stay on his good side."

She laughed at that one. "Yeah. When you don't follow his orders, you have to face his wrath."

"Better you than me." Mark smiled, making sure his dimples were in full view. He stood up and shook her hand. "I appreciate you looking after his patient so well. I will make sure to tell him."

"Thank you." She smiled back at him. "It's not often I get something good told to the doctors about me."

"I'll be back around five-thirty or six o'clock."

"I'll be on until seven," she hinted.

"I'll see what I can do," Mark lied.

"Great! There's a coffee house a couple of blocks down the road."

Mark nodded in understanding, knowing he would never keep that appointment. "I'll see you later, April."

"I look forward to it, Peter," she said with her smile even bigger.

"You can call me Pete." He returned the smile. Mark rolled his eyes as he walked out of the room. He accepted that flirting was part of his job, and that in order to get information from some women, he had to make promises that he would never keep, but he also knew his heart wasn't in it anymore. It wasn't into anything anymore…except Casey.

*   *   *

Through the next couple of days, Mark snuck back into her room. He did his best to avoid April with everything he had. He was relieved to see Casey's temperature dropping, but he was still upset with the Colonel for waiting so long.

"What's her status?" the Colonel asked when Mark walked into the hotel room.

"Her temperature is down to one-hundred-and-one-point-five. She woke up yesterday."

The Colonel studied him for a moment before he said, "I sense a little tension."

Mark pulled a soda out of the tiny refrigerator. "Not much gets by you."

The Colonel sat back in his chair and crossed his arms. "What's wrong?"

"With all due respect, you waited too long, and you know it."

He shook his head. "I don't think so."

Mark glared at him as he emptied the can of soda. Then he crushed it and tossed it into the trash can, watching it drop right in. "I beg to differ."

The Colonel cocked his head to the side as he asked, "What's going on?"

"Why didn't you bring her in sooner?" Mark demanded.

Neither Keith, nor Derek said a word. They saw the discussion coming a mile away, and didn't dare get in between the pair.

"I told you. I didn't want to risk exposing –"

"You did it anyway!" Mark cut the Colonel off.

"Because they were going the wrong way."

"Why didn't you do it the day before? You know, so she and Richter wouldn't have to be carried out of there? What? Were you going to wait until someone died?"

The Colonel leaned back in his chair with his hands behind his head. "She's fine. It turned out okay."

"I need to get out of here." Mark growled, slamming the door behind him.

He walked for over a mile before his mind even remotely slowed. While he never yelled at the Colonel, he knew his tone was disrespectful. Seeing Casey's eyes open this afternoon when he went in delighted him, while having to leave her broke his heart. Could he have fallen for the sister of one of his best friends?

The entire walk back to the hotel, he mulled through his mind of how it was possible. He didn't want to face the Colonel, but he knew he had to do it. Leaving things the way they were, was not an option.

The Colonel met him in the parking lot. "We need to take a drive."

Mark sighed as they walked to the truck. He didn't care where they were going, he just wanted to get 'the talk' over and done with so he could go back and rest in the hotel.

After fifteen silently tense minutes, the Colonel said, "I understand there's something going on."

"Who told you?"

"Both of them. They said you've been on edge since Kirkuk."

Mark looked over him, not sure if he would understand. "What's your motivation for getting out of the situations we seem to find ourselves in?" he asked the Colonel.

He thought for a moment. "Well, the way I look at it, if we don't then who will? The guys we pull out of trouble are the ones who need it the most…they are also the ones the country needs the most. The guys we go after are spec ops guys that are being disavowed when they are putting their lives on the line."

Mark nodded in understanding. Looking out the window, he said, "I get that, but what keeps you going?"

"I don't think about it. I just do it. I know if the situation were reversed that I would want someone coming in after me." The Colonel looked over at him for a moment, before he asked, "What's going on in your head?"

Mark sighed. "I don't know."

"Is this about Casey?"

"In more ways than one."

The Colonel narrowed his eyes for a moment before he asked, "Is there something between you two?"

"No."

"Would you like there to be?"

"I don't know."

"I see."

Mark looked over at him. "Do you?"

"I'm not as cold-hearted as I seem."

"I never said you were."

"You don't need to. I can see it in your faces when I send you guys out." The Colonel sighed in irritation. He didn't want to fight with Mark. "I don't take the missions we go on lightly. I know every time I send you out, that you potentially may not come back."

"As you said, if the situation were reversed, I would hope someone would come after me. I don't want to die, but if it came down to it, I would make that sacrifice to get them out."

"But...?" the Colonel asked, feeling there was more.

"But, I feel as if there's more to this life."

"Meaning?"

"Meaning…I don't know." He shook his head.

"Yes, you do."

"I honestly don't know what's going on in my head," Mark admitted. "I just know that as soon as the plane took off for Kirkuk, all I wanted was to be with Casey. I feel peace when I'm around her. When we're apart, I long to be with her with every fiber of my being. I miss her smile and laughter. I miss her lightheartedness. I miss talking to her. I guess being on edge twenty-four-seven is getting old."

The Colonel did a double-take. Did Mark really say what he thought he said? "Are you saying you're in love with Casey?"

"I'm saying that I want something more to life. I don't know. Maybe it's time to turn in the MK-23s and retire."

"You would….what?" The Colonel's jaw dropped. He spun the truck into the nearest parking lot and threw it into park. He turned and glared at Mark. "You're going to…what are you thinking?"

"I don't know."

"According to Cruise and Mariano, you've been on edge and angry."

"Because I have a lot on my mind. I can sort things out better when I am talking to Casey."

Colonel shook his head. "I don't understand."

Mark looked over at him and admitted, "That's okay. Neither do I."

*   *   *

The day the hospital released Casey, Jesse picked her up so she could get her vehicle and belongings that one of the other firemen brought back to the station. It was a long ride on the back of a motorcycle, but Casey appreciated feeling the wind through her hair. She understood what propelled Jesse to enjoy riding his motorbike. She felt a sense of freedom, unrestraint.

Jesse, along with most of the other guys, were given an antibiotic and released from the hospital on the same day they went in. Casey, on the other hand, was in for four days, and Kim was in for two.

Jesse insisted on following Casey to her house to make sure she got home. "Chief said for you to hold off for another shift before you come in for work," Jesse said, as he leaned against the railing of the staircase leading to her porch.

"That's three more days." She sighed, leaning against her doorway. "That's going to drive me crazy."

"You're not healthy enough to go in tomorrow. Just get some rest and recoup. If you want me to, I can call you to make sure you're doing okay."

"I'll text to let you know I'm okay," she said, secretly hoping that the A.N.G.E.L.s would be hanging around more over the next three days…mainly Mark. She was able to see Mark when she was in the hospital, but it wasn't anywhere near enough for her. He could only stay for five or ten minutes because he was doing his best to duck the nursing staff. "Who knows? I may be sleeping."

"Here's hoping," Jess said. "Nothing personal, but you look like you need it. You're still pretty pale."

She smirked. "Thanks."

He stood. "Well, get some rest and I'll see you in three days."

"Thanks. I'll curl up on the couch and catch up on a couple television series I'm recording."

"Hmm, sounds productive."

"I'm tired of being productive."

He looked at her for a moment before he asked, "Are you okay?"

"Not really."

"Need a vacation from the vacation?"

"I need to get back to work. I think we should plan a vacation at a later date. Chief needs as many of us back for as long as possible. He had to pull a lot of strings to cover what happened when we got lost." She growled in frustration. "I cannot believe we got lost."

"I'm sorry. I promise you it will never happen again."

"I know it was an accident."

He hugged her. "Get some rest."

"Thanks, Jesse. Tell everyone I said 'hi' and that I'll see them on the next shift."

"I will. Now go inside."

She waved good bye as she went into her house, locking the door behind her. She set her purse on the counter, hearing Jesse's bike pull away.

"I thought he'd never leave," Mark said.

Casey about jumped out of her tennis shoes. She gasped as she spun around to see Mark leaning on the doorway of the kitchen. "You scared the living daylights outta me!"

He smirked in amusement. "Sorry."

She took a couple deep breaths before she went in and turned on the living room lamp. Then, she sat down on the couch while Mark sat down on a chair near her end of the couch.

When the light came on, the Colonel, Keith, and Derek walked in the backyard sliding glass door, filling the remaining seats around the living room. The Colonel sat next to Casey, Derek pulled a chair over from the dining room, and Keith took the other chair in the living room.

"How are you feeling?" the Colonel asked.

"Well, once I get my heart out of my throat," Casey said, "I'll let you know."

The guys chuckled while the Colonel said, "At least your sense of humor hasn't suffered."

"No. I'm fine. I just…geez…you scared me!"

"Sorry." Mark sat back in his seat. While it felt good to be with her, he wasn't sure if he was ready to admit it to her yet.

"No problem. Just warn me next time," Casey said, as her heart finally beat at a regular pace once again.

"We wanted to wish you a welcome back home." Derek smiled. "You've been missed."

"Thanks," she said appreciatively.

"We also wanted to see you with our own eyes before we took off," Keith added.

"You guys are leaving?" Casey asked, surprised.

"Just me, Mariano, and Cruise," the Colonel clarified. "We need to go down to Nicaragua. English is going to keep an eye on you, so take it easy on him. He's responsible for your life."

Casey felt the tension in the room. "What's going on?"

"Things are getting hotter out there," the Colonel admitted.

"Meaning?" she pressed.

"There's a target on us."

"How hot?"

"Hot." The Colonel glanced up at her. "It's getting hotter every time one of us is out."

Casey looked at them in concern. "Is it from the government?"

The Colonel shook his head. "Not from ours."

"And technically not from a foreign one either," Mark added.

"Huh?" She was even more confused.

"Through back channels from other governments. However, since we are being 'killed-off' one by one, it should be easing, not getting more difficult." Mark glanced at the Colonel, not sure why he shared this information with Casey. "Why are you telling her this?"

"Because they are losing their grip on us," the Colonel explained. "Since Jack and Marcos are physically dead, and you and I are legally dead, they only have access to Derek and Keith. And since Derek is 'dying' this time around, Keith will be the one with the biggest target out there."

Mark nodded understanding. "Casey too."

"Why am I a target?" she asked, stunned.

"Because of who you know...what you have...and who your brother was," the Colonel said. "You also know us. We've been protecting you for years, and they know that. They also know Jack was your brother and that you hold the money and the code for the strongbox."

"Oh my word!" She threw her hands in the air in frustration. "I want my normal life back."

Keith chuckled. "I don't think your life was ever normal."

"Good point," she conceded.

"But you are going to lead it as if it is and always was," the Colonel added. Then he turned to Mark and said, "And you are going to continue to stay on your toes and in the shadows."

Mark nodded. "Yes, sir."

"We'll be leaving in a couple of hours. Follow standard operating procedures."

"I understand."

Then he turned to Casey, and said, "Don't assume anything. If we text you or leave a message, we will use the code. Be vigilant in observing what is around you and stay on your toes. After Derek gets back, you and Keith are the only two left exposed."

"I understand," she agreed.

"I mean it. Trust no one but us."

"Yes, sir."

"People may look innocent, but you don't know where their loyalties lie. Those around you may not be who they seem."

Chapter 5

Unbreakable Bonds

That night Casey slept soundly in her own bed, knowing Mark watched the house. Remembering that the Colonel, Derek, and Keith were going on a mission, she made sure to include a special prayer of protection for the A.N.G.E.L.s before going to sleep. While she did not have a full comprehension of their missions, she knew they held vital importance.

The first couple of days she didn't see Mark, even though she knew he was there. She wondered if he was upset with her or if something was wrong. Finally, one night she heard two light knocks before she heard three more. She knew the two knocks stood for Angel and the three was Mark, so she put the movie on pause and opened the sliding glass door to let him in the house.

"I didn't want to scare you this time," Mark said apologetically.

"Don't worry about it. I was still on edge after not sleeping all that well in the hospital. Thank you for checking on me while I was there."

"It was my pleasure," he said, sitting on the chair at the end of the couch.

She plopped on the couch near him, and curled her legs under her. "So, what's up?"

He shrugged. "Just miss talking with you. We were doing it on a regular basis there for a while."

"That's true. I miss you too."

He grinned. "Really?"

"Yep."

He sat back in his chair, a little more at ease.

"So, have you heard from any of the other guys yet?" she asked.

"Yeah. They got the intel they need. They're working on a plan to extract the agent now."

"What agent?"

"Never mind." He shook his head. "I said too much. Just keep them in your prayers."

"Always. Have you eaten yet?"

"Yeah. I have my stash of protein bars and MREs out there."

Eyes wide, she asked, "Are you serious?"

"I can't leave you to go get food. I'm responsible for your life. The Colonel will have my head if anything happens to you."

"You should have told me." She got up and went into the kitchen. Looking through her leftovers, she decided on a plate of chicken parmesan and spaghetti with a salad on the side.

"Wow! Thank you." He grinned, his dimples in full view, making Casey catch her breath. "I haven't eaten this good since…well, I can't remember how long it's been."

She smiled, pleased. While Mark enjoyed his meal, she continued the movie at a lower volume. "Good?" she asked when he finished the meal and drained his glass of milk.

"Very much so." He carried the dishes into the kitchen, rinsing them before placing them in the dishwasher. "Gotta clean up my mess."

"Thank you. I appreciate that."

As he sat back down in the living room chair, he asked, "How are you feeling?"

"Much better."

After a minute of silence, he looked up at her and said, "This can't be easy for you – hiding us from your friends."

"It isn't, but it's worth the risk. You guys are important to me."

He looked up at her, pleasantly surprised. He was struggling to read her, whereas he used to be able to read her like a book. "Do you know I've been looking after you since you were seventeen?"

She smiled and blushed as she said, "Must feel like forever for you."

"Actually, it's been quite the opposite. To say it felt like forever implies an almost sense of torture. On the contrary, it's been a pleasure."

She glanced up at him and saw him looking back at her. She thought she might have seen something in his eyes. She decided to keep the conversation light and see where it went. "Seventeen, huh?"

"Yeah. I've watched you enjoy the work you did as a photographer and are now doing as a firefighter. While I understand the change of careers, you have a great eye as a photographer. Look at this picture for example." He got up and went to one of the landscapes on the wall. "I remember this. It was in Queensland – Burdekin Falls, I believe."

"That's right," she said, taken aback by his accuracy.

"I was on that trip with you. The other guys were on a mission for that one."

"Really? I was, what, twenty-nine?"

"Yep. Your birthday was five days before. Jack didn't want you to go, but there was no stopping you, so he sent me. He said it was because he knew I could handle myself and you, if need be. He didn't trust your guide."

"Yeah, Madison was a unique individual."

"Madison was a crook. The only reason he didn't touch you was because I threatened him within an inch of his life if he touched you or ripped you off."

Wide-eyed, her jaw dropped.

"And this one." He pointed toward another one, ignoring her reaction. "I was there for this one too. It was on the island Skopelos in Greece on the Aegean Sea, if I remember right."

"It was. How do you remember that?"

He turned and looked at her. "I told you. I've been looking after you for quite some time." He chuckled for a moment in remembrance, "Jack and I used to joke around that if you knew I existed, you and I would have made a great couple." Then he quickly added, "But you weren't supposed to know I existed."

Casey's heart skipped a beat. So, they did talk about the two of them. "And now that I do?" she asked.

He looked at her for a moment, before turning to another photo in the hallway. "This was the lighthouse of Dun Loaghhaire near Dublin, Ireland. You've been all over the world with one of us with you at all times."

"And now that I do know you exist?" Casey asked again.

He turned and looked at her. He wanted to tell her how much he admired her. He wanted to tell her how he longed to see her sparkling green eyes when they were apart, but he couldn't. He wanted to tell her that her smile lit up his heart. He couldn't say anything.

She walked over to him in the hallway. Standing in front of him, she took his hands into hers, and asked, "And now that I know you exist?"

"Can you lead two different lives?"

"If that's what it takes."

"But we don't even know –"

She put her finger to his lips. "Shhh."

He longed to kiss her. He wanted to know what it felt like to take her into his arms and kiss her soft, tender lips once again.

"We'll take this one step at a time," she said, interrupting his thoughts.

He looked at her for another moment before he shook his head. "You lost Mac less than two months ago."

"I'll tell you what," she said, thinking through her words. She didn't want to push and mess things up between them. "We can take things slowly – no expectations…no thinking…no impressing…just us. That's the only way we can truly know if there is something there."

He reached in his pocket and pulled out the photo he carried around with him. "There has always been something there on my side," he admitted.

She looked at the picture and smiled remembering the moment, before she looked up at him and said, "One step at a time."

He gently wrapped his arms around her body. He would take what he could get.

*   *   *

Later in the week when Casey was off-duty, she was at home watching a movie when her doorbell rang. It was two short and four long.

She sat for a minute in confusion before she slowly got off the couch. She slightly moved the curtain to see Derek, and motioned for him to go to the back door. As far as she knew, he was still down in Nicaragua with the Colonel and Keith.

She ran to the back door and opened it in time for him to come through with Mark on his heels.

"What are you doing here?" Mark asked Derek, as they went into the living room. Derek paced, as Mark sat down on the couch, on the edge of his seat.

"Have you seen or heard from the Colonel or Mariano?" Derek asked, as he anxiously paced.

To Mark, he seemed irritated and on edge, but he also detected the element of fear, and that was unusual for Derek. "They were on assignment with you," Mark said. "What happened?"

"We got separated. The Colonel's instructions were if we got separated to meet back here. I haven't been able to get hold of either of them. Are you sure you haven't heard from them?"

"You guys weren't supposed to check in until 2130 tonight." Mark looked at his watch. "There's still a half-hour until then."

"I tried to contact them, and no one is responding. I needed to know that you two were okay. Something happened, and I needed to know who was okay and who wasn't."

Mark furrowed his brow. "What happened?"

"Remember Hutchins? He was Naval Intelligence from several years ago."

"Yeah, but didn't he die back in ninety-nine?"

"So we think," Derek challenged.

"What does that mean?"

"I saw him."

Mark stared at him in horror. "You…no way. I saw him die."

"I swear to you. He looked like he was only about thirty-five or forty years old."

"That can't happen. He would be at least twenty years older than that by now."

"Wait a minute. Who is Hutchins?" Casey asked.

"He was Naval Intelligence," Mark explained as he got up and paced opposite Derek, rubbing the back of his neck, wracking his brain to remember details of the incident. "We were going in to pull him out from Bagdad, Iraq. He didn't make it." He stopped and looked at Derek. "Are you sure it was him? The age doesn't match."

"I would swear it was him."

"What did he look like?"

"He was about six-foot three, short, light-brown hair, and slate-gray eyes. A big, muscular guy, just like Hutchins."

Casey cocked her head to the side as a thought struck her. She jumped up and got on her laptop, typing in the fire department's web address. She pulled up a photo of Hunter. "Is this what he looked like?"

Mark and Derek both looked over her shoulder as she sat at the kitchen table. "Uncanny!" Mark shook his head in shock. "I never connected –"

"How could he be in Nicaragua when he works at the department?" Casey asked.

"You've been off for two days," Mark pointed out. "No one knows his schedule." He looked over to Derek and shook his head. "You don't think…?"

"No way. There is no way it's him, but he's a dead ringer."

"What happened?" Mark leaned on the chair next to Casey.

"We met with the resistance in the area, and were getting ready to make our move to pull Delgado when we were raided. We split up to give them more targets to go after. I saw several of the resistance fall, but I didn't see what happened to the Colonel or Mariano. I did see one of the men in the middle of the battle pull the bandanna off his face. He looked right at me." The color drained from Derek's face. He shuddered before he continued, "His eyes were gray one moment before they turned pure black. I mean completely black, like he was possessed or something."

Mark shook his head. "The heat. You had to have been dehydrated, or the heat was playing tricks on your mind."

"You're kidding, right? Does this face look I'm making something up or dehydrated? I'm a trained observer, English!" he snapped.

Casey pointed to Hunter. "And you're sure it's this guy?"

"It looks just like him," Derek confirmed. "Unless he has an evil twin out there, it's him."

"Hmm. You go in tomorrow, right?" Mark asked Casey. She nodded. "Let me see if I can get a hold of the Colonel or Mariano. Things may have stepped up a notch."

"What do you mean?" she asked, concerned and confused at the same time.

"We may be fighting something that will take more than one of us to protect you."

Casey gulped, as Mark pulled his cell phone from his pocket. He texted both Keith and the Colonel with the message 'A3' – meaning Mark. When they texted the 'A' for A.N.G.E.L. and the number, it meant the person who texted them was trying to get a hold of them.

Casey nervously got up to keep herself busy. She got each of them ice-cold lemonades while they waited for the response.

About ten minutes later, Mark got a text that said, 'A1.' That was Colonel's way of saying he was okay and would contact if needed. Mark texted back 'No response A5' – meaning no one had contact from Keith.

The phone was silent for around forty-five minutes. The trio nervously sat, not sure what to do. The silence was deafening, so Casey finally turned the movie back on for noise.

When Mark's cell phone went off again, everyone jumped. It was a call from the Colonel. "Yeah," he answered. "No, sir, he came to A7's. He said he could not get you or A5 to respond…Yes, sir, I understand…We will…No problem. We'll wait for further instructions. There's something you should know. A4 said he saw someone he recognized during the fight….He said it was Hutchins, but it couldn't be, could it?...You did?...Yes, sir, she works tomorrow…No problem…Yes, sir, we will wait," he said and hung up the phone. He sighed before he looked up at Casey and said, "You need to call off work tomorrow. He wants you to stay here with us."

"Okay." She nodded in understanding. She immediately went to the kitchen and called off, saying she was sick. For them to ask her to do so, meant something was wrong. When they got a certain look on their face, Casey knew not to question them. It was the same look Jack used to get when something was wrong.

Chief said he understood and would see if someone from 'C' and someone from 'B' could split the shift. Then he said for her to get better, and that he would see her next time her shift swung around. "Done," she said, coming back in the living room.

"Thanks," Mark nodded, as he and Derek pulled out an encyclopedia. They opened it up to Nicaragua.

"Um, I actually have an atlas of South America if you want it," Casey offered. "It's divided into the different countries so you can get a better view of Nicaragua since it's larger."

"Why do you have an atlas of South America?" Mark asked.

"I have atlases from all over the world. Granted, they are in the languages of the countries, so you'll have to translate them to use them, but you can get a general idea."

"But why do you have them?" Derek pressed.

"I had to use them in my travels when I was a photographer. It's a lot easier to point to a taxi driver where I need to go on a map, than to try to explain it in a foreign language I didn't know."

"Good point." Mark nodded. "And yes. Please and thank you."

She went to her bedroom and pulled out the South America atlas before she headed back to the living room. "It's all yours," she said as she handed it to him. "Are you guys hungry?"

"Very much so." Derek looked up with a smile, trying to put her more at ease as he noticed her nervous and agitated state. "Lemonade and food? After coming in from the field, this is a huge blessing."

"No problem." She smiled, pleased and relieved to have something to do. "Mark?"

"Yes, please," he said, and then looked back down at the map. He was in serious mode. "The Colonel said he was in here." He drew a small circle on the map with his finger. "His last report specifically said here." He pointed to a town within the circle.

"When was that?" Derek asked.

"He said it was three hours ago. He also said he had some feelers out about our friend, Hunter. He said he had some suspicions about him when the group was on the camping trip."

"If this is of the unnatural realm, we're going to have our hands full. We can't always see her in the firehouse. We can't get anyone in there either. You're good, but you're not that good."

"Point taken," Mark said. "I will be even more vigilant."

Derek rested his hand on Mark's arm. When Mark looked up at him, he saw that Derek had a look of fear on his face. He looked up toward Casey before looking back down at Mark, and said, "She could have a target. She could be working with the enemy. Depending on when the possession occurred, he could have been planted there since the beginning."

Mark looked up at Casey and sighed. She feverishly worked on getting them food in the kitchen, oblivious to their conversation. "I was hoping to shield her from this type of stuff."

"You know you're not in control of that."

"No, but I know what it's been like to deal with the unseen."

"At least we have a heads-up this time."

"True." He nodded. "I hope it's enough."

Casey heated chicken enchiladas, with corn and green beans on the side. She then cut up an apple, splitting it between the two plates before taking it out to them.

"Oh, wow!" Derek closed his eyes in delight, chewing a bite of the chicken enchiladas. He had to admit that it was the best thing he tasted in a long time.

"I agree." Mark smiled at her, taking a bite. He didn't want her to know about the conversation he had with Derek, so he was doing his best to play it off.

When they were almost done with dinner, Mark's cell phone rang again. "Yes," he answered. "Already taken care of it…Yes, sir, we are looking at a map of it right now…Tomorrow morning? What time?…Mm-hmm, I'll see what I can do…Yep, I will get back to you as soon as possible," he said and hung up the phone. He turned to Derek and said, "Sorry, man, you and the Colonel are going back to Nicaragua. You are taking the Atlas map with you." He looked up at Casey and asked, "Would you mind if we tore out the page?"

"No, go ahead," she said. "It's yours. Anything else I can do for you?"

"Yeah, get me a pen and paper."

Casey grabbed a tablet and a pen from the counter and took it back to him. He tore off the top sheet and used the coffee table to write on the paper so it wouldn't press through onto the pad. He scribbled two male names with social security numbers and birthdates, before he handed it back to her. "You said we are sharing those accounts, right?"

"Yep."

"Then order two tickets to Nicaragua for these two guys, using money from one of the accounts. Make it for as soon as possible after three o'clock in the morning."

"No problem," she said, and headed into the bedroom so she could talk on her cell phone, leaving them to talk privately in the living room.

After working with the airlines for an hour, she got a flight that took off at four o'clock in the morning with two layovers. One was in Mexico and the other in Venezuela. There would be an hour layover in Mexico and a half-hour one in Venezuela. Between the two layovers, it should give them enough time to grab a small breakfast and find their terminal for the last portion of their flight.

Casey wrote down the confirmation number before she hung up, satisfied with the flight she found for them. "Will that work?" She proudly handed the paper with the names and social security numbers along with the flight information to Mark.

"Nice." He nodded in approval. He texted 'A3' to the Colonel, who called back less than five minutes later. The Colonel was pleased with the flight as well, since his flight was getting in at two-thirty in the morning from his current location. From what Casey could tell, he wasn't too far behind Derek in getting a flight out of there.

After everything was set, Mark went outside to keep watch, while Derek slept on the couch. Casey gave him a pillow and blanket before she headed off to bed as well.

*   *   *

When she woke up the next morning, the pillow was on the couch with the blanket folded underneath it, and Derek was gone. It was as if he was never there. The only evidence they were there, was the amount of plates in the dishwasher.

Casey sighed as she got breakfast. She made an extra plate for Mark and set it outside on the back porch steps with a glass of juice, so he knew to come get it when it was clear.

Then, she curled up on the couch watching the news while she ate her breakfast, lost in thought about the events of the previous night. She liked being a part of the A.N.G.E.L.s. She enjoyed being able to help the guys who sacrificially looked after her over the years. When she thought about the dangers these men faced each day, knowing she was able to help them gave her a sense of pride.

She was so lost in thought that she jumped when she suddenly heard two short and three long knocks on her back porch sliding glass door. She ran to the back door to see Mark holding the empty plate and glass…with a grin on his face.

"Thanks," he said. He gave her a kiss on the cheek as he handed her the dishes when she opened the door. He looked around outside, before slipping into the house, going into the living room to sit on the couch.

"Derek and the Colonel got off okay this morning?" she asked.

"I assume so. Derek had their information. You are my responsibility."

"Why did the Colonel want me here? Why couldn't I go to work?" she asked, sitting down next to him in her flannel pants and tank top.

"With someone MIA, he wanted to be sure he knew where you were. While I can keep an eye on you while you are at work, there are a lot of times where you are out of my line of sight." He took a deep breath before he added, "And with this new element, we need to regroup to figure out what exactly we are dealing with here."

"Sooo, I'm going to stay in your sights until Keith is found?"

"You got it."

She smiled. "It might not be a bad thing."

He laughed as he rested his arm around her shoulders. "Problem is, I need to keep an eye on the house too. I need to be outside."

"Well, that stinks," she pouted, folding her arms.

"Relax," he chuckled as he hugged her. "I will keep you updated as much as I can. I do appreciate you putting meals out for me though. This is probably the best I have eaten in years."

"I'll take that as a compliment."

"You know, Jack used to brag about your cooking. And now that I have tasted it, I can see why."

She smiled, pleased. "Thanks."

"On that note, I need to get outside. With Keith missing, and a possible Unnatural out there, I want to stay sharp. I need to keep a close eye on you and the house."

"I understand."

"It's not that I don't want to stay in here with you. Trust me. I would do it in a heartbeat if I could." He smiled, hoping to ease the disappointment he saw on her face. It gave him joy to know she wanted to spend time with him, but it also made him nervous knowing what was out there.

She walked him back to the sliding glass door and latched it behind him as he slid into the early morning shadows of the trees in the backyard. She took a few moments to dwell on him, before she headed into the bedroom to do her devotions for the day. She read about David and Jonathon. It was when Jonathon hid David from Saul. Their bond of friendship crossed bloodlines. Saul was Jonathon's father, but David was his best friend. God blessed their friendship and blessed David, himself, as well. Their loyalty in 'brotherhood' was huge and created an unbreakable bond that even a jealous father couldn't fracture.

As she dwelt on the passage, she thought about the guys her brother worked with over the years. The bond those men had, crossed bloodlines – same as Jonathon and David. It was a bond that left them loyal, honorable, and committed to each other. She was grateful to them, knowing the ones she did. She was also grateful to know Jack was well taken care of while in the field, and that he did the same in return for them. She got down on her knees and prayed for their safety. She prayed for protection, strength, and security for the men that now held a prominent spot in her heart and life.

*   *   *

The humidity was beyond hot and sticky. Keith had escaped the attack on the group and found his way to a cantina in the middle of nowhere. He needed to figure out where the Colonel and Derek were. When they separated, what he saw terrified him. He saw the figure of a man inside a man. The outer shell looked like that of Hunter Morgan, Casey's coworker. The inner spirit though, was an entirely other story. He saw the evil that was within the man.

A young lady came over to his table with a tray in her hand. "You American?" She asked. She stood to maybe five foot three in a flowing skirt with a cotton top. She couldn't have been more than fifteen, so by her age, he guessed that she must have been the owner's daughter. The cantina had six tables, with Keith at one of the three under the extending roof, giving him a slight relief from the sweltering sun. The older man, who must have been the owner, stood behind the bar in the hut. He was drying glasses, keeping an eye on the young lady to make sure she was doing her job.

"Yes," Keith said.

"Drink?"

"That would be wonderful." Keith smiled. "Do you have lemonade?"

"Of course. You want?"

He nodded. "Please?"

She disappeared into the tiny hut. He watched her for only a moment when he felt it. The hair on the back of his neck stood on end. He felt someone or something watching him.

He looked around but saw nothing. The air was eerily still, and the cantina was completely silent. He looked toward the hut and saw the pair talking to each other, but he felt as if he was operating in a dream. That's when he heard it in his head. A voice that said, "And be sure of this: I am with you always, even to the end of this age."

He looked up toward the Heavens, and felt a feeling of peace rush over his body as the knife sliced his neck from his left to his right. As his head slowly fell to the table, he felt the warmth of his own blood as it covered the tiny table underneath him.

While his life ebbed away, he couldn't figure out why he wasn't afraid. He heard the gurgling noise that he emitted, but no words came. He thanked God for not making him feel anything. He praised Him for the peace, comfort, and numbness He provided, as Keith moved from this life to the next. He prayed for his friends – the Colonel, Derek, Mark, and Casey. His last thought was that of God standing there with His arms wide-open.

*   *   *

As Casey prayed, she saw a vision of what occurred in the cantina. She gasped as she opened her eyes in wide-eyed horror. The black form that sliced Keith's neck had the stature of a man with no details. She saw a slight glimpse of its wings before the creature looked in her direction in the vision. She bolted for the sliding glass door to look for Mark. She had to tell him. He had to know.

She went out to the porch and moved one of the porch chairs next to the door before she went back in to wait for Mark. That was their signal over the last several days when she wanted to talk to him.

He was at the door within a few moments. As she let him in, he looked at her in her pajamas without a robe, and asked, "Why did you go outside dressed like that?"

"Keith's dead," she said, still in shock. Her body shaking.

He got a good look at her face. "Um, Casey, sit down. You're pale. Tell me what happened. You look scared to death."

"I was praying."

"Okay," he nodded, as he sat beside her on the couch, "And...?"

"And when I prayed specifically for you guys, I saw a flash of Keith. He had his head down on a table with blood coming out from under it." She looked up at him. "Mark, Keith's dead."

"They'll find him." He hugged her for comfort. "Calm down."

She backed away and looked into his eyes. "I'm telling you he's dead."

"We'll find out when they get there."

"You need to stop them though." She grabbed his arms in a panic. "They could be in danger too."

"Casey!" he said loudly in an attempt to snap her out of her panic, as he slightly shook her. "Look at me. Now, we've done this before. Relax."

"I'm telling you he's dead. His...." she suddenly saw the vision in her mind again. She closed her eyes for a moment. Taking a deep breath, she slowly reviewed the vision in her mind before she looked back up at him. "His throat was slashed. A creature went through the café and slashed his throat. It happened too fast for Keith to react. He never saw it coming. Mark, he's dead. Derek and the Colonel could be walking into a trap!"

He shook his head. "A creature?"

"I saw a black figure. It was in the shape of a man, but I saw wings. Its eyes glowed. Keith was killed by something not of this world."

"They have to find out either way."

"I don't want to lose them too."

"Do me a favor and take a long hot bath. We won't hear from them until tomorrow at the earliest. They have to get down there and then find the town. They are going to have to poke around for a bit too."

Casey nodded, taking several deep breaths to calm herself.

"It's okay. Just relax." He hugged her and kissed her head. He put his hands on either side of her face, resting his forehead on hers so her eyes would look directly into his. "You need to calm down and trust us. We have been doing this for years."

"But Keith didn't even know it was coming," she whispered. "That could happen to you too. If it does, I'm telling you I'll –"

"Don't finish that," he shook his head, "You are stronger than that."

"You don't understand what it will do to me."

"Yes, I do, because if something happens to you it will do the same thing to me." He pulled slightly back from her so he was still within three inches of her face. "Look, I know we have only been at this for a couple of days, but I have liked you for years."

"That is why this is so hard." She looked down, not wanting to look at him.

"Relax, Case." He lifted her chin so she could not help but look into his eyes. "Derek and the Colonel are good. Maybe Keith's just hurt."

"No." She adamantly shook her head. "I saw the creature go into the café. It walked behind Keith and slashed his throat before slipping out without anyone seeing it. Keith looked as if he dropped his head on the table. I'm telling you; I saw it. God showed it to me."

"Just relax. Please," Mark coaxed. After a couple moments of trying to figure out a way to relax her and take her mind off the vision, he said, "Look, before he left, the Colonel told me to ask you to run a couple errands for him."

"What?"

"He wants you to shut down two of the accounts and pull the money. He also wants you to go to the storage shed and pull out Jack's strongbox."

"Why would I shut down two accounts?"

"Because we may need the money, and we're not going to want a debit card trail. Don't worry. I am going to be with you the entire time so nothing will happen to you."

"All right," she agreed. "When are we leaving?"

"How long will it take you to get ready?"

"About an hour."

"You don't want a hot bath first?"

"No, I want to go and get this done."

"Okay. An hour will give me time to get into my disguise too. Hustle up." He stood and hugged and kissed her head again. Then he ducked out of the back door.

She locked the door and sighed, as she leaned against it for a moment deep in thought. Then she headed to the bedroom to jump into the shower, with the dream still weighing heavily on her heart and mind.

*　*　*

Mark knocked on the front door an hour later, dressed in a suit and tie. He carried a briefcase and wore sunglasses to help his disguise. Since it was sunny outside, nothing seemed abnormal. He looked as if he were a business executive or a lawyer.

Casey had on a pair of navy-blue dress pants, a white silk shirt, navy-blue flats, and had her hair up in a French twist. She used her white purse, and carried two small duffle bags with her for the money. She grabbed her sunglasses and keys before they went out the door.

Mark nodded in approval as they pulled out of the driveway. "You look nice," he remarked.

"Thanks. You don't look too bad yourself."

He reached over and grabbed her hand while she drove. "Banks first, and then the storage unit."

She nodded in response.

It took them a couple hours to shut down the two accounts, due to the amount of money in them. The banks, of course, did their best to discourage her from closing out the accounts, so it took quite a bit of time, but she held her ground.

Afterward, they headed to the storage unit. During the drive, Mark had her take several turns that sometimes even brought them about full-circle. He also had her stay on the inner lanes. When she asked him about it, he said it was easier to see if someone was following them by the driving moves they made. Thankfully, no one was.

When they got to the storage garage, Mark stayed outside to keep watch while Casey went inside. Jack's strongbox was in a box toward the back of the storage room, so it took her a few minutes to get to it. The room had a strong cardboard smell due to the boxes. As she pawed her way through the boxes to the back of the storage shed, memories of Jack flooded her mind. Knowing that this man of strength's life was dwindled down to a storage shed full of boxes and a gravestone in a military cemetary broke her heart. He had been a warrior for this country. He had laid his life on the line daily to protect the rights and freedoms people took for granted. She felt he deserved more than that, and she knew it would be up to her to make sure the world knew of his sacrifices.

The men and women of the military deserved honor and respect for voluntarily putting their lives on the line, and not to be discarded due to broken bodies, tortured minds, and hardened hearts. The Bible said in John 15:13 that "Greater love hath no man than this, that a man lay down his life for his friends." Casey was proud to be raised in this culture. It made her a stronger person, allowing her to face the daily struggles she did at work. However, working hand in hand with the A.N.G.E.L.s the way she was of late, gave her an even greater appreciation for their lives.

After about twenty minutes, Casey was finally able to locate the strongbox. She tugged and pulled it through the storage room to the front door, where Mark took it from her. She locked the door behind her, as Mark set the large, metal box in the back seat.

"We need to jet," he said as he climbed into the driver's seat.

Casey didn't argue. She silently climbed into the passenger's seat of the Jeep. To Casey's surprise, they didn't go home as she thought they would. Instead, they went to a hotel in downtown Denver, paying for the room in cash. Mark used a fake ID to get the room.

"And why are we here?" Casey asked, sitting on the bed.

"Colonel's instructions." He shrugged, closing the curtains. After carrying everything in, he locked and bolted the door.

The room had two queen beds, a forty-inch television, refrigerator, microwave, and a small table in between the beds, along with a bathroom that included a shower and tub. The room was by no means an extravagant one. In was a mid-priced, plainly decorated room. As she looked around, Casey noticed it had a strong scent of bleach mixed with a hint of vanilla. The room reminded her of some of the rooms she and Jack had stayed in when they traveled. They would stay on the base where the rooms were white-glove clean. While this room was by no means white-glove clean, it would do.

"Do you approve?" Mark asked, bringing Casey back to the reality of the situation.

"Um, what about my clothes? These are nice clothes. I didn't bring any extra with me. I didn't know we weren't going back home."

He peeked out the curtains for a few more minutes before he was satisfied there was no one watching them, "Trust me. This is safer than your own house – especially with the contents of the strongbox, and half a million dollars in our possession."

"Point well taken," she agreed.

They decided the best way to relax was to find a good movie on the TV. They ended up ordering pizza for lunch. For dinner, they got fast food from a restaurant next to the hotel.

"Now, I know you're used to your cooking, but desperate times call for desperate measures." He winked before biting into his cheeseburger.

"This is all right," she said, looking around the room. They had been there for several hours already. Not much was said between them, as they were both lost in their own thoughts.

"What's on your mind?" he asked.

"Keith."

"You're going to have to let that go."

"I can't. It was so real." She looked up at him and said, "I'm trying to remember the verse in the Bible about visions."

"Um, I think that's Acts 2:17. It says, "In the last days, God says, "'I will pour out my Spirit on all people. Your sons and daughters will prophesy, your young men will see visions, your old men will dream dreams.'""

Casey nodded, still deep in thought. After a couple of minutes, she looked up and asked, "Is that what you think it was? A vision?"

"We'll find out when we hear from the Colonel and Cruise. If what you saw actually happened, it could very well be a vision…especially since you said it came to you while you were in prayer."

"I need a distraction. Tell me some stories."

"I can do that." He nodded, welcoming the distraction from the thoughts that clouded his mind of the Colonel and Derek.

They talked long into the night. Mark shared stories of his growing up. He even shared some stories of Jack, so Casey could have a finite understanding of what he did on the field. They finally went to bed at about one o'clock in the morning in their separate beds. Mark took the bed closest to the window and door, leaving Casey the one closest to the wall.

In order to save her clothes, when she was under the covers, she slipped off her shirt and pants. Silk was a mess when it wrinkled and she knew if she slept in them, it would be horribly wrinkled by morning.

*   *   *

At about two o'clock in the morning, Mark's cell phone went off. He leaned over and turned on the light between the beds to see in the pitch-dark room. It was a text message that read "A1/A4-A5MIA."

"Does that mean what I think it means?" Casey raised an eyebrow at him when he showed it to her.

"It means Keith is not where he's supposed to be, but that the Colonel and Derek are together."

He texted back "A3/A7-SWD."

"What does that mean?"

"That we're together and swimming with the dolphins," he translated, referring to the code. "Swimming with the dolphins" meant they were safe.

A few minutes later, he got another text that simply said, "A1."

"He's going to call in a minute," he said, as he rested back on his pillow.

During the night, Mark had taken off his suit and was lying under the covers in his underwear. Casey had to remind herself to breathe. She reprimanded herself at thinking he looked so good…the temptation was huge. She forced herself to remember that they were on a mission of their own, and that they had to stay on their toes.

Mark's cell phone rang less than five minutes later. "Yeah," he answered. "Yes, we are under. Mission accomplished…Really?" He sat up, stunned. He looked over at Casey in wide-eyed surprise, before he hung his head in his hand

and listened. "Yes, I understand…No, we'll stay here. She's off for two more days…Yes…Okay, we will be here. Call when you get in, and I will give you the location," he said and hung up.

"What's up?"

"Keith's dead."

"I told you." She sat up, holding the blanket on her chest.

"You were right how he died too. How did you know?"

"I told you. God showed me while I was praying."

He shook his head.

"What?"

"I'm wondering if God has given you an ability of visions in the form of dreams."

"Is that possible?"

"We all have gifts."

"What do you mean?"

"Gifts given to us by the Holy Spirit. In First Corinthians 12:7-10, it says, "'The Holy Spirit is given to each of us in a special way. That is for the good of all. To some people the Spirit gives the message of wisdom. To others the same Spirit gives the message of knowledge. To others the same Spirit gives faith. To others that one Spirit gives gifts of healing. To others He gives the power to do miracles. To others He gives the ability to prophesy. To others He gives the ability to tell the spirits apart. To others He gives the ability to speak in different kinds of languages they had not known before. And to still others He gives the ability to explain what was said in those languages.'" You see, there are various gifts given to each of us. I think yours may be the gift of prophesy that shows itself in visions."

"Interesting. Now what do I do with it?"

"Tell me if you get anymore."

"What if it was a one-time thing?"

"Then it was a one-time thing." He shrugged. "Case, there is no recipe for any of this. You cannot limit God. You cannot put Him in a box or lay boundaries, because He will blast through them every time."

"Do you think we're in the last days?"

"It's possible. No one knows the day or the hour, except God, Himself."

"While I have been a Christian for a little over a year, a lot of this is still new to me. Mac and I did devotions, and he told me a lot of different ways to share God's truth, but we didn't walk through this part."

"Really? So, you can share His message?"

She smiled, feeling he was about to test her. "I am pretty confident."

"Okay. Pretend you met me on the street, and somehow we struck up a conversation."

"Okay," Casey agreed.

"So, you are saying this Jesus guy is the only way to Heaven?" Mark asked.

"Yes."

"And all I have to do is believe in His sacrifice, and I can get into Heaven?"

"There's more to it, but that is where it starts."

He shook his head as he crossed his arms. "Too simple."

"Look at it this way," Casey said, thinking of a good example. "If I were to write you a check for a million dollars and told you to go to the bank across the street and cash it – would you?"

He shrugged. "Yeah. Sure, why not?"

"It's the same thing. Only what I'm offering you is worth a lot more than a million dollars. I'm offering you a shot at eternal life in Heaven with God, a Father who loves you and wants the best for you."

"It's the only way, huh?"

"Imagine you were sick and went to the doctor's office, and he told you that you would die if you didn't take a specific medication. Would you do it, or would you ask him if there was another way?"

"I would probably do it. He more than likely knows what he's doing."

"Then why would you not trust the One who created the entire world any less? You don't think He knows what He's doing?"

"Yes."

"Then?"

"Good job!"

Afterward, to calm Casey's nerves, they took some time to pray for Colonel and Derek for protection, strength, guidance, discernment, wisdom, and power. They prayed for the Holy Spirit to surround them, and to put His most powerful angels around them. They also prayed for safety for their safe travels, and for Mark and Casey's safety as well. Knowing what they had was extremely valuable, and that there were already a couple men killed because of it made both of them nervous.

They talked for another hour before Mark off turned the light and they went to sleep in their beds. Casey was grateful to God for placing these men in her life when she needed them the most. While the vision was disturbing, God granted her a sense of peace about it.

She was also grateful God gave the A.N.G.E.L.s the instincts and training to know what to look for and when to take action. She looked forward to seeing what He had in store for them in the future. She said another prayer for safety for this tiny band of brothers before drifting off to sleep again.

Chapter 6

Undercover

The next morning, Casey woke up to Mark running his fingers through her hair as he sat on her bed with his legs stretched out in front of him, watching her sleep. "Good morning." He smiled.

She smiled back at him. "Morning."

"Your hair is so soft."

"Thanks." She reached over, grabbed the pack of gum off the table between the beds, and popped a piece into her mouth before she gave him a piece as well.

"Thanks."

"Did you sleep well?" she asked.

"Yep," he said. Then his face shifted to concern.

"What's wrong?" She sat up nervously.

"I'm worried about the Colonel and Derek. I had the same vision you had – only mine was in the form of a dream last night."

"They are on their way back, though, right?"

"Right." He nodded. "They should be back sometime today."

"So, we will sit tight until then."

"But, I can't guarantee it will be good news when they get back. When he called last night, he wanted to make sure we were not at your house. He is afraid they're watching it."

"Who?"

"They." He looked over at her. "The bad guys so to speak."

"What happens if they are?"

"We may have to pull you. The rest of us are considered dead. It's you they're going to be after next."

"Is it because of what is in that box?" She nodded toward Jack's strongbox, which sat on the floor next to the table.

"Yes. They're looking for it."

"What is it?" she asked.

He gave her a look she had seen more than enough times on Jack's face to understand.

"I get it," she said, putting her hands up in surrender. "I have seen that look enough to know not to question anymore."

"Thanks. You know I love and trust you, right?"

"Right. That's why you are not telling me." She winked at him.

"I'm so grateful Jack taught you so well," he chuckled. "Come here." He hugged her and kissed her head. "Now, go take a shower. We probably have a long day ahead of us, and we're not guaranteed a shower tomorrow."

"Good point."

He got off her bed, and pulled the sheet out from under the comforter of his bed. He held it up for her to stand and wrapped her in it before he hugged her. Then he smiled down at her, tucking her hair behind her ear. "I know how you are about modesty."

"Thank you for your consideration." She lightly kissed his lips. "You are so sweet."

"You know we are going to have to share the toothbrush and toothpaste."

"Is there a hair brush or comb?"

"Nope." He shook his head. "Sorry, you're going to have to run your fingers through that beautiful hair of yours to get it under control," he said, running his fingers through it, watching it fall back down to her shoulders. "Sometimes I have a hard time believing this is real."

"Why?"

"Because I've wanted it for so long. Not to mention that, in what we do, romantic relationships are rare or non-existent. If they existed, they were short-lived. Well, true ones anyway."

"What does that mean?" she looked at him, not sure if she wanted to know the answer.

"Well, let's just say there are many ways to get information from a woman."

She took a step back, stunned.

"Not with you, though. Trust me. With you, it's real."

She narrowed her eyes. "Are you sure?"

"Derek and the Colonel would literally kill me if I hurt you. I would probably kill myself while I was at it. I care about you that much. I can honestly say that I am truly in love with you."

Casey looked at him in shock for a minute, before she saw the tenderness in his chocolate brown eyes. That was something she knew he couldn't fake. She quickly kissed his lips. "All right, I believe you."

He wrapped his arms around her. "Thank you."

She gazed up at him for a long moment, before she reached up and rested her hands on the sides of his face. He dropped his arms down to her waist, as she asked, "What's going through that mind of yours?"

"I don't know." He shook his head. "Are you sure you want to pursue us? You don't think it's too early?"

"It's something I can't ignore," she admitted. "I have had feelings for you since day one. I have never had that before. I didn't think love at first sight was real, but it's standing right in front of me."

"What about Mac?"

"He's probably happy I have found another love."

"You think so?"

"He only wanted me to be happy."

"And…?"

"And, you make me happy."

"For now. What happens when you wake up angry with me? What happens if you wake up and hate me just as quickly as you liked me?"

"I don't think that will happen," she said.

"Why not?"

"Because God would not put you so strongly on my heart if it wasn't something He intended."

"How do you know it isn't lust instead of like?"

"Ask me what I love the most about you."

"Okay," he said with a smile. "What do you love the most about me?"

She took one of his hands and held it in hers as she said, "I love that as strong as you are, you are gentle with me. I love that despite the evil you have seen, your heart is as tender as a child's.

I love the way your mind works. I love to see what it's going to come up with next."

"But you don't know what I do," he said. "I have done bad things. I've killed."

"You killed in defense of another, or of your life."

"I've deceived."

"To get information in order to help someone, I assume."

He nodded in understanding. Then he admitted, "I've used women."

"But you're not using me."

He shook his head as he looked into her eyes. "No. I'm not."

"I can see it in your eyes. I can read your eyes. They tell the true story."

"They've always been my weakness," he admitted.

"Doesn't sound weak to me."

"Well, it's how the unit knows what I'm really thinking."

"Sounds as if they know you well."

"They do," he admitted.

"Doesn't it sound as if I know you well?"

"Yes."

"Does the description sound like someone who just wants your body?"

"No."

She looked at him for only a moment, before gently pulling his face to hers. When their lips connected, the kiss was electric. Their minds were consumed with each other. There was no room for anything else on their mind as they embraced in a tender, gentle, yet passionate kiss.

It only took a moment for the kiss to build. Everything Mark had been holding back suddenly exploded in his body. He leaned down and hungrily kissed her neck.

"Oh, um…." She took a deep breath, putting her hands on his arms. The muscles in his body were tense as he kissed her neck harder.

"I love you," he said. "Sleeping in the bed, knowing you were in the bed next to mine in only your underclothes, made me…." He backed them up against the wall, kissing her lips as he cupped her face in his hands.

"Mark…." She took a deep breath, struggling to keep herself under control as she felt tingles throughout her body.

"What?" He tightly lowered his hands down her sides to her waist.

"We can't."

"I know, but…." He kissed her neck again.

"Need to…slow down."

He buried his face into her neck, breathing heavily. "I can. I am."

"Thank you. It's not that I don't want to. It's just that I want to wait until –"

"I know. I understand."

"Thank you."

He looked up at her with a passionate intensity in his eyes, and said, "We will, when we're married. Until then…." He strongly kissed her for another minute, before bracing his hands on the wall behind her, breathing heavily, and with his voice barely a whisper, he said, "Shower."

"Yes, sir." She nodded, slipping out from under him. She grabbed her clothes on the way to the bathroom. When she got there, she turned to see him pacing between the beds. He looked up at her and winked with a smile. She blushed with a smile on her face, while she headed into the bathroom.

*   *   *

It was a long, nerve-wracking day for them. In order to distract themselves from worrying about Derek and the Colonel, and from temptation of each other, they talked. The more they talked, the more Casey found out how sensitive and kind-hearted Mark was. It made her fall more in love with him with each story he shared. In his job, he couldn't relax. He couldn't be himself. He seemed to relax around her though. Casey decided she liked the 'real Mark' better than the 'military Mark' – but trusted both with her life.

At about six o'clock that night, Mark got a text "A1." He kept his phone in his hand as he said, "The Colonel is going to call in a minute. They probably just landed."

It only took about fifteen minutes for him to call. "Yes," Mark answered. He told the Colonel where they were, and that they were safe. The Colonel said he and Derek would be there in about an hour, and to keep watch for them.

"Um, hate to bring this up, but you do remember I have to work the day after tomorrow, right?" Casey asked, as she sat on her bed with her legs stretched out in front of her, eating microwave popcorn.

Mark picked up a piece of the popcorn and popped it into his mouth, as he sat cross-legged on the bed with her. "Yes, but that might have to change."

"Chief won't like that. He doesn't like call-offs anyway, but to do it two shifts in a row?" She shook her head. "I'll need a doctor's excuse – and it had better be because I was in the hospital close to death."

"That serious, huh?"

"When I do, one person has to stay over from the shift getting off, therefore working thirty-six hours. Then, someone from the upcoming next day shift has to do the same, working thirty-six hours as well. It puts a strain on the guys, and on the over-time pay."

"I see." He nodded, rubbing his chin in thought. "Then we're going to have to let you go to work. You can't lose your job until we're ready to pull you. That will bring up too many unanswered questions."

"What do you mean?"

"If we pull you too soon, they will get suspicious. They're watching you, and know we are watching you as well."

"But you guys are supposed to be dead, right?"

"Yes…and no."

"What do you mean?" She looked at him in irritation. Just when she thought she had the scenario figured out, they threw another curve at her.

"Well, to the real world we're dead, but if you remember, the Colonel asked if you showed his jacket to the MP, right?"

"Right."

"And he said it was to let him know we were watching you, right?"

"Right."

"Well, that lets the military know we are still alive, except for Jack, Marcos, and now Keith, along with the other A.N.G.E.L.s of the past, because they have the bodies to prove otherwise. They will have their suspicions that the Colonel, Derek, and I are still alive, but there will be no proof. However, if you disappear within a couple days of Keith's death, they will know we are alive, and so will the bad guys. Then both sides will be looking for us. If we do it quietly, then neither side will know for sure. They'll question it, but there will be no proof. Without the proof, there will always be doubt as to whether we are alive or not. That's the reason we didn't want you to go to Angelina."

"What do you mean?"

"They could use her as bait to pull us all out. They know deep down that you love that little girl and would do anything for her. If they take her, they have you. If they have you, then they have us. Understand?"

"Actually, I do. It's twisted, but I get it."

"That's how they work." He sighed, shaking his head. "Welcome to our world. Trust is hard in your world…imagine what it is like in ours. Nothing is what it seems. And, just when you think you have it figured out, it takes another turn you weren't expecting."

She shook her head in amazement.

"Now you understand why Jack trained you the way he did."

She nodded. "Yeah."

Jack had Casey in shooting ranges since she was thirteen. Then when they went camping, he would teach her survival techniques. They would also play special memory games during the course of regular everyday occurrences to keep her on her toes. For example, when they were in the grocery store, he would ask her what a woman or man who just passed them looked like. She, of course, wasn't allowed to look at them again. If she was correct three times in a row, they went out for ice cream. If she wasn't, then they finished their shopping, went home, and tried it again next time. One of their traveling games was where he would describe one of the last five cars they passed and she was to tell him not only the state the car was from, but also the license plate number. If she was right three times in a row, she would get a small candy bar. If she missed, they would start over again. Some of the games were frustrating, but the more her eyes were opened to what was going on around her by the A.N.G.E.L.s, the more she understood why. Trusting people was hard for her before all this happened, but it had become increasingly harder over the last several weeks.

"They're here." Mark suddenly sat up as they were in the middle of a conversation.

"How do you know?"

"Shhhh," he hissed. He slowly pulled his gun out of the holster, as he went to the window with one of his eyes closed so his eyes would adapt to the darkness quicker. "Turn off the light," he whispered.

As soon as she shut it off, he pulled the curtain back slightly, searching the shadows as his other eye adjusted to the darkness. He knew he heard something, but he could not see them. A few moments later, he saw two shadowy figures run across the parking lot and up the stairs toward the room. He heard two short knocks and a single one.

"Go to the bathroom and hide in the shower. Do not come out unless I tell you," Mark whispered.

Casey immediately went into the bathroom. She didn't close the door, though, so she could hear.

"Yeah," Mark said next to the door.

The person knocked again, this time two short, followed by four short. Mark opened the door, standing behind it with his gun ready.

The two men came in and sat on the bed. One of them reached over and turned on the light. Much to Mark's relief, it was the Colonel and Derek.

It wasn't until he closed and bolted the door that he called Casey out of the bathroom. "Good," the Colonel said, relieved. "I was hoping you were here too."

They sat down and talked into the morning on what happened to them – in general terms of course. They also discussed work for her, along with a plan if something came up unexpectedly. In the middle of that, they ordered a pizza around ten that night. It was mainly for the Colonel and Derek, who hadn't eaten much on their trip.

The plan was for the guys to split the remaining cash on hand so each had a third. That way if something came up, there was emergency money to get them out of trouble, and if they were the one watching her at the time, to get Casey out of trouble with them.

As far as work, Casey was going to go in on her next shift. She was given strict instructions to stay on her toes more than normal – especially around Hunter. At this point, she was the only one left exposed, and that did not make the Colonel comfortable at all. And with what happened in Nicaragua, they weren't taking chances.

As for the strongbox, the Colonel and Derek were going to hide it the next day in a safe place that everyone would know. That way, if something happened to one, the others could run and take it with them. Casey was the only one with the combination, which not only made her more valuable, but also put her in a higher level of danger than she was already in. The Colonel ordered her not to tell the A.N.G.E.L.s the combination. He said he trusted her to keep it safe.

As a group, they decided not go home that night. Instead, they spent the night as well as the next day and night in the hotel room, mainly to give the Colonel and Derek some rest. Mark stayed up all night while Casey slept in one bed, and Derek and the Colonel slept in the other.

The next morning, the Colonel passed out new pre-paid cell phones to everyone. He had everyone but Casey pull the batteries, and throw out their old cell phones. He made sure Casey had a new cell phone that she was to use only for the A.N.G.E.L.s, while she kept her other one for everything else.

After the cell phones were dispersed, Derek and the Colonel left to hide the box, while Mark stayed with Casey in the room and slept. When they got back, they gave Mark and Casey detailed instructions as to where the strong box was located in the event of an emergency.

They stayed in the hotel room for the rest of the day, talking about what happened in Nicaragua in more detail. Casey was amazed at how accurate her vision had been – it was almost scary.

Throughout the day, Casey also got to know the Colonel and Derek better as they opened up, sharing a bit of their life with her. By them sharing their personal life, it created a deeper bond and trust within the group on all sides. Casey felt honored knowing the group trusted her more. She knew the A.N.G.E.L.s needed each other now that they were only down to her and three of them. The Colonel told her that for better or worse, she was now an official A.N.G.E.L., and she would be treated as such.

She agreed, knowing it could mean even more danger in her life. She prayed God would keep them all safe in the upcoming days so that didn't come to fruition.

Chapter 7

Spirit of Anger

With the occurrence in Nicaragua weighing heavily on her mind, Casey kept an extremely close eye on Hunter throughout her returning shift. He finally asked her about it in the afternoon while she cooked and everyone else took a break doing various things throughout the firehouse. Three firemen watched television less than twenty feet from her, so Casey felt safe cooking with Hunter in there with her. She knew he wouldn't do anything in front of them.

The hair stood on the back of her neck as Hunter leaned on the counter next to her with his arms crossed. "So, what gives?"

"What do you mean?" Casey asked, cutting the vegetables for a vegetable tray. The dip for both of the trays was already in the refrigerator. She already made the meatballs and sauce, which sat in a crockpot on the counter. The meal was meatball subs, along with a vegetable and fruit tray.

"You've been on edge all day today," Hunter pointed out. "It's like every time I turn around, you're looking at me like I've got the plague or something."

Casey laughed out of nervousness. In a manner of speaking, he did.

"What's going on?" he asked.

"Hunter, you're losing it." She shook her head. "I haven't changed anything that I don't normally do." She lied. Hunter terrified her. Knowing what the Colonel and Derek told her about him frightened her beyond words, but she didn't want him to know what she knew.

He studied her for a moment before he asked, "What happened to you?"

"With what?"

"Why didn't you come in last shift?"

"I was sick." She shrugged. "Kind of interesting to find out that you were sick too." She looked up at him. Earlier Jesse told her they had an odd shift with both Casey and Hunter gone.

"Who told you I wasn't here?" he asked.

"Jesse."

"Why would he care?"

She shrugged. "He only mentioned it was different having two people off. Why do you care?"

"Because despite the fact that you seem to hate me, I do care what happens to you. You don't have too many people in your life. Actually, let me rephrase that. You don't let too many people into your life."

Rob, Will, and Tommy looked up from the movie they were watching when they felt the atmospheric temperature in the kitchen shift to an ice-cold.

Casey glared at Hunter as she asked, "What do you mean by that?"

"You keep to yourself. You don't go out much when you are off shift. You don't —"

"How would you know if I go out or not when I'm off shift?"

"You don't mention it," he pointed out.

"Have you not figured out by now that I keep my private life private?"

"You mean to tell me that with as strong as the bonds are here at the station, you don't share what you do on your time off?"

"She doesn't," Tommy spoke up from the recreation area. "That's also her prerogative."

"Why are the rules different when it comes to Carter?" Hunter challenged.

"They aren't." Will shook his head. "We respect her privacy. We don't know what every single guy here does when they are off shift. Why should we hold her to a higher standard than everyone else? Richter doesn't share everything either. It's no big deal."

"It does when we are her only family," Hunter argued.

"But you're not my keeper," Casey snapped.

She looked up to see his eyes turn completely black, and momentarily saw the black shadow of what looked like a demon from her dream standing before her, before Hunter returned to normal. She gulped. Did she push too hard? She knew she would have to tell the A.N.G.E.L.s their instincts were correct. Something about Hunter was definitely unnatural.

"Fine. Suit yourself," he said, and left for the weight room as if nothing happened.

Casey's heart skipped a beat when she saw his eyes and the form. She clumsily cut the vegetables until she calmed herself. She prayed in her head for strength and courage to struggle along the path that God directed her. She had a feeling of foreboding churn through her body. She knew things were coming on the horizon…bad things. She prayed she would survive them.

*   *   *

An eight-hour rotating shift schedule of the A.N.G.E.L.s watching Casey went on for about a year. While Casey was relieved nothing else happened, she felt bad for the schedule the guys had to keep. When they were not on duty, they would rest in her living room, so they always had somewhere to call a home base. She didn't mind though. It made her feel better to have them in the house, than to have her mind preoccupied because she didn't know where they were. It did make things tense, since the guys were continually on edge and pulling consecutive eight-hour shifts for over a year without a day off. Through the course of the year the tense atmosphere of the apartment began to weigh on her.

Regardless of whether or not the A.N.G.E.L.s were watching her, while she was at the station, she had a job to do. A job she looked at with conviction and fortitude. She was on her own as a photographer, but now she was in a position where she prayed for, and took care of, the other firefighters who had her back.

One of her biggest challenges that year was what happened on a scene about three months after they lost Keith. If that wasn't bad enough, she suffered something that jaded her heart and made her angry with God again.

*   *   *

Casey, Pete, Tommy, and Marty were about twenty feet from each other and in teams of two, with three other teams from another department scattered, throughout a one-hundred-yard-long warehouse structure fire. Engine Company Fifteen's crewmembers were closer to the front of the building, when two storage tanks suddenly blew. Casey and Pete dove for the ground and covered their heads. Tommy and Marty were about twenty yards behind, and both flew through the air in opposite directions.

"You go for McCormick, and I'll go for Nelson," Pete said, as he shoved Casey in the direction Tommy flew. On his way over to Marty, Pete called to LT to tell him what happened within the warehouse. LT said to stay with the two injured firefighters and he would send in back-up.

It took Casey a few minutes to find Tommy. She heard him before she saw him. The moans and groans of pain he emitted made Casey cringe. She knew that whatever she walked up to, she would have to be strong for Tommy.

She pushed and shoved her way through the debris to get to him. When she reached where he landed, she was horrified to see him lying with blood covering the ground under him. The railing of the catwalk impaled his abdomen. She ran over to him and quickly opened his jacket.

"Get it out!" Tommy's face was contorted in agonizing pain.

"No," she said, lifting his shirt to see the railing punctured approximately where his liver would be, in the upper right of his abdomen. She knew he wouldn't have much time. "You need to relax and breathe. You are going to be okay. Do you hear me?"

"It hurts, Case," he groaned.

"I need to see if it's through and through."

He nodded, so she carefully slid his arm out of his turnout gear. When his jacket slipped down, she could see a portion of the rail sticking out of his back. "Tommy, I know you are in a lot of pain, but you need to fight for Sally." Casey got on the radio to LT. "LT, this is Carter."

"Go ahead, Carter."

"Sir, McCormick has massive thoracoabdominal penetration."

"Copy. Leave it. Medics are on the way in, and I will set up for life flight."

"Copy." She tuned the radio out, only listening for what she needed to, but otherwise she wanted to focus on Tommy. She turned her P.A.S.S. alarm on manually before she turned Tommy's on as well. She knew this would assist the incoming help to find them easier. "I need you to fight."

"It hurts."

"If you're still feeling it, that's a good thing, but try not to move as much as possible."

"This is not how I wanted to go!"

"You are not going anywhere. Do you hear me?"

He had both of his hands on the railing. He went to adjust, which caused him immense pain, and he let out an excruciating shout of agony.

Casey cringed. "Tommy, you can't move. You're going to make it worse."

"It can't get any worse! I've seen too much to know that….ahhhhheeee!" he yelled through a clenched jaw. "OW! Make it stop!"

"Tommy," Casey pleaded, "stop moving. You have to fight for Sally. She needs you."

He grabbed her arm. "You have to look after Sally for me."

"No, that's your job."

"She's pregnant, Casey. We were going to wait until she was three months along to tell anyone. You have to take care of her for me."

"No." Casey shook her head. She was grateful that the sweat poured down her face, so he would see the few tears that escaped her eyes. "You have to hang on for both of them."

His body relaxed, and his arm fell to the ground, leaving a bloody handprint on her jacket.

"Tommy?"

"It's okay, Casey. It doesn't hurt anymore."

She pulled her glove off and felt for his pulse. It was slow. Casey knew the signs. She knew he wouldn't have much time left. "Fight this, Tommy!"

"I've lost too much blood," he said knowingly.

"You have to hold on. Do you hear me?" she shouted. "You have to hold on!"

"Have you two been fighting again?" Jesse crouched down next to Tommy to look at the wound from the front, while Kim looked at it from behind. Kim looked up at Jesse and shook her head. The amount of blood loss was vast, as it spread on the floor all around them.

"Can't blame her for this one." Tommy chuckled, and then cringed as one last jolt of pain shot through him. With that, his entire body went completely numb.

"Wet these down with this saline while I take his vitals." Jesse handed Casey and Kim each two rolls of gauze and a saline bottle.

Casey wet the gauze, and carefully packed it around the wound. Kim followed suit on Tommy's back.

"Ready?" Jesse asked, with the saw in his hand.

Casey covered Tommy's head with his helmet while she kept a hand on his pulse. It was even slower than before. Kim assisted Jesse in cutting the railing down from the front and back, low enough to be able to move him.

When they finished, they cautiously slid him over to the board, doing their best not to adjust his position. "Stay with us," Jesse said, as he picked up one side of the rescue basket at around the middle. Kim and Casey were on the other side, with Casey near his head, and Kim near his feet. "Careful now," Jesse said, and they maneuvered through the maze of debris from the fire.

"I'm tired," Tommy moaned.

Casey heard the helicopter and knew it was life flight for Tommy. "Hold on a little longer," she encouraged. She looked down at him and saw that his face was gray, and his body was motionless. "Tommy?"

They walked out of the building, making a beeline for the helicopter about fifty feet away.

"Tommy?" Casey gulped. When he didn't answer, she took a deep breath, focusing on securing him within the helicopter.

After they loaded him, Casey slowly took several steps back. In a silent prayer in her head, she begged for God to spare his life. She thought she heard Tommy's voice, but the noise of the helicopter's engine did its best to drown out any distinguishable noise.

"Nelson's on his way to the hospital in the ambulance," Pete said, as he walked up to Casey while the helicopter took off. "He has a broken leg."

Casey nodded, nervously biting her nails.

"He's going to be okay," Pete encouraged.

Casey shook her head, watching the helicopter turn toward the level-four hospital. "I don't know about that."

"Carter, Van den Bergh! Get back in there!" LT shouted at them.

"Yes, sir," Pete acknowledged, before both of them took off back into the building.

*   *   *

After they returned to the station around eight o'clock that night, Casey cleaned up, and then went out the back of the station into the park.

"What are you doing out here?" the Colonel asked, coming out from behind a tree.

"I came to talk to you."

"Why?"

"Because I need you to do me a favor."

He crossed his arms. "What would that be?"

"I need to know Tommy's status. He had a horrible accident at the fire, and I need to know how he's doing."

The Colonel sighed, shaking his head. "Are you sure you want to know?"

"Yes, please?" she asked.

"I'm sorry, Casey. He didn't make it. He was DOA at the hospital."

The words hung in the air for several moments. Casey felt as if she were punched in the stomach. She looked up at him as she felt her heart harden. She had more than enough loss to last a lifetime.

"Nelson is fine," the Colonel continued. "He has a broken leg, but he is otherwise okay."

"Chief is going to have to tell Sally," she said, mentally thinking through the list of what all would need to be done.

"Casey, are you okay?"

"No," she admitted.

He rested his hands on her shoulders as he looked into her eyes. No tears even piqued her eyes. That concerned him more than if she had a meltdown. He looked up to see the back door open, as Chief walked out of the station on his cell phone.

The Colonel didn't take his eyes off the Chief. "You need to get back there. If your Chief is here, then the word is out."

She nodded, before slowly walking toward the station.

"Carter, what are you doing out here?" Chief looked up in surprise when she walked out of the shadows of the park into the lights of the basketball court.

"I didn't mean to scare you." She rubbed her arms due to the chill of the night. "I needed some time alone."

"We need to go back in. I have to call all-hands into the station for a meeting."

"I already know." She looked at him in time to see the shock go across his face.

"How do you know?"

"I was the first one to him. When he went numb and his pulse slowed down, I knew he was going. He was also non-responsive when we loaded him into the chopper."

"I'm sorry, Carter. I know you two were close."

"May I go with you when you go talk to Sally?"

"I'm on my way there now. I had to call her mom to meet us at her house. Are you sure you want to go?"

She nodded. "Please."

"Come on."

They drove silently to Tommy and Sally's house in his Fire Chief vehicle. As soon as she opened the door, Casey knew by the look on her face that Sally understood without them saying a word. Chief sat her down and explained what happened, while Casey held her hand.

Sally's face was stone as she listened to Chief. She knew as soon as she saw the vehicle that her husband would never be coming home again. She and Tommy talked about what to do in case this scenario occurred, so she knew what she had to do. She rested her hand on her stomach, knowing his seed would carry on in their unborn child.

Sally stood up when Chief finished, resigned to fulfilling her new responsibilities by herself from that point forward. "Thank you," she said.

Sally's mom arrived about ten minutes into the conversation. So, when Chief finished, Sally hugged both Chief and Casey before they left. Casey looked up one more time toward Sally before she got into the vehicle. Sally stood there, holding herself, periodically wiping her tears, with her mom standing beside her, resting her arm around Sally's waist.

Chief didn't say a word the entire ride back to the station, while Casey blankly stared out the window. She was done with the feeling of loss. She was angry. God did it again! He took another anchor of hers. She and God were going to have a strong discussion when the dust of this situation cleared. In the meantime, she knew she would have to be strong. She knew she would have to harden herself to her thoughts and feelings and push forward. She would once again bury a great friend and brother. She wasn't sure how many more funerals she would be able to face. When she thought about what she was working within Hunter, she half-wondered if she would be next.

*   *   *

Over the next week, she did her duty. She went to Tommy's funeral, and stood by Sally the entire time, not shedding a tear. She was done with losing people. She was angry with God for taking him. Knowing Tommy would live on in the baby Sally carried was little consolation, since his baby wouldn't have the benefit of having its father around. Casey was confident that

Tommy would have made a great father. It broke her heart that he died so young.

Throughout the several months following the funeral, Mark, Derek, and the Colonel tried to break through Casey's shell. She had a wall around her heart so thick that they couldn't break through no matter how hard they tried. Mark's heart broke for her, but he knew time and God would have to work on her heart together. He knew God could penetrate the hardest of hearts. He held onto the confidence that she was one of His, and he knew God didn't leave His people behind.

*   *   *

Casey and Pete pulled up to the townhouse they were sent to for an ambulance call regarding a domestic dispute. He called dispatch to let them know they were on scene while Casey parked the ambulance along the side of the road. "Casey, I know you can handle yourself, but please let me go in first," Pete asked, as they got out the paramedic bag from the back of the ambulance.

"You are both clear to go in," a police officer said, walking up to them. "Not a pretty scene though." His name was Officer O'Malley. "My partner, Frantz, is inside."

"What happened?" Casey asked. The call came across as a female victim in a domestic dispute.

"Um," Officer O'Malley hesitated. "Well, it was a domestic dispute."

"We got that much. What is the situation?" Pete pressed, a little agitated.

"The boyfriend is in handcuffs, and is pretty bloody himself, but the girlfriend is in rough shape."

"Can you clarify your definition of rough shape?" Casey raised an eyebrow at him, getting impatient with his vague answers.

"She still has the knife in her abdomen."

"She…what?" She looked at him, then at Pete with a look of panic on her face.

Pete grabbed the bag, throwing it over his shoulder, as both of them ran toward the house. They knew the situation went from potentially bad to deadly. The scene they walked into was something she would never forget. Broken dishes and glass covered the kitchen floor. There had been food cooking on the stove, which was now splattered down the wall with the pan resting upside down on the floor.

The house had a strange scent mix of jambalaya, blood, and apple cinnamon from the candle still burning on the kitchen table. There was a tense cloud of anger and hate in the room, as the boyfriend sat on the floor on his knees, wrists in handcuffs behind his back. He had cuts on his face, along with a mark on his cheek that could have been a remnant of the pan from dinner. His white t-shirt was heavily stained with a mixture of blood and food.

His girlfriend lay motionless on the ground. Her breathing was shallow and labored at best. The knife rested about three inches below her navel, slowly rising and falling with her labored breathing.

"What's her name?" Casey asked, looking from her, to her boyfriend, to someone who looked to be a neighbor or a friend.

"Her name is Alejandra," the friend offered.

"Alejandra Montoya," Officer Frantz clarified, glancing at his notes. "She is twenty-five-years-old."

Casey sighed, shaking her head. By the looks of her, she would be surprised if she made it through the night. It was such a shame. She could never understand why someone would hurt the person they supposedly loved that way.

"What happened?" Pete asked.

The officer shook his head, glancing down at the boyfriend.

"We need to know what other types of injuries she may have besides the obvious," Pete snapped. The situation irritated him. In reality, it disgusted him. He would never lay a hand on a woman, and could not fathom what would possess a man to do this to his lover.

"What about me?" the boyfriend asked. "I have injuries too. She hit me with a pan."

"After you went after with a knife!" the friend defended Alejandra.

He shook his head in disgust. "I wouldn't have, if she had dinner done on time."

Casey looked up at him, stunned. "This is because she was late with dinner?" she asked in shock. Her blood began to boil almost beyond her control.

"She knows she has to have it done as soon as I get home, or –"

"Shut up," the officer snapped. "As I have already advised you, you have the right to remain silent, and I suggest you use it."

He sighed, shaking his head again.

Casey wet the gauze down, before she gently packed it around the knife and the wound to stop it from moving. She couldn't take the knife out, or it could cause more damage. The young woman was going to be tricky to move. Casey was not comfortable with moving her at all, but in order for her to have a remote chance, they would have to get her to the hospital as soon as possible.

"What about life flight?" Pete asked.

Casey shook her head. "We can get her loaded and to the hospital before life flight even takes off."

While Casey got the young woman's vitals, Pete patched the boyfriend. The police officer was going to take the boyfriend to the jail since his wounds were superficial. Casey did not want to touch the boyfriend, and Pete could tell by the look on her face that she might cause him more damage than he already had, so he left her to care for Alejandra.

"Ready," Casey said to Pete. She had the board set in place and had immobilized Alejandra's head. Casey had already gathered Alejandra's information from her friend, Daniela Alverez, and she was doing her best to ignore the boyfriend, Lorenzo Jimenez.

"On the count of three?" Pete asked.

Casey nodded, and they gently moved her to the backboard, before then lifting her onto the gurney to move her to the ambulance. She moaned, trying to move her head.

Casey leaned down next to her head, brushing her hair out of her eyes. Alejandra had her eyes partially open. "Please don't move. Just relax. We're going to get you to the hospital for help."

"I'm….cold," she whispered.

"I know," she said, feeling a knot in her stomach. Casey swallowed her tears in an attempt to keep them under control. She knew death would be imminent for the young twenty-five-year-old. "Just know that you're safe now."

She took a staggered breath before she asked, "What about Esperanza?"

"Who?" She looked up at Daniela in question.

Daniela looked down, shaking her head, as she said, "Her baby."

"Is there another victim?" Casey looked toward the officer, horrified that she wasn't notified.

"It was DOA. The coroner is on the way."

"Where?"

"It's dead."

"Where?" Casey demanded, as a flash of anger shot across her face.

"It's on the floor of the bedroom near the crib. When she hit him with the pan, he lost it and ran into the baby's bedroom," the officer explained.

Casey ran for the bedroom, but Pete grabbed her arm. When she looked at him, he shook his head, but she jerked away from him and ran into the bedroom.

The room was demolished. Furniture was strewn about the room in pieces. Over in the corner under a part of the overturned, destroyed crib, Casey saw a little arm. Her heart broke when she saw the tiny fingers still clutching the pink blanket. She slipped on a clean pair of gloves and lifted a corner of the wood to see the baby. The little thing could not have been more than six months old. Casey touched the carotid artery and felt a slight pulse.

"Van den Bergh!" Casey screamed, her heart raced in excitement and panic at the same time.

He came in running.

"There's a pulse!" Her emotions were still in control…but barely. She knew she had to fight to stay in control for Alejandra and Esperanza. Someone had to fight for them.

He knelt down to verify. "She does."

"Quick!" she shouted, throwing the pieces of the bed out of the way.

The baby was a little off-color, but she was alive. Her little brown curls were wet from crying. Casey could still see the tear streaks on her cheeks. When Casey checked her lungs with a stethoscope, her breathing was shallow. Her pulse was slow, almost non-existent.

"Be gentle," Casey warned as Pete picked her up. When he stood up, Casey helped him gently brace her neck in the crook of his arm before they slowly walked out into the living room. "She's alive," Casey announced.

"She's what?" The officer looked at them in wide-eyed shock. "She wasn't breathing when I checked."

"She is alive. Just leave the call of a life to us next time, huh?" Pete said. "That's our job."

"I checked!"

"We don't tell you how to do your job. Don't do ours," Pete snapped.

"Let's get these two to the hospital," Casey said, gently taking the baby from Pete, laying her on the mother's chest. She decided it might help them both.

They moved them both as gingerly as possible to the ambulance. While Pete got them settled, Casey ran back in to grab the bag. When she walked in, the boyfriend was up on his feet.

"Where are you taking them?" the officer asked.

Casey wrote down the number to the station and handed it to the police officer. "You can call the station. They will tell you," she said, and then picked up the bag to leave.

"Why can't you tell me now?" he demanded.

Casey spun around and glared at him for a moment before she said, "Officer Frantz, I am doing my best not to disrespect you. If you cannot figure it out, then go ask your supervisor."

"Yes, ma'am." He nodded, as his face flushed with anger at being reprimanded by the paramedic.

"Oooo! She schooled you!" The boyfriend smirked. "A girl with fire. Gotta like that."

Casey left the apartment with a migraine the size of Colorado. "Get us out of here," she said, climbing into the back of the ambulance.

On the way to the hospital, Alejandra went critical. The baby was not doing well either. When Casey thought about the situation they were just in, she got even angrier. She focused her energy in keeping her patients stabilized, while Pete sped toward the hospital as fast as he dared.

About fifteen minutes after dropping them off in the ER, Pete and Casey were released from the hospital to return to station. Halfway to the station, Pete finally broke the silence. "Are you okay?"

Casey sighed, looking out the window, absentmindedly watching the scenery. "No."

"Want to talk about it before we get to the station?"

She sighed in irritation. "I am going to talk to Harrison." Harrison was the Chief of Police.

Pete shook his head. "Yeah, he wasn't the brightest officer."

"Not the brightest?" She turned to him, as anger shot through her. "He almost cost that baby her life. He assumed it was no big deal to do our job."

"I'm sure he –"

"No!" she snapped. "He tried to call a life. He wasn't even going to tell us. It took the dying woman to tell us about her child. And knowing the dad is the one who not only hurt the baby, but potentially killed the...." She took a deep breath as she looked up, pushing away any tears that wanted to fall. She was done crying.

"Do we need to go somewhere to –?"

"No, let's get back to the station," she cut him off.

"What about –?"

"No."

"Might want to talk to Chief before you go to Harrison," he suggested. "You're a bit wound up."

"Wound up? Really?"

"I'm just saying."

She turned and looked out the window again, making a conscious decision to tune him out until they returned to the station.

When they pulled in, Pete turned the rig off, and looked over at her. "You can't take things personally."

She was so mad by Pete's callous comment that she could not form a kind word, so she chose to get out and go into the station.

Pete jumped out of the rig and caught up to her. "Casey, we need to talk."

"No, we don't."

"Yes, we do. We have to work together."

"Pete, I don't want to fight with you. This isn't about you. It's about what happened on that call."

"You have a lot of anger in you."

"I have a lot of anger toward that guy, who is not man enough to control his emotions. Instead, he takes out his anger on a helpless baby girl and a young mother. He is not a man. He is a young child in a man's body. He should not be allowed to procreate. He should not have the privilege of being graced in his life with a baby. They are helpless. They need adults to guide and direct them, not harm them. A child should not be afraid of its parents."

"I agree, but –"

"No!" she shouted. Then she spun toward Chief's office. With her hands on her hips, she took a deep breath. "I need to talk to Chief."

Pete sighed, turning back toward the ambulance to restock it. "I'll be around if you need me."

Casey knocked on the door. She heard Chief tell her to enter. "Afternoon, Carter. What can I do for you?"

"Sir, we just came from a call, that…." She shook her head, doing her best to form a complete thought. "Chief Harrison needs to know about it."

"What happened?"

"Officer O'Malley, who was on scene when we got there, said the scene was clear, and that it was a domestic dispute. He advised us there was a female with a knife in her abdomen in the house."

Chief shook his head. "Wow, sorry."

"O'Malley wasn't as irritating as his partner, Officer Frantz."

"It couldn't be that bad. They're professionals over there."

"Sir, we had the female loaded and ready to go before the female patient asked how her baby was."

He looked at her in surprise. "The officer didn't know?"

"Not only did the officer know, but he thought it was his job to call the life of that baby. He said she was DOA, and told me not to worry about it. Sir, when I checked her, the baby had a pulse and was breathing. Granted her breathing was labored and shallow at best, and the pulse was extremely slow, but it was there."

"Really?" He grabbed a piece of paper. "What was his name again?"

"It was Officer Frantz…F-r-a-n-t-z," she spelled for him.

"Fill out the report and get it to me as soon as possible. I will talk to Harrison."

"Thank you, sir."

"Now, go work out somewhere and get that anger out."

"Sir, it's just –"

"I know. Trust me. I understand."

"Thank you," she said, and left the office.

She changed into sweat pants and a t-shirt before she filled out her report. She then dropped it off in Chief's office before grabbing a basketball, and heading out to the basketball court.

"Play ya?" Pete asked, coming out in shorts and a t-shirt.

She shook her head with the ball in her hands. "I don't know."

"Are you afraid?" he challenged.

"Am I…you have got to be kidding!" she laughed.

"There's your smile." Pete smiled, happy to hear her finally laughing. Since Tommy's accident several months before, she had closed herself off worse than she already was, concerning several of her crewmembers. "Betcha I can take you."

"Is that a challenge?"

"Depends." Pete shrugged. "What do you want to bet?"

She rested the ball on her hip. "What do you have in mind?"

"What are we betting on?" Hunter walked out of the station with Kim.

"I'm thinking this could be an official 'battle of the sexes' game." Pete rubbed his hands in delight. He enjoyed adding a little friendly competition between the firefighters.

"What are we going to bet?" Kim asked.

"Bragging rights?" Pete shrugged.

Casey shook her head. "Weak."

"You got a better idea?" He challenged.

"Loser has to do the dishes for a month?" she suggested.

"Sounds good." Hunter nodded.

"Not good!" Pete argued. "That's not fair! You already do the dishes."

Casey smirked. "Yep, I could use the break."

"Are you serious?" Pete looked at her in surprise.

"Sure. You guys lose, and I won't have to do them."

"You're pretty confident."

"I'm pretty sure Kimmy and I can take you guys."

"All right." Pete and Hunter agreed.

Due to height, Hunter was paired with Casey while Kim was paired with Pete. Hunter stood opposite Casey at the top of the key with the ball in his hands. "Who takes it first?"

"Ladies before gentlemen," Pete said. He and Kim were down near the hoop.

"Don't do us any favors," Kim said under her breath.

Hunter tossed Casey the ball. "No one ever accused me of not being a gentleman."

She tossed it right back at him. "Take it out."

He tossed it back. "Just trying to be fair."

"No." Casey shoved it back at him. "Take-it-out."

He sighed. "Fine."

He went to shoot, but Casey slapped the ball down as it left his fingers. It hit the ground and bounced back up. Casey grabbed it, spun around, and shot the ball. It hit the backboard before bouncing off the rim. Then it hit the back part of the rim before dropping into the basket.

Casey proudly grinned as Kim gave her a high-five. "Three points," Casey announced.

"We play to ten," Pete reminded them as he took the ball to the top of the key. Kim went with him, leaving Hunter and Casey near the basket. "Don't get cocky just yet," Pete said. "Game's barely started."

"That was a lucky shot," Hunter said, standing in front of Casey with his arms in the air.

"Really?" Casey asked.

"You know I let you do that."

Casey sighed, shaking her head. "Whatever helps you sleep at night."

Kim and Pete struggled at the top of the key. Every time Pete tried to get around her, Kim would cut him off. They were well matched.

"You know there is a time limit. You either have to shoot or –"

"I know," Pete snapped at Casey.

"Now who's snippy?" Casey asked.

"Were you two fighting?" Hunter looked at her in surprise.

"We had a rough call."

"Need to talk?" he asked.

"No. Especially not to you."

Hunter cringed. "Ouch."

"Awww, did I hurt your feelings?"

"I thought we were playing basketball."

"We could, if Pete would ever get past Kim."

"Hunter!" Pete yelled as he lobbed the ball into the air.

Hunter used his height against her. As the ball came toward him, he jumped up, tipping it into the hoop. "Now that is how it's done." He grinned. He tossed it to Casey when it came back down. "Your ball."

Casey took it up to the top of the key, with Hunter not far behind. She tossed him the ball and he tossed it back.

"Any time," Hunter said as Casey dribbled the ball.

She had a hard time looking for Kim. Pete covered her well. "Kim?" she called out.

"I'm here," she said. Kim darted out from behind Pete. Before he or Hunter knew what happened, Casey shoved the ball toward her, and bolted in front of Hunter, who tripped over Casey, sending them both to the ground.

"Oomph!" Casey got out when they landed. Hunter knocked the wind out of her.

They looked up in time to see Kim shoot the ball. It swished through the net. "Nothing but net." Kim smiled proudly. Then she looked down at Hunter, as she bragged, "Three more points. Now that's how it's done."

"Whatever," he dismissed her comment. He got up and reached to help Casey. "You okay?"

"Yep." Casey brushed her sweatpants off from the layer of dirt on the court. "Six-two…four more points, and I will be a whole lot better."

"Yeah, like that will happen," Hunter said under his breath.

Casey shook her head as they headed back up toward the top of the key. It was Hunter's turn with the ball.

"I could just give it to you," Hunter said, dribbling the ball.

"Why would you do that?" she asked. Casey stayed on her toes because she was fairly sure he was trying to distract her.

"We wouldn't want to be accused of taking advantage of you – you know, with you two being girls and all." He winked. Casey wanted to punch him in the stomach for that one.

"Oh no he didn't," Kim scoffed from the bottom of the key.

Pete chuckled. "Oh yes he did."

"Play or get off the court," Casey growled.

He took a step back, aimed, and sent the ball through the air. They watched as it made a beautiful arc, before bouncing off the rim and heading onto the court. The mad dash for the rebound ensued, causing a sea bodies converging on the ball.

"Got it!" Pete said.

"No, I got it." Kimmy reached around him, shoving the ball toward Casey.

Hunter pushed Casey out of the way. She recovered after a couple of steps, and elbowed Hunter in his right arm.

"Hey!" he snapped, rubbing his arm. "Foul!"

"Like shoving me wasn't a foul?" she raised an eyebrow.

"That wasn't a shove…this is!" he said, and shoved her back several steps.

She glared at him as she stood her ground. "I really hope you didn't do that in anger."

"Carter! Van den Bergh!" Chief poked his head out of the back door of the firehouse.

The action on the court came to a sudden halt. "Yes?" Pete and Casey asked in unison as they looked toward him.

"Would you come to my office?"

"Yes, sir," Casey said. She turned back to Hunter and said, "We can finish this later."

"You bet we will," he said, still rubbing his arm.

"Wimp," she said under her breath. Casey smiled to herself. She was sure he would end up with a bruise from that one.

Pete and Casey jogged through the engine bay to Chief's back door of his office. "What do you think?" Pete asked as they stood at the door.

"Maybe from the call," Casey said before she knocked.

"Come in," Chief called through the door.

When they walked in, Chief was at his desk. Police Chief Harrison and Officer Frantz occupied the two chairs across from him. The office had a tense feel to it, and it seemed to become heavier when they walked in the office.

"Carter, Van den Bergh, please find a comfortable spot to rest. It seems we need to talk," Chief said, reclining back in his chair.

"May I ask what this is about?" Pete asked. Casey crossed her arms while Pete rested his hands on the windowsill behind them. Their bodies were instantly on edge as soon as they saw Office Frantz. It seemed to Casey that she wasn't the only one bothered by the call.

"Are you two both willing to stand by your reports?" Chief asked.

Pete looked Chief, offended. "Absolutely."

Casey glanced at the officer, annoyed, knowing Chief's question must have stemmed from him. "I always stand by my reports."

"Well, it seems there are a couple points of conflict between your two reports, and Officer Frantz's report," Chief explained.

Casey glared at Officer Frantz. "Really? In what area?"

"Regarding the child," Chief Harrison explained.

"You mean the child that the victim had to tell me was there?" Casey was angry at the insinuation. "You mean the child your officer had already called the coroner for, yet didn't bother to mention to us? You mean the child we rescued from under pieces of crib, still holding her baby blanket where she was left to die?"

"Enough," Chief stopped Casey from going forward. He glanced at Chief Harrison. "Carl?"

Chief Harrison looked at the police officer. "Care to explain? It seems the coroner's report coincided with the paramedic's reports as to when he was called."

"I checked that child. It didn't have a pulse," Officer Frantz defended himself.

"That child is not an 'it,'" Casey snapped. "That baby girl was alive! You took it upon yourself to call a life…which is not your job."

"Don't tell me how to do my job!" he snarled as he stood.

"Don't try to do ours!" Pete stood up in defense, with a sharp tone to his voice. He stepped slightly in front of Casey to stop the officer in case he got angrier.

Chief Harrison stood up between his officer and the two paramedics with his hands out to keep them apart. "Lady and gentlemen!"

"Your officer could have cost that little girl her life!" Casey shouted in anger.

Pete put his hand behind him to keep her back.

"Cater, Van den Bergh, calm down." Chief stood. "I understand you are angry, and you have a right to be."

Officer Frantz glared at Chief. "They do not."

"Frantz! Calm down now!" Chief Harrison ordered. "That's an order!"

"Your incompetence could have sentenced her to death!" Pete objected, ignoring the police chief.

"She-was-not-breathing!" Officer Frantz enunciated. His face was red, and his voice was to the point of shouting as well. Casey was sure the entire firehouse could hear the conversation by that point.

Casey took a step toward the officer. "Yes, she was! You wouldn't know that though, because you were not trained the way we were." Both the chief's bodies tensed up when she took the step forward. She knew she needed to calm herself. She took a deep breath before she continued. "Officer Frantz, you are trained to do many things, but not what we do. I am not sure if you are new, or just need more time under your belt, but this is a hard lesson for you to learn. You did your job by getting the boyfriend subdued and in handcuffs, allowing us access to Alejandra. You, however, took it upon yourself to call a medical issue, which you are not trained to do. That is our job. It is our area of expertise."

"I am aware of that," he conceded, still irritated, but his demeanor was calmer.

"Then you are aware that you overstepped your boundaries in the function of your job," she pointed out.

"I did not! She was dead!" he yelled, getting angry again.

"By your own admission, you stated it was not what you were trained to do," Chief Blazedale pointed out.

"This is…was this a set-up?" Officer Frantz narrowed his eyes at Chief Harrison.

"Absolutely not." Harrison shook his head. "It was a fact-finding mission. There were inconsistencies, and we needed to flush out the truth."

"I do not appreciate being flushed out for everyone to see," the officer objected.

"If you told the truth in your report, there would not be a need for this meeting."

"Cater, Van den Bergh, you are dismissed. You are no longer needed," Chief Blazedale said to them.

"Yes, sir," they said in unison, before sliding past the police chief and the officer.

"Wow! That was interesting," Pete said when they were out of earshot.

"I'm just glad they got the truth." Casey was disappointed by the officer's actions. Most of the officers she worked with were competent and did their jobs well. While she knew this was an exception, it was an exception that could have cost a baby her life.

"Hopefully he learned something from it."

"Here's hoping." Casey sighed, heading up the stairs toward the shower. "We need good officers on the job."

"But they have to stay out of our way so we can do ours," Pete added, going into the men's bathroom.

Casey took a shower with the meeting weighing heavily on her mind. She tried to figure out why she was so irritated with the officer. She understood part of it was because he lied, and then tried to blame the two of them, but the other part was the entire situation itself.

She also thought about the basketball game. Hunter had been good over the last year, but when they played basketball, he was back to his obnoxious self. She knew there would be a rematch, and she was not looking forward to it. She did not trust him since the incident in Nicaragua. Between what Derek and the Colonel told her, and what she saw in her vision, she had an uneasy feeling whenever Hunter was around. Hunter, however, seemed to finagle his way close to her a lot of the time when they were on shift.

That was the other thing that irritated Casey about the basketball game. She was supposed to play with Pete before Hunter somehow crashed the game. Once he did, it went from a way to work out frustration to a competitive game – making her even more agitated.

The mind games around her were beginning to aggravate her. They were subtle. One would have to study the crew to see them. Pete was Pete. He was who he was with no pretenses. Casey liked that about him. She liked that he was simple and caring, yet strong. Kim, on the other hand, was a different story. She liked Hunter, but he was her partner. She also knew Hunter liked Casey, so she and Hunter both somehow continued to invite themselves whenever Pete and Casey were doing something. Hunter didn't mind dragging Kim into things, therefore creating no need for an extra person. Jesse was caught in the middle of it all. He saw what was going on and did what he could to run interference regarding the situation, but he could only do so much. Hunter seemed to have a way of separating Jesse and Casey whenever they were together.

During all of this, Casey also had to live two different lives. Jesse invited her to do things with him and Carrie-Anne outside of the firehouse. She would accept some of the time, but she also enjoyed her time with Mark, Derek, and the Colonel – only no one could know about it. The guys at the firehouse often said she was going to be a housebound spinster. As far as they knew, she spent a lot of time on her own. They often commented how much they worried about her. Since Mac died, Casey seemed to spend a lot of time by herself…when in reality she spent it with the A.N.G.E.L.s.

*   *   *

Later that day, Jesse sat at the table in the kitchen while Casey prepared dinner. "All right, Carter." He looked up at her from the magazine he was reading. "We have a vacation we still need to take."

"A vacation we need to take?" she questioned. "Wouldn't Carrie-Anne have something to say about that?"

He had been dating a wonderful girl, Carrie-Anne, for about six months. While she did not have Kara's looks, she had more personality and heart than Kara did any day. Casey liked her much better.

"I talked to her about it. She's okay with it."

Casey continued to cut up vegetables. "Oh, like she would say otherwise. She's too nice."

"Say otherwise about what?" Hunter walked in with Kim from an ambulance call. They sat down at the table with Jesse, while everyone else was on the couch watching a football game.

"We were talking about our vacation. I believe about a year ago we said we were going to go, and we have yet to follow through." Jesse looked over at Casey for an answer.

"Why would I need a vacation? I get one away from you guys every two days," she said with a smile, hoping to veer the conversation away from their vacation plans while Hunter was in the room. He was the last person she wanted to know where she and Jesse were going to go on vacation.

"There is nowhere you want to go?" He ignored her attempt at sidetracking the conversation.

"Not really." She shook her head, tossing the cut-up vegetables into the beef broth, which already contained the cooked roast beef chunks.

Hunter looked up at Casey, as he and Kim set up a game of checkers. "Come on. Everyone wants to go somewhere. I get my trip to Africa here in a couple months. We know McFadden wants to go to Australia. We know Jeff wants to go see the Seven Wonders of the World. Where do you want to go?"

"I want to go to France," Kim sighed dreamily, "The City of Love."

"Oh, please." Will shook his head from where he sat on the leather, wraparound couch with the others. "So typical."

She narrowed her eyes at him. "Typical of what?"

"Typical female mindset. Looking for romance anywhere but where they are. You know 'the grass is always greener on the other side' theory?"

"Wow! Talk about your typical arrogant male chauvinist," Kim remarked.

"Do you disagree?" he asked.

"Where do you want to go?" she snapped, ignoring his goading.

"I want to go to jolly ol' England," he said with a fake English accent. Then in his normal voice, he added, "I hear the girls are hotter over there."

She sighed, shaking her head. "Pathetic."

"You have no idea what you're talking about." Scott looked over at him, stunned.

Will scoffed. "Like you would know."

"I've been there. There may be some who have looks on their side, but I like the friendliness of the girls here."

"So, world traveler, where do you want to go?" Will crossed his arms as he glared at Scott.

"I don't know, maybe Egypt. I would love to see the pyramids."

"Jay, what about you?" Hunter asked.

He thought for a moment before he said, "Actually, I would like to go to Hawaii. It might not be on the other side of the world or in another country, but it sounds beautiful, peaceful, and relaxing."

"That's true." Marty nodded. "We went there for our honeymoon – gorgeous place."

"So, is there anywhere else you would want to go?" Kim asked Marty.

"Actually, I want to go to Capetown, South Africa. I would also love to see Kruger Park and Victoria Falls while I am there. I hear both places are spectacular."

"That's on my list, my man." Hunter smiled. "I'll bring you back some photos."

"I'll get there someday on my own," he said confidently.

"What about you, LT?" Jay asked him.

"Actually, I've already been to where I want to go. Patty and I went to Italy for our second honeymoon about five years ago. It's a wonderful place."

Pete smiled. "Well, he's easy."

"What about you?" LT asked Pete.

"Ireland. I know there is a lot of rain, and it's mostly a lot of green, but I would still love to see Stonehenge and the lush green fields. And I really love their accents." He wiggled his eyebrows.

"Uh, yeah." Robbie sighed. "That would be a tough act to follow."

"What about you?" Pete asked him.

"Mexico."

"Mexico? Why Mexico?"

"You really have no idea, do you?" Robbie shook his head in amazement. "The women there are gorgeous! The beaches are breathtaking! Not to mention the Yucatan Peninsula has some awesome Mayan pyramids." He nudged Scott. "May wanna just look south of the border for those pyramids. That country is rich in culture and history too."

Marty huffed. "Take Martes with ya. Maybe then she will shut up about it." (Jessie Martes was always bragging about Mexico and how she wanted to go there. It drove the other firefighters a little crazy.)

"Maybe." He shrugged. Then he looked over at the new guy, Shawn MacAuliffe, and asked, "Where would you want to go?"

"That's a good question," Shawn said as he sat back in his seat. "I guess I would go to Ireland to check out my roots. My grandparents came from Ireland, where the MacAuliffe name is strong."

"Interesting." LT nodded in approval. Then he turned to Vinnie and asked, "Vinnie? What about you?"

He leaned forward and looked each one of the men as he said, "There is nothing more spectacular than America. It has the purple mountains in Wyoming, the geysers in Yellowstone, the Grand Canyon, Niagara Falls, even the mighty Mississippi. It also has the Florida Keys, the Gulf of Mexico, Hawaii, along with many other landmarks like the Space Needle in Seattle, the San Francisco Bridge, Washington DC…and that is not even touching New York City and Lady Liberty. We've got it all here, people."

"I agree, but I enjoy getting to know other cultures and races of people," Hunter said. "It adds so much more to your perspective of the world as a whole."

Casey looked at him in surprise. "That was deep."

"That was a bunch of malarkey." Will rolled his eyes. "You talk as if you've been all over the globe."

"I have. I have lived in Germany, France, Italy, and several places here in America."

"How?"

"I was military for eight years, remember? That's where I got my training as a firefighter/paramedic."

As soon as Hunter said that, Casey looked at him suspiciously, but quickly looked away so he would not see her face. With the beef stew simmering in its pot, she turned her attention to kneading the bread dough that had been rising all afternoon.

"Um, Carter?" Jeff said after about ten minutes of silence.

She placed the dough into the bread pan. "Yeah?"

He draped his arm over her shoulder. "You never said where you wanted to go."

"Yeah. How do you keep doing that?" Jesse looked at her in irritation.

"Keep doing what?" she looked over at him as she washed her hands.

"You continuously avoid answering questions. You somehow get the subject changed before it gets to you. How do you do that?"

"Practice, I guess." She shrugged. "So, dinner is beef stew. It should be ready in about forty-five minutes."

"Smells good." LT gave her the thumbs-up from the couch.

"Did I see you making homemade bread too?" Will licked his lips in delight. "That stuff rocks!"

"Yep. All ready to go." She held up the bread pan.

"Carter!" Jesse snapped. Casey jumped, dropping the bread pan.

Everyone looked at Jesse, stunned, as Jeff barely caught the bread. Jesse rarely snapped, let alone talked with any amount of loudness to his voice. He was one of the more laid back of the crew. LT even sat up a little to look at him from where he sat on the couch.

"Jess, what's wrong?" Casey asked.

Jeff gently set the pan down on the counter before returning to the couch with the other guys, getting out of the way of that conversation. The last time he heard Jesse yell in anger was at Brennon. He did not want to be in the middle if Carter and Jesse got into it. The anger around the station was starting to wear on him. He missed the lightheartedness that used to permeate their shift.

"We still haven't talked about where we're going on vacation and you keep changing the subject," Jesse said. "Cut it out!"

"Geez! You sound like you need a vacation," Casey said, recovering from his outburst. She put the bread into the oven and set the timer.

"Yeah, are ya a little tense there, McFadden? Need to go to the weight room to work some of that out?" Will raised an eyebrow at him.

"Maybe." He shrugged, still agitated. "It would help if Carter would cooperate." He looked at her out of the corner of his eye.

She looked at him in wide-eyed surprise for a moment before she turned toward Will and shrugged. Will shook his head at her to let it go, so she did. There seemed to be a film of anger and irritation throughout the firehouse. Casey decided to talk to LT about it later and see if he could come up with some creative idea to get rid of it.

In the meantime, everyone took a few moments before they settled back down to watch the football game again. Casey took the time, and turned her attention to the kitchen, starting the dishes. After a few minutes, she looked over at Jesse. He fumed in anger, as he flippantly went through the magazine again.

"Jess?" she asked. When he looked over at her, she motioned with her head for him to come over since her hands were in the soapy water.

*　*　*

Hunter looked up when Jesse stood from the table. Over the last year, he did his best to separate Casey and Jesse with no great success. Their friendship had a strong bond. This messed with his plans. His boss was getting impatient with Hunter's performance regarding this mission. Hunter did his best to explain that Casey was different from any other woman he had been assigned to, but they didn't want excuses. They wanted results. Hunter had exactly two weeks or they were moving in and taking matters into their own hands. He had two weeks to save Casey's life. He wasn't sure if he would be able to make the deadline, but he would give it his best shot. His hope was not only to save her life, but also to be with her in the end…even if he had to take matters into his own hands.

*　*　*

Jesse leaned against the counter next to Casey with his arms crossed. "What?"

"Where do you want to go?"

He shrugged. "I dunno."

"Jess, work with me here," she said, setting the clean cutting board into the dish drainer. She then let the water out to clean the sinks.

"Why? You weren't working with me."

"Because I didn't want the entire station to know where we were going," she pointed out as she rinsed the sink. "It's none of their business."

"I'll answer your question if you answer mine."

"Which was…?"

"If you could go anywhere in the world, where would it be?"

"I don't know. You have to remember, I have been all over the world working as a photographer."

"Okay, then what was your favorite place?"

"Hmm." She looked up, thinking. She turned around and leaned against the counter, drying her hands off with a towel. "I liked a lot of the places I visited."

"Like where?" Hunter looked up from where he was playing a game of checkers with Kim at the table.

"This is a private conversation," she snapped.

"Such hostility," he huffed. "Maybe you and McFadden need to go work out in the weight room."

"Shut up," Jesse scowled.

"Aw, come on. We all told where we would want to go. Where do you want to go in this great big world?" Hunter pressed, as some of the guys on the couch turned around to listen.

"As I said, I've been all over the world." She shrugged. "I liked Greece for its beauty, and the ruins. I liked Australia for its natural flora and fauna – not to mention Mount Uluru and the Great Barrier Reef. I liked Italy for its food and unique culture. Rome was the best though, photography wise. I also liked France, England, Ireland, Switzerland, and Scotland for all their landmarks and rich history. Holland has stunning landscapes full of color, while Mexico's people are full of spirit and tenacity – not to mention the Mayan and Mexican history all over the place. I liked traveling around America for all of its natural beauty as well. South America has a lot of soul and character throughout its countries, not to mention its awesome food. I liked Africa for its unique animal habitation, along with those stunningly magnificent Victoria Falls. I also liked China and Japan for its inner strength and beauty. And I liked Russia for its people's heart of courage and valor. There are pluses and minuses to all of them. With many of those places, safety is a luxury."

Jeff looked at her, wide-eyed. "You have been around."

"I told you."

"Were you in the military too?" Kim asked.

"Yes and no," Casey said. "Most of my travels were when I was a photographer."

"You were in the military?" Vinnie asked, surprised.

"No," she said, "my brother was, remember?"

"So, why would you have traveled with him if he was just your brother? I don't understand," Vinnie said, confused.

"Because I lived with him for a while," she explained. "Now," she turned to Jesse before they pursued her any further, and asked, "since it is obvious that I have been all over, where do you want to go?"

He sighed. "Somewhere quiet. I need a real vacation."

"And Carrie-Anne really does not have a problem with you traveling alone with another woman?"

"Well, she did for a while, until I explained our relationship." He leaned on the counter as he said, "Look, I need a vacation. We had a rough year last year. Granted, this one has been a lot easier, with the exception of my personal drama and the loss of Tommy. I'm just tired, I guess. I'm tired of losing good men. I'm tired of walking into over half of the situations we walk into each day at work. I feel like I just need some time to decompress and breathe."

"All right. Let me work on it," she said in understanding. "What dates do you have for vacation?"

"I'm taking my four weeks of vacation, starting in two weeks."

"Will Chief let us take the same four weeks off?"

"He might let us overlap a week or two."

"Okay, let me work on it." Casey decisively nodded. He needed a vacation. He needed to relax. The more she thought about how much Jesse had been there for her, the more she wanted to make his life-long dream come true. She would go talk to Chief later, and then she would work on a flight for him and her to Australia so he could see Mount Uluru and swim in the Great Barrier Reef. She felt that was the least she could do for him.

*   *   *

Hunter knew he would have to pay closer attention to what Casey was doing in order to make his plan work. If Casey and Jesse were going on vacation together, it might be the thing he needed to get her alone. He knew they wouldn't share a room – that wasn't Casey. He would have to find out their travel plans and make plans of his own. He jumped three of Kim's checkers as a thrill of excitement ran through his body. He might make the deadline after all.

*   *   *

After she finished the dinner dishes later that night, Casey pulled LT aside. She explained her observations to him about the crew and the tense feeling around the station. He suggested they take some time and wash the rigs. He said it was to give them a good once-over, but in reality, they always had fun washing vehicles.

He had them all wash as a team. While LT called it a unity building exercise, most of the team grumbled, calling it forced labor.

The first engine was slow, almost a form of torture, as people grumbled and complained the entire time. By the time they got to the second rig, Casey looked over at LT and sighed. He shook his head, not sure what to do. The crew had the second rig already rinsed and ready to be soaped up when she picked up the sponge. She looked around at some of the others who had picked up the sponges and started washing the truck, and those who had the hoses. She knew there was no time like the present to start something, so she glanced at LT who looked at her and nodded with a wink before she threw the sponge at Hunter as hard as she could.

"Hey!" He spun around, looking to see where the soaked projectile came from.

Kim looked at her, knowing she was the one who threw it. Pete poked his head around the corner to see why someone yelled.

Casey crossed her arms. "Awww, are you afraid you'll melt?"

Hunter's jaw dropped. "Was that you?"

"Shame." She shook her head. "And here I thought you were a man. You're just a childish wimp."

"Really?" He looked at her, wide-eyed. Everyone could tell he was upset. No one moved. They were waiting to see what would happen next.

"I told you we would finish what we started on the court later," Casey said.

Hunter was stunned. "Are you challenging me?"

Casey put her hand out for Kim's sponge. "Kimmy, let me see that."

She gladly handed it to her, hoping Casey pushed Hunter too far this time so she could finally have her chance with Hunter.

Casey soaked up as much water as she could out of the bucket. Then she went to Hunter who didn't move a muscle. She released every drop of water she could over his head.

As the water went down his body, he looked at her, dumbfounded. "What would possess you to do that?" he asked, wiping the water off his face when she finished.

"You're angry."

"Of course I am angry. You soaked me for no reason."

Casey sighed as she picked up the bucket of water.

When she headed back toward his direction, Hunter put his hands in front of him. "Oh no. You are not going to do what I think you are going to do...are you? Don't you dare!"

Casey didn't answer. She continued to walk toward him, while he slowly backed away, step-by-step.

He turned and ran around the back of fire engine when she got closer. As he ran by Rob, Hunter snagged the hose from him, turning it on Casey, who threw the bucket in the air in order to block her face from the spray of the hose. It went up in the air, spraying soapy water as it flipped once before landing squarely on its bottom, splashing soapy water on everyone around when it landed. Water from the bucket, along with the hose, got on Rob, Pete, Kim, and Vinnie. LT stood back out of the way, watching with Chief as they stood by his office door.

As soon as the bucket landed, it was a free-for-all. Sponges and hoses, along with buckets of soapy water went flying in every direction. Even where Chief and LT stood, they got wet.

A couple minutes into it, Hunter grabbed Casey's arm and pulled her out of sight of everyone around, to the other side of the ambulance. He gripped her arm so hard, she was positive he bruised it. She gasped as he swung her around to the side of the ambulance away from the other firefighters, slamming her against it with his hand over her mouth. She looked at him in wide-eyed fear.

"Shhhh! If I take my hand off, you are not going to scream, are you?" he hissed.

Casey shook her head.

When he took off his hand, he loosened the grip he had on her arm. "We need to talk."

"About what?" she demanded. The feelings inside her were a cross between angry and terrified.

"You and me."

"You're delusional!"

"You came at me first!"

"Because you can't seem to keep your nose out of my business," she said, getting a little loud. They were not as loud as the guys on the other side of the ambulance though, as the others continued to chase each other around with the hoses, since the buckets and sponges had been expended.

"Shhh!" he hissed again. He glanced through the ambulance windows to see if anyone heard her before he turned back to her. "You and I are attracted to each other."

"Again, you're delusional." She crossed her arms in a huff. "Not every girl falls for you."

"Kim, Zoe, and Bobbi Jo don't seem to have a problem with me," he said confidently.

"Not me," she insisted. Casey stood, feeling angry, trapped, and vulnerable. She knew she would not be able to contain herself much longer before she would snap at him – especially after the day she had.

"Why not?"

"Because you are cocky, arrogant, obnoxious, and, once again, you can't seem to keep your nose out of my business. You continuously push, crossing the line."

"We are a family. There is no line," he said, inching closer to her.

"There is a line, and you have pushed past it too many times."

As she went to sidestep him, he slammed his hand on the ambulance next to her head, effectively trapping her with his body.

"Let me go," she insisted.

"Not until we discuss us."

"There-is-no-us!" she shouted. Part of that was in anger, and part of it was hoping someone would hear.

"Where's Carter?" LT suddenly shouted.

"For that matter, where is Hunter?" Kim asked.

"Now you've done it!" he growled angrily.

She narrowed her eyes at him. "Remove yourself from my personal space."

He chuckled. "What are you, two?"

"Casey!" Jesse called.

"Hunter!" Jay yelled, as they fanned-out through the station.

"Come on." He grabbed her arm, yanking her into the ambulance with him, quietly closing the door behind him.

"They're going to hear us." Casey jumped for the back door, but he pounced on top of her, shoving her to the floor. She knew that would take them out of view of anyone looking for them. "Get off me!"

"Shut up! We need to talk," he growled again, less than two inches from her face.

She looked up to see his eyes shift to pure black, before going back to their normal color. She gulped as she momentarily froze.

"We have to talk about us…and we're doing it here and now," he hissed.

Casey's anger flashed again. She didn't care if he was an Unnatural or not. She was sick and tired of him. "There is no us! If you don't get off of me, I will scream my head off!" she threatened.

He had ahold of her wrists. "Calm down. I'm not going to hurt you."

"Then why are you holding me down?"

"Because when things get too much for you, you run. You don't talk to anyone."

"Because I don't trust you."

"Why not?" he asked.

She thought about telling him the truth, but she didn't want to set-off the demon inside him again. She had to figure out a way to find out why he was there, while keeping the demon at bay. "You won't leave me alone."

"Because I like you, Casey."

She shuddered.

"Is it me…or men in general?"

"Why do you care?"

"Well, it can't be men in general, because Jesse is one of your best friends. On the flip side, you are friends with Kimmy, but not as close as you are with Jesse. Why not? I would think as the only two girls on the shift, you two would bond."

"I don't trust men, and I trust women even less," she admitted.

"Rough way to go through life." He shook his head and sighed as he got off her. "What happened to you?"

"More than you can comprehend."

"Cryptic," he said, as he sat beside the ambulance door. "I like a good mystery."

"Why are you so fascinated with me?" Casey cocked her head to the side, studying him. He didn't want to hurt her; she could see that. She wasn't sure what he was looking for though, so she decided to play his little game until she deciphered it.

"I asked you a question first," Hunter said. "You can't sidetrack me like you do Jesse."

"Why are you so fascinated with me?" she asked again. Now he had her curiosity piqued. He seemed to know exactly where to target her.

"I'll tell you what. We can talk, but we have to let the others know where we are." He went out of the ambulance, and walked around to the other side so the others could see him. Casey could hear the conversation.

"Morgan!" LT looked at him in relief. "Where were you? Why didn't you answer? And do you know where Carter is?"

"Easy, guys." Hunter chuckled. "We didn't hear you. Casey and I are talking in the ambulance. Things got a little heated with us during the basketball game, and since you guys were working out here having fun, we went to talk."

"Where is she?" Jesse demanded, not trusting Hunter's answer.

Casey could hear the anger in his voice, so she knew she had to step in. "I'm right here," Casey said, walking around the ambulance. Despite the fact that he started it, she didn't want him to take the heat for it until she figured out what he wanted. She was tired of walking on eggshells around him. If he showed his true form again, she would have to deal with it, but she wanted to know why he was after her.

"Are you okay?" Jesse asked.

"Yes," she said.

"Where were you?"

"We were talking in the ambulance."

"Why didn't you guys let us know when we called?" LT asked, still upset.

"We came when we heard you calling," she lied. "Look, we still have a lot to talk about. Can you guys handle it?"

"Why don't you guys go talk in the conference room?" Chief suggested. "You can have your privacy in there."

Casey nodded in appreciation, as she walked through the doors toward the hallway for the conference room, with Hunter on her heels.

"Nice," Hunter said, leaving the door slightly ajar as they walked into the room.

She spun around and glared at him. "What?"

He looked at her wide-eyed for a moment, before he crossed his arms and leaned against the table. "You are either a moody little thing, or a really good actress."

"Actress," Casey said, not moving a muscle.

"You seemed perfectly fine in the bay. What's with the attitude now?"

"I didn't want to worry any of the others," she said, as the anger flashed across her eyes. He looked at her wide-eyed again, as she said, "I do not like to lie to my friends or my family, and I will not do it again. If you want to talk, pick a better place and time."

"Listen here." He slowly walked towards her. "We need to find out what the problem is between us."

"The problem is that you won't leave me alone."

"Because you don't trust me. I want to know why."

"Because you won't stay out of my business. You somehow keep shoving your way in the middle of any conversation I happen to be in, or things I am trying to do with another person who isn't you."

"Name one," he challenged.

"The basketball game between Pete and me. The conversation between Jesse and me in the kitchen earlier today. Then the –"

He put his hands in the air in surrender. "Sue me for wanting to be a part of your life."

"I don't want you there."

He rolled his eyes. "That's obvious. I want to know why."

"For one, my brother said not to trust you."

"This is all over one basketball game?"

"That was the start. You seem to keep putting yourself in my business, and I don't like it. You also seem to think that my personal life needs to be public knowledge. My personal life is just that…personal."

"We are supposed to be a family here, but you don't seem to want to share with the rest of us."

"I don't have to."

"Oh no. You get to live your little life all to yourself. You just waltz in here on your shift, otherwise we never hear from you again."

"I do things with Jesse."

"That's it. And it's with Jesse and Carrie-Anne. What else do you do on your time off?"

"That's none of your business."

"Why won't you do things with the others?"

"I don't play well with others."

"Then why don't you just go back to photography?" he asked. "You can be by yourself all you want to."

"Because I like doing my job."

He sighed, crossing his arms. "Look, we care about –"

"Stop it!" she shouted, getting angry as she balled her fists. "This has absolutely nothing to do with the squad. This has to do with you and your selfish tendencies."

"What do you mean by that?"

"Just because you aren't getting what you want –"

"Kiss me," he said, cutting her off.

She looked at him wide-eyed for a moment, before narrowing her eyes at him. "I don't want to."

"Yes, you do. That's why I get under your skin," he said smugly.

"No, it is your arrogance."

"No, it is an attraction you keep denying."

"Because I don't like you."

"Kiss me once," he challenged. "Just once."

"Absolutely not." She shook her head. "There is nothing between us."

"Yes, there is. That's why I irritate you so much."

"No, you irritate me because you're pushy."

He stood there staring at her for a moment before he asked, "Do you have a guy?"

"No." She lied. "Why?"

"Because you don't seem to be interested in any guy."

"Again, none of your business."

"There is someone, isn't there?"

"Nope."

"Are you sure?"

"None-of-your-business!" she snapped.

He grabbed her arms and pulled her toward him.

"Don't do this," she begged.

"Do you like me?"

"No."

"Yes, you do."

"No, I don't. And for you to insist on potentially taking something that isn't yours, will get you into trouble," she threatened. "Now, if you want to continue this conversation, back yourself up several steps. If not, I am leaving."

As she looked at him, his eyes shifted again. She hadn't seen this side of him for almost a year, and thought it was gone, but this was the second time today. His eyes went black as coal before they shifted back to his blue color. She even saw his black form this time. 'The man inside the man' as the Colonel explained it.

Casey gasped as she struggled to get away from him. He went to kiss her, but she slammed her knee into his groin.

"Oomph!" He doubled-over, before dropping to his knees. She kicked her leg up and hit him under his jaw, sending him back into several of the desks.

Casey ran out of the conference room, slamming the door behind her. She stumbled down the hall as her heart raced. She was terrified of what she left in the conference room. She had to figure out a way to keep Hunter in her sights, but not let him anywhere near her again. She turned to look at the conference room door to see if he was behind her. When she turned back around, she ran into the chief.

He grabbed her arms to keep her balanced. "Whoa! What is going on down here? Margo said she heard yelling and a door slamming."

Hunter stumbled out of the conference room, wiping the blood that dripped from his mouth with the back of his hand. He looked up, surprised to see Chief holding Casey's arms.

"He won't leave me alone," Casey said in her defense. She looked closely at Hunter's eyes, but he seemed to be back to normal again.

Chief looked at Hunter. "What happened to you?"

"I fell," he lied.

"Onto my knee," Casey finished, not even looking at Hunter. She wanted a way out, and wasn't giving Hunter another inch.

"Why? What did…what in blazes is going on here?" Chief put his hands on his hips.

"He tried to kiss me, but I didn't want him to," Casey defended herself. "He didn't take 'no' for an answer, so I slammed my knee into his groin before I kicked his jaw."

"Is this true, Morgan?" Chief looked over at Hunter.

"I thought –"

"Wrong," Casey snapped, cutting Hunter off. "You thought wrong!" She stood her ground. "You can't just take what you want. If someone says no, that means no! It's guys like you who –"

"Carter, this is not the same as the call from earlier," Chief cut her off, shaking his head.

She scoffed. "Isn't it? Either way, the guy was being a bully. The difference is I know how to defend myself. Alejandra didn't."

"Is everything okay?" Jesse asked, as he and Pete came down the hall. They walked into a very confusing scene. Not knowing what to do, Jesse asked Chief, "Is there anything we can do?"

"Yes, take Carter to play basketball." Chief crossed his arms, visibly angry. "Morgan and I need to talk."

"Come on, Casey." Jesse rested his hand on the small of her back, as he escorted her out to the basketball court.

"You two weren't talking earlier, were you?" Pete asked, when they walked outside on the empty court. It was dark outside. The court and firehouse lights were the only ones shining on an otherwise dark street. The clouds made it overcast, covering any other light the Earth was trying to give them. "He forced you to talk to him, didn't he?"

Casey looked steadily at Pete, as the rain slowly fell around them, one-by-one at first before slowly picking up speed and size. She could feel the anger boiling inside of her, as it mixed with fear. The trio stood in the silence while the raindrops hit the court around them.

"Did he do something to you?" Jesse finally asked. He didn't want to jump to conclusions, but Casey's behavior wasn't normal.

The rain flowed in a steady stream, soaking Casey, making them colder than they already were. "He tried," she admitted.

"What did he do?" Jesse crossed his arms as he narrowed his eyes.

"He tried to forcibly kiss me," she admitted.

Pete looked at her, wide-eyed. "What did you do?"

"I slammed my knee into his groin, and then kicked him in the jaw. Pretty sure he will remember that next time he tries something," she said, with a slight smile of satisfaction on her face.

Pete chuckled. "Think you effectively ended that conversation."

"And erase doubt in anyone's mind as to whether or not you were attracted to him." Jesse was proud of her, but wished he were the one who had the chance to punch Hunter. He hoped more than anything that this would end Hunter's relentless pursuit of Casey.

"Think Chief will transfer him?" Casey asked, remembering how angry Chief looked in the hallway.

"Are you okay working with him?" Pete asked.

She nodded.

Jesse looked at her, stunned. "How can you?"

"Would you rather have him on a shift where you know you can keep an eye on him, knowing the girls on the shift can kick his behind, or would you rather chance him with Martes?"

"What about kicking his behind back to 'B' to deal Zoe or Bobbi Jo?" Jesse asked. "They can handle themselves."

"Yeah, pretty sure he left that shift for a reason." Pete pointed out, "They wouldn't leave him alone on shift. They harassed him all the time. I felt bad for the poor guy."

"Don't." Casey shook her head. "He probably enjoyed it."

"Are you cooled down enough to go back inside?" Jesse asked, shivering. "It's cold out here."

"Go on inside." She tucked her wet hair behind her ear. "I'm going to stay out here for a few minutes for some fresh air."

"Are you sure?" Jesse asked.

"Yeah. It's quiet."

"All right. If you need us, then yell. We'll keep an ear out."

"I appreciate it."

As soon as they closed the door behind them, Casey glanced out into the darkness toward the park behind the firehouse. She was cold and soaked, but she was sure one of the guys was out there watching, so she cautiously walked out into the park.

Derek came from behind a tree. "Casey, what are you doing out here all by yourself?"

She rolled her eyes. "Had an altercation of the Hunter kind."

He leaned against the tree, with one foot up and his arms crossed. "What happened?"

"He tried to kiss me."

"Oooo! That's not going to make English very happy." He cringed. "Pretty sure English could kill him with his bare hands."

"No worries. I got him."

He stood straight, stunned. "What did you do?"

"I slammed my knee into his groin and kicked his jaw."

"Wow!" He looked at her in wide-eyed surprise. "Um, that's great, but I still have to tell Mark and the Colonel."

"I know."

"Are you okay?"

"Yeah. Just a little...I think the adrenaline is finally coming down," Casey said, as a shiver ran down her spine. "And just so you know, he's still an Unnatural."

"Last time I remember you mentioning that was a few months after Nicaragua. Did something happen?"

"He shifted tonight...twice."

"Wow! Okay, I need to get this information to Mark and the Colonel. You might want to get back inside before you catch a cold. I can't do much for you out here."

"I know."

"Go talk to your chief. I think you guys need to get on the same page. Make sure you keep on your toes around Hunter though. He seems to have a way of getting into your business."

"He does."

"We still have yet to figure out exactly who or what he is," Derek pointed out. "The Colonel has made several attempts to access his past, but he keeps getting blocked."

"I understand."

"Good girl. Now, go talk to your chief."

Casey slowly walked back toward the basketball court, letting the coolness of the rain penetrate the anger that swirled within her, hoping the iciness would put an end to it. The quietness of the outside, with the calmness of the falling rain comforted and relaxed her. Casey wasn't willing to let that go yet.

She leaned against the basketball pole, looking up, watching the rain dance off the court lights. The sounds, senses, and the rain soaked through to her soul. It felt as if God was washing her from the inside out, cleansing her from all the anger, irritation, and frustration of the day's events...the last few year's events for that matter.

As she leaned on the pole, she felt God's peace wash through her. She knew Derek prayed for her while she stood singing God's praises in her head. She ran several songs through her mind while she prayed as well. She took comfort in knowing Derek was watching her, and she could relax because he wouldn't let anything happen to her.

After about fifteen minutes, she finally felt more at peace, so she went in to talk to Chief. After a lengthy conversation about what happened with Hunter, and what her input was as far as how to handle the situation. Chief was satisfied the incident was over, but he still insisted on moving Hunter to 'C' shift for the comfort of the crew. He placed a report in Hunter's file, and suspended him for the remainder of the shift to separate the two of them. Hunter would start the next time 'C' shift came around. After that, he was dismissed.

*　　*　　*

As he closed the door behind him, Hunter leaned against the wall. He mulled through his mind on his next step with Casey, while he eavesdropped on her conversation with Chief. Under normal circumstances, he wouldn't be able to hear through the door, but during the last year or so, he didn't feel 'normal' at all. He felt a lot of anger inside of him. Blocks of time seemed to be missing from his memory as well. He would wake up in his bed, yet feel as if he had been awake the entire night. Furthermore, he had an unusual amount of strength, and his hearing was heightened, like that of an animal. While he didn't mind the new abilities, the anger and lack of sleep made him more on edge.

He put his ear closer to the doorframe to listen to the conversation between Chief and Casey, with renewed interest when he heard her mention her vacation and Jesse.

*　　*　　*

Casey was still on a mission to take care of Jesse. He was a rock for her when she needed him, and she was not going to let him down. She told Chief what she thought and why. He agreed that the two of them needed a vacation, so he gave them two weeks together, as long as Casey took the other two weeks at a different time in the year. It was a fair agreement as far as Casey was concerned.

Her next step was a rather heated discussion about it with the A.N.G.E.L.s. They weren't happy about the Hunter incident, but were pleased that Chief moved him.

The conversation about the vacation made them uncomfortable as well, especially with Hunter shifting in front of her again. However, they understood the need for some time off. Derek and Mark were going to go with Casey, leaving the Colonel to keep an eye on things in Colorado.

The private discussion later with Mark about the trip was a lot more heated. His main concern was her safety. She finally alleviated his concerns, by letting him and Derek share an adjoining room with her, leaving Jesse's room on the other side of them. He and Derek were also going to be doing everything they did. Sometimes it would be from a distance where she might not see them, and sometimes it would be in the same tour group as they were in. Casey would also book all flights together, so there would be no missing each other in flight. They would be within a couple seats of each other at all times. They were going to take care of the travel plans the next morning.

Chapter 8

Trip of a Lifetime

Hunter had a short time to put his plan into effect. He knew Casey and Jesse were going on a two-week vacation in two weeks, and he had to find out where. He decided to tail Casey for the next couple of days to find out what he could.

He sat outside her house, but several houses down the road so he would blend into the neighborhood. Nothing looked out of place, but the hair on the back of his neck stood on end. Someone was close from the other side. He felt it when Casey was around, but this was stronger. It was an overwhelming sense of power. Under normal circumstances, he would talk to his boss about it, but he and his boss were not in agreement at that moment. His boss was a commanding and controlling woman who was used to getting what she wanted. While he respected that, he didn't agree with her assessment of the situation regarding Casey.

He sat up in his seat when he saw Casey and a man walk out of her house. So, there was someone else in her life. He pulled out his cell phone and took a photo of the man. He couldn't get a clear picture though; due to the sunglasses he wore and the distance. The man looked familiar to him. Deep down, something inside him told him he knew him from somewhere…another time, another place. He decided to follow them to see if he could get a better look at the man with Casey. Obviously, someone else was involved, and he would have to move to plan 'B' and take matters into his own hands. Casey's time was up.

*　　*　　*

Mark went with Casey to the travel agency. They pretended they were both planning a trip to Australia, and while they waited for the agent to finish with her client, they chitchatted as if they just met, but got along great. They talked about different things one could do in Australia since Casey had been there before. Mainly, it was all for show for the receptionist.

The travel agent came into the reception area. "Hi, I'm Courtney."

Casey shook her hand as she stood. "Casey Carter."

"What can I do for you?"

"I'd like to book a trip for me and my friend to Australia," Casey said.

"Ya know," Mark said, pretending to be in thinking mode. "You seem to know your way around there. Would you mind if my brother and I hooked-up with you and your friend?"

"Oh, not at all." Casey smiled. "The more, the merrier."

"Great!" He stood up. Then he put his hand out and said, "Colby Leighton."

"Nice to meet the both of you," Courtney said. "So, am I to understand that you both want to book a trip to Australia – you with your brother, and you with your friend?"

"Yes, ma'am." Mark grinned. He spoke with a thick, Texan accent that he normally didn't have. Casey liked it. And boy was he pouring on the charm. All one saw was his smile for most of the time they were in the office.

Courtney smiled, as she led them to her office. "Then, by all means, follow me. This will make my job easier."

They left about an hour later with confirmation numbers, flights, hotels, and a couple of tours. Among the tours were a glass-bottom boat ride and diving on the reef, as well as hiking up the Sydney Harbour Bridge, and a Jeep drive into the Outback to watch the sunset on Mt. Uluru. Casey was confident that Jesse was going to love it. She was beside herself with excitement and anticipation for when she would get to tell Jesse at work in two days.

*   *   *

As soon as the two left the travel agent's office, Hunter ducked in. As they walked away, he noticed that they were excitedly discussing what was on the paper Casey held – probably an itinerary. He needed to find out where she was going.

"Good morning. Can I help you?" Courtney asked, as she walked out of her office.

"Hello, the name's Allen Hutchins." Hunter smiled, pulling every chivalrous quality he had in his arsenal. He knew this would be a tough sell. "I need to book a vacation."

"Certainly, I have fifteen minutes before my next appointment. Please follow me," Courtney said, as she walked into her office. She looked up at him when he sat in the seat across from her "Now, where would you like to go?"

"Where are most people traveling to at this time of the year?" he asked. "This traveling thing is new to me, but I've come into some money recently, and decided I needed a vacation."

"Well, hmm, being that it's October, usually people are heading south of the equator where it's spring. For example, I just had a group of people book for Australia."

"Australia, huh?" He smiled to himself. This was almost too easy.

"Yes. The weather there is nice this time of year."

"Really?"

"Oh! Definitely! Their spring starts in the first weekend of October. The flowers are in bloom and the beaches are open once again. It's gorgeous this time of year."

"Do you have any brochures I can look at?" he asked, hoping she would leave the office so he could grab the papers from Casey's appointment.

"No need. Thanks to technology, I have the brochures right here on my computer." She smiled, turning the computer screen toward Hunter.

"I like to take things home to look at them though. I would prefer brochures." He glanced at his watch, knowing he wouldn't have much time before her next appointment.

"I would be happy to print some out for you. What are your interests?" She slid the paperwork from the previous appointment into a folder, before she rested it in her drawer to file for later. She was pleased everything from the previous appointment was all taken care of and paid for, and couldn't hide her excitement of sneaking another one in before her boyfriend arrived for lunch. She knew he would understand if she were a few minutes late. After all, the commission from another trip would benefit both of them.

Hunter took a deep breath. She was testing his patience.

"Courtney, I'm going to go for lunch." Her receptionist poked her head in. "Or do you want me to wait?"

"Don't worry about me. Warren will be here in about ten minutes. I'll be fine here with Mr. Hutchins until then."

"Okay. See you after lunch," she said, before leaving the office.

"Now, what are you mainly interested in seeing while you are in Australia?" Courtney asked, as she looked up at Hunter, who now stood as he leaned on her desk.

"I don't have time to play around anymore."

"I'm sure you don't." She looked at him, confused. Her eyes became wide, when she saw his eyes turn black as coal, and his body suddenly shifted to some creature with reddish-black skin and scales.

"We need to talk," the creature hissed.

*   *   *

By the time she got to the firehouse the morning of her shift, Casey felt as if she would explode with excitement. She checked the listing, and found that she and Pete were on ambulance crew number two today, with KC Cross and Kim as team number one. The rest were on the fire rig.

Casey tossed her clothes bag on one of the second set of beds in the ambulance crew room, before she ran down to the meeting room for shift-change.

When she got down there, Jesse was already sitting in a chair. About ten minutes remained before the meeting started. Casey sat down beside him with a grin on her face.

"Okay." He suspiciously eyed her. "You look as if you are about to burst. What's going on?"

Casey glanced around the room to see many of people from both shifts already in there, so she pulled him out of the room to talk to him.

*   *   *

Hunter looked up when Casey walked into the conference room and sat down next to Jesse. He narrowed his eyes at her. He discovered her secret. His mission was now to figure out who the mystery man was, as well as how to get to Australia.

When they left the conference room, Hunter went back to reading the newspaper. He took a particular interest in an article.

"'Still No Answers in A Local Travel Agent's Death.'" Kim read the title of the article aloud, as she looked over Hunter's shoulder. "What happened?" She sat down in her seat.

"Don't know." Hunter shrugged. "It seems when her boyfriend came in to get her for lunch two days ago, she was dead. They are looking for some guy named Allen Hutchins, who was her last appointment before the receptionist left, but have yet to find him. I guess it was a bloody mess. It says here the scene was 'almost animalistic.' Weird, huh?"

"The world is getting more and more insane as the days go by." Kim sighed, shaking her head. "Gotta wonder who would do something like that to another human being."

"Yeah. Some people should be caged."

*   *   *

"What's going on, Casey?" Jesse asked when they got outside.

She decided she would be able to see anyone who was coming up to them while outside. "I have a secret to tell you, but you have to keep it."

He crossed his arms. "What is it?"

"Promise to keep it a secret?"

He rubbed his chin, studying her for a moment before he nodded. "Yeah, I'll keep it."

"If you tell, it won't happen. Are you sure you can keep it?"

He chuckled. "This must be big. Yeah, I will keep the secret."

"That means you cannot tell anyone – not even Carrie-Anne. I know you don't like to keep secrets from her, and under normal circumstances I wouldn't ask you to, but this is important."

"Casey, are you okay?"

"Yes. Can you do it? Can you keep the secret?"

He studied her for another moment before he nodded. "Yes. I give you my word that I won't tell anyone."

"You can when we come back, but not before."

"Agreed." He nodded. "Now spill!"

Casey looked both ways to make sure they were alone before she quietly said, "I talked to Chief the other day, and got us an overlapping two-week vacation together in two weeks – the first two weeks of your vacation."

"Cool." He smiled, pleased. "So, is where we're going the secret?"

"Yes."

"Then, where are we going?"

"You have given a lot of your time, patience, and heart to me over the last couple of years. The more I thought about it, the more I could not think of a better way to repay you than to take you on the trip of your dreams."

He had a smile on his face as he shook his head. "Casey, you didn't have to do that."

"It's okay. I used some of the money from Jack. I know he would approve. I also got a discount."

"How did you get a discount?"

"Well, it was really cool. See, I was in the travel agent's office talking to this guy about Australia. And in talking to him, he and his brother were going to go too. So, we talked to the agent, and she gave us a discount since it was technically being booked as a group rate."

"That's…wait!" He looked at her, wide-eyed, when it him where she said they were going. "Casey," he put his hands on her shoulders, looking directly in her eyes as his heart skipped a beat, "did you just say Australia?"

"Yes." She grinned. "We are going to Australia. You took care of me. The least I could do was give you the trip of your dreams – the Great Barrier Reef and Mount Uluru included."

"Casey!" he shouted, and tightly hugged her as he spun her around in the air. "Are you serious?" He put her down, leaving his hands on her arms.

"You promised you wouldn't tell."

"In two weeks, we're going to Australia?"

"Yes. I hope you have your passport."

"I do! This is so cool. This is awesome. Thank you," he shouted, excited, and hugged her again.

She turned him toward the incoming firefighters. "Calm down, we have company."

"Yeah." He turned back toward her ready to erupt with excitement. "Thank you," he said quietly, as he grinned.

"You need to get yourself under control." Casey chuckled. "Think you can relax on that vacation?"

"Oh, yeah! Wow!"

"What's up with you, McFadden?" Will asked. "You look as if you're about to burst."

"I'm excited," he admitted.

"About?"

He put his arm around Casey with a smile that wouldn't stop. "I finally got her to cooperate."

"What does that mean?" Will asked.

"Don't worry about it." Jesse waved him off. "It's all good."

"Whatever." Will shook his head, as he, Marty, and Jeff went into the firehouse. Will was not a morning person anyway. And with Jesse not answering him directly, he didn't have the patience to pursue it at that moment.

As soon as they were in the firehouse, and out of sight, Jesse shouted, "Wooo-hoo!" He cheered and jumped into the air.

"Get it out of your system?" Casey smiled, watching him for a few minutes as he danced in joy.

"Yeah…yes!" he shouted one more time and did a fist pump. "Sweet!"

Casey laughed. "Contain yourself, Jess!"

"Yeah." He looked at her and grinned. "This rocks!"

"I'm glad you like my surprise."

"Like it? I love it!" He hugged her. "Two weeks, huh?"

"Yeah. Can you contain yourself for two weeks…starting in five minutes? We have a shift to work."

"Focus," he said, forcing himself to calm down, as he paced to get out some of the energy. "We're really going to Australia?"

"Yes, we are. Control yourself, though."

"Focus," he said, as he resumed pacing. "All right. We have to release 'C' shift. Focus." He looked up at her with a grin and wiggled his eyebrows.

Casey laughed, as she looped her arm through his, pulling him into the firehouse with her. "Focus."

"I can do this. Keep my mouth shut."

"You got it."

"I can do this," he said to himself. After they passed Margo's desk, Jesse put his arm over her shoulders and kissed her cheek. "Thanks, sis."

"This should cover all thirty-six years of our birthdays."

"And then some. Okay," he said, as they stood in front of the conference room door, "I'm calm. I'm focused. I can do this." He took a deep breath.

"The trip of your dreams depends on it," Casey warned.

"Oh, this is mean."

"But is it worth it?"

"Oh yeah!"

"Good. Then let's go," Casey said, and they went into the room.

Casey sat down by Pete, as Jesse sat down by Will. Chief came into the room and released 'C' shift before starting their day.

*   *   *

Jesse was hysterical to watch all day. People would ask him what was going on, and some would even attempt to guess. They guessed that he was engaged, that Carrie-Anne was pregnant, or that maybe he finally bought a house. He brushed them off, said he was in an exceptionally good mood, and left it at that.

Over the next two weeks on her days off, Casey would go shopping for things she knew she would need for the trip. She bought twenty rolls of film, sunscreen, a new bathing suit, and a few new outfits. She also made sure to pack her regular camera, along with her underwater one for the reef. Casey had everything packed a couple days before they were scheduled to go, making sure it was the right weight for the plane. She was excited for Jesse – this was the trip of his dreams. As excited for him as she was, she was even more thrilled that Mark was going with them, and they would be able to share the trip together.

*   *   *

"So," Jesse asked on their way to the airport, "What do you know about our fellow travelers?"

"Well, they're brothers from Texas."

"Oh boy." He smiled. "This is going to be fun. We're going to have to translate Texan on one end and Australian on the other."

"Aw, come on, where's your sense of adventure? The brother I met seemed like a nice guy. Besides, I've got you watching my back, right?"

"Right."

With that, they drove the rest of the way to the airport, while Casey filled him in on what she knew about the brothers, Colby (Mark) and Clinton (Derek) Leighton. The cover story was that they were the only boys to oil tycoon, Bo Leighton. They moved near Denver about three months ago, due to the opening of a new branch of their business, Leighton Western Wear. After three months of hard work, they were finally confident enough to take a vacation, which was supposedly where Colby ran into Casey at the travel agency.

Casey and Jesse met the guys at the airport, and introduced each other before they headed toward security and their terminal.

It was a long flight, but well worth it. The first day they were in Sydney, they hiked the Sydney Harbour Bridge, along with a couple other small tours. One of which, included the Sydney Opera House. Then the four of them enjoyed dinner together down in the dining room of the hotel, before Casey and Jesse headed out to look around town and do a little shopping.

Casey picked up a souvenir for each of the A.N.G.E.L.s, but she told Jesse they were for her. She also got a t-shirt for her and a matching one for Mark. When Jesse asked her about it, she told Jesse the bigger one was for sleeping.

When they finished shopping, they returned to the hotel and watched a movie, before separating for the night at about eleven o'clock.

About ten minutes after Jesse left, Casey got a knock on the adjoining room door. It was two short and followed by three more in succession. It was so quiet she almost missed it.

"Yeah?" She asked at the door.

She heard two short knocks, followed by four more. She opened the door.

"Hey." Mark smiled, walking in with Derek. "I see Brother Jesse's gone to bed, eh?"

She rolled her eyes with a smile. "You know he went to bed. You guys were probably waiting for him to leave."

"Of course." Derek sat down on the bed. "We waited until we heard his door open and close before we knocked. Good thinking, putting him on the other side of us."

"So, what does Jesse think of the brothers Leighton?" Mark leaned against the dresser with his arms crossed.

"He likes you guys. Your accents crack me up though." Casey chuckled. They weren't using them at that time, but whenever Jesse was around, the Texas slang was evident.

"Well, what's not to like?" Derek shrugged. "We're jus' a couple a' good ol' boys lookin' for a good time," he said with his Texan accent.

Casey smiled as she asked, "So, what have you guys been doing all night while we were out?"

"Watching you shop." Derek sighed. "My word, you are picky."

"Of course. I'm not one who likes to buy just any old thing. I buy things for a reason."

Mark raised an eyebrow. "Oh yeah?"

"Yep."

"Care to explain?"

"What?"

"The t-shirts?" Mark asked.

As soon as he asked the question, Casey smiled. "You're incorrigible." She shook her head. She went to her suitcase and handed their souvenirs to them, leaving hers and the Colonel's in the suitcase.

Mark smiled in satisfaction. "I take it the other one is for the Colonel?"

"Yes. Well, there is one for him and one for me. You guys are a pain to surprise." She handed Mark his t-shirt.

"Where's mine?" Derek pouted playfully.

"Relationships have their privileges. Thanks, hon," he briefly kissed her lips, as he held the t-shirt. "I appreciate knowing that when I'm not with you, that you are still thinking of me."

"How could I not?" she asked. "You are always in my thoughts."

Derek rolled his eyes with a smile. "Enough sappiness."

"Oh," Mark nudged him with his foot, "you love it and you know it."

"Yeah, consider it living vicariously," Derek admitted. "I'm just glad one of us was able to find a good woman who understands the constraints we have to live by."

Casey looked at him, pleasantly surprised. "Thank you."

"Hey, I'm all for it," Derek said. "I wish Jack could have had the privilege of seeing it for himself."

"Yeah." Casey sighed. "I miss him big time."

"Ah-ah-ahhh," Mark said, wrapping his arms around her from behind. "None of that on our vacation." He kissed her cheek before he sat on the dresser behind her. "This is a time for fun and relaxation."

"But still to be on our toes." Then Derek mentioned, "Which reminds me, the doors are staying open between the rooms, the Colonel's orders. Hope you're okay with that."

"It's no problem. It's not any different, than when you guys are sleeping on the couch in the house."

"True. The Colonel also said for you to relax and have fun. He said you deserved it."

"He's a good guy too." She smiled as she thought of the Colonel. "Sometimes I wish I had known you guys when you were a full team."

Mark sighed, shaking his head. "Yeah. We've lost some good ones over the years." He rested his chin on her shoulder as he hugged her from behind, deep in thought.

"Remember Seth?" Derek looked at Mark with a smile of remembrance.

"Who's Seth?" Casey asked, as she held onto Mark's arms.

"Oh! He was a character!" Mark chuckled. As the memory of what happened to him ran through his mind, Mark sighed. "He was killed in Zimbabwe. We were rescuing a POW, when we were found out by some local guerrillas. We almost made it to the rally point when they finally caught up to us. When he was shot, he wasn't more than ten feet from the chopper."

"The Colonel grabbed him by his pants at his waistband, and dragged him to the chopper," Derek continued. "He held pressure on Seth's wounds the entire ride back to the ship. He wasn't about to give up on him."

"Seth was shot in the upper back and mid-thigh. He didn't have a prayer." Mark sighed. "One bullet nicked his heart and the other one hit the main artery in his thigh – which, as you know, the thigh wound alone could kill him."

She nodded in understanding. "Yeah, that one is a bugger when it's cut or hit."

"He was only twenty-three."

"He was the original Angel7," Derek added. "Eight, nine, and ten have stories of their own."

"Who were they?" Casey asked out of curiosity.

"Angel8 was Ariel." Derek smiled. "She was beautiful."

"She was Seth's partner." Mark hugged her closer to himself. "She was also his other-half. When he died, part of her died with him."

"She went to the extreme." Derek shook his head. "She almost seemed to have a death wish."

"That was granted when she turned thirty," Mark added.

"What happened?" Casey asked. "Am I allowed to know?"

"She was on an assignment in China where she was undercover as a girlfriend of a 'big fish' we were trying to catch," Derek started. "It took him a while, but he found out she was the one supplying the information that kept getting him caught. When he did, as a message to all of us, he cut her body up and sent it to the base in pieces."

"Wow!" Casey looked at him, stunned. "I can't believe you guys are mixed up in this stuff."

"These guys play hardball," Mark warned. "That's why we want you on your toes."

"And why we are on your heels as well," Derek pointed out.

"Um, what happened to nine and ten?" Casey asked, not sure if she wanted to know.

"Angel9 was Jen. Jen was Jack's girl for a while." Derek looked up at her. "That is, until she was taken-out at twenty-eight."

"Really? Jack had a lover?" Casey was happy for him, but felt sad for him for having to lose her as well.

"They were a good match," Mark added. "You would have liked her."

"What happened to her?"

"She and Jack were in India, where they were sent in to retrieve valuable information that would put a major dent in the resistance. When the resistance found out, they cornered them. They were both shot, but hers was fatal." Casey could see the memories on Derek's face as he went on, "Keith and I came upon them as the resistance took off, leaving them for dead. Jack held her as she was slipping. It was…." he shook his head. "We brought her back with us. It was a hard one to get through though. Jack was taken down for a little while after that one."

"Was that when he was shot in the shoulder and abdomen?" Casey asked, thinking through the times he came home from assignments that would fit that time period.

"Yeah."

"He seemed unusually upset when I visited him in the hospital for that one," she said. "It took him a good couple of months before he was back to his old self. He was hurt badly, but his heart was hurt worse. He said it was because he lost a close team member. I wish I would have known."

"There's no way you could have." Mark hugged her. "It took us a while, but we got him swung back around."

"What about Angel10?" Casey asked. "Who was that?"

Derek and Mark both chuckled, as Mark said, "He was a character. His name was Ricky, and he had a heart that was as big as he was. It was his sense of humor and his heart that brought Jack back."

"He was good too, though," Derek added. "He was killed when he was thirty-three. He was in Kenya when his plane went down."

"His partner at the time was Keith. Keith was the one who pulled him from the wreckage." Mark sighed. "Even though he was in extreme pain, he still tried to make Keith smile while they waited for the extraction."

"The problem?" Derek said to Casey. "He broke his left leg clean-through at the femur – the bone was even exposed. Keith took his belt and used it as a tourniquet, but it only slowed down the bleeding."

"Jack and I were the two sent in to get them," Mark continued. "Jack carried Ricky to the chopper, while I helped Keith. Keith was banged up pretty badly from the crash as well." He stopped for a moment in remembrance before he said, "Jack talked to Ricky the entire time, keeping him distracted and conscious. When we were almost to the ship, he began to lose consciousness. Jack refused to give up on him, though, and kept waking him." Mark shook his head as he said, "He lost too much blood though. He died in the ship on the way back to the base. He was a good guy."

Casey nodded in understanding. "He sounds it."

"Now, years later," Derek continued, "we've gone from ten to four."

Casey looked up at Derek, questioning whom it was she didn't know. "Four?"

"You are a part of us now…whether you wanted to be or not."

"I don't mind." She smiled. "As I said, I wish I could have known all of them."

"I'm glad we have been able to shield you from the horrid part of it for as long as we have," Mark said. "And since we are close to finishing this leg of the race, I'm glad to have the chance to work with you during it too."

"If there is anything I can do to help, I would count it as a privilege," Casey offered. "What you guys have done, and have gone through, is amazing. Just being a part of you guys makes me feel honored. I respect and admire you guys and your fallen teammates."

Derek looked at her, taken aback. "Thank you."

"Yes. Thank you." Mark kissed her cheek.

"Jack did his best to train me," she said. "So, I hope I can be of use to you guys."

"I'm sure you and your training will come in handy," Mark said.

"It already has," Derek pointed out. "Speaking of which, the Colonel has some information on your friend from the fire department."

"Which one?" she asked. "Hunter?"

"Yes. It seems he was trained for his paramedic/firefighter in the military on the first half of his enlistment. The second half he was Naval Intelligence."

"Oh really?"

"Yes. The Colonel said to watch what you say around him, and what he hears. His concern is that he not only came in a month before Jack died, but also somehow finagled his way onto your shift," Mark warned. "Not to mention the fact that he seems to have a strong interest in you and is obviously an Unnatural."

"I have only seen him shift twice in the entire last year," she said. "Besides, he's no longer on my shift."

"That doesn't mean he's not around," Mark warned. "Don't trust him."

"I don't."

"Well, lovely lady." Mark hugged her. "Hate to do this, but we have a long day tomorrow. Think you can get some rest?"

"Yep."

"That's my cue." Derek smiled, standing. "Come on over when you're ready."

Mark nodded in appreciation. "Be there in a few."

After Derek went through the doorway, Mark turned Casey around in his arms and kissed her. "I love you," he said, looking into her eyes a few moments later. "I love that I'm always on your mind. I love that you're always on your toes. I love that you respect and honor me, and everything we work for. I also love that you love me."

"I do."

He walked her over to the window. The view of the Sydney Harbour Bridge and the Sydney Opera House from Casey's room was spectacular. The water was calm outside, so the lights from the Bridge and the Opera House danced lightly on the water. The stunning view entranced Casey for several minutes, as Mark wrapped his arms around her.

"Why is your unit called A.N.G.E.L.?"

"It's an acronym that stands for: Available to Nurture God's Eternal Love. It means that we are being used by God, to show His love wherever and whenever it's needed. We are kind of God's Special Operations Unit."

"If that's the case, and I'm an A.N.G.E.L., then –"

"Then, you are being used of God. All Christians are His elite force on this planet. He put us here to do His work. Sometimes He uses His spiritual angels to provide those unexplainable miracles we receive throughout our lives, and sometimes He uses those in the physical realm. Consider them support staff. They are those who pray, playing a pivotal role in bringing power and strength to those who need it the most. There are also people who, under the direction of the Spirit, bring a special blessing to His children. They could be something as simple as giving smiles and support to someone who is in their darkest hour, or providing a meal where there is none, or even a mysterious checks or money that suddenly appears when you least expect it, but when you need it the most. The field agents are a unique breed. Some are called missionaries, who have enlisted to do His work daily at home or abroad, and some are those of us who are sent in because we can handle the worst of the worst. We do our best to retrieve and rescue those of His who are POWs for His name. Sometimes we get to them in time, sometimes we don't. But, be rest assured in the knowledge that The Lord's angels are everywhere, and He has them looking out for you."

"I see."

"You're an A.N.G.E.L., and as an A.N.G.E.L., you need to know that there is a group of special operations A.N.G.E.L.s representing each country. Though over the years, some have been battled into extinction. As you can see, our unit has been knocked down to four."

"What happens when we're gone?" she asked.

"Hopefully someone else will come along and pick up the torch. We need more soldiers for Him. That will only happen when people take a chance and talk to others about Him. Hopefully they will come along before we are gone, so we can help train them."

"It's a circle of life thing, then?"

He sighed, as he stared out the window with his arms wrapped around her. "Something like that."

"And we need the next generation to take a stand?" she asked.

"And pray that complacency won't win out over the call."

"Well said."

Mark stood behind Casey, lost in his own thoughts. He knew that with the risks they took, just like the A.N.G.E.L.s of the past, his time might be up sooner than he thought. He also knew that no reward came without risk. "Casey?"

Casey couldn't take her eyes off the serene scene before her. "Yes?"

"Will you, when this is over…will you consider marrying me?"

As soon as he asked the question, Casey spun around in his arms. She spun so fast that he took a step back. "Are you okay?" he asked, slightly taken aback.

Shock written all over her, she asked, "What did you just ask?"

When he realized it was out of surprise and not a bad reason, he took both of her hands into his, and looked into her eyes as he said, "I asked, if you, Casey Ann Carter, will marry me?"

"Are you serious?"

"In our lives, we need to take the good when we can get it. And you, my lovely lady, are one of the best things I've ever had. So yes, I'm serious. Will you marry me?"

"Yes!" She smiled in excitement. She threw her arms around his neck, and hugged him tightly. "I love you, Mark Allen English."

"Good." He chuckled. "It helps a marriage when the partners love each other."

Casey didn't say anything. In her excitement, she kissed him. After a moment, he wrapped his arms around her, and the kiss turned sensual. It lasted for several long minutes, as they relaxed in each other's arms.

Mark smiled as he reached up and tucked her hair behind her ear. "I love kissing and holding you."

"I love kissing and holding you too. Your kisses are so soft. There's so much power behind them too."

He winked at her. "Just wait until I don't have to hold back."

"Any day now," Derek called from their room.

They burst out in laughter as they held each other. "Be there in a minute!" Mark yelled to Derek, before he turned back to Casey and said, "Now, you can't wear a ring because of our cover, but would this work instead?" he asked, pulling out a gold cross necklace with a diamond in the shape of a heart in front of it. It had a tiny gold angel behind the cross, reaching around to the front with its hand holding onto the diamond.

"Yes!" Casey smiled. "I will only take it off for my shower."

"That'll work." He reached around and fixed the clasp, as it hung from her neck, kissing her neck while he was down there.

"Um, Mark, that's not...." Casey took a deep breath. "I thought you had to, um, go."

He looked up at her, with his hands on the sides of her face, and reminded her, "Just wait until I don't have to hold back."

Casey stared at him in amazement. She could not believe that this late in life, God provided her with this absolutely wonderful man. It seemed that God was looking out for her after all.

"On that note, sweet dreams, my little angel." He winked, before he quickly kissed her and left for his room.

Casey turned back toward the view out her window, sighing as she held the necklace. It was beautiful. It was perfect. She was so happy right then; she knew absolutely nothing would be able to ruin it.

*   *   *

The next day, the group headed up north, stopping at a couple small towns on the way. They spent the night in a hotel on the edge of the Outback. The next morning, they went on a two-day drive into the Outback. The roads were marked for them to take, along with a map on how to get to the designated area for the sunset. The four of them shared a Jeep, since it was less expensive for both groups.

"Whoa! Look at that!" Jesse pointed out a couple kangaroos hopping toward a water hole.

Casey pulled over so they could get some photos. They all got out to enjoy the view. They were on their way to Mount Uluru, where they were going to watch the sun set behind it, and then camp out there before driving back the next day.

Derek grinned, taking a couple pictures. "Wow! That's somethin' ya don't see in Texas."

"Only in Australia." Jesse shook his head. "Man, I love this place."

Casey smiled at Jesse's reaction, pleased. "I take it you like your trip so far?"

He had almost a permanent grin on his face since they landed. "You have no idea."

"Thanks for lettin' us tag along," Mark said, taking a couple shots with his camera. "With the extra comp'ny, it adds jus' that much more fun."

Derek leaned on the hood of the Jeep, crossing his arms. "I agree. It's also nice that you're Americans like we are. In a foreign country, it's nice to hear the American accent."

"Yeah, so we can all look stupid together when they're spouting off that Aussie lingo," Casey said with a smile.

"You two don't do too badly in the translatin' though," Mark pointed out. "You seem t' have a pretty good grasp a' it."

"That's just because I have wanted to come here since I was a little kid," Jesse said. "I have been a student of Australia ever since I had to write my first report in school."

"Knowing that makes this that much more special," Casey said, pleased.

"And coming here with my best friend makes it that much more special for me. Thanks, sis," Jesse said, putting his arm over her shoulder.

They watched as several more kangaroos hopped to the water hole before taking back off for Mt. Uluru. They passed several kangaroos that acted as if they were racing the Jeep for a couple of miles, before they turned off toward a water hole. At one point, five kangaroos flanked one side of the Jeep, and three on the other, almost escorting them down the road. The various memories this trip generated was something none of them would ever forget.

*   *   *

They stopped in Alice Springs for lunch, doing a little shopping while they were there. Then they grabbed some food for dinner, taking with them to Mount Uluru. They were going to picnic there while they watched the sun set.

When they arrived, quite a few people were already at the mountain. It was a spectacular sight. They watched the sunset cast its hues of red, gold, and yellow off the mountain as it went down. Casey was amazed, and Jesse was beside himself in awe. Casey saw him even pinch himself to make sure he was really there. This, of course, delighted her to be there for his dream to come true. She prayed the rest of the trip was as incredible as the first half.

*   *   *

The next day, the group enjoyed the Outback for several hours, before heading back to turn in the Jeep. That night they stayed in a hotel, and then headed to Cairns for the Great Barrier Reef the next morning.

"I'm way too excited to sleep," Jesse said, as he and Casey sat on the porch of his hotel room in Cairns at about eleven that night. The view of the ocean from his porch was heavenly – especially since their rooms were on the fiftieth floor. The hotel was across the street from the ocean, but since they were so high, it let for a spectacular view. They were so close. Casey could smell the salt water as the breeze came off the ocean, sweeping those streets that were along the coastline. The roar of the ocean always seemed to relax her.

"I know, but you're going to want the rest for tomorrow. We're going to be doing a lot of physical activity."

"Swimming in the Great Barrier Reef," he sighed, shaking his head. Tears came to his eyes as he said, "You have no idea how special this is to me. This is something I have wanted my whole life…and tomorrow I'm actually going to do it. I've always wanted to see Mount Uluru, but to see it at sunset was…." he shook his head. "And now this? You have no idea how happy I am."

"I'm glad I could do it for you. Seeing you this happy makes me happy too."

He shook his head in unbelief with a smile on his face. "I don't want to go home. I want to stay here."

"I know, but reality will hit in about a week when we have to go back. Then you have to turn your time clock back around."

"You have to do it sooner," he reminded her. "I'll have two weeks to flip it back around. You only have three days."

"Don't remind me," Casey groaned. "And it's actually two days – we lose a day, due to the International Date Line."

"Really? That's so cool."

"For you." Casey rolled her eyes at him. "Not for me."

"Oh, you'll get over it."

"Yeah."

"Case," he took her hand into his, "I'm really fortunate to have the opportunity of having you in my life. I'm grateful to Jack for giving me the privilege to be your brother – even if it is by default. You are truly a good person."

"Thanks." She smiled. "I appreciate that. I appreciate you too."

"Someday, I wish you would take a chance on another man. It's been over a year since Mac died, and I don't remember you mentioning too many other men before him."

"Jesse, I don't –" she started, but Jesse cut her off.

"I know. I don't mean me. I am perfectly happy with Carrie-Anne. I wish you would be able to find someone to make you just as happy. You deserve it."

"Thanks, but –"

"You have to get over this trust thing."

"Jess, do you understand what happened to me?"

"I do. You've told me just about everything, that I know of, about your past regarding men. While I understand your apprehension, you do have a right to be happy. You have a right to find true love. You have given me the trip of my dreams, and made me the happiest man alive right now. I just wish you would find the man of your dreams, who could make you the happiest woman alive."

Casey sighed, smiling, thinking of Mark as she toyed with the necklace around her neck. "Someday."

"Um, I hate to point this out, but we're not getting any younger. We're already thirty-six years old."

"I know. And maybe someday God will give me the man of my dreams."

"What does the man of your dreams look like?" he asked out of curiosity, as he sat back in his chair.

"Well, I would want him to be protective of me, yet be able to give me some freedom as well. I am an independent person."

Jesse rolled his eyes. "Don't I know it."

Casey narrowed her eyes at him, and then smiled so he knew it was in jest, before she went on, "Anyway, he has to be able to protect me as well as my heart. I would like him to be sensitive, smart, honorable, and trustworthy. More on the private side regarding his life…and my life as well. I don't like my life publicized."

"I don't either."

"I would like him to be a man of integrity, and of high morals and principles. I want a man who knows what he wants, and knows how the world works – not someone who is naive. And most importantly, I want a man who honors and loves God, and who is a Christian. And if he's cute too, that will be a bonus."

"That's a pretty tall list."

"I'll only settle for the best."

"No man is perfect, Casey."

"I don't expect perfection. I expect what God wants me to have. If He wants me to stay single, I'm fine with that too."

"Ya know." He rubbed his chin. "You didn't mention anything about money in that."

"I don't care about money. I care about what is inside him. I want to know he's a man of strong integrity and honor. I want a man who knows me well enough that I don't even have to tell him if I'm upset. I want a man who knows when I need a hug and gives it to me."

"That's sweet. I hope and pray you find that man someday."

Casey sighed as she looked out at the ocean. "Someday."

Just then, there was a knock at the door. They had ordered room service that included soda and a pizza so they could sit and look at the ocean while they ate.

"I got it." He jumped up and went to the door.

He was back a few minutes later with the pizza. Then he went back for the two glasses and a pitcher of soda.

As they enjoyed the view and the meal, they were both lost in their own thoughts and feelings.

"Ya know," Jesse said, a couple minutes after they started eating, "I think I've reached the happiest point in my life, right here. Tomorrow will top it, but nothing will top tomorrow."

"Wait until you get married and maybe have a child," she said. "Those will probably top this."

"Not unless I bring them here. You have to understand just how long I have dreamed of this day."

"You'll remember it. And then you will file it in your 'happy times' box and add to it. Trust me."

"I will never be able to thank you enough."

"Then we're even. I will never be able to thank you enough for all you did for me."

"It's not a scorecard. It's called family."

Casey nodded, taking another sip of her drink. The coolness and carbonation felt good going down her parched throat, so she finished her drink. She refilled the glass as they sat quietly for a few more minutes, when she had a wave of nausea and dizziness overtake her. She grabbed her head hoping it would stop spinning. "Um, Jesse?"

"What?"

"I need to go back to my room."

He looked over at her in concern. "What's wrong?"

"I don't…whoa." She shook her head in an attempt to clear it. "Help me back to my room, please?"

"Sure."

He helped her to the door. On the way to her room, she slapped the wall next to Mark and Derek's room door, bracing her arm on the wall for a moment.

"Come on, Casey, you're getting sicker by the…whoa." He took a deep breath as the room spun. "We gotta hurry. I don't feel good either."

He practically carried her for the next couple of steps to her room door. Then he pulled her keycard out of her back pocket to unlock her door. He carried her into the room, helping her to the bed. "I have to go back to my room. I'll see you in the morning," he said as he set the card down on her dresser. He had to hold the walls on the way out the door. He was barely able to secure the door behind him before he made his way to his room.

Casey's head swirled out of control, even with her eyes closed it felt as if the room was spinning. She felt sick to her stomach, but couldn't keep her eyes open as she lay on the bed.

Less than a minute later, Derek and Mark rushed into the room. "What's wrong?" Mark knelt on the floor in front of her, with his hands on the sides of her face trying to get her to focus.

"I don't…." She shook her head to clear it. She felt her eyes roll back into her head.

Mark pulled her back up to a sitting position. "You have to help me, Casey," he said, worry written all over him. "I can't help you if you don't tell me what happened."

"Don't know." She shook her head as she did her best to focus on him. "We were eating, and…." She grabbed her head with her eyes closed. "Did Jesse make it back?"

"I'll check," Derek went to their room and peeked out the door. He was back a moment later. "Yeah. He's at least in the room anyway."

"You were eating, huh?" Mark said, thinking. "Was it room service?"

"Yes," she moaned.

"Were your drinks opened or sealed?"

"Opened. It was soda in a pitcher." Casey lay back on the bed, giving up the fight of whatever was in her system.

Mark moved her to the top of the other side of the bed, facing the sliding glass doors that led out to the patio. He tucked the pillow under her head in hopes that she would be able to rest better. He would have to let Derek know that he was not leaving her alone all night.

"What are you thinking?" Derek asked. The look in Mark's eyes told him that his mind was working on overdrive.

"That the drinks and/or food were drugged," Mark said.

Mark retrieved his cell phone from their room, while Derek went to the other side of the bed next to Casey. "Hey, Casey," Derek moved her hair out of her face, "can you open your eyes for me?"

She shook her head. "Mm-mm."

Mark paced on the other side of the bed, agitated. "I am going to text the Colonel."

Derek nodded. "Good idea."

Just then, they heard someone at the door, so Mark flattened himself against the wall, while Derek turned off the lamp next to them before slipping under the bed.

It took whomever it was a few minutes, but the door opened, and a man walked in the room. He gently closed the door before slowly walking in. "Casey?" he softly called.

Casey strained to focus on the voice. While her brain was foggy, she recognized the voice.

"Casey?" he called again. It was Hunter!

"Mmmm," Casey moaned as she struggled to wake. She didn't know where Mark or Derek were, but if Hunter was in there, Casey knew it was not a good situation for her to be in, especially with the way her body felt.

He made his way over to her side of the bed, and took a plastic bag out of his back pocket. His eyes shifted to pure black as he pulled a rag out of the bag. He was about to put it over her mouth when he heard Mark's voice. "Don't-move."

Hunter jumped. He looked at Mark, so he didn't see Derek's hands come out from under the bed, grab his ankles, and yank.

As Hunter hit the ground, Mark jumped over the bed, landing on top of Hunter. Meanwhile Derek scrambled out from under the bed, and opened the sliding glass door to the porch, giving them more room to work.

Hunter and Mark struggled for a few moments, before Mark got a couple of good jabs at him. As they continued to fight, they both made their way to their feet, punching and kicking each other, while Derek tried to figure out where to jump in.

Just as Derek was about to jump on Hunter's back, Hunter pulled out a knife. Mark and Derek both jumped back with their hands up in front of them. Hunter's black eyes glistened and a heinous laugh escaped his mouth.

Casey barely got her eyes open to see what was happening, but she had to fight the drugs to do it.

In a split second, when Hunter looked from Derek to Mark, with the knife in front of him ready to attack and with an evil grin on his face, Derek kicked Hunter in the lower back.

Hunter bent over backward, going down to the ground. Mark grabbed the knife and punched Hunter in the face. When Hunter's head went back, Derek grabbed him around the neck and flipped him out onto the deck.

As soon as they were out, Mark took Hunter's legs and flipped him over the railing, sending Hunter over the deck. He fell fifteen stories to his death.

She watched for a moment, before Casey closed her eyes again. She couldn't keep them open any longer.

As they came back into the room, Derek shook his head. "That was close." He breathed heavily, as he bent over with his hands on his knees.

"We have to get out of here before someone else comes at her, but she's unconscious," Mark said, with his hands on his hips, catching his breath.

"Well, there's no blood or evidence of a fight, so they're not going to know what room he came from," Derek said, thinking aloud. "Do we want to wait until she wakes up, since we don't know what she's been given?"

"Yeah. We need to pack, though. We'll let her sleep for a couple hours, and then force her to wake." Mark sighed. "I don't like the idea of staying here. That was too close."

"Why don't you call the Colonel while we pack, and see what he says?" Derek suggested, setting Casey's suitcase on the bed to fill it.

Mark nodded as he texted the Colonel. When the Colonel called him, Mark explained what happened. The Colonel was not happy, but was relieved Casey was still safe. He said to wake her up as soon as possible. And as soon as she was coherent, they were all supposed to check out and get out of there. In the meantime, the Colonel would get some things together on his end. He did not want them to fly home. The instructions were to fly to Tucson, Arizona, and he would meet them there.

Chapter 9

The Hornet's Nest

After they got Casey packed, Derek packed his and Mark's stuff while Mark continued to do his best to wake Casey.

"Come on, Casey. We need you to wake up, honey," Mark said, lightly tapping her cheek.

Just then, their room phone rang. "Got it," Derek said loud enough that if Jesse were conscious, he would hear it. He came in Casey's room a few minutes later. "That was the Colonel setting up our 'emergency at home' plan."

"Good." Mark nodded. "Now you have to call for her too."

"I'll give it about a half-hour," Derek said. "That should give you time to wake her. Take her to the shower if you have to. Wake her up!"

"I'm doing my best."

"Treat her as if she were drunk." Derek impatiently folded his arms. "We don't know when: a) they're going to come after her again; or b) if someone's going to come knocking on our door because of Mr. Dead guy down there." He nodded toward the balcony, where even as high up as they were, one could see the emergency lights flashing. "Just throw her in the shower and wake her. You've got a half-hour before we use plan 'B.'"

"All right." He sighed. Mark picked up Casey and flipped her over his shoulder before he carried her into the bathroom. "I'm sorry, Casey," he said, as he set her in the bottom of the tub. Then he reached up and turned on the cold water. He moved the showerhead so the water would hit her directly in the face.

It took Casey a couple seconds before she was able to move enough to block her face from the water.

"There ya go, keep coming," Mark coaxed.

"Shut that off!" she yelled, still trying to block the cold water.

He reached up, shut the water off, and then tossed her a towel. Casey was so relieved it was off, that she dropped her arms into the half-inch of water that had already accumulated in the tub.

"Wake up, or I'll do it again," Mark warned.

Casey rolled her head toward him and asked, "Was it my imagination, or was Hunter in my room?"

He hesitated in answering her for a moment as he dried her hair off with the towel. He decided his best approach in her semi-coherent state was to see what she remembered. "He was, but he isn't anymore."

"What do you mean?"

"What do you remember?"

"Eating pizza and drinking soda in Jesse's room."

"And then?"

"Um." She closed her eyes as she struggled to remember. It all seemed fuzzy, like a dream gone badly. "Jesse helped me to the room. And, um, the next thing I remember was you trying to find out what happened to us."

"Good. Then what?"

She closed her eyes as she struggled to remember. "Um…"

"Keep your eyes open. And you have to stand up so you can dry yourself. We need to get out of here."

"Why?"

"What else do you remember?" He pressed, drying off her arms and back as she stood.

"Hunter coming in and…was there a fight?"

"It was more than just a fight. He tried to kidnap you. Then when we stepped in, he tried to kill us, so –"

"You guys shoved him over the balcony!" Casey looked at him in wide-eyed horror as the vision of what happened flashed through her mind. "That wasn't true…was it? Please tell me that was a product of whatever I was drugged by."

"Yes, it's true. That's part of the reason why we need to get out of here. The other part is that we need to vacate before they come after you again."

"Who?"

"They." He gave her a 'you know what I'm talking about' look.

Casey nodded as she stood there in shock.

"Now, your stuff is all packed, so put on some clean, dry clothes," he said. "Do something with your hair, and let's get out of here."

"Hunter?" She looked at him in disbelief. "It was him?"

"Hunter was more than he seemed to be. His real last name wasn't Morgan, it was Hutchins. He was Naval Intelligence before he went rogue. The firefighter/paramedic training was real, but it was for his cover. His group has been trying to get what is in that strongbox for years. Greedy buggers. We were pawns in the whole game."

"So, Naval Intelligence is trying to get me?" Casey was so confused it made her head hurt.

"No. He is not with Naval Intelligence anymore. He's rogue, and an Unnatural one at that. Look, it's all very complicated, and I'm sure some day we can sit down and spell it all out for you. Until then, we have a dead body downstairs, and a group that's trying to kidnap you. We're not sure why they waited until you were here, and didn't do it in the U.S., but they're trying to get you nonetheless. We need to jet so: a) they don't get to you again; b) so Jesse's out of the crossfire; and c) so the Colonel can finally breathe. He wasn't too happy with the information he received when we called him. Just do us a favor and listen to everything we tell you to do – without questions – until we're out of here. After we've landed and are safe, then maybe we can spell out things. Deal?"

"Deal." Casey nodded. She grabbed her jeans, clean underclothes, a tank top, and a light over-shirt since it was the middle of the night, and changed in the bathroom. When she slipped on the over-shirt, the phone in her room rang.

Since Mark and Derek were still in their room, Casey answered it, "Hello?"

"Miss. Carter?"

"This is she."

"This is the front desk. I'm sorry to disturb you at this hour, but there's an urgent call from the US. It's your cousin. He said your aunt and uncle were in a car accident."

"Put him through immediately, please!" Casey said, slightly panicked. If they were calling her there, then it must be bad.

"Just a moment," the front desk clerk said before getting off the line to transfer the call.

"Casey?"

"Who is this?" Casey asked, stunned and confused.

"It's me," Derek said, walking into the room on his cell phone. "Don't hang up yet."

"What's going on?" She looked at him with the phone receiver in her hand.

"We're setting up your rapid departure. You're going to write a letter to Jesse explaining that your aunt and uncle were in a car accident. You are also going to give him the rest of the itinerary so he can finish his vacation, but you can leave without raising too many questions."

"How are you guys getting out of here?"

"Ours is already done. Go ahead and hang up the phone. The front desk will have a record of the call and the time length. Good job."

Mark came in with a plastic bag in his hand. "Hustle up and put your wet clothes in this bag."

"Thanks." Casey nodded. She was glad it was Derek, because she was trying to figure out how her cousins would have known where she was. She didn't tell anyone the location or itinerary for the trip.

It took Casey a couple minutes to pack and write the letter to Jesse because her head was still foggy at best. It broke her heart to leave in the middle of their trip, but she didn't want him to be caught in the middle of this mess. She wanted him to be safe. Before long, they were on their way downstairs. In the elevator, Mark explained the exit plan.

"We're going to check out while you stay in the hall. When you see us leaving, wait about five minutes, and then check out. We'll meet you outside."

"But, is that safe?" Casey asked. "I know I'm not supposed to ask questions, but I'm nervous."

"Don't be. We'll be outside watching you the entire time. Trust us, we won't let them get to you," Derek assured her.

She nodded, taking a deep breath. "All right."

The guys left her around the corner from the sight of the desk clerk, as they went to the front desk to check out. They argued about what to do with an employee of theirs who was caught stealing, and that they couldn't believe this would happen on their one vacation of the year. If Casey didn't know better, she would have believed them herself. As they walked out of the hotel, their "Texan slang" was in full gear as well.

Casey nervously glanced at her watch to time the five minutes. She wasn't comfortable being alone, especially since the police and emergency personnel were all over the place outside….and who knew who else was looking for her.

Finally, the five minutes were up so she went up to the front desk. While she was nervous, she turned it into an upset emotion since her aunt and uncle were supposedly in an accident.

"Hi," Casey said.

"Good evening. How can I help you?" The lady behind the desk asked.

"I'm Casey Carter from room 1521. I have to leave due to an emergency at home so I need to check out."

"Oh! You were the one who got the call about her family. I'm sorry. I do hope your aunt and uncle are okay and recover quickly."

"So do I," Casey said, signing the exit forms she gave her. When she finished, she said, "Um, I have a friend up in room 1525, Jesse McFadden. I don't want to wake him up, so can I leave him this message so he doesn't worry about me being gone in the middle of the night?" Casey held up the envelope.

"Oh! Of course. I'll slide it under his door tonight." She smiled. She took the envelope and wrote his name and room number on it. "Is there anything else I can do for you?"

"Um, no. I think that's…oh! What happened?" Casey asked, looking outside for the first time, faking concern.

"An accident. If you leave to the right, the emergency personnel would appreciate it."

"No problem. I do hope they are all right. That is a lot of people."

"All I know is that I'm to direct anyone leaving here out of their way."

"No problem. To the right, correct?"

"You got it. I hope you enjoyed your stay with us. I'm sorry you have to leave under the circumstances you do."

"Thank you for your concern," Casey said and left the hotel.

She walked outside, but didn't see the guys, so she walked to the right as instructed. About a block down the road, a taxicab was pulled over to the side of the road with its flashers going.

"Carrie," Mark said, getting out. "We've been waiting for you. What took you so long?" He winked at her so the driver wouldn't see, as he acted upset.

"Sorry, there was a bit of a hold-up."

"Everything's okay though, right?"

"Oh yeah." She nodded, as the cab driver opened the trunk for her backpack and suitcase. Her backpack held all of her camera equipment, film, and cameras, while her suitcase held everything else. Mark and Derek each had only one suitcase.

When she got in, Mark and Derek had her sit in between them. They dropped their Texan accents and spoke normally.

"To the airport in Cairns, please," Derek said to the driver.

"Sure, no worries," the driver said and took off.

About halfway there, he got a call on his radio, "Dispatch to 23."

"Go ahead for 23," the driver said into his CB radio.

"I have a fare for you."

"I'm currently enroute to the airport with the three passengers."

"Three or four?" he asked. As soon as it came across the radio, Derek and Mark immediately tensed, but stayed seated and quiet.

"There are only three, mate."

"Copy. Let me know when you're free."

"Copy. 23 out," he said, and replaced the receiver.

The guys were on edge for a few more minutes, before they saw the driver turn off the main highway, going the opposite direction from the airport. Casey looked over at Mark to see him reach into his pocket and pull out a knife. He took a moment to position it in his hand before he leaned forward, placed the knife on the driver's throat, and said, "Pull over, mate."

"No worries, mate. No need for the knife," he said, as he pulled the car over to the side of the road. As soon as the vehicle stopped, Derek placed his shirt over his hand and opened his door, pulling Casey out with him.

"Pop the trunk," Mark instructed the driver. "Go ahead and put it in park and turn off the engine."

They pulled out all their suitcases and bags. Derek then used his elbow to close the trunk, making sure not to leave any fingerprints. As soon as they stood on the sidewalk with their belongings, Mark took the knife, and in one swift motion, he slit the driver's throat. The blood splattered on the driver's side window, as well as all over the driver, the console, steering wheel, and the window in front of him. Mark tilted the driver's head back and to the side, so it rested on the headrest of the seat. Casey stared at him in horror. He wiped the knife off on the dead man's shirt, and wiped off his door handle with his own shirt. Then he slid out of the car on the side Derek left open for him, closing it with his hip.

"Um…." Casey looked from the driver to Mark, wide-eyed and in shock.

Mark grabbed Casey's suitcase from her and pulled her down the street by her wrist with Derek behind him. "Let's get out of here."

"They know we're trying to get to the airport, and are out of the hotel," Derek said to Mark, still carrying both his and Mark's suitcases.

"I'm thinking their base may be somewhere in Queensland," Mark mentioned over his shoulder, as the trio rapidly moved down the street toward a gas station. "They're everywhere! It's as if we stepped on a hornet's nest."

"Let's go to the bathroom, get you cleaned up, and then grab another taxi – different company – and get our behinds to a different airport," Derek said, looking over his shoulder, "like in Brisbane."

Mark nodded. "Sounds good."

The gas station was only a couple blocks down the road. When they got there, Derek and Casey went into the gas station to ask for the restroom keys, because Mark had some blood on him. He needed to wash it off as well as change his clothes. He also watched the area and the suitcases.

While Mark was in the men's room, Casey was in the women's restroom. With her heart racing, she splashed water on her face and re-brushed her hair. Her hands were shaky at best, but she muddled through. Then she went to the bathroom, washed her hands and brushed her teeth, before she went out to find Mark already out there. Derek had gone into the men's room only a few moments before.

"You look much better," he said, while keeping any eye out for any movement in the area.

They stood with their backs to the restroom doors, so they could keep an eye out in the other three directions. To their left was a fence with brush coverage behind it. To their right and in front of them was the parking lot, as well as the gas station pumps.

"I don't feel better. I'm terrified," she admitted, as she readjusted her backpack. Then she picked up her suitcase, ready to go when they were ready. "So, how do we grab another cab? It's the middle of the night."

"We'll just check with...." a noise on the roof cut him off.

When they looked up, two men leapt off the roof, knocking both of them to the ground. As soon as they hit the ground, two more scaled the fence and covered their mouths with a cloth. Casey tried to scream to Derek for help. As soon as she did, she inhaled whatever was on the cloth, and her head spun out of control. She saw Mark going unconscious as well, and knew they were in danger – they finally had them.

*   *   *

When she woke, a metal cord anchored to the wall shackled Casey's feet and hands. She had a splitting headache. She felt so sick, she thought she was going to vomit.

As she rolled over, she noted that the room measured approximately fifteen feet wide by fifteen feet long. The room itself was about two stories tall, with windows three-feet tall and four feet wide, going along the top of the outside wall of the room. Another bed occupied the room, but it was empty.

Casey rolled back over, faced the wall, and took several deep breaths, slowly letting her air out with each one. She had no idea where Mark or Derek were and that petrified her. She also had no idea where she was, and she knew from the position she was in, it wasn't a good thing.

After about forty-five minutes of lying there, still feeling drugged, the metal door to the concrete room opened. Two big guys came in, dragging Mark with them. His head dripped blood. His clothes had blood all over them, and his fingers were disfigured. If she had to guess, he had at least two or three fingers broken. The guys worked him over to the point where he couldn't even stand on his own anymore. They half-dragged him as he stumbled.

They took him over to the other bed, shackling him to the wall before walking over to Casey. She closed her eyes, pretending to be asleep. Her head spun from whatever they drugged her with, but she would do her best to stay alert as possible.

"She's a pretty one," one of the guys said. Both of them had thick Australian accents.

The other guy shook his head. "Yeah, it's a shame Jackie's the one who gets her."

"She enjoys torturing the pretty ones the most. She is twisted." He sighed, shaking his head.

"That she is." The other guy sighed. "Well, let's get it over with." He unshackled Casey's wrists, while the other guy unshackled her ankles. "It's a shame though."

They practically dragged her to the other room since she was still drugged. They then set her on a chair backward, and one of the guys tied her wrists and ankles around the back of the chair tightly with a rope so she couldn't move. The chair also had a headrest on it, so one of the guys flipped it back and laid her head on it before they both left the room.

A couple minutes later, a woman came in who looked to be about fifty or fifty-five years old, but very fit. She was thin, around six feet tall, had light brown, almost blond hair, and bluish-gray eyes. She pulled up a chair next to Casey. Then she sat on it backward, resting her chin on her crossed arms on the back of the chair.

"Hello, sweetie," she said to her with a thick Australian accent. Casey barely got her eyes open – her head swam. "Are ya comfy?"

"Not really," she mumbled.

"How 'bout ya wake up a bit more, love?" Jackie smiled. "We need t' talk."

Casey struggled for a couple more minutes before she was able to pick her head up to look at her.

"There, that's better, don't ya think? Now, how 'bout you tell me a story?"

"About what?"

She got off the chair and leaned down so she was less than three inches from Casey's face. She jerked her head back by her hair, and said, "Your brother took a box of mine and I want it back. Where is it?"

"I don't know." What she said was true. At that point, Casey had no idea if the Colonel moved it or not.

Jackie took Casey's head and slammed it into the headrest, making Casey's nose bleed, before Jackie yanked Casey's head back again. "How 'bout you cooperate with me? Your friend didn't and he's not looking too good right now."

When Casey didn't say anything, Jackie picked up a syringe from the table that already had a liquid in it. She pulled up Casey's shirtsleeve and jammed the needle into her arm, emptying the stinging solution into her system. Casey gasped and gritted her teeth as she did it, but didn't yell as much as she wanted to.

"We'll just let that soak in a bit before we try again," she said, tossing the syringe onto the table behind her. Jackie then sat backward in her chair again, and rested her folded arms on the back of it. She watched Casey, impatiently drumming her long nails on the back of the chair.

Within seconds, Casey's head started spinning. "Whoa!" Casey shook her head as she fought to clear it. Things were melting together, and she saw flashes of light around the room. Casey struggled to form a complete thought of any kind.

Jackie reached up and tucked a piece of Casey's hair behind her ear. "You're a pretty one. No wonder my son liked you."

Casey looked at her in confusion. "Your son?"

"You would know him as Hunter Morgan."

Casey looked toward Heaven, and screamed in her head, "Oh, God please help me! If she knows he is dead, I will be in more trouble than I already am!"

"Tsk, tsk, tsk," Jackie said, bringing Casey back to her reality, "it would be a shame t' mess up that pretty face."

Casey struggled to get her brain back under control. "What did you do to me?"

"Just gave ya a lil' something t' make you tell me the truth. It helps in situations like this."

Jackie got up and walked behind Casey again. She grabbed Casey's hair, and jerked her head back so hard, Casey thought Jackie was going to break her neck. "Where is your brother's strongbox?" Jackie demanded.

"I don't...." Casey closed her eyes, feeling dizzy. "I don't know."

"Well, maybe you need a lil' persuading." Jackie slammed Casey's head back down on the headrest again, before she went to the table. She took a few moments to look at the tools and weapons that were on it before Jackie went back to Casey. When Jackie did, she picked up both Casey's tank top and outer shirt, rolling them up to expose her back. Then Jackie went back to the table and picked up a whip.

Drawing it back, Jackie landed it right in the middle of Casey's back. Casey couldn't help it. She let out a horrid scream as Jackie dragged the whip across her back. The pain it yielded was almost unbearable as it sliced into her skin.

"Now," Jackie asked again up by Casey's ear, "are ya gonna tell me where your brother's strongbox is since it's not in your storage shed?"

"I don't...." Casey writhed in pain as she gritted her teeth. "I don't know where it is!"

Jackie didn't say anything. She stood, and lashed at Casey's back again with her whip three more times. With each point of contact, the whip sliced deeper into Casey's skin, ripping it to shreds. When she was finished, Jackie rested her hand on the side of Casey's face and jerked it toward her. With tears pouring down Casey's face, Jackie asked, "Does it feel good?"

"Nooo," Casey moaned.

"Do you want me to stop?"

"Yes!"

"Then tell me what you did with your brother's strongbox?"

"I didn't."

"Who did?"

"I don't know what they did with it."

"Who?" Jackie demanded.

"He took it."

"WHO?" she yelled.

"I don't know where."

"My patience is running thin with you. I'm trying t' take it easy onya since you're an innocent in this," Jackie said, as she paced in front of Casey. "All ya have t' do is tell me where it is, or who has it, an' I'll stop."

"I don't know!" Casey shouted, as her back pulsated in searing pain.

Jackie stood in front of her for a moment, before slapping Casey hard across her face, dragging her fingernails across Casey's cheek when she did. Casey immediately felt the blood drip down her cheek. Jackie knelt down in front of her, and held her chin so Casey faced her. "Now, I don't want t' do anymore damage t' your beautiful face, so why don't ya help me by telling me where the box is."

"I don't know!" Casey screamed. The salt from her tears stung the scrapes on her face. She could feel the cuts on her back from where the whip landed, drizzling the blood into small streams as they ran down her back.

Jackie got up and went behind Casey. Drawing her whip back again, she beat Casey with it. It landed across the other slashes, slicing deeper into Casey's skin, as Jackie whipped her six more times.

Casey's horrific screams echoed through the building. Between the ten lashes, the poundings to her head, and the drugs…Casey couldn't think straight. She went in and out of consciousness.

Jackie leaned down and asked, "How 'bout now? Do you remember where the box is?"

Casey slowly shook her head. "Nooooo."

"You know, your back looks pretty bad. Maybe I should wash it," Jackie said, and walked over to the table. She picked up a bowl and took it to the sink. Putting hot water into the bowl, she then added salt to it, stirring it until the salt dissolved. Casey stared at her in wide-eyed horror. Jackie was going to put salt water on the open wounds.

"No, please!" Casey begged, as her body trembled in fear. "Please don't!"

Jackie slowly walked over, continuing to stir the salt into the hot water. "I won't, if ya tell me where my box is."

Casey anxiously looked from the bowl, to her face. "I don't know." Casey vigorously shook her head. "I'm sorry! I don't know! I would tell you, but I don't know!"

"Tsk! Tsk! Tsk!" Jackie shook her head. She poured the contents of the bowl down Casey's back.

The scream Casey let out was a high-pitched, shrill scream of pure pain and agony. She instantly felt the burning as it went down her back like a wall of fury. Casey's body finally couldn't take anymore…and she gratefully passed out.

*   *   *

Two men came in a while later and untied Casey. With one holding each of her arms, they dragged her along with them all the way back to the room where the beds and Mark waited.

Mark rolled over and looked up when the door opened. While he was appalled at the shape Casey was in, he tried to contain himself for both of their sakes. If they knew he cared about her as strongly as he did, they would use her against him to get information.

The guys dragged her to the bed and put her down facing the wall with her back to Mark. They shackled her before leaving the room, locking the heavy metal door behind them.

Mark saw the blood soaking into her shirt. "Casey?" he asked quietly. When she didn't respond he tried again a little louder. "Casey?"

Casey tried to answer him, but her body wouldn't cooperate. She had never experienced pain like this before in her entire life. If the A.N.G.E.L.s experienced even a portion of what she just did, the admiration she already had for them jumped tenfold.

"Oh, Father." Mark looked up toward Heaven in prayer. "We need help. We are children of Yours, and we are in big trouble." He looked over at her again. With tears in his eyes, he saw the blood seep through her shirt. "Father, she doesn't deserve this. She looks...." He shook his head, unable to speak for a moment. He tried to organize his thoughts again, but gave up and spoke what was in his heart. "Father, we love You. We know You are the Almighty One. We know You are bigger than this, and more powerful than they are. Please, I beg You to help her. Please knock her out all the way, so she doesn't have to feel the pain anymore. Her screams were...." he shook his head, as Casey moaned in pain. "I'm pleading on her behalf for mercy. Have mercy on her! Please rain down Your Spirit of comfort, and give her peace and rest. Please protect her from having to go through that again. I don't think she can endure it."

He sighed as he glanced over at her. He shook his head, distraught. "Father, I love her. I love her with all my heart. Please don't make her suffer anymore. Please step in and stop this. The blood...her scream...she's losing a lot of blood, Father. Please help her."

The shackles on his hands and feet clinked as he rolled over to look at her. "I love you, Casey. I'm sorry I couldn't help you. Please forgive me?"

He wanted to go to her to comfort her. He jerked on his shackles, but they didn't budge. For fifteen minutes, he tugged and pulled with all of his might before giving up. His hands and ankles bled, but he wanted to get to her. He turned to see the blood now coating her back. He shook his head as she silently lay there for a few more minutes, when suddenly out of the corner of his eye he saw movement. He saw two shadows cast onto the wall by the moonlight through the window. He looked toward the windows at the top of the room to see two shadowy figures dangling from a rope in front of the window. "What the...?"

After a few moments, the two figures used a glasscutter, and were finally able to break through the glass. One climbed in, still attached to a rope. He swung to the window beside the one he came through and unlocked it, easily sliding it open. When he got it open, the second man came in, also attached to a rope. The first person swiftly scaled the wall, with the second closely behind him. As soon as they both reached the bottom, they unlatched themselves and went to Mark. They picked the locks of the shackles, releasing him.

"Where's Casey?" the Colonel asked Mark.

He nodded toward the other bed. "She's over there."

"Oh my…." The Colonel shook his head, feeling sick to his stomach. "Oh, Casey."

"I don't know how much time we have until they come back." Mark rubbed his wrists. They were raw, but he was free.

Derek and the Colonel immediately picked the locks, releasing Casey from the shackles. "What's the best way to do this?" Derek asked, as he looked at her injuries. "She's unconscious…thank God."

"I've got her," Mark volunteered.

"No," the Colonel said, "you're injured too."

"But she's –"

"I know," the Colonel cut him off. "But you're not in any shape to carry her up a wall. We have to get out through that window in order to get out of here." He pointed up toward where the ropes dangled from the window.

Mark nodded, knowing the Colonel was right.

The Colonel gently picked her up under her arms and slid her off the bed. When she was in semi-standing position, Derek flipped her over his shoulder like a sack of potatoes.

"Let's go," Derek said, going to the ropes.

It took them several minutes to scale the wall, especially Derek. While she wasn't a heavy-weight by any means, she was still dead weight. He was also trying to be careful not to open the wounds any further.

As soon as they reached the top, Derek passed Casey to Mark, who flipped her over his shoulder. "Mark, come on. Let one of us carry her," the Colonel said.

"I am carrying her," Mark said adamantly. "Let's go."

"All right," the Colonel said, giving up, as he and Derek pulled the ropes back up from the room, dropping them down the outside wall. Once the ropes were in place, all three men quickly scaled the wall. When they reached the bottom, they ran into the woods located behind the warehouse where Casey and Mark were held.

"We have to hustle. As soon as they know you two are gone, they're going to start looking," the Colonel said, as they ran through the woods.

"The chopper is a mile that way." Derek pointed to the left, the direction they were already running.

As they ran, they heard gunfire in the distance. The Colonel prayed for safety for the A.N.G.E.L.s he knew were creating a distraction for their escape.

About a mile into the woods, the Colonel stopped. All three guys ducked behind trees, while the Colonel pulled out his flashlight. He flashed it two times short and one long. A moment later, he got a response from the pilot of two short.

"Let's go," the Colonel said, and they ran to the waiting helicopter.

The Colonel got in the front with the pilot, while Derek and Mark sat on the bench seat in the back, with Casey lying across their laps. Mark held her to his chest, as he turned her face up toward his. Then he tucked her arms in front of her. He had of his arms under her head, and with the other, he struggled to put on his headset.

When Derek had his headset on, he reached over and helped Mark with his. Then Mark put a headset on Casey as well to cut down on the noise of the helicopter. "We've got about three hours flying time," the Colonel said into the headset.

"Things are lookin' good, Colonel," the pilot said with an Australian accent, as the helicopter took off. "They radioed ten minutes ago that camp was set up."

"Good, because they need it." The Colonel shook his head. He glanced back and said to Mark, "We need to lift her shirt before that blood dries anymore."

"She's not going to like that," Mark warned.

The Colonel gave him a look of frustration as he stood. "Trade places with me," he said to Derek.

When he got to the back, the Colonel knelt on the floor directly next to Casey. Derek settled into the front seat, watching what was going on behind him.

"Her clothes are going to dry, and it's going to hurt worse," the Colonel explained to Mark. He knew Mark already knew it, but Mark's feelings were clouding his judgement, so the Colonel had to take over. "We have to clean those wounds too. Hey, Fletcher, is there a medical kit in here?"

"Yep." The pilot reached under his seat and handed it to Derek, who passed it to the Colonel.

"You have a good hold on her, right?" the Colonel asked Mark, as he slipped a pair of rubber gloves onto his hands.

Mark shook his head, holding her closer to his chest. He kissed her head. "I'm sorry," Mark said to Casey. Mark held the top half of her to his chest with one arm, and with the other, he held her waist close to him, arching her back toward the Colonel.

The Colonel took a deep breath before he slowly pulled back the overshirt. He shook his head in anguish. "We have to take off this one."

Mark nodded, so the Colonel slipped her left arm (which was her free arm) easily out of the overshirt. He pulled it toward the floor and then slid her other arm out from underneath, and took the off shirt the rest of the way. He held it up for a moment, shaking his head at the amount of blood, wadding it up. He set it on the floor next to him.

Glancing at Mark before looking back to the tank top Casey had on, the Colonel lifted the back of her tank top. It was already sticking to the wounds. "Hold her tight," the Colonel warned.

Mark held her to his chest, with her face looking up toward him and nodded.

At first, the Colonel tried to slowly pull it off. The noise it made as he peeled it, made him shudder. It sounded as if he were peeling her skin off. The closer to the wounds he got, the more he knew what he had to do. "I need to rip it off," the Colonel warned Mark. When Mark nodded again, the Colonel counted, "One…two…three." And then he pulled her shirt straight out, ripping it free from her wounds.

Casey screamed, startling everyone in the helicopter. She looked at Mark, wide-eyed, with tears in her eyes, breathing heavily.

"I know. I'm sorry!" Mark said, shaking his head, not taking his eyes off hers the entire time. This was breaking his heart at his core, but he understood it needed to be done.

She could only keep her eyes open for a moment, before her body went limp due to the amount of pain. She closed her eyes, praying that God would knock her out the rest of the way. She wanted so badly for the pain to stop…and He granted her request, much to her relief.

When Casey stopped moving, the Colonel looked at Mark and said, "It has to come off." Mark nodded in understanding, so the Colonel took off the tank top the same way he took off the overshirt, setting it on top of the other shirt on the floor. The Colonel then unhooked her bra so he could get to the wounds below it.

Mark held her tightly to him, making sure she stayed covered in the front. Mark felt for her, but knew it had to be done. In order for the Colonel to clean the wounds, all the clothing had to be out of the way.

The Colonel took fifteen to twenty more tortuous minutes cleaning each and every wound on her back, lightly rubbing an anti-bacterial solution all over when he finished. The way some of the wounds crossed each other, the skin was torn, ripped, or even looked shredded.

He sighed when he was done. "Do you have an emergency blanket in here?" he asked Fletcher.

"Under that seat back there," the pilot said.

The Colonel took out the blanket. Then with Mark's help, they covered her, leaving only her back and head exposed.

"When we land, we'll take care of you, but she couldn't wait," the Colonel explained to Mark as he got up from the floor. The Colonel lifted her legs, resting them on his lap as he sat on the seat next to Mark.

"That's all right," Mark said, looking down at Casey, as he rubbed his finger on her cheek. "I deserve it for letting them get to her."

"Don't blame yourself." The Colonel shook his head. "Derek said he came out of the bathroom to see four of them throw you two in a car and take off. You were outnumbered."

"You should have heard her screams, Colonel. She was in another room, and I still heard them echoing all the way to where I was. They were so clear, as if she were in the room with me."

"It's over. Soon we will be so deep in the bush, they won't find us. That will give us time to get you two healed enough for travel. Then we'll go under…deep. They will never get to her again."

Mark looked down at Casey, and ran his fingers through her hair before he rested his head back on the seat, knowing they were both safe.

Chapter 10

Angels of the Outback

The helicopter finally landed two-and-a-half-hours later in the middle of nowhere – they termed it the "back of Bourke," "beyond the black stump," "where the crow flies backwards," "the never-never," or Casey's personal favorite, "in the middle a' bloody woop-woop."

As soon as they landed, four other guys carrying a rescue basket met the chopper.

"How are we gonna do this?" one asked, looking at Casey's back and how she lay on Mark.

"What if we just flip her so she's lying on her stomach?" another one suggested. "Do ya think if we slide this in there that you two can lay her down in it?"

Mark looked at the Colonel, and they both nodded, so that's what they did. They slid the basket in the helicopter at the feet of the Colonel and Mark. While the Colonel had her legs, Mark had the difficult portion of Casey to move. He would have to move her, while trying not to open the wounds any worse than they already were. At the same time, he was going to do his best to keep her front covered. He knew the guys were professionals, but he did not want them to see Casey in that way if he could help it. She was his, not theirs.

"Count of three?" the Colonel asked.

"Wait a minute," Mark said, thinking about how to do it. He flipped her from her side onto her stomach while still on his lap. Then he slid both of his arms under her so one was across her chest and the other was across her abdomen, holding the blanket around her arm farthest away from him.

The Colonel took a second to readjust her legs, while one of the other guys turned her head to the side, bracing his hands around her neck to hold it in place so it wouldn't move.

"On three?" the Colonel asked again.

Mark nodded. "Yeah."

"Gently now. One…two…three," he said, and they all slid Casey off Mark and the Colonel into the basket.

When safely inside the basket, Mark tucked the blanket around her so she was covered, but her back was still open. The Colonel wrapped the bottom half of the blanket around her legs, covering them.

The other four guys then pulled her out and carried her to the camp. They set her on a cot in a tent – basket and all.

"We need you to move to the medical tent too," the Colonel said to Mark when he didn't move.

Mark looked up at him, holding his side.

"Um, what exactly is injured on you?" Derek asked, as he nervously looked at Mark.

"My adrenaline came down about an hour ago," Mark admitted. "I really didn't feel it until then."

"Feel what?" the Colonel looked at him, apprehensively.

"I have at least a couple broken ribs and fingers," Mark confessed.

"And you carried her for over a mile?" the Colonel's jaw dropped. "What were you thinking?"

"That I got her into it, and I was going to get her out of it!" Mark snapped. His emotions had caught up with him as well. "She's going to be my wife. I was going to be the one to carry her to safety."

"What do you mean your wife?" the Colonel asked in wide-eyed surprise.

"I asked her to marry me in Sydney, and she said 'yes.'"

"When were you planning on telling me?"

"When we got back. Look, you know as well as I do that in our lifestyle, we have to take the good when we can get it." Mark was borderline angry, along with being in extreme pain.

The Colonel didn't say anything as he looked at him in shock. Derek found out when they were in Sydney, but the Colonel hadn't been informed yet. "All right," the Colonel nodded, resigned to the fact that he couldn't control everything. "We'll work on that later. Right now, we need to get you two in a lot better shape in order to evac from here."

Mark nodded, as he held his side.

"Need a hand, mate?" one of the guys asked, coming back from the medical tent.

"Yeah." Mark nodded. He wrapped his arm around the guy's shoulder so he could help him.

Another guy looked up from the medical tent and ran over to lend him a hand. "Nothing personal, but you're a big guy, mate," he said, wrapping Mark's other arm over his shoulder. They both helped him over to the cot next to Casey.

Meanwhile, a couple guys worked on Casey. One inserted an IV while another took her blood pressure, temperature, and pulse.

"What are we going t' do about that?" One of the guys nodded toward her back. "Her back's a mess, but we need t' clean it."

"I know," the other guy agreed. "I've been trying t' figure that out."

"Hey, Marshall, wanna pass me a lamp so we can get a better look at this?" the first one asked after a moment. The one taking her vitals was at the table putting away the blood pressure cuff, stethoscope, and thermometer.

It was the middle of the night and pitch black outside due to the overcast conditions. The single light bulb in the tent was what they were working with, because they had no natural light to go by.

Marshall turned on the flashlight, and together, the two medics studied the wounds on her back, while two other guys worked on Mark. Mark had many cuts on his torso and arms, and his face had been beaten pretty badly. They also checked his broken ribs, and noticed that he had at least one or two broken fingers.

Marshall sighed, shaking his head. "Someone sliced and diced her."

"What's that?" The other guy pointed to a section on her back that had what looked like crystals of some kind in some of the deeper cuts.

Since the other guy was holding the flashlight, Marshall got up and grabbed a pair of tweezers. He pulled some of the skin back. "Crikey!" He turned his head away, shaking it.

"What?" Mark tried to sit up, but the two guys working on him pushed him back down, mainly because one of them was trying to stitch his forehead where there was a deep cut.

"Is this salt?" the other guy asked, sickened. "Did they pour salt on these wounds?"

"That's what it looks like." Marshall shook his head again. "Hey, Colonel!" He called for the Colonel, who sat by the fire with Derek, the pilot, and a couple other guys.

He poked his head into the tent. "Yeah?"

"Come here. Ya gotta see this," the other guy said, shaking his head in disbelief.

His commander poked his head in the tent. "Harper, can't you do it yourself?"

"But, sir, there's salt in these wounds," Harper objected.

"There's what?" the Colonel came over, stunned. He crouched down so he could get a better look at it. "Oh, Case." He shook his head. "I'm so sorry."

"The problem is that we have to deep clean these t' make sure all that salt is out," Harper stressed, making his point. "How would you like us t' do this?"

His commander sized-up the problem. Since the Colonel filled him in, he knew all the different aspects of the situation. He glanced over at Mark's bulky body, knowing that Mark would probably kill him with them bare hands if they did any more damage to Casey. He glanced back down at Casey, trying to figure out how to do it without exposing her as well.

"All right," he said, with a couple different thoughts in mind. He pitched 'plan a' first, keeping the other two in reserve if 'plan a' didn't go over too well. "What if we put her on the ground, with the tent doors open so the water can drain? You guys just work with her still in the basket on the ground. When you're done, we'll move her back up t' the cot in a new, clean, dry basket so that one can dry."

Marshall glanced down at Casey, before he looked up at his Commander. "With all due respect, sir, that sounds like a good idea with one exception."

"What's that?"

"Her clothes are gonna be soaked when we're done. As it is, her shirts are soaking in bleach to get the blood out."

"What's the problem? Put her in a pair of scrub pants." He shrugged. "And tuck her back in the same way she is now."

"Um," Harper glanced at Mark, before he looked at his commander with the same thoughts Marshall had, "Sir, while I don't have a problem with that, since we have medical background anyway, but um…." He glanced at Mark again, who eyed the guys, wondering how they were planning to move her. "I think big n' burly o'er there may object."

"I'll tell you what." The Colonel stood. He looked at Mark and asked, "What if you help them change her when they're done?"

Mark debated the situation in his head. He knew these guys were more than capable, and he was confident they would do their job properly and with professionalism, but she was going to be his wife, and he wasn't too sure about the idea of knowing these guys were going to see her naked.

"I don't have a problem with it as long as the tent is closed when you change her, and I'm in here. And just you two," Mark said, after a few minutes of silence.

"That's do-able." One of the guys working on him, nodded. "Carson an' I'll bug-out when it's time t' get her changed. We should be almost done by then anyway."

Mark nodded in agreement. "Deal."

"Sounds good." Their commander nodded as well. "Any other questions?"

"What 'bout underclothes for her? Or do we just put her in scrubs?" Harper asked.

"Just put her in scrubs. Give me all her clothes when you're done so I can wash them in the river," the Colonel said. "Anything else?"

Marshall shook his head. "Nope."

"I'm getting her morphine." Harper got off the ground to get it, as the Colonel and their commander walked out of the tent. "The pain this may cause might just wake her up, and I don't think we're gonna like the result. She may tear those even worse."

"Good idea," Marshall said, getting up to grab a pair of scrub pants for her, along with getting the other rescue basket ready as well. He grabbed two extra blankets along with a clean pillow and set the new basket down at the foot of the cot.

"All right," Harper said as he put the morphine into her IV. "We're gonna give this a minute t' soak in before we do the deed."

While they waited, they moved her down to the ground so they could set up the other basket. They put the clean one on the cot and spread out one blanket, open and hanging over the edges, before leaving the other blanket on the table with the clean scrubs.

Then Harper filled a bucket with an anti-biotic solution, while Marshall grabbed a couple clean towels, sponges, and gauze.

"What about ointment?" Marshall asked.

"I think we should save that for later. We're gonna wanna sponge-clean those every eight hours for the first three days. When they're more closed up, we'll rub the anti-biotic ointment on it topped with gauze."

"Sounds good," Marshall said, taking the towels, sponges, and gauze over to a chair, and then moved the chair next to her.

Harper brought the bucket over and knelt next to her. "I'm gonna take care a' this first." He pointed to the scratches on her face. "We'll leave these for afterward." He pointed to the rope burns on her wrists. Marshall nodded in agreement.

Harper took the anti-biotic solution and used one of the sponges to clean her cheek. When he was done, he used some gauze to dry it up before he applied anti-biotic ointment all over the section. Then, he placed a clean gauze pad on top, securing it with medical tape.

"Ready?" Harper asked when he finished.

"No, but we gotta anyway," Marshall said, looking down at her back. "These wounds are already at least three t' four hours old. We have t' get that salt outta there."

They each took a sponge and lightly scrubbed the wounds, before Harper picked up the bucket, gently pouring some of the solution over Casey's back. Harper hoped to loosen the salt that had dried as the water flooded the wounds.

As he poured, Marshall scrubbed a bit harder to loosen what wasn't coming up. They worked on her for over two hours when he hit a spot that was mostly shredded. Casey jumped and screamed, sending several animals that were in the trees near them scurrying into the darkness.

"What's going on?" the Colonel demanded, coming in. Harper and Marshall struggled to hold her down, while she yelled and squirmed, fighting to get free, as the salt stung her back once again from where they flooded it.

"Grant! Get more morphine!" Harper yelled over his shoulder. "We gotta get her calmed down before she opens these even worse."

Casey squirmed, doing her best to get free of them. The salt stung her back again when the water moved some of the salt to several tender areas they had already cleaned. "Ahhh! Stop!" Casey screamed. "Ahhhhhh!"

"Got it." Grant knelt down next to her while Carson struggled to keep Mark under control. He injected five more milligrams of morphine sulfate into her IV, on top of the ten they already gave her, praying it would knock her out. Grant then got back up and got some diazepam, injecting that as well to calm her and make her more comfortable.

She fought them for another minute before she slowed. Her head felt as if it was going to spin off her body. She looked up at Harper, who was on her left, and begged, "Help me."

"We're trying, love," he said with a look of compassion on his face.

Casey nodded, before her head dropped down to the pillow. Her body gave up the fight and allowed her to slip back into unconsciousness.

"We're gonna strap 'er t' the basket," Harper said to Mark. "If we don't, she could do more damage than has already been done. She opened up several cuts even worse than they already were in that one."

"Go ahead," Mark said in understanding. From where he sat, he could see her back bleeding in several areas. He put his head in his hands, shaking it, beside himself with blame.

"Crickey! It looks like they pretty much filleted her back." Marshall sighed, shaking his head in disbelief. Then he looked up at the Colonel as he tied her wrists. "She's not military?"

"No," the Colonel said. "She's a civilian."

He shook his head and sighed. "What did ya get mixed up in, love?"

"Just get her cleaned up so she can rest," their commander said. He nervously rubbed his hand on the back of his neck as he watched them. "She's been through enough."

"Will do, sir," Harper said as he secured her ankles. He looked up at Marshall and said, "I'll keep cleaning while you keep an eye on her respirations. She's got a lot of medicine in her. We also need to keep a closer eye on our timeline to prevent that from happening again. I want her pain free for as long as possible."

While Harper and Marshall worked on Casey, Carson and Grant continued to work on Mark. Carson shook his head as he commented, "Man, they worked you two over."

"You should have heard her when it was originally done," Mark said, watching the guys wash her. Grant wrapped Mark's chest with an ace bandage for his ribs, and Carson dabbed an antibiotic solution onto some other cuts on Mark's face.

Carson sighed. "I can't imagine."

"The last screams were...." Mark cringed in remembrance. "I'll bet that was when they poured in the salt on her back. That was something I never want to hear again for the rest of my life. Let's just say it was a good thing I was shackled to a wall at the time, or...." he shook his head in anger.

"Easy on, big guy." Grant patted his shoulder. "You're all safe out here. No one but the 'roos know we're out here."

Mark nodded, not taking his eyes off Casey.

"Um," Grant knelt down in front of him. He looked at Mark's fingers and said, "I need t' reset these two fingers. You're not gonna like it. You sure I can't give you something for the pain before I do?"

They offered Mark pain medicine several times as they stitched him in some places, and deep cleaned other wounds, but he refused.

"No," Mark said resolutely. "I deserve it."

"Why would you say that?" Carson asked, stunned by his answer.

"Because I let them do that. I let them take us. I was the one with her. I was protecting her at the time. No." Mark adamantly shook his head. "Just reset them."

Grant sighed. "Right-oh."

As soon as Grant re-broke the first finger to set it, Mark jumped and groaned in pain, breathing heavily through it. It hurt him to breathe with the broken ribs before he jumped, but when he jumped, he fought to breathe and control the excruciating pain that emanated from various parts of his body.

"I'm gonna wait 'til this one calms before I do the other," Grant said, sitting back on his feet.

"No." Mark shook his head. "Do it."

"Are you sure? You're obviously in quite a bit of pain right now."

"Do it!" Mark growled.

Grant looked up at Carson, who went over to the table. "Okay," Grant said, keeping Mark's attention on him, and off what Carson was doing. "On the count of three?" Mark nodded, so Grant said, "One…two…three…." And then Grant broke and set the other finger. As he did, Carson went behind Mark and jammed a syringe into each of Mark's arms, emptying the syringe of morphine into one arm, and a mild sedative into the other arm.

Mark groaned in pain. And, as soon as he realized what Carson did, he looked up at him, stunned. "Why?" Mark asked.

"Because you're a good bloke with a kind and gentle heart," Carson said. "You deserve t' rest easy. You've beat yourself up enough."

"I…." Mark shook his head. He was mad, upset, and in pain all at once. He felt an overwhelming sense of warmth as the medicines took over his body. He couldn't think straight. "Colonel!" he yelled. If he was going to pass out, he wanted one of the guys in the team in there with Casey.

"Yeah?" he poked in his head.

"Watch Casey," Mark said, and then passed out due to all the intense pain, the medication, and the stress of the day.

"Whoa!" the Colonel jumped toward Mark, but Carson and Grant were ready for it and were already laying him down on the cot. "What-did-you-guys-do?" Colonel angrily demanded, as he saw his strongest man collapsing in front of his eyes.

"He needed it. He's still beating himself up for that," Carson said, nodding toward Casey. "And Grant's still gotta set another finger on the other hand, as well as bandage up the two he just set. He wouldn't take any pain meds for it, so we took matters into our own hands. We have the medical portion covered, but you're gonna have t' work on his spirit and heart when he wakes."

"He's gonna be ticked when he wakes," the Colonel said with his hands on his hips, getting a full picture of what happened. "But I understand. I'll work with the guys with Casey. Hopefully he will be alert enough to help when they're done, but if not...." He shook his head again. "Just do what you need to do."

"Thank you, sir," Carson said, relieved the Colonel wasn't upset at them. He bandaged the two fingers he set, while Grant felt all of the fingers on Mark's other hand to see which ones needed reset to be on that hand.

It took Harper and Marshall a good three hours to thoroughly clean the wounds on Casey's back to their satisfaction. They wanted to make sure all the salt was out, and the wounds were sterile before applying the gauze. They used the gauze to cover them so nothing in the air could get into the wounds.

Harper sat back on his feet, exhausted. "Done."

"We still need t' work on her wrists and ankles," Marshall pointed out. "Whate'er they tied her with when they were whipping her cut into her wrists an' ankles. I'm glad she didn't struggle after the initial burst of pain, because she could have made those worse as well."

The Colonel went over to Mark and jostled him. "Hey, English, they're gonna change Casey. Are you awake?"

"Um, yeah." Mark partially opened his eyes. "I need to be awake." Mark looked at both of his hands. One had two fingers taped together and wrapped, while the other had only one with a splint on it.

"They're done with you for now. Don't be mad at them. They did their job," the Colonel said, as he helped Mark into a sitting position.

"I'm not." Mark shook his head to clear it. He was struggling to focus. "I need to…will you help me to a chair so I can watch?"

"Yeah, sure." The Colonel moved a chair near the head of Casey's cot, so Mark could clearly see what was happening. Then he carefully moved Mark over, with Mark holding his ribs the entire time. "Do you want me in here?" the Colonel asked.

Mark shook his head. "No."

"All right. Call me when you're done," the Colonel said before he left the tent.

"Okay, what's the easiest way t' do this?" Marshall asked Harper.

"Honestly?" Harper asked.

"Yeah," Marshall said. He probably had the same idea as Harper on how to do it, but he was too afraid of Mark to say it aloud.

"Strip the rest of her clothes off, dry her off with a towel, move her t' the other bed, and then put the dry ones on her there. Do you have another idea?" he asked Mark.

Mark glanced at the soaking wet bed she was in currently, and then the dry bed on the cot. He thought for a couple minutes before he asked, "Can you keep her as covered as possible while you do it?"

"Yep," Harper said confidently.

Mark nodded. "Go ahead."

Harper reached under Casey and opened her pants, while Marshall slid her arms out of the bra. When he finished, Harper covered her behind with part of the wet blanket before he slid off her pants. He was nervous with Mark sitting there watching every move they made. He had worked with Mark a couple times over the years, and knew what Mark was capable of – even in the shape he was in.

Harper threw her pants and underwear into an empty trashcan. The water splattered when they landed. Marshall walked her bra over to the trashcan. He dropped it in with the rest of the wet clothes before returning to her.

Harper already dried her arms and hair off with a towel, so Marshall dried her legs off, resting them on the side of the basket as each one was dry.

When they finished, Harper got a dry sheet and laid it on her back and legs, before he slid the wet one out from under her. He didn't want to put the sheet on her back, but he couldn't figure out a more modest way of doing it. Harper reached under her and braced his arms under her shoulders and abdomen, while Marshall got both of her legs – with one arm under her thighs and the other beneath her knees.

"One…two…three," Harper said, and together they picked her up and moved her to the dry bed, stepping over the rescue basket to do so.

When they got her in, they draped her arms over the top of the basket. Harper slid his arms out from under her, before he turned her head so she faced Mark's cot. Meanwhile, Marshall got the dry scrub pants. Together, each one took a leg and slipped the pants on her.

When they finished, Marshall cleaned the mess on the ground, while Harper pulled the sheet off her back. He tossed it onto the dirty linens from the other basket, before he took the blanket that had been draped over the sides and tucked it under her arms, covering her chest. Then he went over and got a blanket to cover her legs.

"Howzat?" he asked Mark.

"Approved." Mark nodded. "Do me a favor and help me over to her?"

"Sure."

Harper helped him stand up, and then reached around and swung the chair around them so it was by her side. Then, he helped Mark to the chair before he helped Marshall clean up.

"Do you guys have a rubber band?" Mark asked.

"Umm…." Harper glanced around the tent. He went to the medic bag, took a rubber band off one of the bandages in his bag, and gave it to Mark.

"Thanks." Mark nodded in appreciation.

They kept an eye on Mark while they cleaned the mess. Mark ran his fingers through Casey's wet hair, breaking up several knots that were in it. When he finished, he proceeded to braid her hair, tying it with the rubber band at the end. Then he laid it to the side so it would stay off her back.

"I love you, Casey." He leaned down and kissed her cheek that had the gauze on it. "Rest well."

He looked up at Marshall and Harper and nodded that he was done. They helped him to his cot, before they went back to cleaning the linen. Mark rested on the cot next to her and saw that she had a look of peace. He prayed she would stay that way as her back healed from the wounds inflicted on her by evil.

Chapter 11

Charlie

About seven hours after they arrived, Casey finally opened her eyes. She looked at Mark.

Mark smiled, rolling to his side when he saw her eyes. "Hey beautiful. I've missed those gorgeous green eyes of yours."

Casey stared at him in a daze. Flashes of what had happened crawled through her mind like remnants of a night terror. She pulled her hands to her chest and braced herself for a moment before she pushed up on her hands.

"What are you doing?" Mark asked as he watched her.

"What's going on?" the Colonel looked over from where they sat around the fire.

"She's moving."

"Oh, don't do that." Harper got up from the fire and went into the tent. They lifted the sides of the tent so the air could get it, but they left the camouflage netting over the top of the entire camp so it couldn't be seen from the air.

He knelt next to her cot, as he rested his hand on her shoulder. "What are you doing?"

"Need to…move," she said, as she took a deep breath to cope with the pain. "Hurt."

"Want me t' help ya?" Harper asked. "That way you stay covered."

Casey looked down and suddenly realized she didn't have anything on the top half of her body. She lowered the inch she had come up and looked at Mark for help.

"It's because they needed access to your back," Mark explained. "Don't worry. I've been in here the whole time."

"Do ya want t' lay on your side? You can't lay on your back yet," Harper explained. "Give it another few hours an' maybe, but I doubt it. It was pretty sliced up."

Casey nervously looked from Mark to Harper. If she went to her side, it might expose her top half, but her body was stiff from the lack of movement.

"We can keep ya covered if we do it right," Harper offered, almost reading her thoughts. "And, we can probably get a tank top on ya here in a couple hours if we use the right dressing."

Casey nodded, grateful for the help.

"All right." He stood. "You hold the blanket, and let me do the rest."

Casey reached down to her legs and pulled the blanket that was over them up with her. She tucked it around her chest, while Harper went behind her. "Can ya adjust your left arm so I can roll you over?"

It took her a few moments to turn herself toward Mark so her right arm snapped free. Meanwhile, her left hand still clutched the blanket close to her body. Harper gently set one hand on her left-side waist and his other hand on her right-side hip, before he slowly turned her. He had her keep her left leg straight, but bent her right one to brace herself in case she went to sleep again. Then he placed a pillow between her legs to hold them in that position.

"I'm gonna go ahead and clean you back since I'm here." He made a mixture of the anti-biotic solution before he grabbed a clean sponge and went back to the cot. "Here we go. I'll be as gentle as I can."

Casey looked at Mark, doing her best to breathe through the pain. She knew Harper was trying to be gentle, but her back was extremely tender to the touch.

Mark saw the tears in her eyes, so he slowly sat up and grabbed one of her hands for her to squeeze. Even though his fingers were broken, he still let her squeeze as much as she wanted. He still felt he deserved whatever pain was inflicted on him for letting them get caught in the first place.

Harper did his best, but when he hit a tender spot, Casey jumped. Unfortunately, it was one of the worst spots on her back. When she jumped, the sponge jerked and opened the wound. Harper groaned as he ran to grab more gauze.

Marshall came in to see what was happening. He held the gauze with a little bit of pressure in an attempt to get it to clot, while Harper went to get more.

After about ten minutes, they finally got it to clot. Marshall took over the cleaning, while Harper got a dose of morphine ready.

"Ready?" Harper asked. Casey nodded, so he put another five milligrams of morphine into her IV. "Give it a few, and the pain'll slow down for ya."

Marshall finished her back, and then the two of them left Mark and Casey alone in the tent, confident that she would fall asleep soon.

"You okay now?" Mark asked.

Casey nodded, as the warming sensation permeated her body once again, allowing her not to feel the tenderness of her raw back.

"Will you forgive me for not protecting you?" Mark asked.

She looked up at him in surprise. "There's nothing to forgive."

"I didn't protect you."

"We didn't see it coming. There is nothing you could have done."

The Colonel ducked into the tent when he heard them talking. "How's she doing?" he asked.

"In pain," Mark said, upset.

"Let's go take a walk, buddy. She's needs the sleep."

"I don't want to leave her."

"I'll make it an order if you push me," the Colonel warned. "I asked out of respect."

Mark looked up at him, taken aback for a moment before he nodded. He slowly stood, tenderly clutching his ribs. The two of them took off for a walk, leaving Casey to enjoy the painless, peaceful rest that had once again been granted to her.

*   *   *

Over the next couple of hours, Casey enjoyed the blissful peace that was brought on by the medicine. Finally, about ten hours after they arrived, Marshall came in to look at her back. When he finished, he placed the gauze on it as he normally did, using medical tape to secure it.

He handed her a tank top. "Ready to put a shirt on?"

"It's one of mine," Carson mentioned, as he looked over Mark's wounds. "Sorry t' say, your clothes didn't make it – too much blood."

"Oh." Casey nodded in understanding. While she hoped to wear her own clothes, the fact that she wasn't in the warehouse and was alive, was a relief to her. She would have to take what she could and be grateful.

She wrapped a sheet around her body, and then gently took the tank top and put it over her head. As she slipped her arms through the holes, she groaned in pain when the shirt rubbed her back.

Carson looked over at her, concerned. "You didn't open it, did ya?"

Marshall went behind her. "May I?" he asked. Casey nodded, so he lifted the sheet. "Nope. You're good. Keep going," he said, replacing the sheet.

Casey pulled the tank top down, and swung her feet out of the basket to help her keep her balance. When she was done, she put her head in her hands. "Dizzy," she moaned, praying the world would stop swirling around her, as her head pounded furiously.

"Give it a few. You probably still have some of the morphine in ya," Carson pointed out. "There, you're done too," he said to Mark. "Why don't you two make your way t' the fire so we can feed ya."

Casey looked up at him with her head still in her hands. "You want me to move?"

"Aww, come on." He smirked. "I thought you were tougher than that."

Casey groaned as she lowered her head. Mark slowly moved over to her cot. "Come on," he encouraged. "If I can do it, you can do it."

"Give me a few," she said, taking a deep breath, hoping the dizziness and the pounding would at least slow down to a tolerable level. After Marshall and Carson left the tent to get them some food, Casey turned toward Mark and said, "It was a woman."

"Who did that to you?"

"She was Hunter's mother."

"No way!" he said, wide-eyed. "Are you serious?"

"She wanted to know where her strongbox is. What's going on?"

"I think we need to get together and talk about this," Mark said, looking around for the Colonel and Derek. When he saw them by the hill that went down to the river, he whistled. Everyone in camp looked over towards them, so Mark pointed to Derek and the Colonel, and motioned for them to come into the tent.

"What's up?" the Colonel asked, as he and Derek sat down on Mark's cot across from them.

"The woman who did this to me was Hunter's mother," Casey explained.

The Colonel looked at her, wide-eyed. "Hunter? As in Morgan?"

"Don't play dumb with me!" Casey snapped. She was furious. She was still struggling with the medication, but she was livid. As soon as she snapped, everyone in camp looked up at them, stunned.

"Where'd that come from?" the Colonel asked.

"With all due respect, sir," Casey said, snidely, "I've had my back pretty much filleted. And then, just to make sure I would remember it, that woman poured hot salt water over it. I am not in the mood for games. She wanted the strongbox…her strongbox. She said Jack took it, and she wanted it back. Where is it and what's in it?"

"I can't tell you that."

Casey struggled to stand as she moved so she was eye-to-eye with the Colonel. With her hands braced on his shoulders, she demanded, "Tell me! My life, Jesse's life, Jack's life, Keith's life…as well as several other people's lives, have all been ruined, or they have been killed, because of some stupid metal box. What's in it? Why would a woman slice and dice my back because of a stupid metal box? Why would they beat the crap out of Mark because of it? While you people are used to this, I'm not. I am used to putting people back together – not running and ducking while being hunted.”

“Casey, it’s hidden here in the camp with us,” the Colonel said calmly. “I brought it with me so it would be in our sights at all times. As far as its contents, I can’t tell you. As far as that woman claiming to be the original owner, she lied – great surprise there.” He rolled his eyes.

“Well, she sure looked like Hunter, so I doubt she was lying about that.”

“I wouldn’t know. I wasn’t there, you were…and I trust you.”

“Then tell me the truth!” she yelled. She dropped to her knees, as she shook her head and closed her eyes. She braced her arms on the ground to hold herself. The stress, mixed with the medicine, snowballed on her, knocking her to the ground.

“Come on back to the cot.” Mark held his hands on her arms being careful not to touch her back. Everyone in the camp stood by the fire, watching them in shock.

Casey looked up at the Colonel with tears in her eyes as she slowly shook her head. “They almost killed us. I only want to know why.”

The Colonel knelt in front of her and cupped her face in his hands. The pain in his face matched what was in her heart. “I wish I could. I wish you didn’t have to go through any of this.” He shook his head, beside himself. “If I could have taken your place, I would have. This is something we have been doing our best to keep from you. I give you my word though – swearing on your brother’s grave and on all the A.N.G.E.L.s lives lost – that I will not let it happen again. When we get out of here, we are going under. They will never find you again. You’re right. Enough people have been hurt or killed. We are keeping the box so it doesn’t happen again. Trust me when I tell you the contents of that box could cause more death, pain, and injury than has already been inflicted. We love you. This has been killing us just as much, if not more, than it has you. I have had multiple conversations with Mark, because he blames himself for letting them get to you in the first place. Derek and I have had arguments over it. We've pointed the finger enough though. We need to be united in this. If we don't, then they'll win. We need to stand strong until we're all safe. I promised your brother to keep you safe, and I will give my life to do so. You will be safe. From this point on, our mission is to get you deep, keeping you hidden and safe for the rest of your days."

She stared at him in disbelief. "Is that possible?"

"Yes," he said, firmly.

She could tell by the look on his face that he would follow through with that promise.

"I'm holding her up here," Mark said to Derek and the Colonel. "Derek, can you help me get her up to her cot? She needs to lie down."

Derek nodded, before he pushed the basket off the cot so it would be easier. Then he helped Mark get her to the cot, being careful with her back. They laid her down on her side and covered her with a sheet.

"Mark?" Casey asked. Her head spun and she breathed heavily. The Colonel and Derek sat back down on Mark's cot.

"Yeah?"

"Can you get one of those guys? My heart rate is too high, and...I can't...something's wrong. Maybe a fever?"

He looked over at Derek and the Colonel for help. The Colonel called Carson over since he was the closest and told him what she said.

Carson took her pulse, which was extremely high. Then he took her blood pressure and temperature. "She's got a fever, Harper," he called to him. "Her pulse and BP are high too."

Harper said something under his breath before he came into the tent. He sighed as he knelt down next to her. "Right-oh. I'm gonna ask ya t' take a couple pills for me t' lower your fever. Can ya do that for me?" Harper asked, as he held wrist to monitor her pulse.

Casey nodded, so he looked up at Carson, who got her some ibuprofen. He returned shortly with two pills and a bottle of water. Harper helped her sit up slightly to take the medicine, before he gently lowered her back to the bed.

After a few moments, Casey's head spun even worse than it already was. She closed her eyes and relaxed in the peace that was granted to her once again.

*   *   *

Casey looked around and realized she was back in the room with Jackie. Jackie had just finished whipping her back, and then she grabbed the bowl, going over to the sink.

"No, please," Casey begged, as she saw Jackie pour the salt into the water and stir it in. Jackie poured it down Casey's back. In Casey's dream, it looked as if there was fire being poured from the bowl as it rained onto Casey's back.

Casey screamed, struggling to get free of the binds.

"Casey!" Mark shouted.

Casey gasped and opened her eyes. She was sweating profusely. She looked down to see Derek and Marshall holding each of her legs, while the Colonel and Carson braced her waist and upper legs as best they could. Their commander had one of her arms and shoulder, as Grant had the other.

Mark held her head as he yelled at her, "Casey!"

"Make it stop!" she screamed in horrific pain, her body shaking. Her back felt as if it was on fire!

Harper was already on his way over to the table to get the diazepam to calm her down. "Hold her!" He said, and gave her the dose in her IV.

"Please make it stop!" Casey screamed, with tears streaming down her face. She was sweating and breathing hard, while fighting to get free of those holding her down. To her, they were ropes tying her in place, though, not the men who were trying to help her.

"Casey! Look at me!" Mark yelled. "Look at my face. Who am I?"

"Make it stop! Please," she begged. "Please make it stop hurting."

"We're trying. Who am I?" Mark asked again.

The medicine gratefully permeated her body.

"Who am I?" Mark demanded, less than three inches from her face.

"Make it stop," Casey said, moving her head side to side as it began to swim.

"Casey, who am I?" Mark asked calmer, noticing the change in her body.

The guys slowly released the body parts they were holding down as her struggling slowed.

"Please make it stop," Casey begged, feeling as if she was going to throw up. She was so hot…too hot!

Mark moved so he was down at her side. With his hands still on the sides of her face, he asked, "Casey, who am I?"

Casey suddenly stopped moving, and stared at Mark in a daze.

"Please? Who am I?" he asked again.

"Mark."

"Good," he said, relieved. He looked up at Harper and asked, "What are you going to do about the fever?"

"We need her to take these," Harper said, giving Mark the ibuprofen and a bottle of water.

"She's gone, right?" Casey asked, looking around. In her mind, she was still in the room.

"Who?" Mark asked.

"Jackie. She's gone, right?"

"Yes. She's not coming back." Mark shook his head, beside himself. This was killing him on the inside. He felt responsible for the entire situation by letting Jackie get to her in the first place.

"She's not going to hurt me anymore, right?" Casey asked.

"No, she's not going to hurt you anymore. Here, take these," Mark said, helping her take the medicine.

When she was done, she reached up and touched the side of his face. "Mark?"

"What?"

"I'm hot."

"I know. Let the medicine work."

"I love you."

He stroked her hair. "I love you too."

"My back."

"I know."

"When you're back to sleep, we're gonna have t' fix it again. Sorry, love," Harper said, kneeling on the other side of her so he was eye-level with her. "Pretty sure ya did some damage there."

Casey let out a moan, as she momentarily closed her eyes. When she opened them again, she looked up at Mark. "My head."

Mark took her hand and kissed it, before he set it back down on her chest. "I know. Go to sleep." He reached up and rubbed his hand on the back of her neck to relax her.

"I'm hot."

"We know."

She closed her eyes again, moaning, as she moved her head side to side. She almost felt as if she was going to vomit.

"Go t' sleep, love," Harper coaxed. "We need t' get t' your back…sooner rather than later. We don't know what damage has been done."

"She did it," Casey moaned with her eyes closed. They were not going to open anymore no matter how hard she tried. They were too heavy.

"We know," Harper assured her. "We're working on that fever too. You're safe. Just rest."

Mark leaned down and gently kissed her lips. "Go to sleep, Case."

Casey reached up to touch his face. She only got her hand halfway up, before it dropped back down to her chest and her head dropped to the side.

"There ya go," Harper said, satisfied. He jumped up and began working with Marshall to get some solution, gauze, and anti-biotic ointment. He taped several pads together with medical tape. Then he covered one side of it with the ointment, leaving it on the table to put on after they finished, before they came back with the bucket and sponges.

They gently rolled her to her side, to see the blood already seeping through the pads, soaking through her tank top. Harper groaned.

"What?" Their commander looked up from the fire where they had settled back down.

Harper glanced up at Mark, who was still at her side and said, "We need t' take her shirt off again. She bled through. We have t' flip her and do some work on this."

"I'll do it," Mark said in understanding.

They got up to get a clean sheet and some gauze, while Mark slipped the tank top off Casey. He turned her so she was on her stomach with her face toward him. Then he tucked the blanket down under her arms to cover her. After he was done, he called them over. He shook his head at the amount of blood he saw. The pads were already full, and he knew it didn't look good.

Harper peeled back the pads and handed them off to Marshall, before he set to clean her back. It took them a couple minutes to clean the blood off to even see the wounds.

"English, man, I'm sorry," Harper said, shaking his head. "This is…she's not even mine and I'm hurting for her."

Mark didn't say anything. He kept his hand resting on the side of her face. The thoughts he had running through his head were ones he knew he shouldn't have, being a Christian. He was running scenarios on the many ways he could torture and take out those who did this to her.

The Colonel watched Mark for a few more minutes, before he pulled Derek with him, and together they came into the tent. "English, let's take a walk and let them do what they need to do."

Mark looked up at him with pure hate in his eyes.

"I know," the Colonel said, reading his thoughts. "I'm struggling with the same thing. We need to talk. Let's go."

"I don't want to leave her," Mark objected.

"They'll protect her," the Colonel assured him. "They're good at their job. Let them do it."

Derek tried to lighten the mood, so he added, "Besides the fact that they know you will kill them if they mess it up."

Mark glanced from the Colonel and Derek, and then back to Casey. He leaned forward and kissed her lips before he stood up, gingerly holding his ribs. The Colonel and Derek helped him, as they all left the tent out into the woods.

Marshall let out a low whistle as he shook his head. "Wow."

"What?" Harper glanced up from the of her back he was working on.

"He's madder than a cut snake!"

"No doubt! I would be too if someone did this t' my woman."

Marshall shook his head again, as he looked down at her back. "We need t' get her fever down," he said quietly, looking around to make sure none of the others heard him.

"I know," Harper said, as he worked on her back. "Working on that."

"Last time I checked it, was right before she went off. It was 40," Marshall informed Harper. (40 degrees Celsius is approximately 104 degrees Fahrenheit.)

Harper's jaw dropped. "Why didn't you tell me? Last time I checked, it was 39. And that was only an hour ago." (39 degrees

Celsius is approximately 102 degrees Fahrenheit.) "No wonder she was so far gone!"

"I was about to when she went off," Marshall explained.

Harper shook his head before he got up. "Keep working on her. I'm gonna get something t' speed that up. Ibuprofen isn't cutting it."

As Harper went to the table, he caught movement in the bushes out of the corner of his eye. He took a moment before he walked back to Marshall, knelt down, and whispered, "We got comp'ny."

Marshall looked up at him, wide-eyed, and then looked around, straining to see what Harper saw.

"I'm gonna go tell Hawk. Keep your eyes peeled," Harper warned, and then he left the tent to his commander. Harper sat down on the log beside Hawk, and quietly told him what he saw before he went back into the tent with Marshall.

Hawk got up and went to Carson and Grant. All three immediately fanned out into the trees, going in three different directions.

Marshall nervously looked up at Harper and whispered, "English is gonna kill us if something happens t' her."

"Then we'd better not let anyone get t' her," he simply said.

After a few minutes, there was more movement. This time it was a little closer to the tent. Harper and Marshall both snapped up their heads, looking in the precise direction they saw the movement. Marshall stayed with Casey, while Harper stood. Both had their guns drawn, intently scanning the area around them.

Harper went to the table, which was about five feet from where he last saw the movement. He had his gun trained on the tree, as he said, "You might as well show yourself. You're gonna get shot if ya don't."

A moment later, a young Aboriginal man stepped out from behind the tree. He was dressed only in a pair of shorts – no shirt, no socks, no shoes. He also carried a bag of food, with a bow across his chest, and a pack with arrows on his back. He was only about five-seven, had medium-length, black, curly hair that hung just above his shoulders, and couldn't have been more than seventeen years old. As he stood there, he looked around with a grin on his face.

"Who are you?" Harper asked, as Carson, Grant, and Hawk surrounded him on three sides with their guns drawn as well.

"I'm Charlie," he simply said, with his hands loosely draped on his sides, seeming perfectly comfortable even though he currently had five guns trained on him.

"What do ya want? What are ya doing here?" Hawk demanded.

"T' help her." He nodded toward Casey. "Heard her last night. Scared da daylights outta me! She need medicine."

Hawk looked at him, studying him for a moment, before he asked, "What were ya doing all the way out here in the bush?"

"On walk-about." Charlie shrugged. "Take them all da time. Ne'er heard before what I did last night, dough. She had bad dreamtime. Fever…no?" he asked Harper.

Harper looked at Hawk to see if he should answer. Hawk nodded, so Harper nodded as well.

"High…no?" Charlie pressed.

Harper nodded again.

Charlie stood on his toes to see her better and cringed. "Can get ya something t' make dat feel better – heal faster. Got something I can get for dat fever too."

Harper looked at Hawk again for help. Hawk simply said, "You have t' understand that her other half'll kill ya with his bare hands if ya hurt her."

"I know." Charlie nodded with a smile. "I see him. He have a lotta anger in him. He should talk t' da elders. Dey help him."

"Where exactly is your village?" Hawk looked at him, trying to figure out what was going on.

"Jus' down da road…dat way," he said, pointing north.

"How close?" Hawk pressed.

"Day walk." Charlie shrugged. "I could get medicine for her, den go get help. We have Pete, who can help her. I also get elders for your friend. We help."

Hawk studied him for a few more minutes before he nodded. If he were willing to help Casey, knowing Mark could potentially do some serious damage to him, he would go ahead and let him do it. Besides, he had enough experience with the Aboriginals over the years to know they had medicines the military and government didn't even know existed.

Charlie came into the tent, with Harper and Marshall keeping a close eye on him, while Hawk, Carson, and Grant also came in, keeping their guns out as they watched him as well. They also kept an eye out for any more surprise visitors. Hawk didn't like surprises.

Charlie set his bag of food, along with his bow and arrow, on the table before he knelt beside Casey. He shook his head as he looked at her back. "Dat bad."

Harper nodded. "Yeah."

Charlie thought for a minute, looking around at the plants and bushes immediately near them, before he looked back down at her. He touched her forehead and sighed, shaking his head. "Dat high."

"Yep," Marshall said.

"Really high," Charlie said, thinking about the plants around them.

"We know." Harper agreed. He wasn't sure what this funny little man was going to do, but he wished he would hurry. He wasn't sure when the other Angels would be getting back, and he didn't want Mark to see Charlie until they could explain things to him.

Charlie looked around again before he got up and walked into the brush.

"Is he going to be able to help her?" Marshall asked Hawk. "If he doesn't, English is gonna –"

Hawk nodded, keeping an eye on where Charlie went. "I'm aware of that."

"Where'd they go?" Harper asked. "If they come back, and Charlie's in the middle of this, it might not look too good."

"If I see them, I'll run interference," Hawk promised.

"You trust him?" Marshall asked Hawk, surprised. Hawk did not trust too many people.

Hawk nodded. "Yep."

"Right-oh. That's why you're the big dog."

Charlie came back five long minutes later with a couple handfuls of various plants and flowers. He shredded part of them into a bowl on the table. He grabbed a handful of dirt and drizzled it over the foliage. He looked around for a moment before going to a bucket of water that had been boiled for drinking, and dipped a cup into it. He then took the cup with the precious water in it, being careful not to spill any, over to the bowl, and slowly emptied the cup into it. He reached in with his hands and mashed all of the ingredients together. After a couple more minutes, Charlie had mixed it into a decently smooth concoction – well, smooth enough that he was satisfied anyway. He took it to Casey and knelt down beside her.

"Um." Hawk jumped when he saw the Colonel, Derek, and Mark returning. "Just a tic, mate. Gotta take care of something first," he said, and left the tent, intercepting the trio halfway between the tent and the river.

It took him several long, heated minutes until Mark finally relented. They came into the tent, with Mark pulling up a chair by Casey's head to keep a close eye on Charlie.

Charlie smiled at him as Mark sat down, and said, "I'm Charlie."

Mark nodded, not amused. "I see that."

Charlie snickered, shaking his head.

"What's so funny?" Mark snapped.

"I here t' help." Charlie smiled. "Dis anger is for da people dat did dis…not me."

"But, why are you laughing?" Mark asked.

"Because dey in big trouble when ya catch 'em!" Charlie said with a wink.

Mark cocked his head to the side, studying him for a moment before he shook his head, chuckling.

"Funny now…no?" Charlie asked, still grinning.

Mark nodded with a smile, feeling more at ease.

"I do…yes?" Charlie nodded toward the bowl.

"If you can help her, yes."

Charlie dipped his hands into the bowl, and gently set the mud mixture onto Casey's back. Mark watched in amazement as he smoothly spread it over the wounds, even though some were still open and bleeding. His hands glided over her back, making sure every area was coated. As Mark watched him, he saw Charlie's spirit. It was a good, gentle, kind one.

"Need t' do dat e'ery hour," Charlie stressed to Harper and Marshall.

"How will I know what to mix?" Harper asked.

"I make," Charlie said. "Only need t' add water."

"Wait." Mark looked at him, confused. "Where are you going?"

"Need t' get more help. Family dat way," Charlie pointed toward the north. "I get help dere."

"I see."

"You need help too," Charlie said, knowingly.

Mark narrowed his eyes at him. "What do you mean?"

"Your heart need help. Elders help you, while Pete help her. She gonna need heart help too when she wake. I bring da people ya need here."

Mark sat back in his seat with his arms crossed, studying him. This young man had a strange way about him. Mark had been all over the world, and hadn't met anyone like him before. He seemed to be able to assess the situation inside and out in a matter of minutes.

"What about her fever?" Harper asked, concerned. "It's pretty high."

Charlie nodded as he looked down at her, concerned. "Yeah."

He went back to the table and picked up the remaining roots and flowers, shredding them as best as he could. He got more water and poured it into the bowl. After he stirred it for a couple moments, he took it over to Harper and said, "Boil dis for five minutes. When cool, strain it, wake her, an' make her drink. It a tea."

"How often do I do this?"

"Only this one time. When she wake, she gonna be terrible sick for ten minutes. She gonna chunder da whole time. When she done, it should be better. If not, when I come back, I get more."

"Right-oh." Harper said in a sigh. He handed it to Marshall to boil. "Um, she's on medicine right now. I don't know if we can wake her."

"Take her down t' da river. Splash water on her. She wake," Charlie said confidently.

"Got it," Harper said. He still was not sure about Charlie.

Charlie took off into the brush again to get the dry ingredients they were going to need to make the paste. He came back about fifteen minutes later. By that time, the tea was setting on the table to cool. Harper also had several bags ready for Charlie to put the dry mixture into on the table.

Charlie shredded the ingredients, added the dirt, and then separated them into twelve different bags. When he was done, he sealed them. He then took a plastic cup to Harper and handed it to him. "Fill dis to da top – do not spill!" he warned. "Very specific! Den mix 'til smooth. Spread on her back and do not cover. Let air mix with da mixture."

"Um, do ya want me t' clean that before I put on more? Isn't it gonna bleed?"

"Bleed for first couple times, yes…no matter." Charlie shook his head. "Just scrape off, den spread smoothly. It stop."

"You got it." Harper sighed again in frustration. He took the cup to the bags and set it upside down so nothing could get into it, before he went back to Charlie. "Thanks for your help," Harper said, shaking Charlie's hand in appreciation.

"No worries." Charlie grinned. He picked up his bag, bow, and arrow off the table. "I go get more help. Be back in two shakes of a lamb's tail – ten or eleven hours maybe. She be better by den."

Hawk shook Charlie's hand as well. "Thanks, mate."

Mark shook his hand and thanked him as well, before Charlie disappeared into the Outback.

"Um," Marshall looked up from testing the tea, "this is cool enough for her t' drink. We need t' wake her to drink it. I don't want her fever to get any higher. It's too high for my comfort at the moment as it is."

"Crickey! I hope she'll wake." Hawk looked down at her. "If not, this could get sticky."

Mark crouched beside her, and put his hand on the side of her face. "Casey?" He rubbed her cheek. "Can you wake up for me?"

Casey moaned. The fever made her feel horrible. Her entire body ached. She felt as if she was going to vomit, and she wanted to stay asleep.

The Colonel knelt down next to Mark. "Come on, Casey. We don't want to have to take you down to the river and dunk you."

Casey didn't want that either, so she forced herself to partially open her eyes. She was woozy and lightheaded though.

"Good job." Mark smiled. "You're going to have to drink something to lower your fever. If I hold it, will you drink it?" Casey nodded, so he took the cup from Marshall, setting it on the ground next to him. "Lil' help?" he asked the Colonel.

The Colonel went around to the other side of her. "Um…."

"You feed it to her while I hold her up," Mark said, getting a good look at the logistics of the situation. Mark reached under Casey with one arm, while he slid the other one under her head to gently lift her in approximately a forty-five-degree angle. When he had her how he wanted her, he looked at the Colonel and nodded.

The Colonel took several minutes to help her to drink it all down before Mark lowered her. He then slid his arms out and rubbed her cheek.

Casey moaned, moving her head in hopes of clearing it.

"What's wrong?" Mark asked.

"This feels…whoa!"

"Case?" he asked, concerned.

Casey looked up at Mark, feeling tipsy, as if she were drunk. She giggled.

"What the…?" Mark turned to the Colonel for help.

"You're cute!" Casey giggled. Then she shook her head, as the tea mixed with the medicine. "Ohhhhh," she moaned, closing her eyes.

"What?" Mark asked.

"I, um…" she reached up and touched the side of his face.

He put his hand over hers with a look of extreme concern. "Casey?"

"My, um…my legs."

"What about them?"

"They're…I can't move them." Casey sighed, sinking down into the pillow as the feeling slowly poured over her body.

Mark looked at everyone for some kind of explanation.

"She'll be apples!" Hawk said confidently. At least, he prayed she would be fine.

"She's…." He looked down at her, as her eyes finally closed. "Casey?"

"It's the medicine, mate," Harper said. "If it wasn't the medicine or the fever, it's probably the tea that knocked her out."

"No worries," Hawk said. "Those guys have some powerful stuff. Don't know where they get it, or how they know, but it's good."

Mark sighed, shaking his head. "All right."

"Let's go eat, man." Derek put his hand on Mark's shoulder. "It's been a while."

Mark kissed her head before he stood, and they all left the tent.

Chapter 12

Dreamtime

Over the next couple of hours, Harper gently washed off Casey's back and re-applied a new bag of the mixture. Much to his surprise, her back did look remarkably better even after four hours. He was excited to see what was going to happen over the next several hours. He even used a little of it each time for her cheek, which looked amazingly well after only the first couple of hours.

While her fever was still there, it wasn't anywhere near as high as it had been. She woke up about six hours after they gave her the tea and puked her guts out. A couple of the guys held her up with the blanket around her while Mark directed her head toward the bucket he held. They were stunned at how much she threw up, considering she hadn't eaten anything since she was with Jesse at the hotel.

True to his word, Charlie came back about eleven and a half hours after he left. He had four other guys with him, along with one woman.

"Dis is Ollie, George, an' Pete – our elders. And dis is Grace – me blood n' blister." He gestured toward the people with him.

Ollie looked to be about sixty or seventy years old, and was only about five-foot-five. He wore a pair of tan shorts and a white tank top – no shoes. (None of them were wearing shoes.) He kept his curly white hair short, and his white teeth stood out when he smiled.

George was about five-foot-seven, and looked to be about fifty years old. His dark hair was in curly locks, about six inches long all over, mixed with about fifty percent gray. He wore a pair of jean shorts, along with a white, green, and blue flannel patterned, button-down shirt, that was open, with a white tank top under it.

Pete was about five-nine, and looked to be only about forty years old. 'Elder' was not a word anyone would have used for him. His jet-black hair was short, and the dark eyes that all of them had, held a dancing sparkle of life. Pete wore jeans and a royal blue t-shirt.

Charlie's sister (which was what a "blood n' blister" was in Australian Strine), Grace, was very pretty. She had her black, mid-back length, curly hair, pulled back in a low-hanging ponytail. She also wore a strapless sarong tied with a rope at her waist. She was five-foot-five, and looked to be about twenty to twenty-five years old.

Hawk shook each of their hands. "Welcome."

Grace kept looking at Casey, who was asleep in the tent, while keeping a nervous eye on all of the men crawling all over the place. This was foreign to her. The idea that the men were taking care of a woman, and worse yet, that she lay there only partially dressed, was unheard of in her tribe.

"Ollie an' George, are our elders," Charlie explained. "Dey need t' meet with him," he said, nodding toward Mark, who sat by Casey.

Mark looked up at the Colonel and raised an eyebrow.

"Um." The Colonel stood up and shook everyone's hand. When he got to Charlie, he asked, "Why exactly would they want to meet with one of my men?"

"Because his heart needs healing. Dey da one's dat'll fix it, like da medicine fix her back…yes?" Charlie asked.

The Colonel looked at the unconventional band that was before him, trying to assess what everyone's function would be. "And the other two? Who are they here for?"

"Oh! Pete knows recipes better den me. He and his dad, Buri, are da most smart about dat type of stuff. He make better tea den me."

The Colonel nodded toward Grace. "And her?"

"She help Pete. It more proper for da women t' take care of da women," he explained.

"I see." The Colonel nodded in understanding. "That makes sense. Um," the Colonel ran everything through his head one more time before he asked, "And what specifically are they gonna do with English to heal his heart?"

"Dey take him t' dreamtime. No worries. Dey do it tons of times."

"And you? What are you going to do here?"

"I bring dem." Charlie grinned. "I help where needed. You need cook – I cook. You need water – I get. I here t' help."

The Colonel glanced at Hawk, who nodded. Obviously, Hawk trusted them, and the Colonel trusted Hawk, so the Colonel nodded, much to the small band's relief.

Grace put her hand on Charlie's shoulder. When he turned to look at her, she nodded toward Casey, so he nodded. "She gonna help now," Charlie said, as Grace walked into the tent.

Mark suspiciously looked up at her, still not too sure about the entire situation.

"Need t' clean," Grace said, washing her hands in a bowl of water. She dried them off as she went to Casey. She felt her forehead. "Just lil' one," she said to Mark. "She'll be apples."

"Hey, English," the Colonel called him. "Come on over."

Mark looked at everyone, nervous as to what he was walking into. He trusted the Colonel though, so he kissed Casey's head before he headed out of the tent. As soon as he was out, Pete went with Grace, and together they closed the tent walls for privacy.

"Oh! No way!" Mark objected, and turned to go back to the tent, but Hawk grabbed his arm. Mark spun around and demanded, "One of ours is in there with her at all times. If I'm going with them, I want the Colonel or Derek in there."

The Colonel looked at Pete and Grace, who were still putting down the walls, and nodded. "You go with them, and either Derek or I will be in there."

Mark nodded, irritated, but satisfied, and went with Ollie and George into the Outback. He was nervous to leave Casey there by herself, and wasn't sure what he was in store for with these two men. However, he trusted the Colonel who trusted Hawk, so he went.

The Colonel nodded toward Hawk, before he headed into the tent. When he got to the door, Grace looked up, startled.

"No worries," Pete told her. "He's here for her. It's okay."

"Your English is very good," the Colonel observed, going to the chair Mark had been sitting in, resting his elbows on his knees as he leaned forward.

"I worked on a station in Queensland since I was a lil' tyke," Pete explained. "They are good people, and I learned a lot."

"So, are you guys going to be able to help her for real?" the Colonel asked.

"Oh yeah." He waved him off. He knelt down to look over her back, as she lay on her stomach on the cot.

"How can you see under all of that?" the Colonel shook his head, amazed.

"Need t' know what t' look for." Pete looked up with a satisfied smile. "Been doing it for years."

"Need t' clean dat," Grace said, keeping a close eye on the Colonel.

"No worries, Grace." Pete put his hand on her shoulder. "They have different customs. Just do what ya need t' do."

She nodded before she got a bowl of soap and water, and brought it over. She knelt down next to the cot, and then scooped off the mixture with her hands, putting it into a garbage can she had already brought next to the cot. When she finished, she cleaned the wounds with a sponge soaked with soap and water. She made sure to scrub it well, but that was fine. Casey's back had healed quite a bit by that point.

Much to the Colonel's surprise, the wounds were closed. "Wow!" The Colonel looked at it, wide-eyed. "That's amazing!" It looked like a bunch of old scars to him.

"Not completely better, but it's good," Pete said with his arms crossed, and a perplexed look on his face. "The way Charlie described it, I was worried."

"It looked bad," the Colonel said.

"Oh! I'm sure. If it still looks like this, then it had t' be bad."

The Colonel nodded. He didn't understand these people or their ways, but he had been around the world enough to know that each group of people had their own way of doing things...and sometimes their ideas and ways were better than his. He sat in silent prayer for Mark and Casey, as he watched what Pete and Grace were doing.

"What's her name?" Pete asked.

"Casey."

"Casey." Pete gently tapped her cheek after he cleaned it. He didn't bother putting anything else on the cheek since it was mostly healed by that point. The scratches were all but gone.

Casey slowly opened her eyes to see a man whose skin was as dark as an African American, less than five inches from her face. He grinned when he saw her eyes open.

"Who are you?" she asked, struggling to focus.

"Pete."

Casey rolled her eyes at him. How was she supposed to know who "Pete" was?

It was almost as if Pete could read her mind. He cracked up in laughter. "I like this one. She's funny."

"Why? What did she do?" the Colonel sat up to see.

"Her face," Pete said, still laughing.

"Yeah," the Colonel agreed. "She can be pretty animated."

"You get tea?" Grace asked Pete. "She still hot."

"Yeah, I know," Pete agreed. "You work on her back. I got her fever. No worries." He smiled at her to put her more at ease. He and Grace were family. Pete's wife, Victoria, was her sister.

She smiled back, as she continued to clean Casey's back. She wanted to make sure to get every little bit of the mixture off before she decided what to do next. She shook her head though. The marks still left told her that the cuts were originally very deep. She couldn't imagine why someone would do this to another person.

Pete got up, as Casey tried to focus. He went out of the tent for the ingredients for the tea, returning in less than five minutes with a handful of roots and flowers. He had the mixture shredded and boiling less than three minutes later.

"Wow!" The Colonel watched him, amazed. "Charlie was right. You are better than him."

"Charlie's learning," Pete said, as he walked back from the fire where he had the tea set for boiling. "I've been doing this for years." After he got the tea on the fire to boil, he went into the tent and looked at Casey's back, since Grace had it thoroughly clean. He ran his fingers over the scars, shaking his head. "Someone bad did this."

The Colonel nodded. "Yeah."

"Why?"

"For information."

Pete and Grace both looked up at the Colonel, stunned.

"Yeah, I know," the Colonel said. "Trust me. I know."

Pete sat back on his feet, thinking of the best way to fix the scars still left on her back. He knew it was more than an instrument that did this. He knew by the marks on her back, that the whip was just an instrument of the evil behind it. He also knew by the way they looked that something had been put in the wounds as well.

"What was in the wounds?" Pete asked the Colonel.

"What do you mean?" the Colonel asked.

Pete thought for a moment on how to word the question so the Colonel would understand. "When you cut up meat, sometimes you put stuff on it to preserve it. It makes it fresher longer. She's not meat, but her marks tell me that something was in there besides just her flesh. It's what is fighting the medicine t' keep it red…fresh."

The Colonel looked at him wide-eyed, for a moment before he said, "The person poured salt into the wounds."

Grace gasped, covering her mouth in shock, while it was Pete's turn to look at the Colonel wide-eyed. Pete glanced from the wounds, to the Colonel, and back again, before he asked the Colonel, "She was tortured for information?"

"Yes."

The word hung in the air for a moment before Pete said, "She's gonna need t' go through what that other bloke's going through right now. Grace'll go with her, but she needs dreamtime for her peace of mind."

The Colonel shook his head. "I don't know about that."

Pete looked back down at the wounds again. "I do."

"This is done." Harper poked his head into the tent a couple minutes later with a steaming cup of tea in his hands. He glanced down at Casey's back in shock. "Well, bugger me dead!" he said, wide-eyed.

"Looks good, eh?" the Colonel smiled, pleased.

Harper shook his head in amazement. "You're gonna have t' teach me how t' do that."

"No worries." Pete waved him off. "I'll show you before I go."

Harper handed the cup to Grace, as he crouched down next to Casey, running his fingers over her back. "This is really amazing. You should have seen it when she came in. It looked sliced n' diced."

"I believe it," Pete said. "It should look a lot better than it does. It should look like this." He pointed to her cheek. "I'm gonna need something a bit stronger. I'll be back. Grace, feed that t' her while I'm gone," he said, and disappeared out of the tent.

Harper stood up, shaking his head in amazement. "Unbelievable!"

Grace went to the other side of the cot with the tea, as Harper left the tent, still shaking his head, dumbfounded. "You drink…yes?" she asked Casey.

"Yeah." Casey nodded. "Give me a sec." Casey looked around for a moment in order to figure out how to sit up without exposing herself.

Grace glanced up at the Colonel, who understood without her saying anything. "I'll stand with my back to you while you adjust. Sound okay?" he asked Casey.

"Yeah," Casey said, grateful.

When he turned, with Grace's help Casey was able to sit up and turn around in a seated position, with Casey holding a blanket to her chest to cover herself. She couldn't put a shirt on until Pete was finished. When Casey was comfortable, Grace gave her the tea.

"How you feel?" she asked while Casey drank.

"Dizzy and my head hurts, but okay."

"Pain?"

Casey sighed. "I think that's going to be a constant for a while."

"No." She shook her head. "Couple hours…no more. Should be gone already."

Casey looked at her as if she was crazy, and Grace busted out in laughter.

"Can I turn around?" the Colonel asked with a smile on his face at Grace's laughter, imagining what Casey's face looked like at that one.

"Yeah," Casey said, not taking her eyes off Grace.

He pulled the chair over to the side of Casey, opposite Grace, with a smile on his face. He stifled his laughter for her sake, as he saw the look on her face. Casey stared at Grace as if she were nuts. "I didn't believe your back would look as good as it does," the Colonel said. "She's probably right."

"This'll do it." Pete walked in with more flowers and roots. He shredded them into a bowl and added dirt and water, turning it into the thickness of a paste. "She done drinking yet?"

"Yes," Grace said, as Casey chugged the tea and handed her back the cup.

"That one's not as strong. It won't knock ya out, but it will get rid of the fever," Pete said confidently. "Now for your back." He came over with the bowl. "You want t' stay sitting?"

"Um, I want to lie back down. I'm kind of dizzy," Casey admitted.

"Kinda?" Pete questioned.

"I'm dizzy," she clarified.

"On your side?" Pete suggested. "You still can't wear a shirt. Give it a couple hours, and then you may be able to."

"That's fine," Casey said, as she lay on her side, facing Grace. If her blanket fell, she wanted to be facing her instead of the Colonel. "Where's Mark?" Casey asked.

"He with da elders," Grace explained, while Pete spread the mixture on her back.

"Is he going to be okay?"

"Give him day or two." Grace nodded. "He needs t' go t' dreamtime."

Casey looked up at her, not sure if she wanted to know the answer as she asked, "What do you mean 'he needs to go to dreamtime?' What are they doing to him?"

"No worries," Pete said. "You'll find out when they take you."

"When they what?" Casey tried to look at him over her shoulder, but he pushed her back so she wouldn't ruin the mixture.

He laughed at her as he said, "No worries. Grace'll go with you."

Casey looked at her, terrified, and Grace burst out in laughter as well. "No worries." Grace smiled. "Done it before. You be okay."

Casey looked up at Grace in alarm. "I don't know if I want to go."

"No worries. You be fine."

"Colonel," Casey begged, "please don't make me go."

"You won't have to go anywhere you don't want to. Just relax for now." The Colonel rested his hand on her head so she would know he was right there with her.

Casey nodded. Her head was dizzy, so she pushed the thoughts out of her head until she could focus. Then, she closed her eyes to rest while Pete finished putting on the mixture. By the time he finished, Casey had fallen back to sleep.

*   *   *

Over the next couple of hours, her back massively improved. Finally, about twenty or so hours after they arrived, Pete was satisfied. He said the scarring was at a minimum at that point on her back, and he couldn't see the scars on her face at all.

Casey had been able to eat during that time as well, much to the Colonel's relief. It seemed that most of the guys were getting concerned regarding her not eating. While she did eat, she didn't eat a whole lot, because she was worried about Mark. No one had seen or heard from him in three days.

Finally, he came back with Ollie and George looking worn out, but happy. "Hi there." Mark said, walking into the tent with Grace and Casey. He leaned down to give Casey a kiss as he rested his hand on her back. "How are you feeling?"

"Me? What about you?" She looked at him in concern. "No one has heard from you for three days."

He sighed with a smile. "It was rough, but good. I'm glad I went. Now it's your turn." He smiled, tucking her hair behind her ear, as he crouched down in front of her. She wore a pair of scrub pants and a tank top.

"She need t' take clean first," Grace said. "Pete say she can take clean."

"Take clean?" Mark asked.

"Take a bath. I'm going to take a bath down at the river here in a little while. I'm going to go when I finish eating." She looked at him nervously. "Um, I have a question for you." About ten hours ago, she discovered that her necklace was missing, and no one seemed to know where it was. At first, she panicked until the Colonel told her to relax and talk to Mark about it when he returned.

"What's up, buttercup?" He winked with a smile.

"My goodness! You are in a good mood, aren't you?" Casey smiled. She was mentally exhausted and physically tired, but it felt good to see him again.

"Yep. Now, what's the question?"

"Um," she set her fork down on her plate, which was on her lap, "Do you…I really hope you did…."

"Do I…what?"

"Did you take my necklace off me and put it somewhere safe?"

He looked at her wide-eyed, as a flash of panic shot across his face. Then he took a breath to calm his nerves before he asked, "Um, you don't know where it is?"

"No. Last time I saw it was in the hotel when I put it on after I changed from my shower in the hotel room."

"Oh." He looked down, trying to wrack his brain as to when he saw it last.

"Do you remember seeing it on me in the helicopter?"

"No. Quite honestly, I was more concerned with you than with the necklace. Don't worry about it. We'll get you something else."

Casey looked down at her food, feeling sick to her stomach. "It wasn't so much the necklace itself, as much as what it reminded me of." She looked up at him. "Every time I saw it, or reached up and touched it for those few days before we were taken, it reminded me of us standing in front of the window overlooking Sydney, and you asking me to marry you."

Grace quietly stood near the table, listening. She felt bad for Casey. She had not only been tortured, but had also lost something precious to her in the process. Grace had faith that Mark would be able to fix it though. He might not be able to give her the necklace itself back, but he would find a way to make it better.

"I know." He rested his hand on the side of her face. "Don't worry. I'll think of something." He kissed her cheek. Then he slid onto the cot beside her as he said, "I think I need a bath too.

Why don't you finish up while I take a bath in the river, and then you can take one."

Grace adamantly shook her head. "She not take clean in river."

He looked at her, confused for a moment, before he said, "We don't have showers. How is she going to take a bath?"

"In here." She gestured around the tent. "She take clean, den go with da elders."

"She's not going without me," Mark objected. "That's scary!"

Casey looked over at Mark nervously, wondering what they did to him.

Grace smiled, hoping to put him more at ease. "I go too. No worries."

"The Colonel, Derek, and I are going too." Mark stood. "I'm going to talk to them about it. Don't worry." He bent down and kissed her. As he left the tent, he said over his shoulder, "You are not going without me."

"Thanks," Casey said, still anxious.

After she finished eating, Grace brought a couple of buckets of water, which were warmed up on the fire for her to bathe. Grace closed the tent walls, and then went to her backpack. As she watched her, Casey wondered how Grace was planning on doing this.

Grace pulled out three towels, a washcloth, shampoo, and soap from the cabinet in the tent, and took it to the table. "Mr. Harper give dis," she said, showing her the razor that was on the table. "I give dis," she grinned, pulling out a sarong that was three different shades of blue, with an aboriginal sea design. "I also pick deese," she smiled, holding up some little white flowers.

"Thank you," Casey said, excited to finally take a bath, albeit within the tent. She felt disgusting.

"You look nice in deese. Mr. Mark not take eyes off you."

Casey blushed.

"Now, I also bring dis for you because I feel bad." Grace had a slight frown on her face. "Charlie tell me what your back look like." She shook her head out of compassion. "You need t' smell good too," she said, as she pulled out a small jar of oil.

"Thank you."

"Now for da hard part." Grace had Casey take off her clothes. She helped her wash her hair first. While Casey shaved using one of the buckets, a razor, and soap, Grace poked around until she found a toothbrush. Grace then headed out of the tent to find toothpaste from one of the guys. She returned as Casey finished shaving.

Casey then washed her face, along with the rest of her body, out of the same bucket she used for shaving. When she finished, Grace dumped the water, and then went back out to re-fill it with clean water. While she was gone, Casey brushed her teeth.

When Grace came back, she took the clean bucket of water and dumped it over Casey's entire body for one final rinse. Afterward, Casey dried off. Then, Grace helped rub oil on her back and the backs of her legs, while Casey rubbed it on her front. The oil smelled absolutely wonderful to Casey. She made a mental note to ask her what it was later. For now, she was grateful to be clean.

When they finished, Grace took a small handful of the oil and put it lightly through Casey's hair. She said it was partly to condition it, and partly to make it smell good. When they finished, Casey stood up and Grace put the sarong on her. She made sure to show Casey how to do it, so she could put it on herself next time.

Then she took a rope and loosely tied it around Casey's waist for a belt.

Afterward, she had Casey sit down on the cot. While Grace left most of Casey's hair down, she took a portion of both sides and braided the small, country-white flowers into them. Casey would have loved to know what she looked like, but there wasn't a mirror in there.

When she stood up in front of her, Grace had a big grin on her face, pleased with the result. "Beautiful!" she said, and hugged her. "You ready t' see Mr. Mark, den da elders."

"I don't know about the second half of that," Casey admitted. "That part scares me."

Grace put her hands on Casey's shoulders, and said, "It scary…yes, but worth it. Your back, face, wrists, and legs are healing. Now ya need t' heal your soul. Dey be dere da whole time. I be dere too. No worries."

Casey took a deep breath and slowly let it out, before she nodded in agreement.

"Good." Grace smiled, satisfied. "Now, dey waiting. Let's go."

Grace went outside and got everyone's attention, before she pulled the tent door back and Casey walked out. Casey got multiple whistles and comments, as Mark stood in shock.

"Wow!" he said, wide-eyed. "You look great!"

The Colonel winked at her with a smile. "I would lean more toward stunning."

Derek reached up and shoved Mark a couple steps toward Casey. Grace took the cue and shoved Casey a couple steps toward him, leaving only a couple steps in between them.

He reached his hands out towards her, and she reached hers out, grabbing his hands. He pulled her the couple of steps over to him, and he wrapped his arms around her. He deeply inhaled, smelling the oils that were on her. "Wow! You smell good," he whispered. He looked at her, resting his hands on the sides of her face as he leaned forward and kissed her.

Neither cared that they were surrounded by people. They only saw each other.

"I can't wait to marry you, Casey. You are a complete package. Your heart is amazing," he said quietly. "Your spirit is gentle and kind, and you are absolutely gorgeous. I thank God for every day I have the privilege of having you in my life."

Casey looked up into his beautiful dark-brown eyes, and ran her fingers through his blonde hair. "I don't know what I did to deserve you, but I thank God for giving me the opportunity to even know you exist."

"Oh, Case," he hugged her as if he wasn't going to let her go, being careful not to hurt her back, "I love you."

"I love you too."

"I want to take you out of here," he said. "I want to protect you and keep you safe."

"You will."

"Um," Ollie said as he stood, "she need dreamtime. She healed on outside. Now need t' heal inside."

George nodded, looking into Casey's eyes. "Da soul is torn and scarred."

"We kind of need t' keep these guys moving," Hawk spoke up. "I don't know if we can wait three more days. I don't know what the outside world looks like right now."

George looked at him very sternly, and said, "Her core needs t' be healed before her body. Dat more important. It takes as long as it takes."

Hawk shook his head in frustration. While he trusted these people, time was precious. He was responsible for the A.N.G.E.L.s in his care.

George grabbed Hawk's wrist, and brought him to Casey, as Mark stood to the side with his arm around her. "Look at her eyes." George pointed to her face as he said, "Her core is being held prisoner. She needs dreamtime. She need it now."

Hawk looked at her, almost studying her, before he finally nodded in approval.

"Just so you know, we're all going too," the Colonel said, standing from where he sat around the fire.

Ollie shook his head. "She needs t' do dis on her own."

"We're going," the Colonel said firmly. "We will not let her out of our sight again. Come on, Cruise," he said to Derek, who nodded in response as he stood. "He's going," the Colonel said, pointing to Derek. "He's going," he said, pointing to Mark. "I'm going. And he's going," the Colonel said, pointing to Hawk. "The rest of you will hold down the fort."

Grace grabbed Casey's hand. "I go too."

Ollie sighed in frustration, shaking his head. "Right-oh. Let's go."

Casey grabbed Mark's hand as they started into the woods. She was terrified of what this potentially entailed. However, knowing what Mark looked like when he left and what he looked like when he returned, gave her the confidence of knowing that she would have to hold her breath and it would be over soon.

They walked to a small, circular hut about a mile from camp made of mud, tree branches, and leaves. It was solid by the looks of it. The doors were made of thick, brown curtains, and Casey could barely see the glow of a fire from under it.

"We go in dere. You stay here," Ollie said to Hawk, the Colonel, Derek, and Mark, as he pulled back the curtain.

Casey turned toward Mark and gave him a kiss and hug, afraid to let him go.

"You'll be okay. Don't worry," he said quietly.

"Pray for me?"

"Of course. I always do."

"Okay." She took a deep breath and walked into the hut, holding Grace's hand as they entered.

The floor was made of dirt ground, and there was a fire pit in the middle of the floor of the little circular hut. While Casey and Grace sat on one side of the hut, Ollie and George sat on the other, facing them, with the fire between all of them.

"Drink." Ollie held up a cup of tea. He passed it to George, who passed it to Grace, who passed it to Casey. She took a few sips and it tasted horrible, so she closed her eyes and chugged the rest of it. When she finished, she handed the cup back to Grace, who gave it back to George. George set it on the ground between him and Ollie.

After he set it down, they stared at Casey. At first, she tried to figure out what they were looking at, until the room slightly shifted. "Whoa!" Casey grabbed her head. "What's in that?"

They didn't say anything. They didn't move or even breathe. Everything suddenly shifted and swirled around her. It felt like a horrible amusement park ride. Casey put her head in her hands, taking a couple deep breaths for a moment, before she looked back up.

When she did, she let out a horrific scream, startled, as across from her where Ollie sat on the left…was one of those hideous, demonic creatures. Then, on the right where George had been, there was a man with a white robe resembling what the ancient Greeks wore. The man had short, blond hair and brilliant blue eyes. His cheeks were slightly ruddy, as he sat with his legs crossed in front of him, his sword attached to his left side.

The demon looked like the one who had scratched Casey's arm in the dream. It casually sat there with one arm resting on its upright knee, and its other resting on the floor behind him, holding it up. Its wings lazily hung on its back behind it.

"What are…?" Casey looked at them again, stunned. They couldn't be real…could they?

She looked to her right to ask Grace, but Todd Peters from her senior year of high school sat there. Casey screamed and jumped back, only to turn in the other direction to see the man from Columbia who attacked her, and she screamed again.

"What's going on?" Casey demanded as she stood.

She went to leave, but the demon spoke…and she froze in place. "You're not going anywhere, preciousssss," it hissed, pointing up toward the ceiling.

Casey heard hissing and looked up only to see a snake as long as a boa constrictor, slither down from the roof, coiling itself around her upper body. She screamed and squirmed as she fought to get away. It pulled her back down to the ground, so she sat on the dirt between Todd and the man from Columbia, as it held her arms and torso with its body.

Mark poked his head through the curtain to see George and Ollie on one side of the fire, and Grace and Casey on the other. Grace had her arms wrapped around Casey, holding her on the ground while she screamed and struggled.

Ollie looked toward Mark and nodded, so Mark went in a couple steps, and sat on the ground, cross-legged. When he looked back up, he saw what Casey saw. He looked around horrified and in shock, but didn't say a word. He knew he had let it play out, so he sat in continuous, silent prayer.

"Ssssit tight, preciousssss," the demon hissed.

Casey stared at him, frozen in fear. Could this be real? It was as if all of her worst nightmares were wrapped into one.

"Oh, help me!" Casey begged, looking up at the ceiling with tears streaming down her cheeks.

When she looked back down, Jack and Mac sat to the left of the angel, and her parents sat to the right of the demon. The two new sets of people were on either side of the fire facing each other.

"What in the world?" She looked at them, wide-eyed. She was relieved, yet scared, to see Jack, Mac, and her parents. Knowing they were all dead, but sitting right in front of her, terrified her beyond words.

She turned to the man from Columbia, nervous as to why he was there. Then, as she turned back toward Todd, he was within a couple inches of her. She could even feel his breath on her face. He reached around and jerked her head back toward him before he leaned down and kissed her neck.

Casey quickly shifted, as the snake still had a hold of her arms and upper body, and got her legs out from underneath her. She got one knee up and hit him in his chest. He moved slightly back, which was enough room for her to get her foot up to kick him in the stomach, sending Todd back about four feet.

Casey shook her head to clear it, as she still felt dizzy, yet everything seemed so clear. As she watched Todd get back up, thoughts of prom night suddenly flooded her mind. It was as if she was there in the car with him.

*　　*　　*

Todd took Casey up to a lookout point after prom before they were to go home. He said it was one of his favorite spots because of the view of the city. When he put the car in park and turned it off, he rested his arm on the seat behind her.

"Wow! This is beautiful!" Casey said in amazement.

"So are you," he said, eyeing her like his favorite candy.

She looked over to see him staring at her. "Todd, I...." She shook her head. They agreed to go to prom as friends, mostly because his girlfriend had recently broken up with him, and because their families were both stationed on the same base.

He didn't say anything. Before she knew what was going on, he leaned over and grabbed her wrists, flipping her onto her back. He held her wrists to the door so she couldn't get free.

She wriggled and squirmed, getting her feet under him, forcefully shoving her knee into his groin. He grabbed himself, as he got up on his knees. Then she kicked him in the head as she flipped over, opening the car door. She grabbed her purse that had fallen onto the floor and scrambled out of the car.

She got about twenty yards away before she heard the car door close. Then the car started, and she turned to see him pull away. What was she going to do now? It had to be about midnight or one o'clock in the morning, and it was a Saturday night.

She resigned herself to walking, so she headed down the road toward town. She saw several cars on the way down, but ducked behind trees so they wouldn't see her. She wanted to get home where she knew she was safe.

By the time she walked the five miles back to the edge of town, she was exhausted. She called a taxi from the first payphone she found, which was at a gas station. She had the taxi drop her off at the gates of the base, and she walked through the checkpoint.

It was a little awkward since she saw those guys every day going in and out of the base, but she told them it was a nice night to walk home. As far as she was concerned, they didn't need to know any different. That was her business.

Unbelievably, when she looked up toward her house, she saw Todd's car sitting outside of it. She looked around to see if any of the MPs were walking around, but she didn't see any at that moment. She was apprehensive, but knew she had to keep going, despite the fact that she had to pass Todd to get to the safety of her house.

As she walked up to the walkway to the front deck, Todd got out of his car. He called her over, but she didn't move. "Casey, I'm sorry. I don't know what came over me. I would like it if you would forgive me. Please?"

"Todd, I…." She shook her head as she crossed her arms.

"Come on over here and talk to me?"

Casey sighed before walking to the driver's side of the car. As he leaned against the closed door, she left about two feet between them, and she warned, "Don't try anything funny. MPs and Air Force personnel are crawling all over this base."

He stood up and took two steps toward her. As soon as he got within arm's length, he grabbed her and pulled her toward him. She went to scream, but he covered her mouth with his in a kiss. She struggled in his arms, as she turned her head side to side to get away from him.

"Don't," he said sternly up next her ear. He grabbed her hair and jerked her head back. She froze in his arms. "If you even think of telling anyone what happened tonight, not only you, but your brother will pay the price."

"What do you mean?"

"You know who my dad is." He swore and shoved her to the ground. Then he shook his head in disgust as he got into his car and drove off, leaving her in the middle of the street completely by herself.

She was relieved he was gone, but she was scared, and her body shook with what had happened that night. All she knew at that moment was that her sanctuary, her home, was just across the street.

She took a deep breath and struggled to her feet. She stumbled over to her porch where she slowly climbed the stairs. She shook from adrenaline, so she slid down the door to the floor of the deck, holding her knees to her chest as she wrapped her arms around them. She knew she would never find her keys, let alone get the door unlocked with the shape she was in. Instead, she sat with her eyes closed and her head down, taking deep, cleansing breaths while she fought the feelings of violation and humiliation that tried to suffocate her.

She fell asleep on the deck, waking up about two hours later. The base was silent. It was as if she was the only one awake on the entire base at that moment.

She reached into her purse, feeling around until she found her keys and pulled them out. She was still a little shaky, but she grabbed the railing of the deck and dragged herself up to a standing position. Leaning on the railing, she fumbled with the keys until she got the door unlocked and opened. Making sure to lock it behind her, she then staggered to the couch and collapsed on it. She had a sense of relief wash over her as she sunk onto the couch after such a horrid night.

As she lay there, she purposely replaced the feelings of molestation, abuse, and the threats that were made against her…with safety, security, and the loving family she knew she had with Jack. While he was out of town on a mission at the moment, she knew she wasn't too far from his thoughts.

She struggled with those feelings for over an hour, wrestling with what happened. She didn't want to think about what did happen, or worse, what could have happened, had she not fought him off.

She knew she was fooling herself. She knew what really happened that night, but she didn't want to think about it. She finally passed out on the couch, relieved the night was over.

The next morning, she woke up to find her corsage off her wrist, a pillow under her head, and a blanket tucked around her – and she knew instantly Jack was back and she was safe.

She looked up to the ceiling, grateful he was there. She closed her eyes and took a deep breath. When she opened them back up, she sat back in the hut in the middle of the Outback with an angel and demon across from her, her parents to her left, and Jack and Mac to her right. She was also still held captive by a gruesome snake. The only thing that was a relief, at that moment, was that Todd was gone.

"Why didn't you tell me?" Jack asked, hurt that she didn't trust him.

"I did it to protect you. His dad was a General and you were only a Captain. He could have done some serious damage to you and to your career."

"Don't you know that you mean more to me than my career?"

"You just came off the field." She looked down, upset. "You just got back from doing who-knows-what, who-knows-where. The last thing you needed was to be worrying about me."

Jack shook his head in disappointment. She couldn't stand hurting him, and looked down in shame. The last thing she wanted to do was hurt him. She did it to protect him.

When she looked back up, the man from Columbia sat beside her, looking her over with extreme lust and desire in his eyes. It was the same look he had in his eyes the night he attacked her.

She tried to scramble to her feet to get away from him, only to have him move closer.

"Yessss, the Todd inccccident was good, but thissss was a classssic!" The demon laughed an evil, sinister laugh as the angel shot it a nasty look in disgust.

"What happened?" her dad asked in concern, as he looked from Casey to the man and back again.

The man from Columbia was less than five inches away from Casey's body as he leaned up in an arc, next to her face. She couldn't go anywhere. The snake almost seemed to be holding her tighter, cutting off her air.

"I saw her and her guide in a coffee shop that morning," the man from Columbia said, glancing down at her body, before he looked back up into her eyes. "And I knew I just had to have her." He moved closer to her as he said, "I had to wait for my chance. I followed her all day so she wouldn't see me, but another man followed her too."

"He was one of mine," the angel added.

"Then," he smiled, "when she went to the hotel, the man following her left."

The angel glared at the demon. "That was your doing."

"Yessss, I got him!" The demon rubbed its hands together in delight. "It was a delicioussss night! Took one of your precioussss A.N.G.E.L.sss out, and got the key to her core that night too." It laughed a sinister laugh that echoed through the hut.

The man from Columbia looked her over again, moving to within a couple inches from her face. "Yessss," he hissed, as his face turned into the demon right before her eyes. "You were mine from that night on."

Casey screamed in horror, as she tried desperately to back away from this hideous creature, but she couldn't go anywhere.

"She's one of His!" The angel stood up with authority in his voice. "Her heart and soul are His!"

"Ahhhh, but her core isssss mine," the demon said, holding up a key. "This issss the key to her core. She won't give it up…and neither will I. It'ssss locked, forever." It reached up and touched the side of her face as it hissed, "Isn't it, precioussss?"

Casey stared at the demo in horror as she watched its face transform into Jackie's right in front of her eyes. "Yessss, another wonderful day," Jackie cackled. Her face and body were Jackie, but her voice was that of the demon. "Her core wasss mine before, but thisss sssealed it. Your preciousssss A.N.G.E.L.sssss failed." She glared at the angel. As she did, she transformed back into the demon. "They failed…and ssssso did you. Shhhe'sssss mine!" it hissed.

"No! Let her go!" the angel demanded.

Suddenly, Casey turned to see the man from Columbia on the other side of her from the demon. He reached over and touched her face. She couldn't go anywhere. She was trapped.

Just when she didn't think it could get any worse, as Casey trembled in terror, Jackie appeared by a sink. She poured salt into the bowl of water. As she walked over, she let out a foul, sinister laugh. She snapped her fingers, and the contents of the bowl in her hand instantly turned into fire. Jackie continued to laugh as she slowly walked toward her.

The closer she came, the more Casey looked around for a way to get out of this horrific nightmare, only to see the man from Columbia run his fingers down her arm. He kissed her shoulder and then looked up at her, laughing an evil laugh as well. The mocking laughter filled the hut, coming out from every corner. It was almost deafening.

Casey thought she was going to lose it as she stared at the demon. It reached up and rubbed it hand on the side of her face with a malicious look in its eyes. "You're mine, precioussss!" it hissed, and then let out a heinous laugh that blended with the other two.

Casey screamed in pure terror. She looked up toward the sky and shouted, "Father! By the blood of Jesus, I beg you to release me from this. What is…." It was a struggle to breathe, as the snake tightened its grip on her, almost completely cutting off her air. "What is free in Christ…is free indeed!" She gasped for air before she collapsed.

Mark looked up at the angel, who nodded toward him. He called for Derek and the Colonel to come in, and together they stood in front of the door of the tent with a righteous anger, their arms crossed, blocking anyone from leaving. No one was getting out until this was over.

"You can't do anything!" the demon hissed. "She'sssss mine! I won!"

The angel glanced at the Colonel, Derek, and Mark, and then to Jack and Mac, who collectively prayed for strength for the angel.

As they prayed aloud, the angel stood taller. He glared at the trio who surrounded his charge, and said, "What is free in Christ is free indeed. Release her immediately!"

"No!" The demon stood up, as Jackie and the other man slowly moved away to the safety of the other side of the fire. They moved as far away from the angel as they could get in the little hut. The demon stayed its ground while it glared at the angel.

"In the name of the Almighty One, I demand that you release her!" the angel shouted.

A smile slowly formed on the demon's face as it stood up and said, "I'll releasssse her, but I ssstill hold the key." It dangled the key in front of it, on its talon, as it walked through the fire with the other two. As soon as it was on the other side, the snake disappeared, and Casey fell to the ground, unable to move. She was finally able to get the precious air she needed.

The angel nodded toward the Colonel, Mark, and Derek, who went to Casey. While Derek placed one of his hands on her forehead and one on her stomach, Mark was on the other side of her, placing one of his hands over her eyes, and then placed his other hand over her heart. The Colonel took both of his hands and cupped her head, spreading his fingers as he wrapped them from the side to the back of her head, so her entire head was covered with all of their hands.

When they were in place, they all three prayed in a language Casey didn't understand. As she lay there, her body shook worse than it was already.

When they prayed, the angel suddenly began to glow. He pulled his sword out of the sheath. It was glowing as well…almost singing.

The demon, Jackie, and the man from Columbia stared at the angel in wide-eyed horror. They knew what was going on in the little hut, and that they were in deep trouble. The demon narrowed its eyes at the angel. Casey belonged to them!

"Give me the key!" the angel demanded with such authority in his voice, that it shook the tiny hut. "She is His – heart, mind, body, soul…and core. She has asked for it. The penalty has been paid."

"Never! Thissss wassss my masssterpiece." The demon leapt across the fire, landing on the angel, and a struggle immediately ensued between the angel and the demon.

Mark glanced up at the battle going on before him, and then closed his eyes and soaked in the glory of the Lord that had rained down on them in a steady flow. As he, the Colonel, and Derek continued to pray, Mac, Jack, and Casey's parents disappeared…leaving only them, Jackie, the man from Columbia, the angel, the demon, and Casey in the tiny hut.

It was a strange and unique place for a battle, but the stakes were high, so they were going to do their best. As they continued to pray, the angel got stronger, overpowering the demon. Both were bloody. Both gave it their all, not holding anything back.

As the prayers of the trio got stronger, the band of three men shook as well. The battle became more intense. The angel glowed brighter and brighter, until suddenly he shoved the demon across the hut. The demon slammed into the wall, separating the man from Columbia and Jackie. They both looked down at him in horror, trembling in fear, before they looked back toward the angel.

The angel hovered off the ground, glowing so brightly that they had to shield their eyes to look at him. His clothes were as white as snow, and his wounds were instantly healed, as he reared his sword back.

The demon wasn't going to give up though. It scrambled to its feet, just in time to see the angel swing his arms forward with his sword glowing, heading directly toward them! The sword held so much of God's glory that the instant it made contact with the trio, it sliced them through the middle, disintegrating them on contact.

As soon as the angel's arms swung through, his feet touched the ground and he lowered his sword, keeping his hands on it, exhausted. He slowly replaced the sword into the sheath, as he waited a few moments, watching the ash descend to the ground on the other side of the fire.

When it settled, he walked through the fire to the other side and crouched on the ground. He brushed some dust out of the way before he found what he was looking for. He picked up the key, and brought it back through the fire to where the guys prayed over

Casey. Then he knelt down, and placed it gently into her hand, securely fastening it within her fingers.

As he held her hand, he looked up toward her face and confidently said, "What is free in Christ is free indeed."

"Is it finished?" Mark asked, looking up at the angel.

He nodded as he stood. Then he looked down at the powerful men of prayer and faith, and said, "Well done, my little A.N.G.E.L.s. Keep up the good work." With that, he flew straight into the air until he was out of sight.

They watched until they couldn't see him anymore, before all three looked down at Casey.

"She done now," Ollie said, as he and George sat cross-legged on the other side of the fire.

At that point, Grace sat where Jack and Mac had sat. She nodded in agreement.

The guys took their hands off Casey, as they looked down at her. She couldn't move. She couldn't talk. It took everything she had to stay somewhat conscious enough to hear and feel everything.

Mark took a moment before he reached down and scooped her up into his arms. He lovingly looked down at her as he said, "It's finished. Just rest, my love. We're here. You're safe. Just rest."

*   *   *

Jackie sat in her room looking in her vanity mirror. She glanced down at her desk in front of her to see the angel necklace of Casey's. She took it off her when Casey passed out.

Jackie reached down and clasped it in her hand, as she hissed, transforming into the demon. "You may have won that battle, but I shall win the war. You may have defeated the few, but we are legion…we are many. Shhhhe isssss mine. Do you hear me? Shhhe issss mine!" The demon laughed a heinous laugh, as it placed the necklace around his neck. "She is sssssstill mine."

Coming Soon:

The Final Installment of The Holy Flame Trilogy:

Angels Among Us

This is the third and final book in the Holy Flame Trilogy, which follows the life-changing events that surround Casey Carter (a firefighter/paramedic from Engine Company Fifteen of Denver, Colorado) and an elite, special operations unit called A.N.G.E.L. (Available to Nurture God's Eternal Love).

With help from a unique band of characters in the Outback, Casey Carter was able to work through her past. However, would it prepare her for what was to come? The battle is forming. Both sides are amassing their troops as allies align, but will there be enough remaining A.N.G.E.L.s for them to win? Without knowing the day nor the hour, will they be prepared?

What kind of battle would this be if the A.N.G.E.L.s of flesh and blood were battling against the unseen powers of darkness? This may be the deciding factor in Casey's struggle for freedom, but will the remaining A.N.G.E.L.s survive or will it be their final battle?

Revelation 12:12

[12] Therefore rejoice, ye heavens, and ye that dwell in them. Woe to the inhabiters of the earth and of the sea! For the devil is come down unto you, having great wrath, because he knoweth that he hath but a short time.

Books in the Holy Flame Trilogy.

See what the other A.N.G.E.L.s have been assigned -

Books in the Grace Restored Series

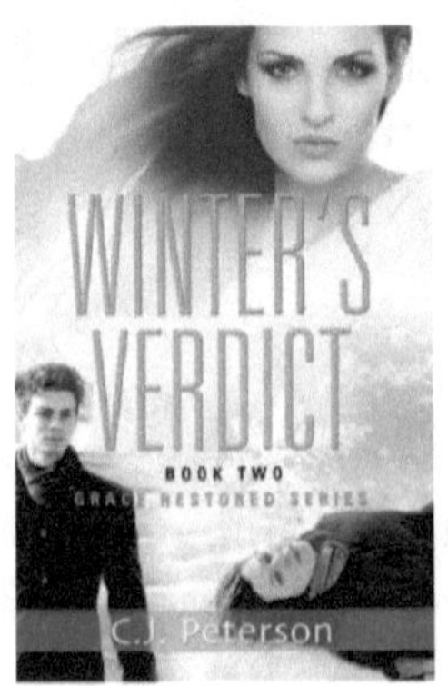

The next generation is taking over. In the Award-Winning
Divine Legacy Series.